JO & LAURIE

JO & LAURIE

MARGARET STOHL & MELISSA DE LA CRUZ

putnam

G. P. PUTNAM'S SONS

G. P. PUTNAM'S SONS

An imprint of Penguin Random House LLC, New York

First published in the United States of America by G. P. Putnam's Sons,
an imprint of Penguin Random House LLC, 2020
First paperback edition published 2022

Visit us online at penguinrandomhouse.com

THE LIBRARY OF CONGRESS HAS CATALOGED THE HARDCOVER EDITION AS FOLLOWS:
Names: Stohl, Margaret, author. | De la Cruz, Melissa, 1971– author.
Title: Jo & Laurie / Margaret Stohl & Melissa de la Cruz.
Other titles: Jo and Laurie | Description: New York: G. P. Putnam's Sons, [2020] | Summary:
"After the publication of her surprise bestseller *Little Women*, Jo March struggles to write
its sequel, while also deciding her true feelings for her best friend,
the boy next door, Theodore 'Laurie' Laurence"—Provided by publisher.
Identifiers: LCCN 2019059388 | ISBN 9781984812018 (hardcover) | ISBN 9781984812025
Subjects: CYAC: Authors—Fiction. | Family life—Fiction. | Love—Fiction.
Classification: LCC PZ7.S86985 Jo 2020 | DDC [Fic]—dc23
LC record available at https://lccn.loc.gov/2019059388

Book manufactured in Canada

ISBN 9781984812032

1 3 5 7 9 10 8 6 4 2

FRI

Design by Eileen Savage
Text set in Winchester New ITC

For all of you, dear readers.

Make your own happy endings.

~

"You've got me, anyhow. I'm not good for much, I know, but I'll stand by you, Jo, all the days of my life. Upon my word I will!" And Laurie meant what he said.

—Louisa May Alcott, *Little Women* (1868)

I believe there are some natures too noble to curb, too lofty to bend. Of such is my Lu.

—Abba Alcott, on the subject of her daughter Louisa (1850)

Before You Begin . . .

THE STORY THAT we now think of as *Little Women* was originally published as two separate volumes written by Louisa May Alcott in 1868 and 1869.

In those pages, Jo March—one of young adult literature's most beloved writers and sisters—writes and publishes the story of her life with her family at Orchard House.

Our own reimagined story takes place *between* the two volumes, after the success of the first, as Jo struggles to write the second.

Just as we expect "Lu" did.

—MS & MdlC

LITTLE WOMEN

The Offices of Roberts Brothers, Publishers and Bookbinders
Washington Street, Boston, Massachusetts
1868

ittle Women? That's the title?" The author looked concerned. Above her light brown eyes and beneath her threadbare linen cap, the chestnut curls that framed her face were shaking. Miss Josephine March was all of seventeen years old, and though her girlish curves were slight, her spirit was immense.

There was nothing *little* about her, or her characters.

Or so she had thought.

The book in question—a volume of domestic stories, loosely inspired by her own family—was one she hadn't wanted to write, had in fact steadfastly *refused* to write, until her editor had offered a notably *unrefusable* royalty, instead of the usual piffling advance. Only then had she dashed off a dozen chapters in a fit of pique. To her dismay, he'd loved them, and she'd had no choice but to finish the final chapters, which she'd come to deliver now.

And lo—insult beyond injury—it would be called *Little Women*.

"Isn't it perfect?" Mr. Thomas Niles beamed at her over his spectacles. Her editor at Boston's (moderately) respected and (moderately) solvent Roberts Brothers Press, Niles felt he had developed some (moderate) expertise in the publishing industry. His authors, at times, disagreed.

This was one of those times.

"Far from it!" Jo drew a worn cambric handkerchief square from her pinafore pocket and dabbed dramatically at the corner of her left eye, although both author and editor knew there was no actual tear to be wiped away.

Only fury, and there's not a cambric square big enough in the world for that—

"It's dismissive!" Jo seethed. "It's pap!"

"Oh?" Niles pushed his spectacles back up the bridge of his bulbous red nose. "How so?"

"It's . . . trite!" Jo dropped the handkerchief upon the bundled pages in front of her. They were tied with string, the requested final chapters, as painstakingly inked as the others before them. Her hands hovered, as always, just above the parcel; it was never easy, letting go of the fruit of *so many* stolen hours in her damp writing garret under the attic eaves, where she'd burnt her last saved stumps of candle-wax—as well as her fingers—and ruined her eyes in the service of one of these so-called *little* stories. *The nerve!*

Niles sighed.

"Trivial!" Jo huffed.

"When you say *trivial*," Niles began, "do you mean—?"

"For starters, that's not a title, it's a literal restatement of the very essence of the plot," Jo interrupted.

He eyed the parcel hungrily. "Yes, and I'm told it's charming."

Jo's head-shake was very nearly violent. "It's not *charming*. I'm not *charming*." After making a living writing her customary *blood-and-thunder* tales—or so she thought of them—this business of feminine tradition and treacle was all very unfamiliar. To be fair, with the exception of her sisters, Jo knew and liked hardly any girls at all.

"You're *very* charming, Miss March. Nearly as charming as your book," Niles said, looking amused. "And a tribute to little women everywhere." He pulled a tin from his outer vest pocket. "Peppermint?"

Buying time with sweets, again. Niles offered them up only when he found himself in a tough conversational crossroads, Jo knew.

So that's it, then.

There really is no changing the title.

"Thank you, no." Jo looked out the window as a horse and carriage clattered up Washington Street, spraying mud in every direction, including onto the glass of the (moderately) well-kept Roberts Brothers offices. She tried not to wring her hands in despair and failed. "I suppose it is what it is. Perhaps it doesn't matter what you call it. I dashed the thing off in weeks, and for what?"

"Money," Niles said. "The almighty dollar. Which you happen to need, not unlike the rest of us. Speaking of earning your wage, are those the chapters you owe me?" He reached for the bundled pages between them.

"It's not about earning my wages," Jo said, tightening her grip on the manuscript. "Not *just* about that." She'd written it on assignment, because Niles was experimenting beyond the standard Continental Gothic that came flowing from Jo's pen so easily.

And, yes, because of the money.

The result was a collection of domestic moments, sure, but it had surprised even her; it wasn't just feminine drivel, even if the title might perhaps now doom it to be. She hadn't expected it to come as quickly as it had, or as pleasantly. Not that she would admit that to her editor. "Money's not a reason. Not a proper one, anyway." *Even if we are poor as rats.*

"Many people—*most*—seem to think otherwise," Niles said, yanking his handkerchief from his pocket and mopping his brow, which was beginning to perspire as they argued. He was never without a handkerchief; decades of sobbing authors, Jo suspected, had trained him thus.

"Not all people," she sniffed.

"Certainly my investors do. You aren't the only family with war debts, you know."

Jo had no answer for that, for he was right. She supposed she would never be considered a real writer now, never be taken seriously by the public. Never invited to lecture at the Athenaeum with Ralph and Henry and . . . *Who was that other chap?* Perhaps this was what happened to feminine scribblers who aspired above their little place in the Concord world.

Strike another blow to the weaker sex—and all that rot.

"Charming," she sighed.

"Ideally, you've written equally charming last chapters as well." Niles eyed the stack hopefully. "Seeing as my typesetters have very nearly caught up with you."

Jo snorted, which was a good indication of her feelings concerning the process that put her words on the page. Lottie Roberts, who manned the letterpress, had once changed *"Christopher Columbus!"*—Jo's most oft-uttered oath—to *"My Heavens!"* and Jo had never forgiven her. This was, truthfully, not an isolated event; *"Blazes!"* had been mysteriously printed as *"How sad!"*—*"Hell"* as *"The Down Below"*—*"Blow me down!"* as *"No!"*—and *"A French pox upon you, Adventuress!"* had been eliminated altogether.

"Your typesetters go too far." She glared, repeating the warning not to change a word of her text for the twentieth time.

"Yes, well." He snapped shut his peppermint tin. "When women of polite society are allowed to speak like common sailors, you are welcome to terminate their employment yourself, Miss March."

"And I look forward to the day, sir." Jo pursed her lips.

"I am confident you shall meet it." Niles smiled. For despite all indications to the contrary, the two were fond friends. Niles reminded Jo of her father, who had left Concord years earlier to join the Union army as a chaplain. Mr. March had come home only once in all that time—when the Union prevailed and the war was won, three years ago. Shortly thereafter, he'd left once more to volunteer in the Reconstruction efforts in the South, helping to build schools and churches for previously enslaved people. And though his letters usually came frequently, the March women felt his absence keenly.

But Jo still had Niles, and if they fought, they fought well, each considering the other the more harmless version of their species. (The dollar a story Niles paid to run Jo's wild romantic adventures didn't hurt, either. Neither did the fact that subscriptions to his circular, *The Tall Taler*, had gone up by forty-three since engaging her. *Forty-three!*)

"Call it what you will. No one will read it, anyway." Jo tapped her fingers along the brown-paper-wrapped parcel. "I don't know why you believed you could sell it."

"Perhaps." Niles nodded.

"I should have used a different name instead of my own," she sighed. "Eustacia. Thomasina."

"Possibly." He nodded again. "Eustacia Emerson is lovely. I'm quite partial to Thomasina Thoreau, but Hildegarde Hawthorne could also do just fine." He winked.

Hawthorne. That was his name, the other Athenaeum chap!

"Fine." She picked at the string about the parcel. "Take my daft little book of scribbles and do with it as you will."

"I've seen dafter. Trust me."

"Trust you? You have no sense of anything, least of all publishing! Why, you couldn't sell *Romeo and Juliet* if I wrote it for you."

"Admittedly a bit somber for my taste—I do prefer a happy ending to my *sensation stories*. So do our *Tall Taler* readers. Why couldn't Romeo have married Juliet and settled down in a nice Tuscan villa? A sequel by any other name . . ."

The author bit her lip; it kept her from responding in a discourteous manner.

"Now give it here," the editor said, sliding his fingers impatiently across the blotter atop his desk and taking the manuscript from her hands.

"Take it." She scowled.

Manuscript obtained, Niles traded his peppermints for the bottle of peppermint schnapps he kept in the bottom of his drawer for special occasions.

"A toast!" he offered, pouring two thimblefuls into two cups.

Jo grudgingly accepted.

"To our *Little Women*!" her publisher cried. "And to the bright future of Jo March, Thomas Niles, and Roberts Brothers! May 1868 prove to be a banner year for us all!"

Jo clinked her glass against his. It seemed rude otherwise. With a final sigh and a shake of her curls, the author drank to her defeat. The editor drank to her success.

Little Women it was.

1869

~

One Year Later

1

HAPPY ENDINGS

*C*hristopher Columbus! I don't believe it," Jo said, shaking her head at the small mountain of carefully inscribed paper envelopes covering the round dinner-table of Orchard House, the Marches' neatly kept cottage farm. "Who are these people? They just keep coming."

The old cottage didn't answer.

Jo shifted uncomfortably in her horsehair-cushioned seat, and even the soft lawn collar of her new day-dress didn't make her feel better. This could partly have been due to the particular circumstances of the dress itself; Thomas Niles had sent one for each of the March women, all the way from Boston by carriage, at an expense never before undertaken by any Orchard House resident, with a note: *For Our Dearest Little Women, with Greatest Admiration for Our Most Productive Partnership, and with the Hope of Many Future Successes. Respectfully, Mr. Thomas Niles, Editor & Partner, Roberts Brothers.*

The dress was fine. It was the implication of the note that made Jo squirm. Two thousand copies, sold out almost from the start! Certainly, the book's popularity had surprised everyone, particularly its eighteen-year-old author. But future successes? Beyond Mr. Niles's promotion to partner? That meant future books about her family. And successes meant *expectations*. Expectations she wasn't sure she could meet. She'd wanted the book to do well, naturally, but—

"Believe what?" Amy, Jo's little sister, called up from the root-cellar, where, as usual, she was foraging for something better than the dull piece of bread and scrape of butter she customarily had for her tea. The last of the raisins, most like. "Coming from where?"

"Where else? That book, of course!" Jo shook her head. Her chestnut ringlets were bound up in rags that were meant to make her look exotic, but only succeeded in making her look like one of their old homemade rag dolls. (*Perhaps,* as her older sister, Meg, had pointed out, *because they're made from the very same rags.*)

Nineteen-year-old Meg was distressingly traditional, which accounted for her taste in the most tediously earnest boys—the one thing both Jo and Amy could agree upon. Otherwise, the three March girls did not agree on much, though they loved each other dearly.

A small shout echoed up the cellar steps. "Don't yell. You know it upsets *Marmee*." Jo heard the sarcasm in the tone; she could imagine the smirk on her little sister's face.

"Don't . . ." Jo picked up an envelope and tore off the corner with her teeth. "Do *not* start!" There was a pause—and a crash—and

Jo imagined the baskets of last year's potatoes that had most likely been upset on the stone cellar floor. It was a bright sunny day in May, and Jo wished she felt more sanguine about her success and less rattled by its expectations.

Then she heard Amy's voice. "You were the one who gave her that treacly nickname, Jo! She's *Marmee* forever now, in *thousands and thousands* of copies of a book everyone in the world mistakes for our real life!"

Jo tossed the letter over the grating and into the dining-room fireplace, picking up another. "Oh, you ridiculous tartlet. Blame Mr. Niles! He insisted."

The stomping that accompanied the declaration brought Amy up the stairs and into the small, warm dining-room where Jo sat.

Amy flung herself into the creaking wooden chair across from her sister. "What are you doing, anyways?" But she instantly forgot her question upon spying a ceramic bowl in the center of the table. "I didn't know there were oranges! Oh, Jo! Such fancies we have now!" Oranges were a rare delicacy, shipped all the way from Florida or raised in a greenhouse, and only the wealthiest households were able to afford them.

It was true. Though it was still a bit soon for Jo's royalties to make the March family much in the way of actual dollars, Jo's career now brought certain niceties into the house on a regular basis. And Jo had to admit, the more-than-modest success of the book had been satisfying, if bewildering, to acknowledge. It had completely taken her by surprise, and if a few obnoxious reviewers had dismissed her work as *slight feminine rubbish*, her pride was somewhat assuaged by the very real physical comforts said scribblings had brought them.

Jo pulled the fruit bowl away from her sister, thumping it back to the table, where it had been holding a pile of letters down. "Mama's saving those for preserves," she scolded.

"Hannah hasn't let Mama Abba make preserves in years," the youngest and blondest and prettiest of the March sisters answered back.

Youngest and prettiest and by far the most irritating, Jo thought. *At least I got that part right.*

"So what's gotten you all up in arms?" asked Amy.

Jo turned back to the table in front of her and motioned to the pile of mail with a touch of incredulity. "These are letters from my readers."

Amy was making a little pile of orange peels on the table. "All those? For you? You're *no fun* at all! Why would anyone write you?"

"Precisely the question." Jo quirked an eyebrow. "I haven't the faintest idea. Perhaps because they feel that I write to them . . . well, *for* them."

"You mean in the *book*?" Amy had gone wide-eyed, as if the idea of Jo's newfound regard—or more specifically, her little tome's—had only now struck her. "At least they aren't thronging to our actual house, I suppose. Your readers."

"Could you imagine their disappointment? Upon learning the home of the Great American Authoress was this damp and earwiggy place?"

"I suspect they'd be more shocked by your earwiggy curls," Amy sniffed, with a self-satisfied toss of her own neat braids. "And what do these letters say?"

Jo stared at the pile. "Some begin by asking for an auto or a photo—neither of which I can afford to send. But really, they want the very same thing. All of them."

"Well, what is it?" Amy asked, impatient now.

Jo sighed. "They want to know how it all ends, which apparently means who marries who."

"Well, they have a point. How *does* it end?" Amy cocked her head, sucking juice from her delicate fingers.

Jo snorted. "It ends the way it ends! Isn't it enough the way I left it? That I become a writer? That Laurie goes off to college, and our father returns from war? That a very serious boy proposes to our very pretty sister—and that you, scamp, learn the error of your ridiculous ways?"

Amy smirked. A curl of orange peel fell to the tabletop.

"You're hideous." Jo flicked the peel gingerly off an envelope. "You should live in a barn."

"*I'm* hideous? While you're the one telling the whole world about the time Mr. Davis struck me and made me throw away my pickled limes?" Amy leaned forward and pinched the soft white bit of Jo's wrist.

It was true; some of the more popular chapters of Jo's little book had involved Amy's misbegotten transgressions at their old school—in particular, a scene of the littlest March smuggling a sack of concealed treats into her desk and being punished as a result.

Amy had sworn to never forgive Jo, though she'd enjoyed her newfound fame all the same. "*Of course* that character is inspired by me," she'd say to anyone who asked. "Really, I created her myself."

"Maybe you shouldn't be such a ravening little *pickled piglet* every second of every day. Besides, those limes did, in point of fact, fund the purchase of those very oranges," Jo teased, "so I assumed you approved of those sorts of things."

"And so I do, those things. Most things. Though Meg was right that it was a curious choice to invent a neighboring dowager aunt who absolutely despises us all . . ."

Not this again.

"You know why." Jo frowned. "It was just, everything was a bit too—"

"*Treacly*, I know, I know. The great and temperamental Jo March can only handle so much sugar in her spice." Amy looked at Jo sideways. "If only we did have a rich aunt."

"Anyway, it's not about me," Jo tried to explain, as she had a thousand times before. "It's about the story. They all come with their own shape and spirit, you know. I can't control how they turn out."

"Why not?" Amy demanded, shoving a section of *lime-funded orange* into her mouth. Even the scent was intoxicating, especially within the rather more pedestrian walls of Orchard House. The smell of adventure and faraway lands.

Well worth the price of the limes, Jo thought.

Amy kept going, dribbling juice as she spoke. "You're the writer, aren't you?"

"I am, and use a napkin, you monster." Jo pulled a folded

square of cloth from beneath the pile of envelopes, brandishing it at her sister.

"What? This?" Amy grinned with an orange-peel smile instead of teeth. Still, she took the napkin, spitting her peel into it. "I still don't understand."

"I only write the characters for what feels like a moment, until the characters sort of . . . take up the quill on their own . . . and begin to write each other. Tell each other their stories. They breathe on each other, and make each other live. And from then on, I'm just an eavesdropper, Amy."

"But you crawl upstairs with your quill and your ink-pot, and that's when the story begins. I've seen you do it a thousand times."

"That's where it all starts. But the early bits are just, I don't know. Pantomimes made with paper dolls . . . paper dolls and promises, I suppose."

A final wedge of orange halted in mid-flight as Amy shot her big sister a look. "What about Beth?"

Two pink spots appeared in Jo's cheeks. "What about her?"

Amy put down the orange. "You changed what happened to her. You let her live. You *wrote* her, Jo."

Jo looked at the orange peels in the palm of her hand. She couldn't bear hearing Beth's name mentioned, not even by Amy, who had loved her as much as Jo had. "That was Niles's idea. He said the book was too sad otherwise."

Is that it? You did it for Niles?

Or did you do it for yourself?

Unlike what had happened in real life, in Jo's book, Beth, the third March sister—younger and sweeter than Jo, older and wiser than Amy—had recovered from scarlet fever and lived. It was the least Jo could do for poor Bethie, whose absence in the house was still a shadow they lived under, an ache they all felt.

The angel of Orchard House.

Because the truth was, since she'd passed, Beth was still somehow there but not there in the house—same as her abandoned, porcelain-faced dollies, still in their old room, sealed in the close air of the cedar chest at the foot of the empty daybed.

The chest Jo walked past no less than ten times a day.

In some ways, I've begun to imagine myself a well-worn Roman step . . . , she had written into her tear-smeared journal. (Never mind that her "Rome" was only the capital city of her heart's imagination, and that Jo had yet to venture farther than Boston.)

> *. . . just a sanded bit of stone in an empty stairwell, still carrying the deep grooves and depressive dents of every passing sole that ever touched it. A meaningless monument to absence made permanent. To eternal loss and stillness. To the impressions that remain, whether or not we ask them to, long after their makers have turned to dust.*

"Your editor said the truth was too sad for your book?" Amy gave Jo a pointed look. "He wasn't wrong, you know. Though some girls like sad books. Poppet does."

Jo looked past her sister to the little grating that hid the fire, forcing herself to breathe, in and out, again and again, as far as the nipped-in waist of her new day-dress would allow. Beth had known her best—and worried about her—for Beth had seen how dark Jo could get and, more to the point, how lost she would feel without her Beth. And so Beth had made her promise—

No, stop.

It was still too painful. Jo could not let herself dwell on her memories. On the grief that had wrung out Orchard House in the days after the scarlet fever had taken the second-youngest March.

It was only writing her book, her *Little Women*, that had allowed Jo to begin to feel even some relief.

Jo took Amy's discarded orange peels and tossed them into the fire with a brisk, no-nonsense motion, as if she were sweeping out all her sorrows with them. They curled up into little black husks, making the whole house smell like oranges.

2

THE SEQUEL PROBLEM

No more sad truths. No more ghosts, however angelic. Not this afternoon.

Jo inhaled sharply and changed the subject. "I thought we might go into town and get you a new ribbon tomorrow."

"You did?" Amy sounded shocked—and gleeful. "Can we?"

"I believe so." Jo smiled as she tossed another letter onto the pile. "Roberts Brothers wants a sequel, you know. Now that the first book is selling, Mr. Niles says if I were to do it, he could finally offer us the sort of money that could properly change our lives."

Amy sat up. "Really?"

"They've had to reprint it, you know. They're even in talks to make *Little Women* into a theater piece in London's West End." Jo couldn't hide the pride in her voice at that fact.

"Oh." For once in fifteen years of her life, Amy had nothing to say.

"A literary society wants to bring me on a steamship to Paris for a speaking engagement."

Amy's mouth fell agape. "Paris?! You? Because of *a book*?"

"Yes, me. They want me to speak next year." Jo frowned. "Why else do you think the fruit baskets and the flower arrangements and the sweets and the dresses keep coming?"

But Amy hadn't heard a word after *Paris*. "Speaking engagements! The theater! The River Seine! *Resplendid!* Oh, truly! As famed as if you'd written *The Orphan of the Rhine!*" Amy clapped her sticky-sweet hands together. "Think of all *those* oranges! And grapes! And the cherries we'll have this summer! Oh, cherries!" Cherries were Amy's favorite and hard to come by for those of modest means.

Jo shook her head. "I can't think of it. It's all become . . ."

"*Wonderful?!*" Amy's eyes widened.

"Strange. And . . ."

"*Incredulous?!*" Amy clasped her hands dramatically.

"*Confusing.* Because it isn't real, you noodle-head. My book's based on us, but my characters aren't us, not really. We're not *those* little women." The title still made her cringe a little. "So how can I keep writing them?"

"So?! If we aren't, then who is?" Amy was spluttering now. *"The cherries, Jo!"* Her face had gone pale. *"Think of the cherries!"*

"I do! It's all I think about! Why do you think I wrote the stupid thing in the first place? Father's war debts . . . and all the costs of maintaining Orchard House . . . the animals and the gardens . . . coal and milk and butter and meat and sugar . . . setting aside something for Mama Abba's future . . ." Jo tried not to feel resentful of her father for leaving them alone, but some days were harder than others. While she rarely said it aloud, she couldn't help but wonder what she would have been free to write if she didn't so keenly feel the pressure to earn. *Then again, as a member of the gentle sex, would I have been encouraged to write at all?*

"Animals? Gardens?" Amy was still spinning. "You mean *ball gowns*! And *petty-furs*! And the *Grand Tour*! We can travel the world, Jo! We can go to Rome and Sardinia and Capri, where I will paint and you will write and Meg will . . . come with us!"

"Amy!" Jo shook her head. "Stop swooning. I don't think I can do it. I've even tried to plot it out in my head. But I'm not . . . a romantic. Not this sort." She sounded strange as she said the words, mostly because she herself wasn't entirely certain of what she meant by them. "*Good Wives*. That's what the title is meant to be, of the second part. Roberts Brothers wants us all married off, Niles says. What madness! If I can't imagine it, I can't very well write it, and I can't sell a book I can't write."

Amy laughed. "Jo March! Of course you can! You've been writing romance since I was five! I've been more swooning damsels and lovelorn dashers in your plays than anything else!"

"That's not the same."

Amy ticked them off on her sticky fingers. "Roderigo of the North, Alphonse the Odious, the Countless Count . . ."

"This time it would be us, Amy. Even if . . . it's not. I can't write romances for *us*."

"*Poppycock!*"

"Amy March! That mouth!" Jo tried to be scandalized, but in

truth, it was always a bit thrilling when one of the other Marches cursed.

"You're just scared."

"I'm not!"

"Of course you are," Amy scoffed. "You've had a bit of luck with your first book, and now you're afraid you'll do something wrong and spoil everything." As usual, her sister had hit the nail on the head, or, as she was more likely to say, *the head on the nail.*

"Don't be ridiculous!" Jo could feel her temper rising with her voice. She reached to pull the nearest golden curl, but Amy squirmed away.

"Don't wrestle me like I'm Laurie!" Amy howled. "And don't be prickly, I'm just telling the truth!"

Could she be right? The little potato? Jo thought about it. *She may just be right.*

"Don't be such a fraidy-cat," Amy said, earnestly. "Give the people what they want, Jo. Give them the sequel they deserve! You owe it to your readers . . . not to mention the London West Enders."

"Do I?"

"Of course you do!" The youngest sister was no longer listening. "As for me, in the sequel, make sure I marry a count! No—a *prince!*"

Jo couldn't help but smile. Her little sister was nothing if not predictable. "Pierre, the *Prince of Pickled Limes*?"

"No! Christophe . . . the *King of Cherries!*" Amy shouted as Jo chased her around the chair.

The wooden door pushed open as Meg March followed their mother inside, trailed by Hannah, their loyal servant and, in many ways, a member of the family. Hannah had helped raise the March girls from infancy. Jo truly didn't know how Mama Abba would have survived their father's absence without her.

"What king?" Meg asked, pulling off her plain, round-brimmed bonnet. The splintering straw was shaped like a coal scuttle, Jo thought. Way too homely for their sister. Even if they could have afforded a ribbon or two, it was near impossible to get Meg to really enjoy anything.

Regardless, Meg was generally held to be the first great beauty of the March family, with her rich dark hair and doll-like porcelain complexion—perhaps even more fragile than a doll's, like a teacup Jo might drop, or a silk stocking she might tear.

When Meg blushed, Amy said it looked like watercolor paints splashed across her cheeks. But Meg only looked delicate. In truth, Meg was as tough as any March sister, inside and out. She could beat Jo up the attic stairs and shinny up the old oak before Amy had reached the lowest branch. The rest was all feminine artifice and girlish manner—as per the style, and the society, of the day.

What a fat lot of rot, Jo thought.

Poor as the March family was, she didn't know why her older sister bothered with feminine artifice at all. She herself certainly didn't. Yet Meg did always seem to care what other people thought of her. And now Jo could not stand that her horrid *little* book had become a source of some awkwardness between them. But it had, because Jo had written that their neighbor Laurie's otherwise unremarkable tutor, John Brooke, had proposed to Meg, and Meg had accepted him, when in truth they had never even exchanged a word with each other.

"What king? Why, the king I'm going to marry in Jo's next book! The Cherry King!" Amy announced, even as she held up an orange.

"Amy! Those oranges were the last of the fruit basket the *book man* sent! I was saving them for the preserves!" Hannah scolded. "Now we've nothing to send to the picnic on Sunday." Hannah sighed, but she drew her arms around Amy. "Next time, stick to the raisins, dearest."

"You just wait for my wedding. All the preserves in the kingdom, Hannah. They'll be yours—and you won't have to can a one." Amy winked wickedly.

"Lovely, my dearest. Are we invited to the wedding ceremony, then?" Mrs. March asked, draping her shawl over the little hook on the wall. "I'm not sure I have something suitable enough for the wedding of a proper king."

"You'll need Parisian silk," Amy decided. "With the finest whalebone stitching, sewn right into the seam like a corset. It's *au currant*," she said.

Like the raisin. Jo smiled. She never corrected Amy anymore. The idiosyncrasies of Amy's speech would surely give way to womanhood soon enough, and Jo found herself already missing them. Plus, they had been such great material in *Little Women, First Part*—which was what Mr. Niles had now taken to calling the first book, in hopes of pressuring her into the second.

Jo sighed.

"Au courant," Meg corrected. She always corrected her sister, as the French tutor and governess that she was.

Amy ignored her, as the ungoverned student that *she* was. "And petticoats and puffed sleeves . . . opera gloves . . . and satin brocade slippers . . . and ribbons! Loads and loads of ribbons."

"Don't worry." Meg smiled at their mother. "Jo will write you something *lovely* . . . but then make sure everyone knows your dress is borrowed." She rolled her eyes at Jo. "I told you that Belle lent me her dress in secret!"

"Better borrowed than scorched!" Amy made a face at Jo.

If Amy had suffered the shame of the pickled limes, Meg had endured the shame of the borrowed dress, having scorched the back of her own—even though Jo had given herself that particular shame in the story and set it at Mrs. Gardiner's party instead. Still, everyone who had been at the real Moffat ball knew which March girl that particular scorch mark had belonged to . . .

This is why I can't write the sequel. Who knows what it would do to them? I've already wounded Meg's pride by pairing her off with Laurie's tutor when he's never even said a word to her.

"Now, what fun would a dress be with no scorch marks?" A booming voice followed them inside, and the sound made everyone smile.

Jo pushed back her chair. "Exactly. That's what makes it a story, you ninnies."

Theodore Laurence—affectionately called Laurie—burst into the room, lighting the whole place up as he entered, just as he always did. Laurie was Jo's best friend, their next-door neighbor, and, luckily for Jo, the sort who didn't care too much for books—not even hers, not even when he appeared in them.

Quite the opposite; he insisted he'd never even read them.

Today, though, he carried inside an armful of paper envelopes, dropping a few at every step.

"Get out of my sight, you horrid boy!" Jo groaned. "Shoo! You're banished. I can't handle you and another one of your deliveries *most foul*."

The Laurences lived across the road from the Marches—and routinely brought in their mail as a favor. Laurie took his duties as Jo's postman with a great deal of mock seriousness, just as he did every new opportunity to tease her.

"Oh, you can handle me." Laurie laughed. "At least, you always have. Quite well, if you don't mind my saying."

"It's true, isn't it?" Jo smiled, despite her annoyance.

A sweaty lock of sun-streaked gold-brown hair flopped into his eyes, covering half of his cheerful, ruddy face. "I have always belonged entirely and devotedly to you, since long before you had such a great many passionate fans, *Milady Shakespeare*."

He tried to manage a bow, but it looked rather like a stagger and only sent more letters flying. Though an athlete, Laurie could often be awkward; though intelligent, he could often be a fool; though rich as a Cherry King, his tastes tended toward the acquired rather than the obvious. Jo suspected he'd had more than enough of *finer things*, and was interested in something more substantial. What that might be, however, she could not bring herself to yet imagine.

She reached out to place her hand gently upon his flushed cheek. "It's true, dear boy. Even before I had a single reader, I had a singularly devoted you."

She kept smiling as she reached for his ear . . .

"Undeniably." Laurie's eyes were on hers, as they so often were, these late-spring days. "I remain your first and your greatest—"

. . . and twisted as hard as she could.

"*OWWW! SWEET GODLESS HEATHEN BEAST! What sorry man would have you?! Atrocity, thy name is woman! This must be hate mail!*"

With that, Laurie howled and tossed the whole load of envelopes into the air, where they flew like so many handfuls of confetti about the room.

As befits the wedding of a Cherry King, Jo thought. *Just so long as it's not mine.*

3

~~~~~

UNWRITTEN

*T*he next day, Jo found herself in front of Meg's students while Meg found herself in bed with a spring cold and a borrowed volume of *The Necromancer*—Flammenberg's latest, just translated from the German. Jo was irritated that Meg had gotten her hands on it first (just as she'd done with the Dickens before that!), especially since, in return, all Jo had gotten were two very bored children squirming in front of their equally bored substitute governess.

"Why must we practice our handwriting again?" The older daughter (*Beatrice, or Bethany, was it? Belinda?*) regarded Jo with some skepticism. Jo didn't blame her; the lesson was so sodding dull, Jo would have wanted to break her own slate over her teacher's head had she been asked to do it herself. At that moment, their makeshift parlor classroom seemed very much the prison it was—to pupils and teacher alike.

"Why, indeed?" *These are Meg's students*, Jo thought; *they'll need a Meg-like answer.* Unfortunately, Jo rarely had a Meg-like anything, let alone an answer. Instead, she leaned forward and stared into the child's eyes. "So that, *Sweet Countess Belinda*, when called upon to handwrite pirate maps with immense clarity or else be made to walk the plank, you are not fed to the sharks."

"Really?" Belinda's braids snapped as she startled to attention.

Jo sighed. "No."

"It's for writing tidy market-lists," the girl's brother said from his own blot-stained paper, a smirk on his lips. (*Leopold? Leon? Lewiston?*) "And tidy recipes. That's what girls do, Belinda."

Jo frowned at him. "Girls do a *great many things*, my esteemed *Master Leopold.*"

Belinda looked up at her thoughtfully. "*Until* they get married?"

"Course not," Leopold snorted. "*When* they get married. That's their job. The cooking and the laundry and the shopping-lists."

"Oh." Belinda sounded disappointed.

Leopold smiled. "Now, the man of the house, he could very well be a sea captain out walking the plank. I intend to go to sea, myself. To India."

"Only India?" Jo raised an eyebrow.

"India has tigers in it," Belinda said, wistfully.

"But we're respectable, so at least you won't have to be a governess," Leopold said, looking at Jo. "Will she?"

"*Will I?*" Belinda looked nervous.

Jo thought about answering both of them—*with a sound slap*— and then thought the better of it, given the March Quaker streak and her family's general distaste for violence. "These are all excellent lines of questioning. And seeing as the rather *delicate topic* of relations between the sexes seems to hold such interest for you," she said, sternly, "I've just the thing."

She pulled out a dog-eared copy of Byron, the most scandalous of her entire collection—which accounted, truthfully, for the dog-earing bit. "Copy the entire page of verse, please. Top to bottom. With care. Lord Byron deserves your best handwriting."

As soon as the ledgers came out and the book was propped open, the room fell utterly silent. Leopold was immediately glued to the page, and Belinda's eyes went wider and wider as she read in silence, her mouth forming a small O.

Jo watched with satisfaction as their hands shook, copying (*savoring!*) every inappropriate word and graphic descriptor, while the clock plodded most non-Byronically toward her freedom.

When she could take it no longer, she stood and stretched, pacing the length of the carpeted hallway outside the parlor prison.

This was why she wrote the first book, wasn't it? To be free? Freedom, after all, was the whole point, was it not? Byronic or otherwise. Freedom to create, to do as she pleased. Freedom from poverty and servitude. Freedom from war debts, from worry about who would pay the coal man and the butcher. Freedom from having to be the kind of girl who grew up to only write grocery-lists.

Freedom to go and write whatever she liked . . .

Like Good Wives, *for the Roberts Brothers?*

Jo paced the hall.

If not for that, then what? Why bother?

But the thought triggered another, a memory of the last time Jo had posed such a question. It was the fateful night Amy had burned Jo's first finished manuscript to ash in a fit of spiteful sisterly pique. The shock of the loss had sent Jo spinning to her darkest place, hurtling her into one of her bone-chilling, soul-killing winter moods that—no matter how merry she seemed—was always waiting right outside her own heart's door. Beth had sat with Jo in bed for hours that night, gently patting her older sister's heaving shoulders while she sobbed and threatened to never write again.

"Why bother?!" Jo had cried.

"Mama Abba says you're writing your way out from the shadows to the light, every day," Beth told her. "Writing your way back to Orchard House, and to us, as you build your castles in the air. So you can't stop, you see? You must never stop, Jo, because I need you here with me. In *our* castle."

"I must never stop or we shall never have anything to eat but bread and water," Jo moaned into the quilts, sobbing harder. "Never mind any castles."

As Jo thought of it now, she wondered if it were still true. Like perhaps all writers, Jo wrote not just because she wanted to, which she did, and not just because she needed to earn a wage, which she did, but because she must. Because she needed a way—and a place—to live. Despite the darkness. Even if only a castle in the air.

Jo had always known she was meant to be a writer; it had forever been her earliest memory and the most important thing in her life. She couldn't remember why or when she'd first believed it might happen. She'd just always known—and with an absolute surety she'd never felt about anything else—that she could be one, at least in terms of natural talent and proclivities.

She was perhaps *wild and queer*—as she liked to say—and truly rubbish at a great many things, but at this one thing in particular, this writing thing, she was good. Better than good.

She, Josephine March, was meant to be a writer of books. A great many books. Her mind, her soul, her imagination—sometimes it even felt like her very body itself—were bursting with all that she had to say. And now not only had she written a book, but she had published it as well.

She was a writer.

So why couldn't she write?

4

VEGETABLE VALLEY

I hate writing," Jo announced the next day, standing in her stockings and petticoats on the back veranda. She'd been trying to work all morning on her manuscript, with no luck at all, and had given it up for the moment.

Instead, she'd wandered outside, as she so often did when her muses abandoned her, to pester her sisters as they worked in the broad-striped family kitchen garden—lanes of bold colors and patchy greens—that occupied the full length of the house, all the way from the back of the veranda to the fringe of forest thicket lining the property.

Vegetable Valley, Jo called it. When she found herself particularly stumped, she would come outside to rub a few tomato leaves and smell the life on her fingers. Today, though, not even the newly hatched tomato leaves seemed to have any effect.

Standing on the edge of the porch, her quill still tucked into her ink-stained cap, she looked a bit like a privateer . . . on laundry day.

Give me back Meg's little pupil prison. Anything is better than this.

"No, that's not true. I don't hate writing; I absolutely, positively *loathe* it." She took a carrot from the woven basket that sat at the edge of the cellar door and began to clean it against one of the few unspoiled folds of her writing apron. "*Good Wives* are now *Dead Wives*. I'm going to tear up my new contract."

"And good morning to you, Josephine." Mrs. March looked amused from the ancient rocking-chair at the corner of the porch, where she was snapping peas. She eyed her daughter as she did most mornings, checking for signs of Jo's shifting temperament as if it were another Concord spring storm.

Jo smiled ruefully.

"Did you sleep at all last night, my dear Jo? I'm beginning to worry about you."

"I don't know, Mama Abba. Day, night . . . they're all starting to blur." She bit into the carrot, crunching loudly as she continued to bemoan her fate. "I loathe it. (*Crunch.*) I loathe myself when I try to master it. (*Crunch crunch.*) I loathe all of Concord (*crunch*) and Orchard House (*crunch crunch*) and this . . . this *carrot* . . . for being . . ."

"Here?" Amy suggested, looking up from her sketch-pad, over near the rose garden.

Jo held high the half-eaten carrot, waving it wildly as she spoke. "The scene of my probable and most tragic demise."

Mrs. March chuckled and snapped another pea spine. Meg looked up from her place in the middle of the vegetable beds, but kept quiet—and kept weeding.

"Oh," Amy said, her hand with the charcoal hovering above the page.

"Does no one care?" Jo wailed.

"Jo. Please." Meg sighed. "We all know you hate writing; you say it every time you have to write. We are not unsympathetic. On the contrary, we are *well aware* of your *writing storms.*"

Amy rolled over on her stomach, giving up momentarily. She went back to studying her face in the dull reflection of their mother's good mirror, sketching herself with a satisfied smile. "There. I've got the nose bit just right."

"And?" Jo said, insulted, ignoring her little sister.

"And it doesn't seem to change anything. If you hate it so much, quit!" Meg sniffed. Her nose was still reddened from her cold, but she had determined not to waste another day in bed—which was just as well with Jo, as it had given her the opportunity to start devouring *The Necromancer* before Meg could change her mind.

But now, with a deadline plaguing her, not even Herrman and Hellfried and their supernatural cohorts or Flammenberg himself had been able to distract Jo for long. The most passionate of the March girls was suffering the worst of all worlds: no time for reading, and no success with writing.

She was left, as a result, with no alternative but to resort to the most trusted and time-honored, if most time-consuming, occupation of all writers—belly-aching about needing to work instead of working.

The ritual did require an audience, however; for a great many years, that service had been dutifully performed by Beth. But Beth was gone, and Jo was left alone with her ill humors—which was what had brought about this little visit to the garden now.

"Quit?" Jo snorted. "Quit?! What else is a person like me supposed to do? *Govern children?!*"

Meg arched an eyebrow. "I should say not. After yesterday's little Byron assignment, you've been banned from my students for life."

"Well, there you go. I'm doomed. Doomed!" Jo paced up and down between rows of cabbages, the family cat trotting behind her. "I hate writing and I hate this book." She grabbed each side of her ink-stained, raggedy writing cap and yanked it down the sides of her head. "Frankly, I believe the feeling is mutual. My silly book also despises me. My editor will fire me."

"Then I suppose it's a very good thing you aren't a writer," Meg said, yanking out crabgrass with both hands. "Wait—oh. *Oh, dear. Too late!*"

Jo looked at her sister suspiciously; it wasn't like Meg to joke. But the oldest March child kept a straight face as she continued to pull weeds out from around a particularly knotty root.

"What's the real problem, Jo?"

Jo did not answer Meg immediately. Instead, she paced Cabbage Lane, turning around at the intersection of Tomato Hill and Zucchini Park. Finally, she stopped in her tracks.

"What's the real problem, you ask? How are we to distinguish between *real problems* and *imaginary problems*? When my *real problems* concern themselves with matters so entirely *fictional*, so utterly—"

"Hand me that trowel?" Meg tossed another handful of muddy grass.

Jo did. She squatted on her heels in front of Meg, rattling the bucket between them dramatically.

Meg let go of the root and wiped her hands on a rag. "The real problem, Jo. I'm still waiting."

Jo shook the bucket in frustration. "Is my current *poverty of imagination* not a real problem?"

"Indeed," Amy said, poring over the mirror.

"Indeed, Jo. And we shall help you fix it," Meg said patiently, as she had to her little sisters a thousand times before.

"Indeed?" Jo rattled the bucket again. "How are you going to help me fix it, Meg? Will you pay a visit to Mr. Niles tomorrow? Write my pages for me, the day after?"

"I suppose so, if that's what it takes. You're my sister." Meg picked up the trowel again. "I've been fixing your problems since the day you arrived. What makes you think I can't fix this one?" She had a point.

"Weddings and balls and gardens and carriages, Jo." Amy was quick to rattle off Meg's particular specialties. "She's written whole pages of them, in almost every issue of the *Pickwick Portfolio*—you know she has."

The Pickwick Club had been their favorite childhood game of all, writing news articles and bits of ephemera for their home-grown newspaper in the style of the characters in Dickens's novel *The Pickwick Papers*. They all had roles: Meg as Mr. Pickwick; Jo, Mr. Snodgrass; Amy, Mr. Winkle; and even Laurie as Mr. Weller.

Beth had been Tracy Tupman. The old Pickwick nicknames still occasionally reappeared, a lovely reminder of when all four sisters had been together. But that was long ago, now.

Even so, every time any of them read a passage from Dickens—or "old Charley," as Jo had a habit of calling him, as if he were a bosom friend rather than a writer she'd long idolized—it brought all those pleasant memories flooding right back.

"Not whole pages, Amy." Meg blushed.

"Yes, pages, *Mr. Pickwick*," Jo said, a bit shamefaced, because it was a truth among sisters—especially these sisters—that what could be said of one could be said at least partly of the others; Jo had dragged her sisters along into her writing attic garret, as often as not. "Old *Winkle* has a point."

"Only because you insisted, *Mr. Snodgrass*," said Meg.

"Very well." Jo pulled herself to her feet. "It's a story problem. Quite a lot of them, actually."

Meg nodded. "About?"

"My sisters and their prospects. The March girls—I mean, the fictional variety."

"Prospects?" Amy sat up. "Go on."

Jo looked at Meg. "Am I really to do this with you? Here and now? In Vegetable Valley?"

"Why ever not? Was I not your champion editor, Mr. Snodgrass?" Meg smiled. "Of all Pickwick's most esteemed editorial board?"

Jo's face took on a suddenly grave expression. "Ah, most certainly, Mr. Pickwick! Most certainly, indeed."

"Then, proceed, dear Snodgrass. If I may call you that." Meg lay back on her elbows, despite the garden mud, which was unlike her.

"Very well, Pickwick. If we are not to stand on formalities." Jo pointed to a nearby cabbage. "Let's say that hideous deformed leaf-head is your future husband, John Brooke."

"Not again." Meg twisted to have a better look at her leafy green ball of a suitor. "Please don't, Jo. It's so awkward. I've hardly spoken to him, and now half of Concord believes him to be my intended!"

"Plus, he's a cabbage!" Amy laughed.

Meg rolled her eyes. "Must he be?"

"Absolutely." Jo plucked a long twig free from one of the saplings lining the muddy garden path. "Yes," she repeated firmly.

"What prospects!" Amy shook her head.

"But that cabbage doesn't look like Brooke." Meg frowned.

"Not a bit," Jo said, feeling a bit cheerier now. "But he is . . . rather serious, like your John."

Meg looked distressed. "Jo, you know he is not *my John* and has never been! I can't even look the man in the eye since your book was published."

Jo shrugged and ripped loose a fat, many-stalked rhubarb plant, tossing it into the dirt next to the cabbage. "And that's you, Meg. You've put on a few pounds since the wedding. I suspect . . . well, yes, you're with child."

"No!" Amy howled.

"Already?" Meg pursed her lips. "Are you certain?"

"As the grave." Jo looked somber.

"Ah, very well. A baby's a blessing, as Mama says," Meg said.

"*Babies*. Twins, in fact." Now Jo was almost enjoying herself.

"Twins? Oh, Jo, that won't be easy." Meg grimaced. "What a thing to do to your sister."

"Horrid business." Jo nodded.

"Do they at least have names?" Meg asked. "My babies?"

Jo picked up and swung a stick, beheading a daisy from the clipping garden on the other side of the path. "Daisy. That's one."

"Daisy?! Why Daisy?" Amy began drawing daisies along the page.

"I don't know. I suppose because I could reach the daisies."

"Why not Rose?" Meg asked.

"The roses are on the other side of the house. Do you really want to make me walk past the woodpile? It's practically a mansion for spiders!" Jo swung the stick again, clipping off the tops of the basil bush.

Meg tossed her rag back in the bucket. "Fair enough. Daisy, then. What about the other twin?"

Amy scoffed. "The boy? Who cares?"

"John Brooke the second. After his father," Meg said, blushing as she bent back over her weeds. "We could call him Demi!"

Jo pointed her stick at her elder sister. "Please don't fall in love with your beloved imaginary baby's fictional father, Meg. You'll only regret it."

Amy looked interested. "Why not? What's wrong with him?"

"I haven't decided yet. Perhaps he's a terrible drunk. A terrible, stinking drunk!" Jo laughed.

Meg was horrified. "Jo! No!"

"Is he, Jo?" Now Amy was intrigued.

"Of course not!" Meg looked appalled.

"He is if I say he is." Jo threw the twig as hard as she could, sending it flying into the trees. "See? *This* is why I didn't want to have to write all this girlish nonsense!"

Meg scrambled to her feet. "Those are *my twins* you're talking about! That's not nonsense, Jo!"

"They're a daisy and a . . ." Jo grabbed a stone from the path. "Rock."

Meg grabbed the rock from Jo's hand. "You're a horrid thing! I don't want a rock for a son! That's my Baby Brooke!"

Jo shook her head. "You're missing the point, Meg. Your family is happy. Daisy and Baby Brooke are the apples of your matronly bosom . . ."

"Eye," Meg corrected.

"That, too. You live over there . . . in that shoe. Which is a cottage. A dovecote. You love it. You do all sorts of—I don't know— sweeping and laundry and mending things there."

Amy watched as her big sisters negotiated Meg's future family in the middle of the garden bed.

"I see. Not a bad life. But what about you? Don't you need a suitor?" said Meg.

Jo laughed. "Me?"

"Yes, you." Meg folded her arms. "Since you have been so bold as to have married me off to a man who doesn't even know my name, you need a suitor as well."

"She has a point," Amy said. "Turnabout is fair play and all that."

Meg considered their middle sister. "Perhaps a professor."

"To ensure that I die of boredom?" Jo rolled her eyes. "Fine. Professor Bore."

Amy folded up her sketch-pad. "Bore isn't a name. Bayer? Baer?"

"*Bhaer.* There you go. He's from Europe. Positively Continental. You'll love him," said Meg, pointing to a head of German lettuce. "Wait, not a professor, a prince!"

"A prince? Whatever would I do with a prince?" Jo made a face.

"What about me?" Amy demanded. "Can I at least go on a Grand Tour? I'll meet the prince, and Jo can have the professor!"

Jo looked at the vegetables. "Hmmm, it might work. Your husband, Prince Arthur?"

Amy folded her arms. "No, I loathe the name Arthur. I've an idea! Laurie's as rich as prince! What if we met over there? While I'm painting the Colosseum!"

"But what about Arthur?" asked Meg.

"Arthur . . . fell in a well . . . and broke his neck."

"How sad for him," Jo said. "And for you."

"It was. I wept piteously and tremendously into my best lace handkerchief until Laurie came to console me in a horse and buggy with chocolates." Amy stuck out her chin. "I want Laurie."

"You can't have Laurie," Meg said. "It doesn't work in the narrative. You and Laurie don't even like each other all that much. Actually, I take it back about the German professor. Obviously, Jo has to marry *herself* off to Laurie."

"*Obviously?!*" Jo sat up, spluttering indignantly. "I do not!"

"Jo does not!" Amy crowed, equally so.

"In point of fact, Jo does." Meg yanked a worm-ransacked, half-green tomato from the vine. "It's written in the stars, just as Jo wrote about Roderigo of the North. In Act the Third, our scandalous *Laurence Lovers* elope, and it breaks Mama's heart."

Jo was aghast. "Foul plagiarist! You can't just *steal* Roderigo's Act the Third!"

Amy tossed her head. "I still think my ending is better."

Meg threw the rather sad-looking vegetable to a still red-faced Jo. "There you go. That's a Jo March of a tomato if ever I've seen one."

Jo looked like she wanted to hurl the lopsided green orb at her sister's linen-capped head.

Amy giggled, in spite of her commitment to a good sulk. "You mean *Jo Laurence*, now that they've eloped."

"*Christopher Columbus!* Enough!" Jo roared. "No wonder they call you the weaker sex!"

Amy and Meg burst out laughing.

Jo's pink-spotted cheeks were now bright red. "Fine. Take Laurie. I don't want him. But you have to live here. I can't write back and forth across a whole ocean and between two countries. I'll be describing cities until the cows come home."

"What about Beth? What happens to Beth? In the book, I mean," asked Amy. "Since she's meant to be still alive in your book."

A momentary silence rose up between them. The elder March sisters looked at each other askance. How could they imagine a future without their sister? What would their lives have been like if she had lived?

"Beth becomes a famous pianist, of course," said Jo, staunchly.

She tried not to think of Beth's final days, of the way Laurie had played all her favorite melodies on her little piano, over and over and over—

"A pianist? Of course," said Amy, approvingly. "Which means she'll be touring the world over, just like me. I'm a *vray artiste*, Jo. I'm not meant for Concord."

"If you stay, I'll let you babysit the twins," Meg said, attempting to sound cheerful, even though her face had gone decidedly pale. "Daisy and what's-his-name. If you're responsible. Twins are an enormous responsibility. You'd need to be patient, and kind."

Amy looked stricken.

Meg faltered. "I mean, I'll have to ask Brooke, but seeing as I'm the mother of his children . . ."

Jo looked at Meg like she was speaking gibberish. "We're talking about a rock and a daisy. I think Amy will be fine."

"I'm sure," Meg said, brightly. "And I'll show her what to do."

"Also? You probably die in childbirth, on account of the twins. I haven't decided. But if that's the case, Brooke will be eternally grateful for Amy—seeing as she'll most likely be the only mother your poor children ever know. Perhaps they'll even marry each other after you die."

"*What?!*" Meg and Amy both shouted.

"You're killing me off?!" Meg looked horrified.

"You're dooming me to twins?" Amy looked terrified. "Can't I be the one to die?"

"Fine! No one gets married in the sequel!" Jo huffed. "I shall write a Manifesto of Femality! One to rival Margaret Fuller's own! Where women give themselves to service and to fulfillment of their art!"

"Sounds terribly didactic," said Meg. "And a bit dull."

Amy pouted. "No princes? No castles? No Laurie?"

"None! As the author, after all, these decisions are best left *entirely* up to me."

"Like the limes?" Amy hissed.

"And the borrowed dress?" Meg scoffed. "Or our dowager aunt?"

"Exactly," Jo said, rising to her feet. "Now off to the garret I go, to destroy your horrible lives." She was feeling a bit better.

A good scrap with her sisters was, at times, an even better distraction than rubbing tomato leaves.

And as she savored the teacup-sized triumph of the writerly life, she wondered again how anyone could content themselves with any other sort of horrible life at all.

5

HOT AND COLD

*P*erhaps one day you'll be happy that the famed authoress Josephine March wrote you into her stories," Laurie said, tugging on one of Amy's curls, already damp with the unseasonably thick heat of the late-spring afternoon. It felt practically like summer.

Amy had regaled Laurie with tales of their Vegetable Valley futures the entire way to the church picnic. Once they'd arrived, Meg had done her best to find a shady spot for their blanket, beneath the spreading oak trees—but even in the shade, this particular Saturday was unbearably hot. And even by Concord standards, any event hosted by the First Unitarian Congregation was certain to be a notoriously dull affair.

"Stop!" Amy said, pulling her blond curls away. "I won't. Besides, it's no fun at all. Her versions of us aren't proper versions. We're all scrambled together and boiled down again . . . like syrup."

Laurie sat up, surveying the picnic spread Meg had laid out from Mrs. March's hamper. "It doesn't sound too bad, especially not when compared to my fictional future, which apparently includes moving back to Italy to become a musician and living the lonely life of a wandering wastrel. You don't hear me complaining about it." Jo had shared Laurie's fate with him that morning.

"Orphan wastrel," Jo corrected. "And there may be a hump involved; it isn't settled yet."

"Well, keep me informed, just so I know what size vests to buy. These sorts of topics aren't addressed in *Sensible Etiquette of the Best Society*."

"Naturally," Jo said soberly, only the merest twinkle in her eye acknowledging the game she shared, in perpetuity, with her bosom friend. "Speaking of complaints—how long must we stay here?"

"Longer than this," Meg said, surveying the crowded grass between their blanket and the church.

"Fine." Jo took a butter knife from the basket and turned to Laurie, who sat immediately next to her, as he always did. "Please plunge this butter knife through my heart, Laurie. I beseech you, dear boy."

"I will not," Laurie said. "Stab it yourself." He kept his head bowed beneath the straw hat he'd stolen off Jo's own head, but his cheeks were still flushed a bright red. "Are you going to eat that lettuce? Trade you?"

Jo tossed another piece of chicken down to his plate, which tipped unevenly on the blanket in front of him, spilling fried-chicken bones and butter-sandwich crusts. "But it would be a merciful death," she said, reaching for the strawberry in Laurie's hand.

He pulled it away before she could take it. "What fun would that be? I live to punish you, my murderous pet."

"Oh, I know." She reached over him to grab it in a most unladylike manner. "And you do it so well."

They laughed together. That was how dull the afternoon was.

"*Blazes!*" Jo sighed.

"*Damnable blazes,*" Laurie agreed.

"Shush!" Meg hissed at them from her perch across the blanket, where she'd been doing her best to ignore the tomfoolery. "Stop it! You two cannot *be yourselves* at a church picnic! There are decent folk here."

"Any decent folk in particular, Meg?" Laurie teased.

"Theodore Laurence," Meg huffed. "Behave yourself!"

Jo reached for the untouched chicken drumstick on Meg's plate and stole it, taking a bite before she handed it over to Laurie. "Feed the beast and he'll be quiet."

"Please," he answered, attacking the drumstick himself. "Well played."

"At least we won't starve to death," she consoled him.

"No," he said, his mouth full. "We're more likely to die from boredom first. Because this isn't one of your stories. It's Concord." A bit of chicken fell to the blanket, and Meg made a face.

"True." Jo nodded, eyeing the crowd. "I'd give them all the

Black Death. Buboes for the lot of them! That would spice up an afternoon."

"Only that?" Laurie grinned.

Jo considered the crowd. "Give me a minute. Galloping consumption . . . and a raft of marauding pirates . . ."

"You deserve each other, you monkeys. You're unfit for company, especially a church social. At your age, you both should know better," Meg grumbled.

"He's a year older. He's worse," Jo said, pointing at Laurie, who nodded agreeably.

"Loads worse."

Even Amy, who had both shoes off now, looked at their older sister, annoyed. "We're just trying to survive, Meg. You can't expect *les savages* to have manners."

"Put your shoes on, you little heathen." Meg was increasingly out of sorts, sitting stiffy in gloves and long sleeves and another one of her plain bonnets.

"Are you sure you don't want to take your gloves off? You're going to faint," Jo said. "Then we'll have to carry you home, which is difficult to do . . . *properly.*"

Laurie eyed Meg. "I bet I could do it. Throw her over one shoulder?"

Jo looked Meg over as well. "I suppose I could take the legs?"

"Wouldn't we just use a wheelbarrow?" Amy asked, shoving the last of the lettuce into her mouth. "I saw one over in the church shed."

Meg snapped, "No, thank you. No wheelbarrow will be

required, and my gloves are not about to leave my fingers, as long as we are in mixed company—with gentlemen—at a church social." Her bonnet bobbed with indignation.

"Gentlemen? Here?" Laurie laughed.

"She doesn't mean you, you toad," Jo said, poking him in the ribs.

"Well, if this *fine social occasion* is meant for gentlemen, then can we be excused?" Laurie asked. "Since Meg wouldn't let us swim in the creek in our knickers on the way here, I want to jump in the swimming-hole on the way home."

"*Knickers?!*" Amy said. "That wouldn't hardly be fair. I only got to take off my *shoes*, and Meg still complained!"

"In Italy we swam naked," Laurie said, causing all three March sisters to blush. "We jumped off the boat at Otranto, just near the lighthouse, and outswam the Medusas. Sorry, was that coarse?" he asked with mock innocence. Laurie's mother, who had died long ago, had come from that country, and he forever used it to tease at the Marches' rather more prim New England sensibilities.

"The Castle of Otranto?" Jo asked. "From Walpole's book?"

"The very same," Laurie said. "There's a dull place, I tell you. Nothing but Turkish cannonballs all strewn about. And dust."

"I'm finished." Amy stood up. "I'm going to find my friends. I made a plan with Poppet to go spy on all the most horrible boys."

Poppet was their Hannah's niece—as well as Amy's long-time friend—and there was no end to trouble when the two were together.

"You and Poppet?" Jo raised an eyebrow. "Again?"

Amy shrugged. "There's a lot to spy on. They're very horrible boys."

With that she ran off, nearly bowling over a tall, dark-haired young man with deep brown eyes, a serious expression on his handsome face, and a slight hitch in his walk. A war-wound that had not completely healed. A sign of the times, which, like so many of the fathers and brothers and uncles of Concord, he wore without complaint, almost without comment.

It was Mr. Brooke, Laurie's tutor—and Meg's fictional suitor.

"Miss March?" He bent over their blanket. "Would you be so kind as to accompany me for a walk down to the edge of the creek?"

Meg held a gloved hand above her eyes to block out the sun and to try to identify the speaker. As soon as she did, she turned a deep pink that had nothing to do with the weather. "You're too kind . . . Mr. Brooke."

Jo looked at Laurie, wryly.

Mr. Brooke smiled. "I wouldn't like you to become overheated. It's such a frightfully warm day," he continued.

Here was the tutor in question, the one who had so dashingly swept Meg off her feet in the pages of Jo's book. *At least John Brooke has the dignity to never mention it,* Jo thought. In fact, it was the first time he had spoken directly to Meg, and something in his earnest brown eyes made Jo wonder if he had the courage to do so now precisely because of her book. After all, she had only written him as Meg's suitor because the poor fellow had spent whole months mooning over her sister without so much as a word.

Not that Mr. Brooke had time for pleasantries. Since he took his wound in the war and had been sent home, he'd become a teacher. Twice a week he took the train back and forth between Concord and Cambridge, dividing his time between his duties as Laurie's own tutor and as the sole instructor of a private preparatory course in ancient Greek and Roman readings. The Cambridge position had him tutoring local boys set to follow their fathers directly to the Harvard Club of Boston. "The Blasted Brookesian Brahmins," Laurie called them, just gleeful to have escaped attendance himself, though his grandfather often threatened it.

Not that anyone Brooke taught needed help securing a Cambridge future. Their family names—Adams and Peabody, Coolidge and Cabot, Forbes and Endicott—were already carved across the stone faces of half the buildings surrounding Harvard Yard. Still, Brooke dutifully plowed through Virgil and Homer and Catullus with the lot of them, just as he did with Laurie. The poor fellow was nothing if not dutiful.

Meg hesitated, as if only just now realizing the implications of the two of them walking together. "Please don't feel even the slightest obligation, Mr. Brooke. I shouldn't want people to think . . . simply because my sister, well, and the story . . ." It was unbearably awkward, and she blushed the color of a spring rose.

The effect was breathtaking, and not lost on Mr. Brooke.

Jo found she could not look away, almost as if she were trapped in the front row of some dreaded holiday pantomime.

Now he bowed. At least it was an awkward bow. Still, Jo eyed him with suspicion.

"There can be no obligation where there is affection, Miss

March. I would be honored. Truly." He smiled, and for the first time, Jo noticed the warmth in his voice. Begrudgingly.

"Oh! Mr. Brooke! In that case, a walk would be lovely," Meg said, holding out her gloved hand and allowing herself to be pulled to her feet.

Laurie and Jo exchanged a glance. "Well, I'll be," said Laurie with a grin. "Perhaps truth shall follow fantasy, after all."

Jo threw a strawberry at him in annoyance as Mr. Brooke extended a stiff elbow to her elder sister.

"Do you think she might actually like him?" The thought came to Jo, sudden and strange. "Could Meg be *flirting*?"

"No," Laurie said dismissively. "That? That's not what flirting looks like."

"How would you know?" Jo looked over at him.

"Because I'm told I'm an excellent flirt?" He kept his eyes fixed on Meg as Mr. Brooke plucked a willowy cat's-tail from the riverbank, presenting it to her. "At least, better than that."

"Really, now? Who, pray tell, would have told you that?" Jo felt her face turning a confused sort of pink. Was it the thought of her best friend looking at another girl the way Meg was looking at Mr. Brooke right now? Or was it the thought of losing her sister to a happy ending Jo had never meant to happen?

"Look, wouldn't your sister be, you know, giggling or something? Isn't that what girls do? When they flirt?" He reached for the biscuit that sat untouched on Meg's abandoned plate.

"How should I know? And that's the last of them." Jo held out her hand expectantly. "Fair is fair."

Laurie ripped the roll into two halves. Jo took the bigger biscuit half, and Laurie smiled.

They sat in companionable silence for a while, wilting under the sun, until Laurie suddenly got to his feet. "Damn the heat. Damn the gloves. Damn Brooke." He looked down at Jo and held out his hand. "Would the lady be so kind as to accompany me down to the damnable swimming-hole? So we can swim in our damn knickers like the good Lord intended us to?"

Jo looked up at him. Her girlish hat was now cocked at a ridiculous angle on his sweaty head, and his shirt was covered with crumbs.

"Not Italian-style?"

"This is Concord, milady. Not a Turkish cannonball in sight. The natives would never allow it."

Why not? Another adventure, and Jo was always up for a dare.

So she smiled and gave him her hand. "I thought you'd never ask."

THE WATER WAS bracing and cold, if Medusa-free. While not the Adriatic, it still took the breath from their chests and the blush from their faces. There, surrounded by moss and overgrowth, splashing in the same dark green water they'd been swimming in since they were children, everything became and remained as normal as it ever had been or ever could be.

It was a place for secrets, the swimming-hole. Their secrets. It always had been.

It was true that most girls wouldn't have gone swimming in their britches with the boy from next door—but most girls weren't bohemian writers setting out to make a name for themselves as the voice of their generation, and most boys weren't Laurie.

Besides, they weren't only best friends—they were loyalists. Neither one of them would ever tell.

"I'm meant to write this book," Jo finally said, treading water.

"You will," Laurie said, treading next to her.

"But I hate it."

"You won't."

"I don't know if I have another one in me." She felt her knickers swishing back and forth beneath the water.

"Then don't write it?"

"But I have to! For money, Teddy. I signed a contract. *Good Wives.* The Roberts Brothers say the story's not finished the way it is."

"They do?" he asked. "Is it or isn't it? Wouldn't you know? Aren't you the writer?"

"You would think."

"So?" The word gurgled out with a mouthful of pond water.

"So I don't want to write it," Jo said, simply. "I can't make it . . . tidy. Tie up all those loose ends in a nice, neat bow. They're ours to tie . . . or untie. I won't do that to my family. Marry them off like that."

"So . . . don't." Laurie was looking at her strangely now, almost as if he had never seen her before. She could only imagine what she looked like, soaked through her two undershirts, with at least one, maybe two vines in her hair. Not that she cared, although it was maddening to realize she might, a little.

"Don't write it? Just like that?" She kicked her legs beneath her.

"Just like that," Laurie said.

"But it's meant to make us our fortune," Jo said, mulling. "My family, I mean."

"A fortune? From a book? I'll be damned." He went under the water, then came bursting back to the surface, shaking and spraying water from his hair like a hound. "Do you care?"

"Spoken like a true Laurence." Jo tipped her head back until the cold crept all the way up her pooling brown hair to her forehead. She kicked harder, grazing his leg with her toe.

"Was that a yes?" He looked confused.

She yanked her head forward, letting the water drip into her eyes. "Not everyone is a Laurence, Teddy."

"But you're a March." He grabbed a handful of the ferns growing out of the bank, holding himself above the water enough to stop kicking. "Marches don't care about that sort of thing. That's part of their—your—magical . . ."

Jo leaned on his shoulder and he pressed his chin against the top of her head, putting an arm around her to help keep her head up from the surface.

"Magic," he said.

"Really." Jo smiled, moving slightly away so that she could look him in the eye.

His eyes twinkled. "You're the writer."

Now she could feel his pruned fingers against her arm as he

supported her weightlessness easily against him. "Life could be easier. Just because we don't talk about it doesn't mean it's not a weight on Mama Abba . . . on all of us. But that doesn't make it a virtue, either. Not for my family. Not for me."

He pulled her arm around his shoulder so that he was holding her steady. "You *and* your family, Jo. That's what makes Orchard House so wonderful."

"Please *do* give me a church sermon in your underwear in this watering-hole." She rolled her eyes, feigning annoyance. "That would be such a lovely follow-up to that already perfect picnic."

He laughed. "I'm allowed to think you're wonderful, Jo. I've never pretended not to."

She rested her chin on his cold shoulder. His shirt stuck to his muscled body like a second skin, and she found herself looking away. "Being poor doesn't make anyone wonderful, just like being rich doesn't."

"I didn't mean that," he said quietly, letting one hand fall on her back at her waist, as if to better support her. "I just mean—you shouldn't worry about it. Grandfather and I . . . we'd never let anything happen to you. To any of you."

She knew he spoke the truth. She'd seen it herself, they all had, when Beth needed special doctors, special medications, special treatments.

Jo shivered. "That's the thing. I don't want to *let* anyone—not you, not your grandfather—*let* me do anything. I want to . . . *let* myself . . . if there's *letting* to be done."

Even if it means writing the damnable book.

She had done well so far, hadn't she? She and her sisters didn't need to make rich matches and fortunate marriages. That wasn't the story that she was going to tell. Not at all!

"You're the writer," he repeated, though he didn't move his hand away. How strange it felt, the growing warmth pressing through the cold, cold water. So comfortable and familiar and welcome, and yet . . . and yet . . .

"We should go," Jo said, suddenly breaking free from his arms. She kicked across the pond and climbed up the rock, shrugging back into her clothes, dripping wet. "Race you home."

Laurie's only answer was a great leap past her, leaving his coat on the shore.

And with that, they raced all the way back to Orchard House— chasing and hollering and stumbling, frightening every chattering magpie along the path—until they collapsed in the garden, breathless children again.

6

DRAFT ADVENTURES

*I*t took a short three weeks for Jo to finish her first draft.

From late May to mid-June, she largely didn't come out of her attic garret; she ate bread or apples or cold boiled potatoes for most meals, and worked in solitude at all hours of the day and night, burning her way down through her last bits of beeswax. She didn't see much of Theodore Laurence, either, who had seemed—puzzlingly—to have disappeared.

Her mother and sisters, fortunately, were used to such behavior by now—as was the family cat, who stayed up with Jo most nights, until inevitably curling up to collapse in exhaustion on ink-smeared stacks of paper as the sun rose.

After the three weeks, the poor thing was so covered with black inky spots that Jo had taken to calling her Midnight. The attic, her Bestiary.

When Amy asked, one morning at breakfast, what she

was writing about, Jo only offered the most Jo-like of replies: "Something truly terrifying. Our fates."

Meg quieted Amy with a single sisterly look, and after that, everyone knew better than to ask again.

Once Jo had finished the raw words, it took another several days for her to ink a final copy, another day to get up the nerve to bring it in to Roberts Brothers, and then another week for Thomas Niles to read it.

What an *interminably* long week it was!

Not even the traditional Independence Day festivities—the Sunday School parade to the Old Hill Burying Ground, or the reading of the Declaration of Independence—could distract an anxious author awaiting judgment. To Jo, even the triumphant ringing of the Old North Church bell sounded positively ominous.

The very next day, the author appeared in person at the Roberts Brothers offices, where her editor broke the news.

The news was not good.

THOMAS NILES SLID the tin of mints across his desk apologetically. "I'm sorry, Miss March. I've discussed it with my investors at great length. We just can't publish this."

Jo stared. "What are you talking about? You asked for another book and I wrote it. You wanted a sequel; there's a sequel."

"But that's not it."

"What do you mean, that's not it?"

"I'm afraid that's not the *right* sequel."

"I'm the writer, aren't I? I wrote it, didn't I? How is it suddenly not right?" She'd made Meg a bravely stoic nurse helping soldiers in the war, and sent Amy off to Europe to become an artist. Independent women, all. Paragons of self-determination, moral clarity, and spiritual fortitude. "What seems to be the problem?"

"The problem, Miss March, is that I can sell two kinds of stories. Sweetness or scandal. True love conquers all, preferably culminating in a ball, a wedding, a nice piece of land, and dimpled babies—"

"Or?"

"Or the Josephine March special. Roderigo and Rodanthe. Rugged heroes, heaving bosoms, love and loss . . . and *boom!* The point of no return. Murder. Betrayal. An inheritance lost and gained. Everyone dies at the point of the blade."

"I see."

"Or there's always creatures, I suppose. Winged, horned, spewing flaming dung—up to you."

"Flaming dung?"

"Or mermaids . . . mermaids are big this year! Huge!"

He tossed her pages back on his desk. They scattered out of order, floating off the table and down to the floor.

Jo felt a wave of anger, then frustration, then exhaustion. The shame only came about last. "Well, I suppose that's that, then. I'm sorry, Niles. I've let you down."

"Sorry? You're my *author*, Miss March. I'm your *editor*. It's your sworn *duty* to let me down, over and over again, just as it's *my* duty to set you back on your path again, over and over again. You cajole; I threaten. You threaten; I cajole. This *literary husbandry* is the very foundation of our glorious profession. Our lives rather *depend* upon it, I'd say."

Jo managed a small smile. She knew when Niles was coddling her, but she appreciated it all the same.

She took a steadying breath. "Now what?"

"Now? Now you fix it, Miss March." Niles waved his hand at her imaginary process. "Go back to work. Do whatever it is you do. The sisters are a mess."

"*Mess* is a rather general term," she said, trying not to scowl.

"Beth is hardly in the story, for one thing."

"That's not true." Jo squirmed in her chair. She'd avoided saying what happened to Beth for a reason. She couldn't imagine Mama Abba reading about Beth's death and reliving the pain all over again; it was all any of the Marches could do not to weep every time one of them so much as spoke of her. Even their letters to their father had hardly mentioned Beth since the funeral.

Because her pain isn't a story, and because her story can't have an ending. She can't be gone both in the book and in life.

My Beth can't have an ending.

Niles sighed. "Then there's the matter of Jo."

"Jo? What's wrong with Jo?" That one she hadn't expected.

"I wouldn't know—that's why I'm asking," said Niles, exasperated. "You don't seem to want to say what happens to her at all."

"She has a long and storied literary career, *obviously.*"

"But whom does she marry?" asked Niles.

"Marry?!" Jo felt the rage bubbling up inside her chest as her face reddened. "I . . . she . . . doesn't know what she wants, just like my readers don't know what they want."

Now she could feel the blush warming and spreading across her entire face, perhaps her body, as a sudden image of Laurie came to mind. Laurie laughing in the damp noon heat, his shirt-sleeves rolled about his elbows. Laurie racing boat leaves in the creek, his trousers rolled about his ankles. Laurie and Jo, at their swimming-hole a few weeks back, with far more than wrists and ankles bared between them—

She tried to shake it off, but other thoughts crowded in. Everything she had wondered, might have wondered, might have wanted; everything she couldn't admit, not even to herself—

Christopher Columbus!

"Perhaps she'll never marry. Or marry every cabbage in the garden. Or eschew cabbages entirely, discovering she has a proclivity for . . . for tomatoes!"

"Tomatoes?"

"She—*we* don't know, Niles. That's the whole point!"

Now Niles was tapping the manuscript between them for emphasis. "But your readers do know what they want, Miss March. They want their little whalebone-corseted hearts set afire."

Her skin was hot as a furnace now.

"We do also have brains, Niles."

"Yes, brains that want happy endings. Weddings. Not Romeo and Juliet snuffed in Verona. Romeo and Juliet in domestic bliss in their Tuscan villa. You are—*Jo is*—allowed to want those things. And dare I say? To have them."

Jo reached for the tin of peppermints. It was all too much. She opened the tin, hesitated, leaving it open. "I won't do anything that hurts my family."

"Hurt them?" Niles stood up, pushing off from his desk. "How are you hurting them? With any luck, you're making them rich beyond their wildest dreams."

"Theirs or yours?" Jo arched an eyebrow. He arched one back.

"You're being unreasonable," they said, one to the other, almost in unison.

She rose from her chair and plucked her gloves from the desk— sending another page of her abandoned manuscript sliding to the floor. "I'm going."

He shook his head. "I'm sorry, Miss March. If you didn't want to write about your family, you should have said so before you signed our contract. Your family is what readers on two sides of the pond have bought and paid for. I thought we discussed this."

Jo shoved the peppermint tin across her publisher's desk, sending the candies rolling in every direction.

"And I thought I already said no."

"Let me at that Niles," Laurie growled, pacing the length of the Orchard House dining-room. "I'll flatten him. *Christopher Columbus*, I will."

"You won't," Jo moaned. "You can't." Her voice was muffled, as she had collapsed in a heap at the dinner-table.

Meg and Amy sat on either side of her, protectively; they had been taking turns patting her heaving, sobbing shoulders since she'd returned home from her meeting.

"Watch me." Laurie glared, though there was no point to it, as Mr. Niles was not there to see or care. "It can't be that bad," he muttered at no one, for the fifteenth time.

"It is. He hated everything. He said they all did." Jo could barely get the words out. "It's back to the beginning. There's no way around it. They want romance. Weddings. The full Vegetable Valley."

"Is it really so awful?" Laurie said, now crouching next to Jo.

Jo dropped her head into her arms. "I won't make a scandal of the March family."

"I don't mind," Amy said, squeezing a walnut between the jaws of a little nutcracker. "I'm naturally *tempestuous*, you realize. Scandal-wise."

"What a surprise," Meg said as the nut exploded, sending bits of shell shrapnel scattering across the crocheted rug.

Jo sat up in spite of herself. "You can't rescue me this time, Teddy. You can't solve everything and save everyone, as much as you want to try."

He looked at her helplessly. "I have to do something, Jo. Let me do something."

She straightened in her chair. "No, Laurie. Let *me*. I have to take care of this. And I will . . . I just don't know how. Not the way Niles wants me to."

Laurie went back to walking the room; an out-of-sorts Jo always meant an even more out-of-sorts Laurie. That much they all knew.

"Roberts Brothers Press? They're no different from the rest of them, publishers and editors and newspapermen. All a barrel of snakes!"

"Mr. Niles isn't like that," Jo said. "You don't know. They can't all be like that."

"Grandfather says so, every time we go to New York. He says you can't listen to people like that."

"People like that?" Jo looked appalled. "What people? Tradesmen? Workmen? *Writers*, Laurie?" When the two friends fought, this was why. Laurie could never really imagine any sort of life beneath his own set of rooms on the second floor of the Laurence house, and Jo could hardly imagine the view from up there. Two windows connected them; that was all. One had given a youthful Laurie a glimpse of the March family parlor, and the other had given the March girls a view into Teddy Laurence's sitting-room.

Two windows. A few dozen panes of wavering glass.

Was it really ever going to be enough to bridge the whole worlds—of day-dresses and kid leather gloves and carriages and careers; of farms and root-cellars and weeding and candle-stubs— between them?

Jo wondered.

"Come on, Jo. It's a coarse business." Laurie was still pacing, red-faced. "Men like that? They're dishonorable. They only speak lies—"

"Or worse. The truth." Jo sat up.

"I don't understand a word either of you are saying." Amy took a handful of walnuts from the mason jar on the table and began to crack them. "But here. You'll feel better."

"Will I?" Jo asked sadly.

"Of course you will." Meg put a cup of tea in front of her. The cup and saucer rattled the quiet in the room.

Jo didn't move.

The sisters looked at each other. "What's happening?" Amy whispered. Meg raised a finger to her lips.

Laurie touched the cool window glass with his fingertips, staring out into the shadows. A moment later he sighed as if he'd suddenly made up his mind about some question he couldn't bring himself to ask.

He looked down at Jo. "So, then. Romance? That's what we need, Mr. Snodgrass, old chap?"

Jo felt the smallest simmer of relief—as always—at the reappearance of their old nicknames. "So it seems, Mr. Weller. I believe *little whalebone-corseted hearts* are to be *set afire*, as it were."

"I see I shall have to bequeath you something of my considerable understanding of the subject, Mr. Snodgrass. Sadly, even your most *Vegetarian* fates hardly merit a bit of melted whalebone at all."

Amy laughed. Meg elbowed her.

Laurie stepped closer to the table, looking affectionately down at Jo's mop of brown curls. He took her usual bundle of paper from its place on the top shelf, then placed her old ink-pot in front of her with a thump. "And at what temperature does whalebone melt, *precisely*, Mr. Snodgrass?"

He held out her quill.

"I don't believe it's entirely clear, Mr. Weller." She bit the inside of her cheek to keep from giving him the personal satisfaction of so much as even a chuckle. Still, she dipped her quill into the ink.

"I suppose marrying vegetables is somewhat tiresome." Laurie sat backward on the chair next to Jo. A heap of long arms and even longer legs spilled awkwardly in either direction from the chair back. "So I'm assuming that instead of marrying a cabbage, Jo dies in a shipwreck off the coast of the New World, *old chap*?"

NANTUCKET, Jo scratched, without missing a beat. "They go down like a stone. *Old chap*."

"With her young Florentine lover?"

VENETIAN, she wrote, perking up. "Passionately so."

Laurie nodded, matter-of-fact. "Proper remains?"

NOT A ONE, Jo scribbled back. "Utterly dashed to pieces against the shoals." The thought made her smile. That damnable Laurence boy. There was no staying in a properly miserable mood when he was around.

He knows me too well.

Laurie watched her, increasingly amused. "And her life's work, Mr. Snodgrass? Forever lost? Pages floating on the waves?"

AT THE BOTTOM OF THE SEA. Jo frowned. "In the

lifeless arms of the Venetian, possibly. Or, you know . . . the author."

Amy looked intrigued. "Was he rich? This Venetian?"

"Penniless." Jo smiled as she wrote. "But not so much a German Emerson. More of an Italian Byron, really."

"Scandal upon scandal," Laurie said. He clapped his hand upon Jo's back. "Sure to sell loads. Highest marks, my dear Snod. Congratulations. You've done it. Now just, you know, write it all down."

"Oh, is that all?" Jo laughed.

He yanked her up from her seat, forcing her to her feet. "What are you waiting for? Get up to your garret and write, Snodgrass!"

"Let me use your study, dearest Weller, and perhaps I shall."

"Even better." He bowed and offered her his arm.

"Wait for me," Amy said. "I've just got to put away the nutcracker."

But by the time Amy returned from the cellar, Jo and Laurie were already out the front door, with the rejected manuscript harmlessly hidden under Laurie's arm.

"Wait!" Amy cried. "I can catch up—"

"You have chores to do before dinner." Meg shook her head at her youngest sister. "Let them be," she said. "Those two."

"But I never get to go, and it's such a tremendous house with so many paintings to look at." Amy sulked. "And they're not even talking about anything. They never are. Just loads and loads of nonsense."

Meg patted her sister's arm. "Only they know what they're

talking about, Amy, but I do believe—in their own way—it's not nonsense."

"Shipwrecks and sunken manuscripts and Jo's Venetian?!" Amy looked at Meg, confused. "If that's not nonsense, what is it?"

Meg circled her arm affectionately around her little sister's slender shoulders. "He's Jo's Cherry King, don't you see?"

"I do," said Amy. "But does *she*?"

Meg pinched her chin fondly. "Fair question, Mr. Winkle."

It really was.

7

ENCHANTMENT

*D*eciding to slander the character of your family in the pages of your as-yet-unwritten novel was one thing. Actually doing it, as it turned out, was quite another.

Jo had taken to working in the upstairs study of the Laurences' house, as if she needed the physical space between herself and her real family in order to turn them into the things they were not, the things that they needed to be, at least on the page.

Laurie had taken to lurking about the house while she did—or, as he liked to call it, *helping*.

It was slow going—for both!—but Jo was determined to make it work. "*Roderigo and Rodanthe!* I have to do this, Laurie. It's my job."

He glared from his current perch, draped across the divan, a pillow balanced on his face. "I don't like it."

"My having a job?" Her eyes widened.

An exasperated groan came from beneath the pillow. "You

not having any fun. Which means me not having any fun, drearily enough. I only wish I knew how to unchain your beastly days from my own. We used to have such a romp, Jo!"

"Go have fun, then." She sighed. "Romp all you like. Romp for both of us, my boy. You shouldn't have to suffer just because I'm suffering. You're not the writer, as you're so fond of telling me."

"Good thing, too. That's all I mean to say." Laurie rolled off the divan, wandering across the room to busy himself with re-arranging the books on Grandfather's shelves. More of an artist and a musician than a reader, he tended to sort them by color, to Jo's endless chagrin.

"You don't understand. I've never *not* been able to write a book before." Jo was now out of her chair and banging around Laurie's drawing-room as if she owned the place—which, she reminded herself, no matter how many years they'd spent next door to each other, she didn't and never would.

"I know," Laurie said, settling back onto his favorite perch, the piano bench. He started to play a sweet melody—Tchaikovsky's very newest, that had just arrived from the Continent: "None but the Lonely Heart." Jo only knew it because he'd made a point of playing it for her before, whenever he was in one of his more plain-tive moods.

She sat down next to him, almost automatically. It was hard not to, when he played for her. His hands moved absently over the keys, the melody sweet as honey. It was soothing, sometimes hypnotic.

She leaned her head on his shoulder. She liked the feel of his arms moving beneath her, even now, when her mind was occupied with other, more horrible things. "I've never *not* been able to do anything before, come to think of it. Not if I truly cared about it."

"Dancing," he teased, his eyes twinkling.

"Depends on the quality of the slippers, I suppose. And whether anyone will see us." She lifted her head, swallowing a smile and remembering how she had written about how they'd met in her first book.

"Dull-witted parlor talk?" He looked at her sideways.

Jo considered. "How dull?"

His hands moved more quickly now. "As dull as feather-hatted ladies? As a church picnic? As Grandfather when he drones on about my taking up the law at Harvard?"

"Those are three different dulls, entirely," she protested.

"Not if you're me."

"Fine," Jo said, giving up. "Some things are perhaps *a little* harder than others. But not *writing.* Not for me. That's supposed to be the easy bit, Laurie. Maybe my only easy bit."

"I agree," Laurie said, turning his focus back to the piano.

His head rocked carelessly, longish locks of brown curls hanging in his eyes like the forelock of a pony. Jo knew the look well, the one that came with the moments when he became suddenly oblivious to everything but the music. The moments when he was even foreign to her.

This is what it looks like, then. From the outside.

His hands moved across the keys in ripples, pushing ahead only to draw back again.

Making something.

Jo knew how it felt to be in a room with other people but to still be utterly alone. To be lost to herself in a world only she knew existed. To rejoice in the thrill of it, to dread the end of it. To feel the guilt and the fear that nothing in the world of the living might ever again feel so true, or come so close.

The fear that I live in the wrong world. A castle in the air, made of shadows and light, where no one can reach me . . .

Now Laurie sang the words as effortlessly as he played.

> *None but the lonely heart*
> *Can know my sadness;*
> *Alone, and parted far*
> *From joy and gladness.*
> *Heaven's boundless arch I see*
> *Spread out above me.*
> *Oh, what a distance drear to one*
> *Who loves me!*
> *None but the lonely heart*
> *Can know my sadness;*
> *Alone, and parted far*
> *From joy and gladness.*
> *Alone, and parted far*
> *From joy and gladness.*
> *My senses fail,*
> *A burning fire*
> *Devours me.*

None but the lonely heart
Can know my sadness.

His voice was clear and tender, but as always, the effect was not without a certain sorrow, though Jo never could say why. She'd also never dared ask, unusually enough.

He has a shadow-castle of his own. I can hear it.

His melodies come from heartache, she thought. *Even my jovial Laurie.*

Perhaps all melodies do.

Jo suspected it had something to do with his mother, who seemed to have been an Italian soprano with no small reputation of her own, in her day. Jo tried to imagine her now, beautiful and bosomy, powdering her face in some dressing-room while a cherubic Laurie toddled around, upsetting vases of roses from undaunted suitors and generally destroying everything in sight. Then she tried to imagine her beloved Teddy, wailing and reaching for his mama when she was no longer there . . .

The last notes faded away.

"So?" he said, letting his hands drop into his lap. "What do you think you should do?"

It took Jo a moment to remember he was talking about her book.

She sighed. "I just . . . I don't know if I'm telling the right story. And it matters, Laurie," she finally said. "At least to me. Whether or not anyone else seems to understand."

"Why, the story matters, of course it does. But you can't

possibly have time to write if you spend every waking moment worrying about *what* to write. Take it from me."

Jo frowned. "Whatever would you know about worrying?"

Laurie laughed. "Nothing at all; that's absolutely my point. My expertise lies in *not* worrying!"

"Ah, the plight of the forever gentleman." She rolled her eyes. "Well, some of us must both work and worry. We can't all practice Teddy Laurence's fine *foolosophies*."

"But I'll teach you!" Now he leapt up from the piano. "What you need, Miss March, is a change of pace . . . or at least a change of scenery. That's why I've made a plan for us, a good one. Come on." He grabbed her hand, a delighted look on his face.

"What?" She laughed, pulling away.

"A surprise!" Laurie loved a surprise more than anything. They were all his little productions—a version of theater, not unlike Jo's parlor-room plays, she supposed.

"Please. No settee jumping in the drawing-room, Mr. Laurence!"

"Aw, don't you trust me, Jo?" He looked remarkably earnest for Teddy Laurence. *And for the moment, remarkably unfoppish,* she thought.

She smiled at him fondly. "Of course not."

He nodded. "Very sensible. Still . . ."

Plans, indeed!

It had taken two days to convince Mr. Laurence to allow his ward to go to New York City, let alone with one of the March girls.

(*"Running off to that thieves' den? My own grandson? And with a decent, sweet thing like Josephine March? Forty fits! That's what you'll give me!"*) It had taken three days after that to talk Mama Abba into allowing Laurie to bring Jo along with him; she'd only relented, in the end, because she had an old neighbor-friend—Mrs. Kirke—who ran a boarding house in Greenwich Village, which was where Laurie and Jo found themselves now.

Their train had arrived too late for lunch and too early for dinner, so they sat together at the long-planked table in the communal dining-room, drinking tea and eating chocolates, laughing at the characters they'd seen on the train and in the streets along their way.

When Laurie took a flask of his grandfather's brandy out of his satchel and dripped a capful into each of their teacups—*"Let's have a little Grandfather's tea, shall we?"*—they only laughed harder. It was all very scandalous.

The boarding house was plain but clean; Jo suspected Laurie had never stayed in such a humble room, but he managed not to say anything terribly obvious, and she loved him for it. And for her part, well, New York City loomed larger than she had realized it would. For almost the first time, she wondered if she were not *quite* so brave as she let on.

"You have to let me do this, Jo," Laurie said.

"Do what?" Jo asked now, stirring another lump of sugar—and by that, she meant another capful of brandy—into her tea. She raised her glass. "Here's to Grandfather's tea."

"Grandfather's tea," Laurie said, clinking his teacup to hers—but he put his down without sipping it this time.

"Let me treat you, old girl. Take you out. Show you what a proper weekend in the city can be like." He sat up, excited by even the prospect of such an adventure. "For inspiration! A new adventure every night—you'll have loads to write about!"

Jo shook her head at his excitement. At times like these, he was as young as one of Meg's pupils. "We're here, Teddy. Isn't that enough?"

"No, Jo. It's not." He stood up. "Not for you. If I'm to be a proper muse, it's my *duty* to inspire you."

"Muse? You!" Jo laughed. Laurie looked hurt. "Inspiring it would be, but you live in Concord just like I do, dearest heart. How would either of us begin to know what a *proper weekend* in New York City is like?"

"I asked." He held up a handful of tickets and papers. "Grandfather called his solicitor. I've arranged whole days of proper New York plans. Nights, even. Come on, Jo! Be a sport and humor me. Just this once—it'll be such a grand lark!"

Now Jo was caught off guard. "Tickets? Laurie—to what? The opera? Art galleries? Museums? You shouldn't have!"

"Oh, *I* didn't. As I said." He grinned. "Really, Jo? Why would I myself have *opera tickets*? I live in Concord just like you do! I just, you know, sent a few telegrams . . . spoke to a few rather well-situated chaps . . ."

Jo shook her head in wonder as she pored over the tickets—then put them down on the table linen between them. "What of our agreement? You were to catch up on your college reading, and I was to try to write, remember?"

It was true that Laurie was meant to begin school in Cambridge in September, regardless of how he felt about it—and there was a fairly daunting reading-list that stood between him and his arrival in Boston. That said, not only had he failed to open a book yet, he'd also been threatening to not go at all for weeks now, which was how Jo felt about her failure of a writing project. The looming fall was bearing down on both of them.

"Gah," Laurie said. *"Reading."*

"Do you not think, dear boy, I might be the *slightest bit* offended by the low regard in which you seem to hold my *entire awful profession*?"

"We needn't both be writers," Laurie said. "That would be unbearably dull. Besides, I read your book."

"Liar." She glared.

"Fine." He laughed. "But I will, one day. Write a few more, and I'll read those, too. Write enough and you'll convert me to your *entire awful profession* yet, Miss March. Until then, I will confine myself to being, if not your muse, your . . . let's say, *Master of Inspiration.*"

"Do you mean my Master of Procrastination?" Jo frowned. "We were to be in hiding, remember? You with your Plato's *Symposium* and me with my scandalous yet scandalously un-written novel? I didn't bring anything nice enough for a proper weekend—and even if I had, it still wouldn't be nice enough."

"What are you talking about?" Laurie looked confused. "You always look nice enough—don't you?"

Jo put down her teacup. "You don't notice, because you're a

boy. But my gowns are all wrong, my slippers are from two seasons ago, and these aren't even opera gloves."

"Operas have gloves?"

"Laurie, you're hopeless."

It was only then that she saw the twinkling in his eye and realized he was teasing her.

She blushed. "You're teasing. You're awful. A horrible bore."

He winked. "At least I'm not a cabbage. At least I'm not Professor Bore."

"At least that," she said, smiling into her tea. "Odious fellow."

"Grandfather took care of everything, I'm told. It's all upstairs, and meant to be a very girly surprise, and beyond that I have no idea what's in anything or how any of it works, so please don't ask me to tie things and clasp things and buckle things like Amy always does." He looked so truly befuddled that Jo laughed aloud.

"Oh, what love," she said, and he took her hand before she realized she had said it.

"You're magic," he said, simply. His eyes had locked on hers, and she found she could not look away. "I've said it before. You're a magic person, Jo. I sometimes think you might be . . . an enchantress."

She felt the two pink spots deepen on her cheeks, and there was nothing she could do to stop them.

"Stop!" she said, as much to herself as to him. She drew her hand away from his. "For all you know, what I am is a witch."

"Of course," he said, sitting back in his seat with satisfaction. "A witch. It's so obvious now! How could I have gotten that wrong?"

She laughed and shook her head. "Oh, Laurie. How are you even possible? I sometimes think it doesn't matter what I say."

"Not a bit."

"You honestly don't care what words come out of my mouth—you've already accepted me for them, haven't you?"

"Why wouldn't I? So long as you're the one saying them? I know we have our rows, but we always come out on the other side, don't we?"

"Always."

Laurie looked as if he wanted to say something more, then stopped himself.

"What?" She sipped her tea, feeling happy and dizzy and alight with the prospects of the weekend.

Laurie looked uncharacteristically serious. "You're my best friend in the world, Jo. You have been, for as long as I can remember. I can think of very few words you could say that would change how I feel about you." He drained his teacup and put it down. "Unless you were, say, Plato . . . and all the words were a frightfully dull *Symposium*."

Jo let out a laugh, despite herself.

"But let's suppose even Plato has a *few* good bits . . . that I'll discover . . . one of these days . . . possibly."

"You really never give up, do you?" Jo sighed. "I love that you can be like that, my boy. If only I could be that way with myself."

"Do you want me to show you how I do it?" Laurie asked. "Because I can. I'll show you the trick. It's simple—I swear it."

Jo said nothing, but she found it hard to look away. She also found she wanted to. It was like that between them, sometimes. She wanted to be near Laurie, to stay within the bubble of light that he carried with him; but once she was that close, she found she was too afraid to show herself. Whether to him or to herself, she couldn't say.

Either way, one moment everything would be perfectly normal. They'd be laughing and teasing and running the meadow path like wild things.

The next moment, he'd look a certain way—or look at *her* a certain way—and she'd find herself staring down at her own slippers, like a tongue-tied schoolgirl who can't bring herself to look her first maidenly crush right in the eye.

Just one look.

Sometimes, one word.

The constant push-pull of her emotions exhausted her, dizzied her. Or perhaps it was only Grandfather's tea.

She found herself studying her slippers.

Laurie lowered his voice and leaned forward. The room was suddenly so still, she could hear dishes clattering and maids chattering in the next room. But as he spoke, she heard nothing else, and it seemed to Jo like they were the only two people on earth.

The words were close and quiet in her ear.

"Love yourself like I love you, old friend."

He pressed his two hands to her one. His voice was light, but she recognized the tremor of truth as he spoke, and she knew he was deadly serious.

She felt the air close around her. Her heart beginning to pound.

Her old familiar shadow-lands, waiting just behind the door to her heart. Now a tidal wave of panic beginning to rise. As if she were trapped in her own skin and had no choice but to wriggle free. As if her life depended on it, and she didn't know why.

It's Teddy. It's still just Teddy. You're not afraid of him.

You're not.

She let go of his hand.

"That's quite a trick." Jo shivered. "I'll try to remember."

"It's all right," Laurie said, his fingers still grazing hers. "I won't let you forget."

Jo's teacup clattered in her hands and she stood up, not knowing what else to do. "Stop. Stop talking foolishness. I'm going to write and you're going to open your Plato or I'll cast a spell and banish you away to college forever."

He raised both hands. "Not another word."

8

A Proper Weekend

*B*etween Grandfather's tea and her own pounding heart, Jo had completely forgotten the promised surprise.

But when, at last, Laurie agreed to go do his reading, Jo went upstairs to her small, plain room in Mrs. Kirke's boarding house, and there it was.

Not so much *it* as *she*—

"Christopher Columbus!" Jo exclaimed.

Because it was Meg. Still holding her gloves in one hand. Sitting in the worn wooden chair by the window, peering out at the crowds of people passing by on the street below.

For a moment, Jo stared in disbelief. Truly, the day had been surreal enough that she thought it entirely possible she was imagining things; to that end, Jo wouldn't have been surprised to open the door and see President Grant himself sitting there.

"Took you long enough!" Meg cried.

Jo smiled at the sisterly scolding. *Not President Grant.*

"Meg? Meg!" She flung herself across the room and into the arms of her older sister, almost before Meg could rise to her feet. "But you hate trains! And cities! And crowds! And . . . whatever are you doing here?"

"What do you think? I'm your surprise." Meg looked annoyed. "Did he not say? Oh, fiddlesticks! Laurie was to tell you there was something waiting for you upstairs. And that something was to be me. I don't know why he had his heart so set on the trick of it. I took a later train and just arrived, and Laurie made me sneak up the back stairs, that scamp."

Jo laughed now, finally catching on to the joke. "He made you sound like a parcel of clothes! That ridiculous boy."

Meg smiled back. "I did bring you a parcel," she said, now pointing to a paper bundle on the bed, tied with twine. "Mama Abba had them made up for you but forgot to slip them into your bag. She's not so good at surprises as Laurie, I suppose. So here I am."

"Mama! Oh, no, I hope she didn't spend too much." Jo began doing the frantic mental calculations every writer did in their head every month, especially the sort who worked at *The Tall Taler*.

Meg put a gentle hand on her sister's shoulder. "No, Jo. It's a gift from old Mr. Laurence. For your first trip to New York City. What a gentleman. He made certain Mama Abba was the one who chose your things, to make sure she—and you—would approve."

Jo smiled at the thought of her mother folding the little bundle before her. It was a relief, to be sure, but still, to have Meg come all this way just to deliver her a bundle of clothes seemed a tremendous lot of bother. "Did Mr. Laurence come with you? I can't imagine Mama Abba would let you come alone. Or that you would dare attempt it."

Meg blushed a deep pink, looking back out the window. "I didn't. Not exactly."

Jo gave her sister a queer look. "Then how—exactly?"

Meg's mouth twisted into a half-smile that she couldn't suppress, though Jo could see she was trying. "John—Mr. Brooke was my escort."

"John?!"

"Mr. Brooke, Jo."

Jo found it hard to even imagine the long hours of a rattling train ride down the Hudson Valley sitting across from the solemn and silent John Brooke. "How tedious your trip must have been! You really should have ridden down with Teddy and me."

"Actually, he was . . . very kind. I feel like I know him much better now, and he seemed pleased enough to spend the time with me." Now the pink spots on Meg's cheeks deepened into a particularly becoming shade of rose.

Jo touched her sister's face. "I expect so. Especially if you were blushing like that all the way to Hudson Station!"

"He was being a gentleman. That's all," Meg sniffed. "Obviously."

"Obviously." Jo gave her sister a teasing look. "I just hadn't expected to see my literary matchmaking have such an effect."

"Don't be ridiculous." Meg pulled off her bonnet, shaking her curls free to her shoulders. "It was nothing. And both Mr. Brooke and I are only here because it was Laurie's idea. He thought the two of us would enjoy *a little escape*, as he called it."

Two? Of us?

"But that old brick? He hardly speaks! How did you manage hour upon hour of conversation?"

Meg pulled loose the ribbon of her bonnet. "We managed well enough. He's friendly, if a bit shy of me. After all, let's recollect the whole English-speaking world thinks you want us to marry."

Jo scoffed and fingered the twine on her bundle. "I'd hardly say the *whole* English-speaking world cares about John Brooke. If any of my readers care a whit, I suspect it's only about you."

Meg smiled, folding her bonnet on the neatly made bed. "We had a bit of a laugh about it, at first. The awkwardness of it all. Once that was out of the way, we found all kinds of things to discuss."

"What sorts of things?"

"What it's like to be tormented by having a writer of books in your family. What it's like to be tortured by having a scamp in your tutelage."

"Well, that surely took hours." Jo rolled her eyes.

"It did."

"Wonder of wonders," Jo said, crossly. She flung Meg's discarded gloves onto the floor and took their place on the opposite chair. "Well, I can hardly imagine old Babbling Brooke with us for an entire week. I hope this isn't Teddy's way of trying to marry you two off in real life."

"I imagine it was Laurie's way of being kind. Really, Jo, I don't know why you think everything is a marriage plot! It's only *you* who thinks about marrying everyone off all the time!"

But to Jo, it *was* a plot, and an obvious one. Much worse, it was a betrayal. *Theodore Laurence*, she thought, *don't you dare play matchmaker with my Meg.*

"I could never be interested in Mr. Brooke, anyway," said Meg.

"Why not?" asked Jo, surprised.

Meg flushed, as if she had already made up her mind. "Because."

"Because he's poor like I wrote in my book, and 'Aunt March' thinks you're throwing your life away? Oh, Meg, that's just fiction. You can marry anyone you please, even dull old Brooke if you truly want to," said Jo.

"Of course I can't," said Meg. "I must find a Laurie of my own."

Jo was stunned. "A *what*?"

"Marrying well is the only way I can help the family. You help with your writing, Jo, but what can I do? I'm not a famous author like you."

"Good heavens, I'm not famous by any means," said Jo, even as that statement was becoming less and less true. "And you mustn't speak that way. It's not becoming, and it's not the Meg I know."

"Don't look at me like that," said Meg. "Like you think I'm . . ."

"Amy?" Jo couldn't resist.

"A . . . a trollop!" Meg snapped. Jo raised an eyebrow. Her sister was flustered. "It isn't the very easiest thing, you know. Having

American authoress Josephine March for a sister. Being *the other* March sister. The one who didn't die. The one who isn't renowned. The one who isn't an artist, or a scamp!"

Jo looked taken aback. *Meg's hurt, you ninny. She's hurt and you didn't even see it.*

Meg kept going. "When our sister died, you had your garret to disappear into. Amy had her—"

"Mirror?" Jo volunteered.

"Sketch-pad!" Meg was agitated now. "What did I have? What do I have now? What's left for me, Jo? Being *a governess*?" She rubbed the back of her hand against her eye, and Jo suddenly felt as if her own heart were breaking.

"What's left, Meg, is for you to keep being Meg March, the best of us. My hero, and my beloved, *absolute loveliest* surprise. Let's not ruin it by squabbling," Jo said as she took her sister's arm.

She meant it, which Meg knew—as sisters do—and so peace was struck just as war had been declared.

Also as sisters do.

"Come on." Meg smiled, suddenly picking at the bundle. "Let's see what Mr. Laurence and Mama have sent you to wear."

Jo groaned. "Must we?"

"Yes, we must. This is New York City, and we're here to inspire you. If we're all to be characters in a Jo March story, we should at least dress the part."

Jo flung herself down on the bed, rumpling Meg's bonnet. "Fine. But if they're the least bit frilly, I'm giving the whole lot to you. I don't do frilly."

"You don't? What a shocking piece of *entirely new* information," Meg snorted.

"I said, the whole lot," Jo growled again.

"Even better," said Meg as she undid the bundle. "Now, what have we here?"

THAT WEEK WAS unlike any other in the history of the world, or at least Jo's world. Seven days of perfection, almost to the point of fiction. Even Mr. Brooke tagging along couldn't dampen her spirits.

Perhaps her sister was right.

Perhaps they all were characters in a Jo March story now.

In truth, she'd imagined such days before, but she'd always imagined them as the stuff of *The Tall Taler*—not Jo's rather more *Small Taler*, as she had come to refer to her own domestic life. While a week at Mrs. Kirke's boarding house was hardly the stolen rendezvous of thwarted lovers or shipwrecked castaways at some faraway Castle Otranto—as Jo herself might have written for Niles in the past—it was still so exotic, when compared to her pastoral Concord life, that it might as well have been.

That week, Jo and Meg had no *goblets of mead* to toast with, but tiny cups of strong coffee. No *nectar and ambrosia* to feast upon, but thick slabs of toast and jewel-colored berry preserves. No *brocade-and-ermine capelets* or *filigreed tiaras* to don, but clever new boots with a row of inlaid mother-of-pearl buttons and a pair of hand-stitched kid gloves—thanks to Mama Abba and the elder Mr. Laurence!

If the two girls and their male companions faced no *dueling pirates* and *dastardly fisticuffs*—the one exception being a rather heated exchange between Laurie and a leering, rough-mannered paperboy—they did find plenty of crowds to battle past and whole city blocks to navigate.

And though sadly lacking in both *galloping consumption* and *fainting spells*, Jo found no shortage of other maladies of the heart and soul.

Because this week, if there were no Roderigos, there was a Teddy.

Every morning, the two good friends, usually accompanied by Meg and Mr. Brooke, set out for another day of carefree adventure in the city. Jo and Meg (with two new day-dresses to show off, as if they'd stepped out from the pages of *Godey's Lady's Book*, Jo thought) and Laurie (with a trim new suit from the Laurences' personal tailor that he cared not a whit about showing off) walked the streets of Manhattan until their feet ached, marveling at tall buildings and small discoveries as the city unfolded before them.

Together the four of them ate *filet de boeuf* and sipped champagne at Delmonico's, attended lectures on France under Napoleon III, visited the site where Roebling was planning his elegant new bridge across the East River to Brooklyn, and even picnicked on the Green at Central Park.

Their days ranged from the exceptional to the overwhelming. One morning, they found themselves studying the gilded frames at the museum; that same afternoon, they accidentally wandered into the infamous tenement neighborhood of Five Points—west of the Bowery and south of Canal—where they encountered a scene of such squalor that it made the poor Hummels back home in Concord seem positively rich in comparison: mothers begging for food for their children, young boys fighting each other in the streets, and even a bar brawl that tumbled out onto the sidewalk.

After this last, John Brooke quickly urged Laurie and the ladies back north. ("Really, Mr. Laurence, what were you thinking, bringing ladies into this—this *den of iniquity*?")

Although Jo was secretly a bit thrilled to have seen said infamous den of iniquity with her own eyes, if only as fodder for future stories, Meg relived it all with such a heavy heart as they crawled into their warm bed that night that Jo was ashamed. "That mother with her babe! I shall never forget the sight! The poor thing had such a fever, I could feel the heat from three feet away!" Meg had cried.

They didn't say the obvious thing, of course. That it was their sister Bethie who would have taken the child to her bosom. Beth who would have wept at the needs of such a family, just as she had at the Hummels. If it had been winter, she would have pressed her own cloak into the hands of the first desperate mother she encountered, then wrapped her own scarf around the cold shoulders of the next.

Yes, and then contracted scarlet fever and died of it.

Which is precisely why your little sister isn't here, and you are.

Because, while life is not fair, it is logical.

Jo lay in bed that night feeling the heavy darkness settled upon her once again.

Danger was one thing, of course; destitution, especially that of poor women and their children, was quite another. Mama Abba, like Beth, would have urged Jo to see the poorer residents of the great city less as potential characters in her private dramas—less the personification of misfortune itself!—and more as human beings.

So Jo tried to do, for the sake of the poor creatures as well as her own soul.

And for her lost soul.

For Beth.

Still, every day brought a new discovery, most more pleasant than Five Points. When Jo and Meg, Laurie and Brooke returned to the little boarding house on the dark end of each day, they recounted everything they'd seen and heard, said and done. The younger two raced each other like schoolchildren as they bolted up the stairs and across the landing, each to their own little doors; the elder two lingered, taking their quiet leave at the bottom of the stairs as they went their separate ways. Jo—in such a hurry to write down everything she'd seen and heard, the better to remember it and write about it later—nearly forgot about Meg and Brooke's budding, or not-so-budding, romance.

Because the truth of it was hard to untangle.

The more Jo watched her sister and Mr. Brooke together, the more she was certain that Meg had feelings for him, whether or not she would ever allow it. Her sister's face and entire manner brightened in his presence, a rose in bloom. And Jo had to acknowledge that John Brooke, as staid and serious as he was, was a good man, a decent man, and Meg could do worse than to throw her lot in with his.

Jo desperately didn't want her sister to leave her, but she also deeply wanted her sister to be happy. And she could hear Meg's question, lingering still—*What's left for me, Jo?*

If only she knew the answer.

But romance or the lack of it aside, the week seemed to Jo but one long moment, suspended in a suffusion of pleasant new opportunities and even pleasanter old memories and—pleasantest of all—Laurie's generous, boyish laughter. The result was a sunbeam and a bubble and a dream of the rarest and realest sort; unsurprisingly, the more—and yet, somehow, less—pressing matters of Plato (still unread) and books to write (still unwritten) fell by the wayside.

It was not a week of writing, but not for lack of effort. Jo dutifully sat at the uncomfortable little mahogany writing-desk in front of the window of her room every night—gas lamps in the street illuminating her blank papers along with the moonlight and the candle-wax—but still no words came. When she forced them out, by way of threatening and bargaining and cajoling, she'd only find herself crossing them out, crumpling the page in the starker light of the next morning. She was as absolutely, irrefutably stuck in New York as she had been in Concord. Finally, she told herself she had no choice except to abandon quill and ink altogether.

You shall write about this someday. But not today.

Today you are too busy living it.

It was enough, for now. It had to be.

On Friday afternoon, when a summer storm drifted into the city, Laurie suggested another ramble. "A good day for tea, isn't it? And Grandfather's given us a whole list of tea-rooms to try, what do you say?"

"Yes, please!" Jo snapped shut her journal. "Let's have an adventure."

"No, thank you," Meg demurred, smoothing the ribbon at her tiny waist. "I'd prefer to not muddy a perfectly lovely day-dress I've only just had made."

"And I shall keep Miss March company. I have some long-overdue correspondence I need to catch up on, I'm afraid." Mr. Brooke nodded at Meg, who blushed.

"As you like," she said. Jo responded with a meaningful look.

Meg meaningfully ignored it.

9

SAILING AWAY

Within the hour, Laurie and Jo set off on their adventure. Laurie procured a poorly made umbrella at twice the usual price. (*"Forty cents, Teddy! That's what I would have to earn, for the price of a few steel ribs and a shoddy bit of oiled cloth!"*)

Now properly armed against the elements, they roamed onward, down the length of Broadway, in search of a particularly Parisian tea-room that the elder Mr. Laurence had made them promise to visit.

Before long, they reached the edge of a great, crowded wharf, and beyond it, the even greater gray harbor. Beyond that, the vast expanse of the Atlantic yawned at them.

"Ho, Jo! Look!" Laurie gave a shout and pulled Jo excitedly toward the broad platform before them, over to the place where the wooden walkway was crowded with passengers and families and friends, whole streams of people arriving and departing, along with the loved ones assembled to see them off and welcome them home again. Sailing ships of all stripes floated there, great three-masters meant to cross the Atlantic and a number of steam vessels as well, including the famous sidewheel steamer the SS *Baltic*, one of the fastest ships ever made. The dock was a threshold, teeming with people going to and fro. *Like a train station,* she thought, *only a thousand times bigger and more frightening.*

Laurie let go of Jo's arm and stepped across the walk, leaving both his friend and their umbrella behind, as if the ships were magnets and he was powerless before them. The scene did not have the same effect upon Jo; the longer she stood watching, the harder it was to know if she was exhilarated or terrified.

She closed her eyes and tried to decide the matter for herself. She knew she was being ridiculous. She'd always wanted to go to Europe; she couldn't imagine anything she'd wanted more. So why did the sight of the shipyard set her spinning? Was it the feeling of freedom all around her? Or the feeling of being trapped in some way?

I'm not afraid. And I'm not being wild and queer. I'm not. It's Teddy who's being strange, ever since we arrived. Strangely charming. Strangely gallant. Strangely handsome.

What's so very wrong with that?

But now all Jo could feel was the fluttering nervousness beneath her ribs, the great knotting lump that should have been her nearly empty stomach, the goose-bumps pricking up along the seam of exposed flesh at her wrist, just beneath her new linen puffed sleeve. The thought of all that water beneath her, the fathomless dark depths of the ocean and herself in it, cold and alone . . .

"Smell that!" Laurie took a great whiff of air, wagging his head. He looked back at her. "Come closer! You've got to *feel* it!"

As she stepped forward to his side, she could see what he meant; the wood-planked platform was vibrating beneath their feet as the crowd shoved between and beyond them.

Now the two friends stood side by side at the edge of the harbor. She angled the umbrella to cover them both, but he didn't even notice.

"It's such a *city*, Jo!" Laurie's face was ruddy with excitement, just as it had been all day. "And those enormous steamships. Beyond them only the big, wide ocean. Then nothing at all until London and Paris and Rome, whatever we want." He was in one of his moods.

Unstoppable and unapologetic, Jo thought. She had come to know his moods well, and to love them better.

She kept her eyes on the ship nearest them, which steadily swallowed a ramp full of departing passengers into a shadowy opening in its hull. It swayed in its berth with the rocking motion of the waves.

"Shall we join them?" Laurie took her gloved hand in his warmer, larger one.

She let her eyes flicker over to him. His face was sparkling with mischief; he didn't seem to notice the change in her mood at all. "Is that a question?" she asked.

He squeezed her fingers. "Every boat is a question, don't you think, Jo? Whether or not to get on and sail away, forever and ever, world without end?"

Jo couldn't help but smile. He looked like one of Meg's pupils, all wonder and eagerness at the thought of tigers and India and gangplanks. "No end at all?"

"Why not?" He said it again, eyes still on the steamer ship. "Don't you just want to climb that ramp and go?"

She tilted back the umbrella for a closer look. "Is that what you want, Teddy? For me to wave you off with this rather fetching new lawn pocket square your grandfather gifted me? Cry *adieu* from the dock while you sail off to the high seas?"

"Don't be daft, you turnip-head. You'd be standing next to me on the very tip-top deck. The highest one." He scrutinized the *Baltic*, then pointed. "That one, I think. Right up . . . there."

She considered the specks lining the upper deck of the vessel in question. "It's awfully high."

"For you?" He scoffed. "Not high enough. If I know my Jo, you'll be captaining that ship by the end of our first day at sea."

"Then we'll make it to London in no time. Perhaps we'll make it in time to see *Little Women* in the West End." She laughed.

"We'll sail this fine, seaworthy vessel down the Thames ourselves!" He saluted the sea briskly. "Aye, Captain March! Next is Paris! You shall have your shipwreck yet, Milady Authoress!"

Jo burst out laughing. "Oh, you're such a *boy*, Teddy!"

"Why, had you forgotten?" He took another deep breath of the salty, steamy harbor air. "Don't I look like one?" He turned toward her now, offering his face up for inspection. "Eh?"

She regarded the familiar features of his face for a moment, then sighed. "Who knows?"

"I beg your pardon?" He sounded insulted.

Jo reached up to pinch his cheek with one damp kid glove. "If you want to know the truth, dear boy, sometimes I forget you have a face at all."

"Hey now!"

"Sometimes you just look like . . ." She considered it.

"Like what?" His eyes met hers.

She shrugged. "I don't know . . . like me, I suppose?"

"You?" He quirked an eyebrow. "That's a new one."

"It's not, actually. Not remotely. I just don't tell you half the things I think."

"Not half?"

"Not a fraction."

"Now, that's hardly fair, seeing as you know my innermost thoughts."

Jo smiled. "All right, then. To me, you look like . . ." It was hard to put the truth into words, even if it was just a truth about her dearest friend. "I don't know, *me*, but *not me*, exactly. More like . . . an appendage?"

"Your foot? Maybe a hand? I'm trying to decide how insulted to be."

"No, Teddy. A soul . . . or maybe a sunburst? Like sunshine itself. Like the sun."

It sounded ridiculous. There was nothing Jo hated more than not being able to speak the truth, especially not to those she loved best. Especially not to Laurie.

But the truth is a hard thing to speak, especially when you don't know it yourself.

"A ball of flame and light? Are you a blind goose? What else do I look like? Better yet . . ." Laurie caught her fingers in his, and her stomach tightened. He pulled her toward him until they were face-to-face, a still island in a circle of crushing passersby. "What does *this* look like to you, Jo?"

There it was. The current that ran between them, whenever she let it. Whenever he walked into the room, or even passed in front of his window all the way across the lane from hers, it was there. She felt it now. Crackling with fire, with life, with something. Some unspeakable *Teddy-ness*. Every time she glanced his way or caught his eye by accident, it was another trembling tilt of the candle, another drop of hot wax against cold fingers. She didn't know if it was pleasant or painful, only that it was . . .

You know exactly what it is, honestly.

Why do you lie to yourself? To him?

How long do you think this strange truce with the truth will hold?

"What does this look like?" The words came from her lips before she realized she was saying them. She took a step backward, smiling awkwardly. "Happiness. Summertime. Childhood. My best friend . . ." She stopped short, ducking away beneath their shared umbrella, looking down at her muddy boots.

You little idiot, you'll ruin everything. You have to fight it. Fight or run!

"Jo," Laurie began, from the other side of the umbrella. His voice was low.

She could hardly breathe. *What's the matter with me?*

"This is silly," Jo finally said, clutching at the umbrella handle, shivering. She felt light-headed, like the storm was closing in on all sides. "It isn't letting up, Teddy. The weather. Perhaps we should head back to our rooms. Change out of these wet clothes."

Laurie beamed. "Jo, I have to tell you something. Another surprise."

"Perhaps I've had enough with your surprises. Perhaps not today." She looked away, down the street. "Look—is that the tearoom? Can you imagine, this whole time, it was right there."

"Jo, just listen—"

She kept her eyes fixed on the glass doors of the little restaurant. "And we can't stay long. We've got tickets to a show tonight, don't we? The opera? Isn't that surprise enough, already?"

"Si. Verdi, the Italian master." His voice tensed as it always did when he recounted any of the operas his beloved mother had treasured in his youth. "*La Traviata*, the tale of the fallen woman, something the Italians pride themselves on knowing quite well, if memory serves."

And like that, the moment had passed, just as it always did. She could sense the hurt in his voice; he was sulking. "But Italians aside, your biggest surprise is tomorrow."

"Bigger than Meg and John Brooke?" Jo poked him between the ribs. "Come on, let's go stuff our faces with pastries and tea, and you can tell me all about it, Teddy. Please. You know how you love spoiling your own surprises." She felt like she was begging and she didn't even know why. She wanted to hike up her muddy linen skirts and bolt.

But it was too late. The umbrella was sliding out of her hands. He was taking it from her. Taking her will and her courage with it.

Don't.

The umbrella was in his hands now, all forty cents of it.

The rain was going to fall. There was nothing she or anyone could do to stop it.

That was the nature of rain.

"Don't be afraid," he said.

"I'm not," she answered. Then she turned and fled.

10

⁓୨⁓ ⁓ଡ଼⁓

SILK THE COLOR OF MOONLIGHT

The table was already piled high with all the delicate sweets and savories of a posh afternoon tea—and Jo was midway through her third crustless cucumber sandwich—by the time Laurie found his way into the tea-room. He sat down across from her, dropping the wet umbrella at his feet with a shake of his even wetter mop of hair.

"I'll never understand you, Josephine March."

Jo handed him a cup of Earl Grey. She had pulled herself together, somewhere between the second and third sandwich. "I know, old friend. To be fair, I don't understand myself."

Laurie grinned ruefully. "But I'll never give up trying."

"I expect you shall, one day—and I shan't begrudge you for it."

He sighed and pulled four paper rectangles out of his waistcoat pocket, sliding them across the marble tabletop toward her. "Here. Your biggest surprise."

Jo felt a welcome flush of relief at the change of subject. "Tickets? Another opera?" Teddy's love of music was heartfelt, and she would not have been surprised if he'd had them going to one concert or another every night of their little expedition into the city. Concord's musical culture left something to be desired, especially after the Laurence boy's Continental childhood. Perhaps he would never become a composer himself—as Jo knew he secretly wished he could—but that didn't seem to stop him from appreciating the genius of others. Just as Jo herself appreciated his own gifts, when he played.

"Not quite." He grinned.

"Oh, Teddy." Jo shook her head. "It's all too much."

"My sworn duty, Mademoiselle March. I'm your Master of Inspiration, remember? And it seems inspiration is a demanding master, especially for an author. If I am to do my job, every sunrise must hail an inspiring new surprise. Isn't that what I promised when I persuaded you to come away with me?" He took a sip of his tea and held the warm cup to his cold face.

"When you say it like that, you make it sound so scandalous," Jo said, picking up the tickets without even glancing at them. She was in high spirits now. *"The Marauding Bride and Robber Groom, to Their Horrid Grave.* Translated from the German. In three parts!" she joked.

Laurie took the tickets from her hand, waving them in her face until she finally focused on the small scripted words printed across them—

Mr. Charles Dickens

—»»»— —«««—

Steinway Hall
14th Street
One Night Only

"*Christopher Columbus!*" Jo stood up, nearly upsetting the cream pitcher and sending a plate of pastries clattering over the edge of the table.

Laurie caught the plate with one hand, scooping up a scone with the other. He took a bite and grinned. "Not quite. I do believe *those* tickets would have been even harder to get, though not by much. But a berth on the *Niña*, the *Pinta*, or the *Santa Maria* would have been a fair sight cheaper, to be sure. The queue for these tickets was *five thousand readers* long, Jo."

Jo sat back down. Her face had gone pale. "Charles Dickens? *The* Charles Dickens? *Here?*"

Laurie was exuberant now. "Tomorrow night. Eight p.m. sharp." He beamed. "At the Steinway theater. A private box at the opera pales in comparison."

"Oh, Laurie." Jo was speechless, a rare thing indeed.

"You hold in your hand the last four tickets in all of New York City, and they're yours—well, ours—even if I admit they're wasted on this lowly Master of Inspiration." He raised his teacup to her. "Long live the *Pickwick Portfolio*, my dear Snodgrass!"

"Why, this is the very fount of inspiration itself! I don't

believe it!" Jo put one hand on her fluttering heart. "I read that he was coming to America but . . . this weekend? What luck!"

"Luck, indeed! I've been planning it for *ages*." Laurie looked proud of himself. "I've done everything I could to keep you from the newspapers this week. You've no idea. Nearly every story has been about the poor fellow and his wife."

"Oh, Teddy." Jo looked dazed.

He finished his cup and immediately started on hers. "Seems like a regular enough chap."

She shook her head. "Theodore Laurence! I can't believe you did this!"

He sat back in his chair, genuinely pleased. "Well, not just me."

Jo was having trouble looking away from the tickets. "I will fly at your grandfather with such a *glad* embrace, it will knock the air straight out of him!"

"This wasn't just my grandfather. I had to call in every favor in the book, high and low. Talk about great expectations. Then again, how could we, the publishers of the esteemed *Pickwick Portfolio*, not be in this particular audience?"

Jo still couldn't speak, such was her excitement.

"Think of it as a glimpse of your future, Jo! One day everyone shall fuss just the same over you, my friend!" He beamed at her.

Jo laughed delightedly. Then—a realization. "Now I understand why Meg came all the way to New York City to deliver that parcel from Mama Abba!"

"Obviously, as the titular *Mr. Pickwick*, Meg had to join us. I only hope *Mr. Winkle* won't have burned Orchard House to the ground by the time we return."

"Blast!" Jo's eyes narrowed at the thought—the memory, rather—of her littlest sister's wrath and her own lost manuscript. The one Amy had burnt up in the fire three years ago, and Jo had immortalized in her book ever since.

"Well, yes." Laurie ran a hand through his unruly brown waves. "Let us just say that the fourth member of our little *Portfolio* was not *entirely pleased* to miss such a grand occasion—but Mr. Winkle's mother was *entirely clear* that Mr. Winkle's tender age would make the journey impossible."

Jo was aghast at the idea of Laurie having to navigate a disagreeable Winkle. "Thank you. Truly." She didn't know what else to say. Entirely too much had been said and not said already. But her heart was bursting, she was so overwhelmed—and she could not keep such feeling to herself. "The March family is so lucky that you showed up one day in sleepy old Concord, all those years ago. I can't imagine what my life would have been like without you, Laurie."

"That . . . is not a thing anyone needs to imagine, Snodgrass." Laurie put a gentle hand on her sleeve. For once, she didn't protest.

"I suppose not, Weller."

She handed the tickets back, Laurie pocketing them once again. "Now, are you going to eat the rest of that sandwich or what?"

Jo shook her head. "It's quite possible I'm never eating again."

Laurie picked up her plate. "They say he does all the voices. I hope so, at that rate!"

"It would be enough even if he refused to speak a word." Her eyes were still shining. "I never thought to breathe the same air as Dickens. Never."

"Excellent," Laurie said, his mouth already full of bread. "Let's be off, then. I've one last stop to make before the opera."

INSIDE THE CARRIAGE, moods continued to lift as the welcome distraction of an errand gave both friends some relief from the afternoon's heavier topics. And at least the storm had stopped, though the clouds still rolled gray and thick across the sky.

Laurie whistled Verdi while Jo looked out the window. Charles Dickens! She still couldn't believe it. She felt like she was in a dream, flying low above the city streets and away from her old life, her old self. The idea of introducing herself to him as the author of *Little Women*, perhaps striking up a friendly correspondence with him, overwhelmed her. It wasn't that she'd never encountered other authors before. She'd been to lectures at the Boston Athenaeum, loads of them.

But this was *Dickens*.

Would he scoff? A girl like her, so young? An authoress, really?

She wouldn't be able to bear it if he laughed at her. No, she would not confess herself an author. Not to Dickens. If he laughed, if he dismissed her book as the scribblings of a *little woman*, she would die on the spot. She was sure of it. She would never be able to write the sequel, at the very least.

Quit your whinnying, she thought crossly. *He's Charles*

Dickens. He's probably never even heard *of a book called* Little Women, *much less cared whether you are its author. You'll never get close enough to speak to him, anyway.*

In such a mood, they stopped the carriage at Mrs. Kirke's boarding house to pick up Meg, who climbed inside with a dismayed look at the muddy hem of Jo's still-damp dress. "Gracious, Josephine!" she declared in horror. "What have you been doing? Wrestling in the mud? And on such an auspicious week?!"

Jo had been trying to rub out the soiled spots, but it was no use. "You were right to stay home, Meg. This is my best dress, and it will never dry in time."

"Jo always looks perfect," Laurie said, in a jolly tone. It made both girls laugh.

"Laurie, you are hopeless," Meg said, with a sigh.

"Utterly," Jo agreed.

Meg surveyed the offending dress. "She can't possibly go to the opera like this."

"What have I done?" Jo studied her sodden gloves, wiggling her damp toes with regret. "New clothes are entirely wasted on me, I confess."

"I wouldn't say that," said Laurie, who looked hurt.

But it was no use. Jo sank back in her seat, dejected. "It's true. One solid afternoon of rain and Cinderella is officially back to her old self."

Laurie smiled. "Cinderella is *La Cenerentola.* An entirely different opera, by Rossini. I saw it in Rome, with my mother."

"That's beside the point, Teddy."

"Nothing is beside the point, my cinder princess." A short while later, Laurie pushed open the carriage door just as it slowed in front of a glass-windowed boutique painted in a distinctly Parisian blue. (Or so Jo thought, but truthfully, having never been to Paris, it was at least what in her manuscripts she would have called a *distinctly Parisian* blue!)

Red geraniums were clustered in painted boxes along the glass. A placard at one side of the entrance read a distinguished name, along with a word Jo knew only from novels—HOUSE OF WORTH, COUTURIER PARISIEN.

Jo stared from the relative safety of the carriage. "Teddy, what have you done?"

"*Rien.*" He offered his gloved hand. "At least, nothing of consequence."

She hesitated. "I can't."

He looked even more hurt than he had a second ago. "You can."

"I can't, Teddy. I can't go in there like this!" She plucked helplessly at her skirts again. "I'm a disaster. You can't spend your money on me. Not for clothes. I won't let you!"

Laurie hesitated, looking from one March sister to the other. "But I already made the appointment," he said. "It would be rude not to keep it."

Jo groaned and slid down on the carriage seat like a bored schoolgirl. "I refuse to let you dress me up like a paper doll simply to avoid being *rude*."

Laurie glanced at Jo with such a look of disappointment that it nearly took her breath away. He glanced at Meg, ready to plead his case.

Then Jo had the best idea. The most brilliant idea she'd had all day, maybe her whole life. For—what had Meg said? The words came crowding into her mind: *The other March sister. The one who didn't die. The one who isn't renowned. The one who isn't an artist, or a scamp.*

"Let Meg be the one," Jo blurted.

Laurie and Meg both turned to face her with a look of such shock, she nearly laughed. "What?" they cried in unison.

"If you must spend your money on clothes for the March girls, give them to Meg. Oh, Teddy, they will look so much better on her than on me! And I can wear Meg's old evening dress instead of my wet things. Please, please—you must!"

A number of expressions crossed Laurie's face as Jo watched. First hurt, then surprise, and then a certain sense of acceptance. He saw the wisdom of such a decision, surely.

"I couldn't—" Meg began.

"But you must," Jo cut her off.

Laurie gave up. "Very well. If you won't let me do this for you, Jo, then I shall do it for Meg." He offered Meg his hand with a flourish and she took it, adjusting her skirts as she hopped down from the carriage door.

"Jo, no—"

"Meg, yes."

Meg's smile was at once so familiar and so particular that Jo found she could not take her eyes from her sister's face, not even as they heard the tinkle of a distant bell and followed Laurie through the open door.

The great stack of blue cardboard boxes rising from the brass-cornered counter in front of them was impressive. A trio of smiling attendants in well-cut black woolen dresses and neat chignons hovered at every side of it.

Laurie murmured at the nearest, who nodded to Jo and Meg with a reassuring smile.

"Which of you is Mademoiselle March?" Jo pointed immediately to Meg. "*Bonjour* . . . welcome."

"French? You're . . . that's French." Meg looked at Laurie, wide-eyed. "What have you done, Laurie?"

"Be brave, dear Meg," Laurie said, nodding at the attendant. She removed the lid from the box at the very height of the stack. Pale rose-colored tissue rustled as it erupted from the inside. Moments later, something gossamer, something made from dreams and wishes and fairy dust, emerged, slipping into the attendant's deft hands. When she held it high, it reflected the light from the delicate brass chandelier that hung behind the counter.

"Oh," breathed Meg, and Jo squirmed from happiness. That her sister, her dearest Meg, would get to wear these clothes to the opera . . . nothing could have made her happier.

This is what's left for you, Meg.

Everything.

Jo squeezed Laurie's hand and grinned so happily that his expression brightened immediately. He was giving her pleasure—so much more than she could even describe—just not the pleasure he'd planned to give. "You must thank your grandfather for us, Teddy."

Laurie hesitated, then confessed. "This isn't from Grandfather. It's from me. I had it made for you. Well, for you, Jo—though it should look equally lovely on Meg." He looked away.

"More lovely," Jo insisted. "She'll be a vision, Teddy!"

"The House of Worth," Laurie went on, now with more enthusiasm. "You know the fellow, Charles Worth, he's awfully famous for this stuff. He made all the dresses for Jenny Lind, all kinds of royalty. Some or another princess, I believe—oh, that Empress Eugénie, the one from Spain. The silk for your dress came into the city on one of those boats we saw at the docks—I was going to show you then, if I could find it. Oh, Jo, I've had this on my mind for awfully long."

"Teddy," she said, smiling, "don't be hurt. You know it will suit Meg far better than me. And I will have a new dress, too, after all. New to me, anyway."

The attendant held out the dress for Meg, who fingered the fabric as if it were a butterfly's wing.

"Mademoiselle March?" A second attendant held open a navy velvet curtain, where a matching velvet divan awaited. A dressing chamber. "Please, would you like to try it on, *Josephine*?" She pronounced it with a deep French accent, and Jo's plain old name sounded suddenly *très chic*, even to Jo herself.

Meg just stared. She was too petrified to correct the attendant who'd called her *Josephine*.

"Go on, Meg," Jo said. "Put it on."

Meg watched as the attendant hung the gown in the little room. "I . . . I can't."

Laurie took her by the hand. "Of course you can. We want you to."

"We do," Jo said, happily.

Meg hesitated. Then inclined her head ever so slightly toward Laurie. "You meant all this for Jo," she whispered. "How can I?"

He whispered back, "If you don't, I shall have to give it to the poor-house." Then he smiled and pulled her toward the curtains. "The House of Worth. I'm sure it will fit. Monsieur Worth came highly recommended; he's Lady Carmichael-Carlthorpe's personal couturier."

"Who?" Meg looked confused.

"No one . . . an old family friend. I said I wanted Jo to have just one dress that was every bit as unique as she is." He was flustered, and Jo couldn't help but smile. "This was where she said to go."

And then all anyone could do was stand there marveling at the gown in front of them.

Laurie pointed. "See how there's almost no crinoline or bustle at all? It's called a . . . polly . . ."

"*Polonaise*, monsieur." The attendant smiled at him.

He nodded, relieved. "That. Made for Princess Alexandra. It's apparently the style now, a princess line or something."

Meg smiled incredulously. "Are you explaining *crinolines* to me now, Theodore Laurence? As if you've ever worn one?"

He scratched his head, trying to remember. "I think it's

hand-stitched . . . I know there isn't another one like it in the world, because it was made after a very particular drawing."

Jo was incredulous. "A *drawing?*"

His face turned red. "One of mine."

"Teddy? *You . . . drew me . . . a gown?*" Jo was practically apoplectic at the thought.

Now his face was the color of one of the more purple beets from Vegetable Valley. "Only sort of. Monsieur Worth's dressmakers made it fashionable and all that. I just sort of . . . inspired it, I suppose. Master of Inspiration that I am and all."

"You did all this for me?" Jo shook her head. Today had escaped her, utterly. "This is beyond inspiration, Teddy."

Laurie struggled to express himself. "It's from a portrait of my mother when she was young, in Paris. She was laughing and so happy and so alive . . . Well, it's the one picture of her that always reminds me of you, Jo. The dress isn't the same, of course, but an approximation of it." He pushed a lock of brown hair out of his face with a sigh. "I can't explain it any better than that. I just wanted you to have something that would make you feel . . . the way my mother taught me to feel about Verdi."

Jo squeezed his hand, keeping her eyes on the length of silk the color of moonlight.

Meg is here, so I can hold your hand and tell you how wonderful you are and nothing will be strange and everything can stay perfectly jolly between us.

Couldn't it?

Part of her was already regretting her refusal of Laurie's gift. She had to admit that. But another part of her—the biggest part, if she were being honest with herself—was far more pleased that she and Laurie both could give this moment to Meg, who was already stepping behind the curtain to have the attendant dress her, pale with shock but giving the tiniest smile of pleasure. Like the copy Jo had once seen of Leonardo da Vinci's *Mona Lisa*, as if Meg had heard a secret she didn't dare tell.

Jo gave Laurie one last, grateful look and disappeared through the curtain after her.

And as the recipient of the look watched her go, he marveled that the House of Worth was so aptly named.

A few minutes later, Jo emerged dressed in Meg's old evening dress, a newer version of the modest white tarlatan Meg had worn to Sallie Gardiner's debut, which had had such a prominent place in *Little Women*. It was understated and drew no attention to its wearer, as fitted Jo perfectly. Her new kid gloves and matching boots would do well enough for the evening. She was elated.

Meg, on the other hand, emerged from the dressing-room in a gossamer haze, silvery silkwork flowing down from her bosom—like the clearest, coldest water from a Concord brook in the peak of summer—embroidered with the tiniest, most delicate threadwork, in the pattern of soft silver lilies . . .

Not unlike a certain watering-hole.

Jo felt her heart stop. It had been meant as a private language between herself and Laurie. Something he was trying to tell her.

But now it was Meg who would wear it, not Jo. She had refused his gift. Refused him, in fact, and given her sister to him in her place.

Oh, Laurie.

All Jo could do was hug her sister, hard. When she pulled away, she could see Meg's face was as dazzling as the dress. "You look glorious, Meg. You'll be the most beautiful girl in the room."

"If I am, it is only because of the most generous gentleman in the room." She smiled at Laurie. "Thank you, Laurie. Truly. Both of you."

"*De rien*, Mademoiselle March." Laurie bowed with a smile, giving Meg his arm as he escorted her outside to the waiting carriage.

Waiting to take them to the opera, to Verdi, *La Traviata* and the tale of the fallen woman.

As Jo followed behind, now carefully holding her dress—*Meg's dress!*—above the puddles, it occurred to her for the first time that Meg and Laurie were not so very far apart in age, after all.

A Laurie of my own.

That was what her sister wanted. She had said so herself, hadn't she?

Jo March, what have you done?

11

Presenting Lady Hat

$\mathcal{S}$ome moments pulse more brilliantly than others, as if time itself could have a heartbeat of its own. Jo felt it as she walked into the theater in Meg's old tarlatan dress, watching her sister moving through the crowd on Laurie's arm. The cascade of silk nipped at her waist, darted at her bosom, tucked along her hip, and her matching silk-gloved hand rested on the arm of one of the most eligible young men in Massachusetts, if not all of America.

As heads turned and the elegant couple made their way through the well-heeled crowd, Jo felt as if the future were already written, and she simply had to turn the page to keep reading.

If only I can bear it.

For the third time, Laurie looked back to Jo, offering his left arm.

Jo shook her head. Meg was the pretty one, the charming one. In her elegant and fashionable attire, she would be the talk of New

York society for days, if not weeks. Who was that girl with the Laurence boy? Where had she come from?

Jo felt positively inconsequential in comparison.

Perhaps that was the way things should be. Meg *should* be the one who received everyone's admiring glances, not regular old Jo March, the somewhat-known scribbler from Concord. She could still move through the world largely unseen, as a writer should.

So why did it bother her so that Laurie and Meg seemed to be taking such pleasure in each other's company, suddenly? That the crowd parted with a whisper, admiring the lovely couple, even while Jo walked in their wake?

Invisible.

If, all of a sudden, Laurie preferred Meg to her, that shouldn't bother her in the slightest. Why would it? He would still be her dearest friend. She couldn't wish a better suitor for her lovely, calm, devoted sister, who deserved nothing so much in the world as a man who would appreciate both her beauty and her temperament.

Could she?

Better to lose her to Laurie than to some strange man who would take her far from home, where they might not meet more than once or twice a year, Meg bearing his children and slaving over his household, ruining her sweet disposition with child-rearing or poverty, or both. On the contrary, marrying Laurie would be a boon to their whole family, raising all their fortunes. Laurie could never hope for a better wife than serene, beautiful Meg, truly the best of all the March sisters. How happy it would make Mama, and Father, and even Amy.

Jo could be the maiden aunt, tending their children, writing her books by night, with no thought of marriage or children for herself. Unencumbered. The best thing for everyone. Truly.

Jo had practically resigned herself to the certainty of their betrothal when they reached a private opera box, where they were met by John Brooke. His eyes widened at the sight of Meg in her elegant gown, at least until he dropped into a stately bow.

"Mr. Brooke!" said Meg, failing to hide her excitement. "Laurie neglected to mention you were joining us this evening."

"Miss March," he said, his fingers trembling as he lifted Meg's gloved hand for a greeting kiss. "You have never looked lovelier. Not even your sister could describe such beauty in the pages of her books."

Jo raised an eyebrow. *I don't know about that.*

Laurie elbowed her.

Still, it was nice to see the ladies at the House of Worth had not wasted their efforts, to judge from the way Brooke was looking at Meg.

To be fair, Meg was looking at Brooke as if he were the Prince of Persia.

Now Laurie snuck a conspiratorial glance at Jo and winked. "Please, the two of you should take those seats," he said, pointing to the front row. "I've promised to explain the whole opera to Jo, so we'll be back here getting shushed." That much was true.

"I expect nothing less." Mr. Brooke smiled, offering Meg his arm.

"As always," Jo said, gamely.

Brooke led Meg to the front of the box, leaving Jo and Laurie to sit together behind them. Laurie didn't seem the least reluctant to let Meg go. As the lights went down, and Meg and Mr. Brooke settled into their chairs, he hardly glanced at them.

Lowering into her own seat, Jo wondered if she'd imagined the whole thing about Meg and Laurie. It would hardly be the first time. The authoress Jo March did have a bit of an imagination, after all. Seeing Meg in that silvery dress, her hair done up in the latest fashion, her arm in Laurie's—it would probably have given anyone ideas.

Jo watched as Meg and Brooke put their heads together, speaking so softly, no one else could hear.

"You see it, don't you?" Laurie whispered.

"Shush," Jo whispered back. *Why, are you jealous?*

"I knew we'd be shushed, but I didn't expect it to come from you," he hissed.

She was irritated. He was right, of course; there was definitely something there.

It was never just fiction, the idea of Meg and Brooke.

If only Meg would admit that. And if only everything wasn't so confusing.

Soon plain old Jo March, in her borrowed tarlatan, found herself taking in Verdi's greatest masterpiece from a private box at the Grand Opera House.

The luminous center-stage *prima donna*, whom Jo observed through a pair of gilded opera glasses, opened her mouth, and the most astonishing sounds came out. Jo had never heard anyone sing like that—high and sweet and powerful, all at once.

As every thrilling note crept up and down her spine, Jo became quieter and quieter. For once, she had no words at all. She was too busy *feeling*. But what was she feeling as she watched Meg and Brooke put their heads together and whisper? When she watched Laurie absorbed in the music, a small smile on his lips?

It seemed that one night, one series of small, nearly insignificant moments, had changed them all irrevocably: herself and Meg, Laurie and Brooke. And that there would be no going home again, not to the people they'd been before.

What is happening?

It was all impossible, this business of love and marriage, suitors and family and money. Why anyone would voluntarily spend ten minutes worrying over any of it was beyond her. Much less writing—or even reading—a whole novel about it.

Perhaps I should have stuck to Tall Talers.

Meg should stay home with the family, where she belonged. Except of course that wouldn't make her happy. Brooke made her happy. That was all too clear now.

As the music rose and the lights brightened, Jo felt a steely resolve. Beth had never even had a chance to sit in this opera house and listen to Verdi. Meg had to live her life, had to find her happiness. If she did love John Brooke, then she must accept him if he asked.

Time was so short, for all of them.

Jo glanced at Laurie, who already had the look in his eyes, the one that meant he was lost to *La Traviata*.

And with that, she closed her own eyes and let the music carry her away.

AT INTERMISSION, LAURIE reached around to grab the crimson velvet back of Jo's chair. His face was still glowing; he hadn't looked away from the stage for the last half hour. "Oh, Jo, now do you see why we had to see Verdi? Isn't it splendid?" For the moment he seemed like her old friend, excited about his Italian music and memories of his mother's country.

"It was perfect, Teddy. You were so right." She took his gloved fingers in hers, squeezing tight. Now that the lights were up again, she found her eyes straying to her sister. In front of them, Brooke said something low in Meg's ear, and she smiled, winningly.

Laurie bowed his head to whisper in her ear. "I believe love is in the air tonight."

She looked at him. Everything beyond their crimson-draped balcony box—the noise of the crowd, the grandeur of the stage, the glow of the lights—began to fade away.

"Whatever do you mean?" Jo hardly managed to get the words out.

"Why, Meg, of course."

Jo's mouth was suddenly dry. Perhaps she had misjudged everything, after all. "You're smitten with Meg; of course you are. She's beautiful."

"Meg?" Laurie asked, taken aback, as he turned to her with a flash of his dark eyes.

"You have my blessing, if that's what you're waiting for," she began.

"You're joking," he said, loudly.

Jo wanted to shush him again. "Am I?"

Laurie threw back his head and let out a peal of laughter, loud enough that half the opera house turned and looked at them. "Oh, Jo! You goose." He lowered his voice to a whisper. "You think I'm in love with Meg?"

"Of course not!" Jo hissed. "I just thought . . ." Then she stopped, because in truth she had no idea what she thought, what she wanted, what was happening. Tonight had folded everything back on itself a hundred times already.

"Please," Laurie begged, amused. "Were you *jealous*, Jo?"

She could feel her face turning the color of the opera curtains. "Of course not, you vile thing!"

He looked at her fondly. "I know what you thought. Meg is very lovely in *your* dress, but we're no match, Jo. Surely you know that."

Jo stared down at the kid-gloved fingers folded in her lap. She was starting to wonder. *If Meg is no match for him, then who is?*

"Mr. Laurence! Is that you?" A woman's voice came from behind the curtains at the back of their box. "I heard you from six boxes down."

Laurie sat up, startled.

Jo smelled the powdered, perfumed, lace-edged bosoms

before she saw them, though they would have been difficult to miss. Frankly, they were difficult to not look at, as they occupied the curtained entrance to the box almost entirely.

Their owner was a particular beauty—stunning in a manner unlike any that Concord had ever seen and ever would—or so Jo guessed.

As Laurie rose to his feet, it became obvious he had spent a great deal of time looking at this literal *bosom friend* himself, judging by the familiarity with which the two now greeted each other.

"Hullo, old Hat!" Laurie gave her an emphatic kiss on each cheek.

"Hello, darling!" said the beauty.

"I didn't know you were back in town. You didn't mention it when last I saw you! I thought you were leaving for Paris for the summer," said Laurie.

"Changed our minds!" said the lady. "Imagine that." Her laughter spilled across them, as if she'd tossed a handful of silver pieces into their laps.

Jo snorted. Meg and Brooke now rose to their feet to see who had arrived.

"Hat?" Jo echoed.

"I don't believe we've met." The lady Hat held out a pale, slender, soft-gloved hand. "I'm Lady Harriet. And surely you must be Laurie's dear Cousin Jo! I'd know you anywhere."

"Lady?" Meg blurted, in an uncharacteristically un-Meg way.

"I—I . . ." Jo stammered. "Cousin?"

Laurie was red-faced now. "We're not *actual* cousins, Hat. I keep telling you that."

"Just as I keep not listening to a word of your endless prattle, dear boy." Harriet chuckled sweetly. "Now, do try to be less of an unbearable beast and introduce me to your friends properly, please. You know how I loathe disappointment."

Laurie swept his arm into a melodramatic bow, reaching for Harriet's hand with, Jo noticed, yet another emphatic kiss. "Lady Harriet Carmichael-Carlthorpe, formerly of Sussex, briefly London, now perhaps seasonally or, one hopes, eternally New York City. Or so it seems most men of my species hope and pray, at least to hear Hat tell of it."

"Fervently," Hat sighed. "The praying. I find it quite trying, actually, the dull repetition of masculine veneration . . . you know." She winked at Jo, who realized she was still staring, and not at Lady Hat's face.

"I can't imagine," Jo said, forcing her eyes upward. "I mean, I truly can't."

Laurie looked from Jo to Lady Harriet, and back to Jo.

"And now, dear Hat, it is my great honor to present Miss Jo March of Concord, formerly of Concord, briefly of New York City, now perhaps seasonally or, one hopes, eternally—"

Harriet regarded them imperiously. "Of Concord?" She did not move her eyes from Jo's.

Jo found herself blushing. "It does seem likely."

Laurie shook his head. "Don't interrupt, Hat."

"I couldn't, quite literally, as the excellence of my upbringing forbids it," said Lady Harriet, now glancing at Meg in her silvery silk and, interestingly, at John Brooke. "And who are these friends?"

"May I present Miss Margaret March and my tutor, John Brooke."

Lady Harriet smiled in acknowledgment. "Aha, the tutor! I do enjoy meeting a man of education. Mr. Brooke, I don't know how you manage with Mr. Laurence here, but I commend your bravery during the war."

"Not at all," said Brooke, taking a step toward her. "How are you liking New York?"

"Very well," said Lady Hat. "To be fair, the weather has been a bit off, but I find it improving more and more by the minute. Rather suddenly."

Mr. Brooke took her hand. "Charmed."

"Are you?" She smiled.

Meg stiffened under her crinoline, until Lady Hat turned her considerable attention to her. "So Miss Margaret, are you yet another Concord cousin? A *Cousin Meg* perhaps?"

Now Laurie grabbed Jo's gloved hand and kissed it as well. "*Cousin Jo* is, most emphatically, not my cousin, but rather my—"

"Special friend?" Hat said, suggestively.

"I was going to say my beating heart itself." It sounded like a joke when Laurie said it, but also not. "She and her sister Meg."

"Hence the dress." Lady Hat smiled. "I thought it was intended for Miss Josephine?"

"She wanted Meg to wear it tonight," said Laurie, with a twinge of sadness.

Lady Hat went on. "It turned out rather better than I expected, I'll give you that. Even for the House of Worth. Charles does work his magic." She shook her ringleted head. "Do you recall the day I took you there? How incredibly lost you were, on Prince Street?"

"Surrounded by fabric and feathers? Would you imagine I was otherwise?" Now both were laughing. It took Jo a moment to catch up.

Hence the dress. She was there when he ordered the dress. *This dress, my dress. Here in New York, with Teddy. Lady Carmichael-Carlthorpe. Teddy's "old family friend."*

Jo pulled her hand away. Her heart was pounding. "Of course. And I must thank you for helping Laurie with his most generous and . . . adventurous errand."

"Any day with Laurie is an adventure."

"And with you, Hat," said Laurie, giving her an impudent wink.

Was it possible Laurie was flirting with her? The bosoms?

Just then, an emphatic noise came from behind the box curtain. "Theodore Laurence! Is that you? How utterly charming to see you, and so fortunate, as tomorrow is the Ducal Ball!"

Lady Harriet, Theodore Laurence, John Brooke, and the two Misses March all turned to face the speaker—an older and even more buxom version of Lady Hat, in an even more ridiculous degree of finery and plumage—as she pushed through the curtains. This was, apparently, the Dowager Lady Carmichael-Carlthorpe, or, as Lady Hat said, "Mummy."

"Madame," Laurie murmured, rising from a rather grand bow with a deferential nod, while it was all Jo could do to wriggle out the smallest bob of a curtsy. Beside her, Meg made a small noise of terror in the back of her throat.

"Do say you'll join us, my dear boy—I haven't seen your grandfather since Biarritz."

Laurie smiled at the mention of the elder Laurence. "Ah yes, for the Ducal Ball. How could I have forgotten? And so the great Carmichael-Carlthorpe clan is assembled to grace all Manhattan with its presence?"

The broad-faced, lavender-scented matron smiled with a heave of her lacy . . . collar. "Not *all* Manhattan, my dear boy."

"*Uppertens* only, if you please. Strictly *first quality* for the Ducal Ball. Otherwise you'll frighten Mummy." Lady Hat yawned.

Jo was, of course, familiar with the horrid phrase; the *Upper Ten Thousand* New Yorkers, the upper crust, had been much discussed as of late in almost every magazine that had also carried one of Jo's own little submissions. But to hear it spoken? To hear Laurie, of all people, laugh at such a thing?

Jo, ever the chaplain's daughter, felt ill.

"Behave, Harriet. Of course, we'll just be entertaining a *very few* well-bred, properly positioned families. Including, *naturally*, the Laurences of Boston," the dowager said.

"Naturally." Lady Harriet smiled. "Oh, and do bring your friends, Laurie. Where are they from again? Boston?"

"New York City, mademoiselle," said Mr. Brooke. "But I was mostly brought up in Providence."

"And we are from Concord," said Meg, awkwardly. So there it was. There was little else to say about it.

Lady Harriet smiled at the sisters. *"Conquered? That's too bad. Here I thought the Union soldiers had won it all back."* She tipped back her head and laughed at her own pun.

Jo coughed. Meg's eyes widened in horror.

The dowager lady leaned closer. "Harriet means *no harm*; it's just that she finds herself in possession of a *most wicked* sense of humor, especially around *unsuspecting Americans*. To be sure, it's a *rather grievous* character defect, as *I'm certain* you'll agree."

Perhaps it was the tone of the banter, or the scent of the powdered ringlets, or just the cloying crush of the lacy frills. Whatever the cause, Meg clutched at Jo's arm. Jo could feel her sister's legs buckling beneath all the silk.

"I think . . . I need . . . air," Meg said.

Jo couldn't agree more. They all needed air. Air that didn't smell like privilege and powdered bosoms, like jealousy and judgment.

A deep breath of fresh Concord air.

12

⤳⤳◦⤶

GREAT EXPECTATIONS AT
STEINWAY HALL

*T*he telegram arrived by breakfast the next morning. The telegram, and then the trouble. Just four clipped lines: DUCAL BALL—CARMICHAEL HALL—EIGHT SHARP TONIGHT—CHARLES ELIOT ATTENDING.

The telegram's meaning had been conveyed clearly enough, at least to Laurie: Grandfather Laurence wanted Laurie to represent the family at the famed Carmichael-Carlthorpe Ducal Ball. Beyond that, the details didn't matter; clearly some Carmichael or another had sent a telegram to Mr. Laurence via his solicitor—the only way the old man received telegrams—after the curtain had fallen on Verdi.

"We can go? The four of us?" Meg was nearly bursting with the news. A society ball, especially *this* society ball, would be worth the trip from Concord alone.

But Jo was angry. It was amazing, she thought privately, how quickly a certain set of people could make the rest of the world fall in line. Even people as powerful as the Laurences. The speed implied some urgency, whether due to the proximity of the event itself, or the desirability of Laurie's attendance. Which of the two it was, Laurie was too much of a gentleman to say, which only made Jo more cross as the morning progressed—not that she would admit it. Not to him.

"If you need to go, just say it," Jo said, pacing about the drawing-room of the boarding house.

"It's just the bit about Charles Eliot," Laurie said glumly.

"Yes, about this Mr. Eliot—why does your grandfather care if he's going to be at a ball?" asked Meg.

"You know how my grandfather feels about my going to Harvard."

"Of course I do," said Jo.

"Of course we do," Meg repeated.

"Eliot's the new president. Only just arrived."

"Oh." Jo sank into the hard cushion of the nearest wing-chair. "Well. That clarifies things. Is he friends with Mr. Laurence?"

"They're not close. All Grandfather's said to me is that Eliot's threatening to abolish the Greek requirement, which would put poor Brooke out of half his line of work."

"Really? I can't imagine you'd be too put out by that, yourself."

"Of course not. It's ancient Greek. But still—Brooke."

"Well, what does Brooke expect you to do? Go argue on behalf of studying ancient Greek, in your atrocious ancient Greek?"

"Brooke? Of course not. Though he's said he's going. I suspect he wants to make his case in person, or else gape at old Hat again."

Meg looked pale.

"Well, then?" Jo asked. "What's the problem?"

Laurie sighed, sinking into the arm-chair next to Jo. "I expect Grandfather just wants me to go to the ball to act the fine gentleman. You know, sort of play the game a bit. Make an impression on him."

"Is that important?"

"Yes? No? How should I know? It's important to my grandfather, so it's important, right? Isn't that what you say when you're arguing his side of everything? Which, by the way, you seem not to be doing at the moment?"

Jo sighed. "Laurie. Surely your grandfather won't expect you to miss this. It's *Charles Dickens*. He hasn't been to the States since before the war."

"I know, but my grandfather sent direct orders."

Jo was starting to see that arguing was pointless. "Fine. Go to your ball. Go hobnobbing and Harvarding about with your fancy society friends. Meg and I will go to see Dickens."

"Jo." Meg made a noise of despair. "Truly, it's why I came. But—a ducal ball? After you've written so many imaginary ones, in all our little plays? How can we miss the very thing itself?"

"I suspect we shall manage," Jo said, irritated.

Meg was less resolved. "If we go to Dickens, we'll miss the ball. And if we go to the ball, we'll miss Dickens."

"That is, generally, how the laws of the physical universe seem to work, yes. One place, one time," Jo answered, wryly.

Although normally an audience with Charles Dickens would

have been the most exciting thing Meg had ever witnessed, it did not compare to a true society ball, apparently.

One where Mr. Brooke would be in attendance as well—as Jo would have predicted.

"How are we to decide?" Meg looked distraught.

The idea that there was even a decision to be made was baffling to Jo, who was hurt her sister would prefer Brooke's company to her own—hurt that she would abandon her, hurt that their childhood game meant somehow less to her.

Jo changed tack. "Meg, you wouldn't make me go alone? And have Laurie waste the ticket?"

"Of course not, Jo. No self-respecting *Pickwickian* would do that." Meg looked truly distressed.

"Jo," Laurie groaned. "It's not the ticket I'm worried about, you nincompoop. I'm not going to leave you unchaperoned at night in New York City."

"Our *chaperone*? Is that what you think you are?" Jo laughed.

"I didn't mean it like that."

"You don't think we can handle ourselves at a *literary event*? Which one of us, might I ask, is the author here?"

"Jo, don't be like that," Meg chided. "Laurie is trying to be a gentleman."

"Laurie *is* a gentleman," said Jo. "He will go off to his gentlemanly world—to the *uppertens*—and you and I will go off to ours, Meg. We shall all be alarmingly fine on our own, and possibly a good sight less dull than we might be in some other people's company."

"*Jo*," Meg said. A warning: Meg was letting Jo know she was close to crossing the invisible line between her usual teasing and true disrespect.

Laurie bowed his head in mock supplication. "Your company is never dull, Miss March. I might go so far as to say upper*ones*."

The compliment was lost on her.

Jo glared. "And yet oddly enough, Mr. Laurence, I, for one, am finding this whole morning to be exceptionally tiresome."

When she stalked out of the room, her volume of *Great Expectations* in her hand, he knew better than to stop her.

Jo AND MEG, Laurie and Brooke had negotiated a truce as they slipped across the cobblestones of Fourteenth Street, where Steinway Hall and Charles Dickens awaited. The agreement was thus: Laurie, Meg, and John Brooke were to accompany Jo to the Dickens event, then all but Jo would travel together to Carmichael Hall. Once there, Laurie would send the hired carriage back to Steinway Hall to await Jo at the close of Mr. Dickens's appearance. Jo would make her own way back to their rooms in the carriage and then send it back to the Ducal Ball for the rest of them.

Jo could not contain her excitement, could hardly stop talking, could barely catch her own breath—all to the continual amusement of Mr. Brooke and Meg. "Can you imagine it? That we are seeing this inconceivable spectacle with our own eyes?"

"I'd rather witness it through your eyes," Laurie said with affection as he pulled her just out of the path of a passing carriage, though Jo hardly noticed.

As they crossed Fourteenth Street, the atmosphere was that of a great carnival, or a festival, Jo thought. The air was electric, wild with excitement. A throng of readers had camped out on blankets, forming a long line that snaked all the way from the entrance to around the block. From the look of it, readers had come out by the thousands.

"Look at them, Laurie. All *those readers*!" Jo was breathless. She pulled her cape around her shoulders. Underneath she was wearing the well-cut dress Niles had sent to her at Orchard House, in congratulations for the success of her publication, as if it held some badge of writerly authority stitched into its hem. She barely even noticed how glum Laurie's mood grew as they came to the entrance. He said little, dutifully tramping next to her, his hands stuffed into his pockets.

"Mr. Snodgrass! Are you quite delirious?" Meg called from a few paces behind, where she and Mr. Brooke lagged.

"Quite beside myself, Pickwick," Jo shouted back. "Quite."

But even so, she found herself increasingly nervous with every step, as if she herself would be performing on the stage that evening instead of Dickens, which was also ridiculous.

Now she looked over at Laurie, who had taken her hand to pull her through a particularly clogged corner. "I wonder if he'll read from *Great Expectations* or something new. Something unpublished?"

"This way. Watch the step," Laurie said, looking back to catch sight of Mr. Brooke and Meg behind them before shrugging at Jo. "You mean like his overdue sequel?"

"Teddy!" Jo hit him with her fan. "You mustn't spoil tonight! This is very important."

"You don't have to tell me, Jo. I'm the one who got the tickets, remember?"

"I do! And I will be forever in your debt, Theodore Laurence. Josephine March in the presence of Charles Dickens himself. I could die, Teddy."

"This was supposed to be our grand finale, the culmination of *Pickwickery* years in the making, the greatest night of the whole trip!" He was cross, indeed—probably because they were in sight of the main doors now.

"Must you really go, Teddy? I'm bereft that you and Meg aren't getting to see him."

"Do you imagine I'd miss it if I didn't, Jo?"

Now they stood side by side in the great throng of book-clutching readers nearest the entrance.

Jo nudged his shoulder, and he nudged her back, finally smiling. "Oh, I'm just sad I'm missing the chance to sit by the side of the beloved authoress Josephine March, even if her curls do still smell like the fireplace poker."

She sniffed. "Chestnuts, actually." She turned to look, and sure enough, Meg was holding a paper cone full of them, Mr. Brooke still putting away his coin purse. *I wonder how many lessons those cost,* Jo thought. She didn't even want to imagine the price of the tickets.

"You have your tickets?" Meg asked, offering a chestnut.

Jo waved it away with the slender envelope, which she clutched so tightly her fingertips were starting to lose sensation. "Glued to my hands."

"Don't lose sight of them. Not in a crowd like this," Mr. Brooke said.

"I won't." Jo leaned to kiss Meg's cheek. "Have fun at your ball—but no duels, fisticuffs, or revelations of long lost and perhaps previously shipwrecked siblings, please."

"Those only happen at *your* balls, Jo." Meg teased.

"Mine and Roderigo's," Jo said, a wicked twinkle in her eyes. Then she turned toward the entrance—

Laurie looked suddenly concerned. "I don't know, do you really think you'll be all right if we go? You'll wait right here until the doors open?"

"Yes, *Grandfather.*" Jo smirked. "We've already been over this. I promise, I won't wander off and I won't speak to strangers."

"Don't be flip, Jo," said Meg. "You *are* taking a chance, being here alone."

"With affection, I can take care of myself," Jo said, exasperated.

"With affection, when you say *with affection* it means *with irritation*," Laurie snorted. "And I didn't say you couldn't take care of yourself, did I, Miss March?" Now he winked. "Maybe I'm just worried for the strangers."

Jo pointed. "Now. Go!"

And with a squeeze of his arm and a quick wave to Meg, Jo was off.

13

~୬୧ଚ ଚ୨୬~

AT THE DUCAL BALL

At her first sight of Carmichael Hall—the family's palatial house on Fifth Avenue, glowingly lit from within—Meg's breath caught in her throat. Gleaming carriages were lined up two and three deep to drop their charges at the front door, including men in top hats and enormous starched white collars, women in gowns of glowing gold and blue brocade, hair wrapped around their ears in intricate braids and whorls, flowers and fronds tucked in the folds. From all over the Eastern Seaboard—and Europe, too, Meg had to remind herself—people of the most exclusive levels of society had gathered for the ball.

And Meg March.

Despite Jo's comments about the *uppertens*, which normally would have shamed Meg as much as anyone, she was excited to be there. Excited to see it all with her own eyes, just this once. She felt certain she could return to her boring, impoverished life in Concord—could deny herself every luxury from this point forward, including nice gowns, new gloves, and the company of high society forever—if it meant she could come to this one event, this one glorious night.

She remembered the time she had attended Belle Moffat's coming-out, borrowing one of Belle's dresses and feeling like an interloper, and how Major Lincoln had shamed her by complaining the Moffats had turned her into a doll, beautiful and spoiled. Jo had unfortunately memorialized the whole thing in her novel, doubling Meg's shame.

Tonight there would be no Belle Moffats, no Major Lincolns. Tonight, in her House of Worth polonaise, in the company of Theodore Laurence and John Brooke, she was every bit a duchess. And she would not let her enjoyment be diminished a whit.

Even if Laurie himself seemed to regard the whole thing with dreary resignation.

From inside the carriage, he shrank into his elegant suit. "Well," he said, groaning out the word as if it pained him, "I suppose there's no more putting it off."

"You'd think you were going to Judgment, the way you talk," said Brooke, "rather than a society ball."

Meg put her hand on Laurie's arm. She knew he was missing Jo and felt a momentary stab of pity for the dear boy, who was trying—and failing—to woo the most stubborn girl in New England. But her excitement was too great to keep bottled up for long. "The sooner we go in, the sooner it will be over," she said. "You can tell your grandfather you did his bidding. No one can ask more than that."

He smiled at her. "I'm glad you're here, Meg. I couldn't bear it without . . . well, without a friend."

And so Laurie helped her out the door of the carriage and up the stairs through the warm and warmly lit front door.

If only Sallie Gardiner could see her now, in her Parisian finery, walking into Carmichael Hall on Laurie's arm! How she would enjoy recounting it all to her friends in Concord later: the chandelier in the foyer dripping with crystals and creamy candlelight, the cool white marble floors, the gilt tables and vases of flowers, the tables piled high with sugared fruit and bowls of cherries. She smiled to see them, remembering Amy's appetite for the sweet things.

Perhaps tonight Meg would meet her own Cherry King.

She looked briefly at Brooke, who seemed already to be searching the room for Lady Hat, and felt her eyes smart with tears. For even in her House of Worth gown, she was still a poor girl with no prospects who could barely afford to buy gloves. The wealthy, beautiful Lady Hat would have the eye of every man in the room—even a good man like John Brooke.

Brooke gave her a polite bow and headed into the crowd.

Steady, Meg. It was her little sister Beth who came to her mind's eye now. *Remember who you are and where you come from. Remember everything and be cheerful, because this chance will never come again.*

"I'm right here, Meg." Laurie gave her arm a squeeze. "Never fear. I won't leave you to the wolves."

She wondered if he could feel her trembling. "Goodness,"

she whispered. "I didn't know there was so much wealth in all the world!"

"The Carmichael-Carlthorpes are a very old family," Laurie explained. "They can name their ancestors back to the Norman invasion. Look at all the portraits—no one with such an ancient lineage ever lets anyone else forget it."

"I don't see how anyone could." Meg laughed, feeling a bit better already. She did see several oils of various Carmichaels, or perhaps they were Carlthorpes, hung in prominent locations in the drawing-room, in the halls, in the dining-room: stern-faced men and women, all looking terribly important and desperately miserable. One or two had the look of an Old Master.

"None of them seem very happy, do they?" asked Meg.

"Maybe a bit gassy," Laurie teased. "Especially that one." He pointed, stopping in front of a particularly sour-faced fellow.

"Laurie!" Meg hit him with her fan.

"You know, Miss March, that's the second time a beautiful woman with your name has hit me with a fan tonight," Laurie said lightly. "So I suppose I am either doing something very right or something very wrong."

Meg studied her companion's face. "Is that truly a question, Mr. Laurence?"

"Everything is a question, Miss March," he said, studying the painting. "As is the further question of whether or not to ask them."

"At least you're happier than he is," Meg said, moving on to the next painting.

Laurie followed her. "Happiness is not a trait much desired in one's ancestors, I've found." With a nearly imperceptible sigh, he leaned forward to scratch a fingernail lightly against the portrait of a pale-skinned burgher in an enormous white ruff. "The more miserable the better, in fact. Something about money not being able to buy happiness, and all that."

"The Marches must be the happiest family you've ever met, then," Meg said wryly.

He laughed, his melancholy entirely forgotten. "Positively giddy."

She put her hand on his arm. "Thank you again for bringing me, Laurie. I shall never forget this night."

"I'm sure your sister will never let you forget it, either." Now he gave her a rueful smile. "I would give up my entire fortune *and* all my ancestors to be listening to Dickens right now with Jo rather than trying to make an impression on some dowdy old Harvard president."

Meg patted his cheek with one gloved hand. "Then let's make it a quick impression, so you can get it over with."

"I like the way you think, Miss March," said Laurie, and gave her a mock bow. Meg took his arm and let him lead her deeper into the belly of the beast.

"THERE YOU ARE, you *wicked, wicked* things!" Lady Hat called out, descending upon both of them with a tray of sugar mice. "I thought perhaps you'd thought better of coming. Mummy was *positively devastated* at the prospect of missing you."

"Hullo, old Hat," said Laurie. "You remember Miss March, of course."

"Of course! How well you look tonight, Miss March. Is Cousin Jo not with you? I hope she's not ill?" Lady Hat wore layer upon layer of peacock-hued crushed silk; a lone peacock feather emerged from the elaborate coil of braids and curls at her crown, and bounced when she spoke.

"Thank you," Meg said, "but no. She had a previous engagement to attend."

"I see," said Lady Hat, looking more closely at Meg, who suddenly felt like a prime *filet de beouf* in a shop window. "And in your Worth! Every time I see it, it's more lovely than the last. Or perhaps it's just the lady wearing it."

Every time. Meg felt her face burn, as Lady Hat had perhaps intended. But there was no question of wearing a different dress; nothing else owned by either March girl would have been suitable for an occasion as fine as the Ducal Ball. "Thank you," she said, simply. "It brings me great joy."

"But nothing compared to my own," Laurie said, gallantly. "Which is why I insisted she wear it again tonight."

Meg felt a burst of happiness, and the two smiled at each other.

"Of course you did," Harriet said, studying the two of them. Then she leaned in close and whispered in Meg's ear: "I hope I'm not embarrassing you, but you look as though you had trouble with the laces on your polonaise, my dear. If you come with me, I'll have my lady's maid do them up for you properly. We might even have a few pomegranate flowers to adorn your hair. Shall we?"

Jo had been the one to help Meg with the laces earlier, and it was like the middle March sister to make a mess of the job, especially on such an important occasion. Meg tried not to grimace. *Hopeless Jo! Couldn't you do a careful job this* one *time?*

But she remembered her earlier admonition to herself: *Remember who you are.* She would not let herself be pampered and petted a second time, not when she remembered so well how she'd felt when Belle Moffat had turned her into a doll. When she'd gone to Vanity Fair, or so she'd thought at the time. Belle Moffat's coming-out couldn't hold a candle to the Ducal Ball, but laces or no laces, she would not let Lady Hat fuss over her. Meg March was no longer just a girl, longing for silk stockings and her first glass of champagne.

So she gathered herself into a smile, then replied, "It's quite all right, Lady Harriet. My sister did my laces since, as you must know, we have no lady's maid. And I think my hair doesn't quite need any more adornment right now. I'm sure it would only get in the way during the dance, don't you think?"

"Indeed, in the way of the dance, and in the way of the view— as I, myself, greatly prefer to see Miss March's face," Laurie said with a bow.

Meg touched his arm affectionately. "Silly boy."

"I see," Lady Hat said, though she clearly did not, for she looked bewildered, as if she were unused to being refused anything. She handed off her tray of sugar mice to a passing servant and said, "Well, I suspect the particulars of your *Concord customs* are lost on me. But you *will* let me know if you change your mind."

"Of course," Meg said, going on to lavish Lady Hat's own dress and the decorations for the ball with sincere praise. She didn't want the other girl to take her refusal as an insult. "I've never seen such loveliness," Meg was saying. "Your kindness in including me tonight will never be forgotten."

"Never," Laurie repeated, though it was Meg who he now regarded with admiration. Truly, this was a side of the eldest March he had never before seen and would not soon forget.

"Tosh," said Lady Hat, smiling and taking Meg by the arm. "*Any* friend of the Laurences, you know." She led her, crooked laces and all, toward the ballroom, looking back over her shoulder at Laurie only once. "Do you mind, dear boy?" she asked. "I simply must make Meg here my pet."

"Just be careful she doesn't bite you," said Laurie.

Lady Hat's laughter floated over Meg's head to him. "Theodore Laurence! How can you talk so about our *dear* Cousin Meg?"

Laurie gave Lady Hat a wicked grin. "I was talking about you, old girl," he said with a nod. Then he straightened, looking at Meg questioningly. When she nodded his dismissal, he turned back to the crowd, straightening his vest. "I'm off to dance with Harvard, then."

"Good luck, Laurie!" Meg called after him.

He disappeared from sight.

As Lady Hat and Meg stood in the doorway to the ballroom, the musicians struck up "Crystal Schottische," and the beautifully gowned and perfectly suited dancers began to spin in a slow, glorious whirl around that vast gilded space.

This is a ball, Meg thought, breathing it all in. *A real one.*

Lady Hat watched her with fascination. "I can see why Laurie is so fond of you. You're a *bit* breathtaking, aren't you?"

"You are too kind," Meg demurred.

"Now! You must let me help you, Cousin Meg. I am determined that tonight you will be the most admired girl in the room." She spoke as if it were a game—a favorite one. "With whom should you dance? You shall have your pick, if I have my way!"

"Which is, I imagine, most often?" Meg ventured.

"Oftener." Lady Hat winked.

Meg blushed all the way to the roots of her hair. What an impertinent girl this Lady Hat was—it was no wonder Laurie liked her. She was an *uppertens* version of Jo, Meg thought, though it was only her wealth that allowed her to say outrageous things and get away with it. With Jo it was simply her character. Everyone knew there was no help for it, and all attempts to correct her would be met with disappointment.

The very rich and the very poor have so much in common, Meg thought. *No one expects them to conform to social niceties. It's only those of us in the middle who must constantly prove our worth on both sides.*

Beside Meg, Harriet was already running down a list of eligible young men, none of whose names Meg recognized. And none of whom, she noticed, included either John Brooke or Theodore Laurence, the only men in the room Meg actually knew. She was slightly horrified.

"Now then," said Harriet. "Who sounds like a good partner

for you?" She pointed with a gloved finger, ticking off the targets across the room, one by one. "Steel? Oil? Coal? Finance? The odd lesser lord?"

"I shouldn't even guess," said Meg, haltingly.

"Then I should!" Harriet winked again. "Railroads it is!"

Meg was flustered. "I—don't—"

"Oh, but you do!" said Harriet. "Here comes Mr. Brooke. Let's ask him, shall we?"

"No, please, Lady Harriet—I couldn't possibly—" said Meg, nearly ready to faint now as John Brooke crossed the room, coming closer.

Remember yourself, Meg.

14

A Departure

*M*y dear Brooke!" cried Lady Hat, putting a hand posses-
sively on Brooke's arm.

Meg couldn't help but notice, which was perhaps the whole
point. "Now then, you know our friend Meg better than I; who
would be a good partner for her?"

Mr. Brooke was caught off guard. Meg looked away. "Miss
March might have her pick of all the young men, I'm certain. As
for partners, I couldn't say. My own acquaintances here are few, as
I don't normally travel in such fashionable circles."

"Tosh!" said Harriet. "You're the equal—nay, the superior—to
any man here." She drew closer to him. "A soldier. A philosopher.
And, I daresay—a hero."

I will ram that peacock feather down your pretty throat, Meg
thought.

"How could you know that?" said Brooke. "You've only just
met me. I might be . . . a pirate, for all you know."

If it was at all possible, Meg realized, Brooke was flirting with Harriet.

Brooke. *Flirting.* With *Harriet*.

"I'm certain Mr. Laurence would never hire anyone except a first-rate scholar and gentleman for his grandson's tutor," said Harriet, "much less as *chaperone* for our dear Cousin Meg."

"I'll do my best to live up to your enormous expectations, *mademoiselle*."

"See that you do." The feather bobbed.

Meanwhile, *Cousin Meg* was trying, and failing, to turn into wallpaper. She couldn't bear what she was hearing.

"Now then," said Harriet, "why don't you dance with her first, Mr. Brooke?"

Mr. Brooke bowed stiffly to Meg, then said, "I should be happy to."

Meg's joy in the evening shrank. She didn't want Brooke to dance with her out of pity. "Oh, please," she whispered. She was mortified. "We needn't dance at all."

Harriet and Brooke didn't seem to notice. "Aren't you a dear!" said the lady to Brooke, sending them off to the dance floor together. "And when you've danced with her, I shall find her another partner."

"Perhaps you would save me a dance as well?" Brooke asked Harriet.

"Of course."

Oh, no. Meg thought she would shrivel up and disappear.

Brooke gave Lady Hat a gentlemanly bow, then took Meg by

the arm toward the dance floor. "Thank you," she said in a low voice as they moved out of earshot of Lady Hat. "It is very kind of you to dance with me."

"No, Miss March, it's I who should thank you," said Mr. Brooke, giving her a warm smile, as if Harriet were already forgotten. "I've been waiting all night to ask you to dance. I'm glad the lady gave me a chance to do so."

Meg blushed, relaxing just a little bit.

Mr. Brooke—John—did seem more like his old self.

Maybe I imagined the whole thing, she thought, and went twirling to the dance floor on the philosopher-hero's arm.

ACROSS THE ROOM, Laurie watched with interest.

He saw his old friend and tutor lead Meg to the dance floor for the waltz. He saw how pleased they both looked, turning around and around the ballroom floor in the newest dance, only just imported all the way from London.

Which was why Laurie had just now asked Brooke to chaperone Meg home for the evening, instead of himself.

Nothing would suit them better, he was sure of it—and if a dance led to a growing friendship between his tutor and his friend Miss March, so much the better. It would keep her in Concord, near her family, which would be good for everyone.

Myself included.

He could see other things, too. He saw the way Harriet watched Brooke and Meg dancing, how quickly she found him again when the song was over, how often she hooked her arm through Brooke's. Poor Meg looked aghast but said nothing.

That old game.

It was like Harriet to set her heart on Brooke, a man without title or money, a man whose mere presence in Harriet's affections would irritate the dowager no end.

Harriet had done this once before, with a poor musician of Laurie's acquaintance in London; that time, she'd threatened to elope with the man, causing all kinds of scenes between herself and her mother. It had been the talk of the town for months. The romance of poverty, the thrill of illicit affair, all that rubbish—Harriet reveled in it. Only her mother's threat of disinheritance had persuaded Harriet to drop the entire scheme, which Hat had done in the end—furious and in tears.

It was possible that was the reason the Carmichael-Carlthorpes had come to New York in the first place. No one had said as much to Laurie, but he could see the wisdom of it: the dowager taking her daughter away to America for her own good, trying to put the incident—and the scandal—behind them.

Except that Harriet had quite a talent for finding trouble wherever she went. She never suffered from a lack of suitors, impoverished or no.

Laurie didn't see that Brooke was any better of a choice than the musician had been. Not only was he poor and lacking in land or titles, but Brooke had spent the last few months entirely smitten with Meg March. Anyone could see that much.

Surely not even the prolific charms of Lady Harriet Carmichael-Carlthorpe—not to mention her enormous wealth—could turn Brooke's head in a single evening.

No, indeed.

Nothing so fine as the forty apple-trees of Orchard House, here.

Lady Hat caught his eye from across the room, raising her glass of champagne to him.

Laurie grabbed a glass off a passing tray and raised it in return.

She laughed, disappearing into the crowd.

He downed the glass in one gulp. "Harvard be hanged."

And with that, he was off.

Making his way back to the front door, where he'd told his carriage driver to wait "just in case," Laurie slipped out into the hot summer night. The carriage—parked over on the next block—was all in readiness to whisk him to Steinway Hall.

Laurie clambered inside, telling the driver to make haste. Down Broadway they clattered in the dark, the horses jolting around mud-holes and crowds of people shouting after them, up to the front door of Steinway Hall. Laurie argued his way inside—finally producing a receipt for the tickets in an amount so substantial that the doorman gave up and let him pass—and slipped down the dim aisle.

The stage was still empty, the lights up. The buzz in the crowd was so electric, Laurie knew it would be only a matter of moments until the principal attraction—Dickens himself—took the stage.

Laurie searched the crowd for one head of slightly mussed curls in particular.

There.

He could see her, just a glimpse, from rows away. How it was, he couldn't have said, but he could always spy her. Crossing a field, all the way from the road. Walking a crowded street, from down the block. A particular gesture of her hand, the bend of her head. The lines of her he knew by heart. The colors he knew best.

The speed of her. The liveliness. The spirit.

He watched from the aisle. She was talking animatedly with an older man sitting to her right.

He smiled.

No peacock feather here, just a slim velvet ribbon in the mussed curls of her hair.

The seat to her left—the seat that Laurie had bought for himself—was still empty, as if she was waiting for him.

The others had long been given away, but this one seat she had kept.

Just in case.

Just as you would have for her.

Laurie could not say when it had happened, or why. There were no moments to pinpoint, no lines to quote. The truth of the thing had inched up around him a season at a time, finally bursting into blossom with the apple orchards adjoining their two houses. Laurie had grown up learning how to love her. It was the only lesson he was ever any good at, because Jo herself had taught him, even if she hadn't known she was doing it.

She had made him.

And now, she was the thing that made him happy, made him whole, made him anything at all worth being.

He never wanted to be anywhere but by her side.

Hang Harvard.

He took a deep breath, feeling for the small velvet case in his pocket.

The one that held his mother's ring.

The one he'd been carrying around with him all week. To the Green in the sunshine. To the docks in the rain.

This was why they had come to New York. This was why they had come to see Dickens. He had wanted everything to be perfect, and at the very last minute, Grandfather had scuttled his plans entirely.

Grandfather, and Harvard, and Lady Harriet.

And—

Who the blazes is she talking to?

Jo didn't see Laurie at first, so engrossed was she in her conversation with the older-looking man. Dressed a bit shabbily—his cuffs were frayed, and the hat in his lap had definitely seen better days—the fellow seemed to be saying something about the work he'd done in the war. Laurie heard the words "battlefield" and "photography."

Jo could barely contain her excitement. "And so you were there? At Gettysburg?"

"Yes, but I was too far away to witness the conflict while it was happening. I could hear the cannons firing and see the smoke."

"But you walked the battlefield after, with Mathew Brady, the famous photographer?"

"I did. It was . . . difficult work, to say the least."

"I can imagine."

As Laurie moved closer, he could see the flush of interest on Jo's face—her eyes bright, her attention all focused on the photographer. And equally so, the smile of pleasure from this unknown man whose work Jo found so fascinating.

It was an intoxicating thing to be the object of Jo's attention—as Laurie himself had been, once upon a time.

As I long to be again.

Laurie drew nearer.

"And what brings you to Dickens this evening?" Jo was asking.

The man looked proud. "I'll be taking his photograph later. It's all been arranged."

"Christopher Columbus!" Jo exclaimed. "That means you'll get to meet him!"

"That's true." He nodded. "It *is* a bit exciting, I'll give you that. Though I'm meant to not let on, professionally speaking."

Laurie could see the scheme forming behind Jo's eyes.

"I don't suppose—" she began, then faltered.

In a moment she'd be inviting herself back-stage with this older photographer in an effort to meet Dickens in person. Or worse—the photographer would do so himself. Dickens or no Dickens, Laurie wouldn't let himself be usurped by an old man in fraying cuffs.

He pulled his hand out of his pocket.

The box stayed put.

Now is not the time.

Laurie stepped forward, into Jo's line of sight, and said, "Aren't you the American authoress Josephine March?" He offered a sweeping bow. "And would you be saving that seat for anyone in particular?"

Heads swiveled from every direction. Heads, followed by whispers.

"I beg your pardon," Jo's seatmate began, indignantly.

Jo looked momentarily startled—until her face lit with pleasure. "Oh, Teddy! You came!"

"You know I could never choose a society ball over you, Jo." He slipped into his seat and took Jo's hand. The photographer noticed, giving Laurie the merest nod and Jo a look of regret. Laurie ignored him completely.

Jo didn't notice because the audience was quieting. Dickens had just arrived.

"Just in time," said Jo.

On-stage, Dickens strode tall and elegant to a table at the center, where a book lay open. Waiting.

For a moment, Laurie felt certain the author must have seen him slipping into his seat near the stage—watched him sliding his hand into the hand of the young woman waiting there in her authoress's dress, her face rapt.

And so, too, he believed Dickens himself could surely see what Jo could not or would not: that they were meant to be.

Just then, the great man gave Laurie an imperceptible nod—or so he imagined—and began to read.

"*My father's family name being Pirrip, and my Christian name Philip, my infant tongue could make of both names nothing longer or more explicit than Pip. So I called myself Pip, and came to be called Pip. . . .*"

There was rapturous applause and Laurie chuckled, then leaned toward Jo and whispered, "So he *does* do voices! I told you. Well worth the price of the ticket."

"Stop, Teddy!" She touched her head to his, hesitated, then— "Was the ball a terrible bore?"

"You weren't there, Jo." He shrugged. "Of course it was. You know I'd rather be here with you. More than anywhere."

She squeezed his fingers hard, her face shining with excitement. "I'm so glad," she said, and for the barest second, his heart leapt with hope.

15

⤳⤳⟲⟲⟲

A Quarrel

*B*y the next morning—and by all accounts—it seemed the night had been a great victory, indeed. A shining triumph of a night, in a city indifferent to such glories. All of which made for a rather difficult business of going home.

But it was time to return to Concord, regardless of whether anyone seemed particularly happy about it. Jo had already crammed her authoress dress into her trunk and was trying to get the lid latched when Meg came in with the Worth gown on her arm and a forlorn expression she now punctuated with a heavy sigh.

Jo pushed harder. "For goodness' sake, Meg, you aren't still mooning over old John Brooke, of all people. So he danced with you. That's what people do at balls."

Meg gave her sister a frown. "I'm not *mooning* over anyone. Besides, you're one to talk. Why don't you tell me the story of how Charles Dickens himself shook your hand and said *Miss March* fifty-five more times?"

"Perhaps I will! Because he's *Charles Dickens*." Jo gave up on her bag and thumped across the room. "I can't seem to find my cloak."

The elder March smoothed the silvery fabric of the gown, straightening the embroidery. Despite her protests, she *was* still thinking of the ball, and of John Brooke. Of how good it had felt to have a friend there who knew her and liked her for who she *really* was—a girl without a dowry, in a dress that originally had been meant for her sister—especially after Laurie disappeared.

Meg hadn't told Jo everything that happened the night before. She hadn't told about the whispers that ran around the room when Lady Hat discovered Laurie had left Meg behind at the ball. Meg knew immediately where he'd gone; there was no question his heart was with Jo at the Dickens event, the surprise he'd arranged so carefully and then had to abandon at his grandfather's whims.

But no one else knew where he was, or why.

Or why Lady Hat, in particular, seemed to care.

Meg also hadn't known that Laurie had arranged for Mr. Brooke to be Meg's escort. Not at first. At first she only felt Lady Hat practically *gloating*, her face shining with mischief at the discovery as she danced a waltz with Brooke. "What!" Harriet said, loud enough for the entire room to hear. "Gone and *left her*? Our dear *Cousin Meg*?"

Then the humiliation when people stared and whispered. *That poor girl*, they must have been thinking. *That poor, poor girl, to be abandoned at the biggest social event of the year!*

It was only when Mr. Brooke insisted on dancing with her

a second time that the whispers stopped and Meg could enjoy herself again. At the end of the evening, when Mr. Brooke said Laurie's carriage had arrived for them and asked if he could escort her home, she went with him gladly, gratefully—a true gentleman who never said a word to embarrass or frighten her.

And when they came into the drawing-room of the boarding house and he bid her good night, he'd kissed her cheek.

For just a moment, Meg had let herself imagine what it would be like to be Lady Harriet, rich and worldly and admired everywhere she went.

"Thank you for your charming company, Miss March," he'd said. "I hope I may enjoy it again sometime."

He'd called her charming! But then, he'd said the same about Harriet. Meg had to admit he'd spent half the night flirting with Harriet and the other half with her.

Why did Meg care? Like Jo had surmised, Meg wouldn't allow herself to feel those feelings for him. Jo's book was astute. In it, Meg originally meant to refuse Brooke because of his poverty, but had only accepted him to spite "Aunt March." Meg had to make a rich match. She couldn't be as silly as their parents, who had given away their fortune to live in genteel poverty, as Jo's book told the world. Meg wanted more for her children. She wanted them to have everything she never had.

What were their names? That Jo had given them? Daisy and—
She'd forgotten already.

And yet, Meg hadn't stopped thinking about it—that dance, that kiss—all night. Not when Jo came in and flung herself down on the bed. Not when her sister went on all through breakfast about Dickens and *Great Expectations*. Not when she'd retold the story of the timid girl who had tapped on her shoulder and asked if she really were the *American authoress Josephine March*, and in that case, if she would sign her program.

All the while, Meg had taken out her memory of her night—of her Mr. Brooke!—and turned it over and over in her mind's eye, as if it were something so soft she could not help but reach for it, yet something so delicate she was afraid to touch it at all. Perhaps a novel she wanted to read so badly she had slept with it under her pillow. Or a Christmas present she'd only just been given and had yet to unwrap.

As much as she loved her sisters, this was for her, and her alone.

Meg didn't tell Jo any of these things. Jo would tease and taunt her about *old Babbling Brooke*, but Meg wasn't sure she was ready to share it yet. Or that she even knew what any of it meant, for her or for him.

Him.

Even that small word sent a shiver through her.

Under my pillow you go. Meg carefully folded the Worth dress into her own small trunk and closed the latch. "I was only thinking there may never be another occasion for either of us to wear this. That's all I meant to say."

It was the strangeness—was it sadness?—in Meg's voice that snapped Jo out of her own dark mood. She stopped fussing about her cloak and turned immediately to her sister. "But you wore it brilliantly, Meg! Truly, you were the very picture of beauty itself. Beyond that—if you ask me—it was a terrible waste, even for our Teddy. I do wish he hadn't done it." No one ever had to ask Jo anything; Jo simply volunteered her opinion anyway.

Just then, the maid knocked at the door. Jo leapt up to let her in.

"Mr. Brooke wants to see Miss Meg," the maid announced shyly in a pronounced Irish accent. "Waitin' for you in the drawing-room, miss. Some question about the travel arrangements."

"Thank you, Bridget," said Meg. Her voice was calm, but her heart thudded.

Meg rose to go. "The only waste is that Laurie went to a lot of trouble buying an incredible gift for you that you won't even wear. You can't very well be cross at him for that."

"I'm not cross," Jo said, crossly. Meg looked at her. "At least you didn't burn the back of this one," said Jo with a sigh. "If you think it's a waste and neither of us shall ever have occasion to wear it again, maybe you should leave it here with Lady Hat? I'm sure she'd find a use for it."

"I'm sure she would," said Meg, wincing at the very thought of the flirtatiousness between Harriet and Brooke. "But she already has enough fine gowns. We'll take it home and put it away, Jo. Maybe one day you'll wear it as a wedding dress."

Jo's face crinkled up into a look of horror. "The only thing I'm married to are my books, Meg. You'll wear it for a wedding dress before I do. When you marry Mr. Brooke, perhaps."

"Jo! That's the last thing on my mind," Meg insisted.

But Jo gave her a sly look, as if she knew what Meg was thinking and wasn't fooled at all.

AT THE TRAIN station, where the porters loaded their trunks into the cars and the passengers scurried to and fro to find their seats, Meg and Jo, Laurie and Brooke climbed aboard for the long ride back to Concord.

It had been a late night—and a long week—and they were all a bit gloomy at the thought of returning home.

After the Dickens reading, Jo had been so inspired, she'd spent half the night making notes for her novel, even going so far as to write a new scene, so provoked was she by something the great man had said about the evils of modern society.

And, perhaps, by the tap on the shoulder.

She wondered if she would ever get used to meeting her own readers in person. It was one thing to think of them as envelopes, or even oranges. It was quite another to see a face, to shake quavering hands, to hear how Jo's words had found their way into a new home.

What an odd life this is!

Jo had thought she would write on the train, but as she stared out the soot-streaked window now, she was too preoccupied. She thought of her writing garret in Concord, which somehow seemed even smaller now—and after the adventures of Manhattan, a trifle cramped and dull.

Meg, too, was quiet, lost in thought. She only wished she had a moment to be alone again with Mr. Brooke, to determine the depth of her feelings for him, or his for her—were that the case. *But I don't know up from down*, she thought.

Charmed or charming.

A kiss on the hand or on the cheek.

Concord or Kensington.

But all Mr. Brooke and Laurie could do was argue about the student's utter abandonment of his reading-list and his lapse of study in Greek.

"You're snapping at each other like little old ladies," Jo finally said.

"Jo!" Meg frowned.

"Sincere apologies," Mr. Brooke said, looking distressed.

"Come now," Laurie groused. "We were just having a bit of lively discussion."

Jo snorted. "Lively discussion? If I had the money, I'd hire a private car so I could write in peace and quiet." She crossed out the last sentence she'd written.

"You would not, and you know it," Meg observed, with a shake of her curls.

Jo knew she was right, but still.

LAURIE COULD NOT shake the mood, either.

There's no escaping the row ahead, old boy. Might as well soldier up and accept it.

He knew Grandfather would hear that he had not, after all,

made the acquaintance of the Harvard president; had, instead, left the ball early to go see Dickens. The old man would have some choice words for his grandson, surely—about duty and honor, about his place in society.

Gratitude. My mother, whom Grandfather never approved of. The Laurence name.

He suspected there would be a further row, about leaving Meg there, for surely Brooke—or else the Dowager Lady Carmichael-Carlthorpe—would tell the old man everything.

If only Grandfather didn't know Hat's mother quite so well.

Laurie sighed. He didn't want to admit that he felt a bit like he deserved that one, himself.

And he especially didn't want to imagine what Mrs. March would have to say to him.

Mr. Brooke eyed him from over his Greek text.

Laurie turned back to his small window and its rushing stream of soot and scenery.

That's not the worst of it, though, is it?

Why you're so out of sorts?

It wasn't, and he knew it.

Because he had a much bigger problem than Grandfather and the dowager, or Mrs. March and Meg, or even Harvard and Mr. Brooke.

It was Laurie himself—at least when it came to one person in particular. The only person who mattered, who had ever mattered.

Jo.

He had still failed to say the one thing to her, the thing that he had wanted most to say. She seemed as far away from him as ever—close in proximity, but not in her affections.

Not the way she was in his.

And I'm so afraid that I'll never be able to reach you, Jo.

He let out a great sigh. The girl was impossible.

In fact, it was Laurie's great sigh that first gained Jo's attention, across the aisle. "I know," she said, sympathetically. "It does seem terribly dull to be going home already! But think of all we shall have to remember and talk about for years to come."

"It's not that," said Laurie. "Only that I was thinking how angry Grandfather will be that I left the Ducal Ball after less than an hour."

"As he should be," said Mr. Brooke, over his tome. He gave his young charge a disapproving frown.

Laurie looked from Brooke to Jo to her sister. "Meg, do you mind switching places with me for a bit? Mr. Brooke was just telling me he'd love to show you some basic Greek conjugations."

"Of course," Meg said, looking only somewhat embarrassed, as clearly Mr. Brooke had said nothing of the kind.

Mr. Brooke gave Laurie an odd look, then held up his Greek ledger. "I thought you'd never ask."

As Meg and Mr. Brooke fell into conversation, Laurie slid into the seat across from Jo.

"Don't worry so much about your grandfather, Teddy. You had great fun seeing Dickens," said Jo. "Better for both of us that way."

Laurie only smiled. "Great fun, yes. But it will come at a cost."

"Not your cost, surely," said Jo.

"Yes, mine," sighed Laurie. "Most likely. I suppose I'll soon find out. You know, this may come as a shock to you, but I'm rather behind in my studies," he said ruefully. "It's quite possible that there will be no place for me at Harvard next year."

"No wonder your grandfather was fussing about it." Jo shook her head. "I'm sorry, Teddy. But you said it yourself: Dickens was a must. How could you miss it?" As she spoke, she dabbed at a spot of ink that had dropped onto her skirt.

"That's not it." He leaned toward Jo. Then stood, holding out his hand. "I can't do this here. Come on."

Jo followed Laurie down the aisle of the swaying car and through the doors. Now they were standing on the platform between the hurtling, whistling, rattling train cars.

"How is this a better place to talk?" Jo shouted, holding on to the rail.

"It's not. But I have to say it. It can't wait." Laurie clutched the rails in both hands. "I promised myself I would do this while we were in New York, so this is my last chance, Jo."

Jo frowned. Laurie took a deep breath.

"I needed you at the ball. I didn't want to be there without you. Why do you think I left to come find you?"

"I thought because—you know," Jo said, loudly.

Laurie shook his head. "I don't know, Jo."

"Because you enjoy Dickens," she shouted. "Not to mention you did purchase *two* tickets. Well, four, actually."

"I left for you. Because that's where I wanted to be. *With you* is always where I want to be." It was glorious, to finally get it out, to not be carrying it around, a secret weighing on his heart. Like the velvet box in his pocket. "I—"

Jo held a hand up. "Teddy, stop it. Just stop. I don't—I can't. Please don't."

"You have to hear me out, at least one day, Jo." He tried not to sound desperate, but it was how he felt.

Jo looked pained. "Not today, Teddy, please."

They stood on opposite sides of the platform, facing each other across the coupling, where the train cars pitched and shook and groaned at each other. Listening as the swaying steel rattled beneath them.

Laurie sighed. "Fine."

The train was picking up speed as it pulled out of Manhattan, fleeing north into the Bronx and following the curve of the Hudson toward New England. The trees grew thicker as the houses grew sparser, but here and there the glint of the water shone through the trees.

North. Concord. Orchard House.

Home.

The whistle sounded, and Laurie shoved the door open to the next car, pushing his way inside.

16

ANOTHER SEQUEL

A dark cloud hung over Orchard House.

After the trip, Laurie grew sulky, avoiding Jo whenever he could. She could see him pout by the windows at the Laurences' estate, turning away when he caught sight of her face in the glass. If he went out to get the carriage or walk into town, he refused to even look in the direction of Orchard House, as if it were not simply Jo but the entire cottage itself that pained him.

"Where's Laurie?" Amy pouted. "It's as if he's suddenly decided he's too good for us! That, or that we're frightful *dollards*."

"Dullards," Meg said, automatically.

"It's hardly our affair, what Laurie thinks of us—or what he chooses to do or whom he chooses to do it with," Jo scolded. "Most likely he isn't thinking of us at all, but rather occupied getting ready for school in September."

Meg wisely said nothing, just as Mama Abba—the well-trained mother of daughters—had instructed her.

But where Laurie had been, there was now a hole in the March family, and it wasn't only Amy who noticed.

Jo missed him, but she was determined to "buckle down" and work on her sequel, as she had not in New York, where there had been too many distractions.

I don't have time for the silliness of boys, their hurt feelings and pouting expressions.

Not when there's a book to write and money to earn.

And truthfully, there was that.

Money that Mama Abba needed to run the house, or that could be sent to Father for food or boots, or that could buy new shoes and a coat for Amy, who had grown since last winter.

The need for money, and for someone to work to earn it, was not something Laurie would ever understand, Jo thought, as she often had. With Father still down South on a quixotic mission and the March family's fortune squandered, Jo's little bit of writing income was her family's main source of support at the moment.

Jo was essentially the man of the house, and she took that responsibility seriously.

Someone must.

A new book, and the bit of income it afforded, might finally free them from the grip of poverty. She might be able to pay off Father's war debts, even secure a dowry for Meg. Art lessons for Amy. The idea of the family being comfortable again—and on the strength of Jo's quill—gave her such pride she could scarcely breathe.

Such hope.

She couldn't let Laurie change everything, not because of his boyish fixation on her. They both needed to be smarter than that, and if Laurie wouldn't, then Jo must.

It was only alone in her garret, late at night, when Jo sat with her toes tucked up beneath her night-dress, petting the cat, and wondered at the great brokenness between them.

DESPITE ALL HER efforts, however, the idea of romance was still in the air. Since returning from New York, there were other disturbances.

And these, too, were allowed whatever space and time they needed to work themselves out, as dictated by Mama Abba's wisdom—as, again, the mother of girls.

Meg went about sighing all the time and looking at her reflection in mirrors, patting her hair and her clothes with an air of dissatisfaction. More than once, Jo had found her elder sister staring out the window at the road as if waiting for someone, all the while ignoring some bit of sewing or a loaf of rising dough in front of her.

"What is it out there?" Jo whispered playfully in her sister's ear, as Meg took in the view of the little lane between their house and the Laurences'. "Do you see fairies?"

"I think she's under an enchantment," Amy echoed. "That, or a toothache."

"I believe this is something closer to a fever," Jo said, giving Meg a poke.

But Meg just blushed and refused to answer.

More than once, Mama Abba had to bring her back to the present with a simple "Meg," spoken in her firm but gentle voice, and Meg would startle and go back to whatever chore she'd been neglecting.

How dreary were girls in love! Jo found herself stomping out of the room whenever Meg got that dreamy, distant look on her face. Over John Brooke! It was stuff meant for novels, not real life, where there were chores to be done and money to earn.

And John Brooke is hardly the stuff of a protagonist, Jo sniffed.

But if the feminine airs of the house were definitely starting to irritate Jo, Amy had positively wept with envy when Meg told her about the Ducal Ball and Lady Hat, museums and the opera, the rooms of crystal and marble. "Oh, Meg! How lucky you were, to be there to see it! I shall never get to attend such an event, never!" Only the promise that one day, when she was older, Amy would get to wear the silvery House of Worth polonaise herself (and be the envy of every girl in Concord) gave her reason enough to pause her complaining.

"I shall wear it with my best rose ribbon," she said, pausing to smooth it flat with her palm, again and again, on the dinner-table.

"You won't, though, because in another week of this nonsense, you will have worn it threadbare," Jo said.

But it was no use, and the fact that Meg was only her old self when describing balls to Amy only made Jo more bothered.

Even Mama was starting to irritate Jo. Every day her mother would bring her a bit of toast and a question—

"So, darling, how *is* the story coming along today?"

"Fine," Jo would answer some days.

"Horridly," on others.

"Same as when you asked yesterday," finally—because whether or not it was there, what Jo heard was her mother's gentle reproach that she hadn't finished it already.

Even old Hannah, the servant, seemed always to be wanting to ask her questions about the book, such as who would live and who would die. "Just not my girls, Jo. Not you, or Amy or Meg. I can't have *that* again, not even if just in one of your stories."

And if Jo reassured anyone at all, about any of it, the questions only brought more questions.

"I don't know!" Jo would protest. "So please let me alone so I can find out for myself!"

Because it was true.

She didn't—she simply *did not know* the fates of her characters. Not yet.

With any luck, the proper ending would come to her one of these days. Or at least she hoped it would.

So Jo continued to chase it, hiding herself away in her attic garret, scribbling away as fast as she could on a new version of the story, one with less ordinary feminine courage and more danger.

Once again, she married Meg to Brooke—she suspected that, this time, neither of them would object—but then that was too boring.

So instead, she killed him off in a distant war. Like Lord Byron, freedom-fighting abroad. A heroic death. *Something* more interesting for old Brooke to do than talking ancient Greek and visiting her sister, which he did any afternoon when he wasn't in Boston, meandering past the hedge to sit in the parlor with Meg and drink tea.

Filling the hole that Laurie was leaving behind.

Jo couldn't imagine what they found to talk about so often. One could only tolerate so much discussion of the weather.

And balls!

So Jo made their fictional lives more interesting. She sent Laurie to school and Brooke into a foreign army, giving Meg a tearful speech begging him to stay. The next day she'd rip up the page and have Brooke break Meg's heart by casually mentioning his recent visit to a society lady whose attention he'd caught. (From what she'd gathered of the Ducal Ball from both Meg and Laurie, this bit of the story might not be confined to fiction.) Then she'd send Brooke home from the war, wounded in action, a shattered man unable to work or support his new bride.

Jo's fingers were black with ink by the end of the first week home. She finally settled on marrying off Meg and Brooke in the usual way, finished the book, and sent the pages off to Niles.

They were quickly sent back to her.

That ending was declared "too nice" for his editorial sensibilities, so Jo killed off John in a fit of pique, leaving his lifeless corpse on the battlefield, and leaving Meg a widow.

There were no twins this time, the better to let Meg find love again. So there was, at least, some solace.

But when it came to choosing a second suitor, Jo came up empty. The perfect man for her dear Meg just wouldn't come to mind. Perhaps Laurie would be an acceptable substitute—they certainly had enjoyed each other's company in New York, enough to make her believe, momentarily, that Laurie and Meg might one day be more than friends.

But somehow, that didn't feel possible anymore.

Jo was beginning to think her sister was too good for the fickle Laurence boy, who by all accounts had flirted with Lady Hat under her very nose—and then had the audacity to demand Jo's undying loyalty for life. He didn't know *what* he wanted, or whom. He was no better at this than she was.

Boys!

So how should plain old Jo March manage to figure him out?

Since Laurie was determined to punish her for being herself and for following her passion—as he wasn't allowed to follow his—she decided to let his fictional double suffer *without* his happy ending.

So the authoress wrote him off entirely, sent him to London to work in his grandfather's office, toiling away in obscurity forever.

Dollard, as Amy would say.

After doling out such a fitting punishment, Jo found the writing a little easier than she had, if only by an imperceptible margin.

As before, the fictional family took inspiration from the real one, but all the details were changed. In the novel, Jo sent herself and Amy to New York for an adventure instead of herself and Meg. The youngest March, so pleased to wear the latest fashions, fainted dead away at the opera (from an overcrowded, overheated room), but in swooning managed to catch the eye of a dashing new character named Roderigo, an Italian with a waxed mustache, an *entire orchard* of lime-trees, and a secret, possibly sinister past.

For several days Jo agonized over the source of her Roderigo's secret. Perhaps he'd run away with a bishop's daughter and afterward lost his family fortune to political unrest. Or perhaps he was swindled by his own brother, since the two of them had once loved the same woman.

No, she had him beg Amy to elope with him to Australia, where he had the chance to regain his fortune in a mining company.

Amy denied him, of course, tearfully refusing his offer on the grounds that it would break Marmee's heart.

As it would.

She promised to wait for his return, but instead he was lost in a shipwreck in the Pacific, and Amy spent the rest of the story weeping lovely big tears into her pillow, tended to by Beth, who had taken over Meg's old job as governess to the Kings.

Beth, Jo thought. If only the real Beth had such luck. On the pages, Jo could bring Beth to life, let her play with her dolls and her piano, have her bring the contentment she had always ushered into Jo's life and the family's house.

But when she put the quill down, once more Jo felt her heart seized by the loss of her, the sister who had been the kindest of them all.

It was too much to bear.

Real life was never as satisfying, nor as just, as fiction was. It made Jo furious whenever she wrote about it, even thought about it.

In real life, poor girls remained poor, and fathers lost their fortunes in quixotic business deals, and wealthy people swept in and upended everything.

Sisters, even the most beloved, sometimes died.

Silences fell.

Promise me, Beth had said right before she took her last breath.

Promise me, Jo. Write your way back to the light. Stay in the land of the living. Don't follow me into the silence.

Jo wiped her eye with her sleeve and picked up her quill.

Oh, Beth, I'm trying.

She turned back to the page, and to fate—this time, her own.

So what of the tomboy Jo March?

In the novel, Jo met a friend of Dickens at a reading of *Great Expectations* at Steinway Hall, a literary scholar with frayed cuffs and kind eyes. They spent a week enjoying each other's company at lectures and readings and cafés. But the man's health was poor from hours spent holed up in musty libraries.

Tragically, he died of consumption over the winter, leaving Jo bereft but determined to continue his work.

He also managed to leave her *just enough* in his will to attend a ladies' college outside of London, a very modern place with exquisite ancient buildings and execrable food.

Heaven.

In the novel, Jo March began a correspondence with Dickens himself, starting by breaking the tragic news that his dear friend had died.

Dickens wrote back encouraging letters about her novels,

using his connections with an editor in London to have her newest creation published to great acclaim. Thus began a great literary friendship.

It was all very Pickwickian, until (on her way home to America in triumph, no longer an obscure authoress but a genuine phenomenon) Jo had herself kidnapped and removed to Australia by pirates. There she escaped her captors by hiding a key under her tongue, undoing her locks, and running away in the middle of the night.

As one does.

She was about to gain passage on a ship home to Boston when she met Amy's Roderigo getting off a steamship in Sydney Harbor. He had survived the shipwreck and was sending a letter home to Amy to let her know he was alive, but that he had been maimed in attempting to escape and could not bear to let his beloved see his mutilated form.

I am doomed to love your sister forever, he said to Jo, weeping as he pressed the envelope into Jo's hands, *but I can never be hers now.*

Let her find someone else and be happy.

And so the fictional Jo March returned home, sadder and wiser. Each of the sisters had her own special adventure, but ended up where she'd started: living together at home with their mother and the servant, Hannah.

Only this time, because of Jo's success as a novelist, they would not be destitute but live as rich old maids, able to order the world to their liking.

Fin, she wrote, and readied the manuscript to take to good old Niles.

It was the end of summer, the end of August, and Jo March had finished her book at last.

WHEN MR. NILES announced he didn't like this direction for the book, either, Jo nearly threw it at him. She was starting to suspect that he didn't know *what* he wanted. That he should write it himself if he didn't like any of her efforts.

"I'm sorry, Miss March. It's just not right still. It's too . . . much."

"Too *much*?"

"Much too much. Roderigo maimed? Giving Amy up forever? Readers would have my head, and yours, too."

"I can take that part out. The maiming."

"It's not just the maiming, Miss March. That is just one example out of a dozen. You'll have to start over, I'm afraid, the better to serve both your characters and your readers."

A great weariness came over her, as if she'd been drugged. "I can't start over, Mr. Niles," she said, feeling tears starting at the corners of her eyes. "I can't bear to look at it another minute."

"You must," he said. "Your way lies somewhere between feminist determination and melodramatic whimsy."

Jo wanted to clutch the sheaf of papers to her chest and run, not walk, to a different publishing house. Any publishing house. Any that would let her write what she wanted without constantly telling her she was wrong. "You were the one who asked for more melodramatic whimsy, if I recall. You said you could sell sweetness or *the Josephine March special*."

He nodded. "I remember. But this is not what I meant. It's . . . well, lacking in good taste. Though I'm sorry to say it."

"Shakespeare was constantly writing shipwrecks and kidnappings and dramatic changes in fortune. No one ever says his work is *lacking in good taste*."

"Shakespeare was not a young lady from Concord."

Jo had never in her life uttered a scream—she disdained girls who did—but she very much felt like uttering one now. Everything she did was wrong. First it was too little. Too quiet, too staid, too idealized. Now, it seemed, she'd gone too far in the other direction: Shipwrecks and kidnappings were all too much.

Because she was a *young lady*.

From Concord.

Did Lady Harriet have to deal with such nonsense?

Jo suspected not.

But if Jo were ever to have a prayer of getting paid, of buying new boots for Amy or new gloves for Father or paying off her family's war debts, she'd have to start again.

Start fresh, Niles said. Give them excitement and romance, but make it realistic. In good taste. Cleverly wrought. Well-paced. With truthful yet heartwarming encounters between several flawed if likable characters.

"Sounds easy enough to me." Niles looked at her from across the desk. "Don't you agree?"

She didn't agree at all. Absolutely did *not*.

But all she said was, "You'll have your sequel by the end of the month, Mr. Niles. At the very least before Thanksgiving, I assure you." It was early September now, and she could dash the thing off in two months, she was sure.

"But will it be . . ."

"The *right* sequel? I suppose you'll have to tell me that for yourself, won't you? You and your partners. Somewhere between dull and whimsical. In good taste."

She would not scream. She would *not*.

"I trust you, Miss March. If you tell me you have written the ending your readers would want—on both sides of the pond—I will believe you. You know what they want. Them, and you. They want a little adventure, a little romance, but mostly they want the girls to decide their own fates. Not to be flung about by chance."

She thought of the girl who had tapped her shoulder at Steinway Hall.

What she would have wanted.

Jo wanted to protest that was exactly what she had written: that the little women of her story had determined their own fates. They had not let the men decide for them. They each got to choose: one married and widowed, two unmarried by their own choice, and Beth gloriously still alive in the book. But together still, as they should be.

They belonged to themselves, and no one else.

It was clear to her that Niles, and perhaps all men, had no idea what it was that *little women* actually wanted from life.

Niles didn't see it that way. He seemed to think it was she, *Jo*, who didn't know what she wanted. "When you know what you want," he was saying, "you'll know how to end the story."

She wasn't sure she understood him. "Me? What do I have to do with it?"

"When Josephine March, the author, knows what she wants, Jo March the character will as well. Do you understand?"

Jo gave a great sigh and sank down in her chair. "I don't think I actually do, Mr. Niles. But I suppose I shall have to endeavor to, for your sake."

"For both our sakes," Niles said, and offered her the tin. "Mint?"

17

Heartache

*S*o it happened that the next day—as Jo was deciding that even Dickens would have run mad with an editor as fickle as Niles—who should visit her writer's garret but Theodore Laurence himself.

She answered the knock expecting to see Amy with tea and toast, but instead it was Laurie, his face long and his eyes contrite. "Mr. Weller requests an audience with Mr. Snodgrass," he said. Though he tried to keep his tone merry, his face said exactly the opposite: He was in earnest.

She dreaded Laurie in earnest. It didn't suit him at all.

Jo had just been deep in consideration of burning her latest manuscript draft. Instead she looked up and with practiced irritation said, "This isn't the Pickwick Club, Teddy. I'm working."

He sat on a tuft of rags, his knees nearly up around his ears. *When did he grow so tall?* Jo wondered. *How long has it been since he's been up here?*

"Meg told me you were done with your book."

Jo decided then and there never to tell Meg anything again as long as she lived. "I was," she replied, "but once again, Niles has squelched all my efforts. So I am back to square one. As in, *once more*."

"Oh," said Laurie, eyeing the sheaf of papers sitting on an upturned washtub, a leaking quill sitting on top. "Sorry to hear it."

"Not as sorry as I am."

A moment passed as they sat in silence.

He looked over at her. "And how do I make out in this version?"

She smiled. "Murdered in the street by ruffians."

"Oh?" Laurie's eyes lit up. "Defending your honor?"

"Refusing them half a penny for the poor-box," she said, almost gleefully.

Laurie scrunched up his face. "A stingy fate for a friend, don't you think?"

Jo squinted at him. "A friend? Is that what you are now? A friend wouldn't disappear for a month over a simple quarrel."

It was September now, the air was crisp and bracing, and yet upstairs in the attic it was as humid as an August day due to Jo's mounting anxiety over the latest draft.

Laurie pressed his hand to his heart and gave her a small bow. "That's why I'm here. To beg your forgiveness. I am sorry, for everything. I was an idiot."

Jo nodded. "That's the first thing you've said in ages that I agree with."

He stood and shut the door behind him, in his familiar way,

and she felt a momentary return of the old panic. Anything he said to her now, he could say within earshot of her mother and sisters, surely.

She looked back down at her papers. "Must you close the door?"

He sighed, and turned back to her with a somber expression. "I'm afraid I must."

Perhaps she had made a mistake in letting him get so close, and giving him the wrong idea. Boys liked to joke about girls being swoony, always talking about romance and love, but in Jo's opinion, boys—especially Theodore Laurence—were as ridiculous as any girl she'd ever known.

Then, as if to prove her point, he sat down on an overturned basket and said, "I'm sorry we fought, Jo. I'm sorry for everything. I believe—I was jealous."

She avoided looking at him. "Jealous? Of what?"

"Everything. Your writing. Your freedom, most likely. The space you keep between your art and whatever else might distract you from it."

Jo listened.

"You can pursue your writing when I must give up my music to go to university. All this business about business, and no thought at all of what I want."

She was suddenly caught up with rage. Jo would have cut off her hair and dressed as a boy herself if it meant she would get to attend university.

The whole world lay at Laurie's feet—money, travel, society, every opportunity Jo herself would wish—and he'd give it all up to sit in obscurity every day, writing and rewriting the same rotten story at an editor's whim?

Jo would never have squandered an opportunity like Harvard. All those books to read, all those things to learn! And here he was, moaning about it like he was being sent to prison.

Money is wasted on the wrong people, she thought. Foolish boy, never to be grateful for his grandfather's generosity.

Jo set down her quill. "I'll make you an offer: I'll take your place at Harvard, and you can stay here and write my book for me."

"Deal." He reached out to shake her hand. "So long as it's a concerto and not a book. And I can compose it on a piano and not at that horribly cramped little desk."

The wistful look in his eye softened her anger. Because, deep down, she knew it was all true, all of it: the entitlement and the opportunity, the wistfulness and the loss.

His music is the mother he misses. The life he will never know. The book I cannot remember how to write.

She took his hand and gave it a firm shake. "Now then, I can cut off all my hair to make you a girl's wig, but we will have to do something to give you a bosom . . ."

He laughed. He didn't realize she was only partly joking.

Nor had he let go of her hand yet.

"I had hoped . . . ," he started. Then he looked out the window, uncertainty crossing his face.

He turned back to her. The pause became longer as he searched her own expression.

If he were waiting for her to say something to prompt him to continue, he was going to be waiting a *very long* time.

The little garret seemed to grow even quieter. She could hear her own heart beating. Meg and Amy arguing over the tea, downstairs in the parlor. Outside, a dog howling his way down the dusty middle of the lane after a squirrel, barking like mad—but still the sound was better than what she knew was coming.

Jo could see it in Laurie's face—despite their earlier quarrel, he was still set on romance, and he was still set on her.

Foolish fickle heart, to choose so wrongly for itself.

"I was hoping," he began again, "that during our time in Manhattan, we would have come to an—an understanding."

"An understanding of *what*?" She raised an eyebrow.

Laurie suddenly found something very interesting on the toe of his left shoe. "Of the future," he said. "Our future. Yours and mine. I did try to bring it up on the train ride home."

Obstinate boy!

"Oh, Teddy, please don't!" she groaned. "I've already told you—"

His face erupted. "I will, Jo. I will and you must hear me now. It's no use; we've got to have it out, and the sooner the better for both of us," he answered, flushed and excited all at once. "I tried in New York—so many times. But you wouldn't let me. But we must, old girl. Listen, please."

Jo gave a great sigh and threw up her hands. Here it was, at last—and now she must be done with it.

Laurie continued, "I've loved you ever since I've known you,

Jo. I couldn't help it; you've been so good to me. I've tried to show it so many times, but you wouldn't let me. You wouldn't even wear the dress I had made for you. Now I'm going to make you hear, and you must give me an answer, for I can't go on so any longer. I can't leave it until I return from Harvard. You might meet someone while I'm gone, and I can't have that, Jo. I can't." He knelt before her and took her hand in his.

"I thought you'd understand! I wanted to save you from this," said Jo, who found this situation a great deal harder than she expected. Her hands were trembling even as she pushed him away.

"Save me from what?" he implored, still kneeling.

"From me," said Jo, simply.

My messes and scrapes and moods and shadows. My queer temperament and career. My inability to live on the same plane of existence as every other person on earth...

"Jo."

Her eyes were wild. "I wish you wouldn't care about me, not in that way."

"It's no use, Jo; I do care. I care so much. I know I'm not good enough for you, but I hoped you'd love me, and I thought that you might—" And here there was a choke that couldn't be controlled. Jo felt tears come to her eyes as well.

He took another breath. "Because I love you, Josephine March. I always have, and I always will. I think you know that, because I think you love me, too. I read your book, Jo. *It's all in there. The two of us.* We're meant to be together."

"Teddy?!" Jo was stunned. *"You read my book?"*

"Of course I read your book," said Laurie, looking aghast at the very idea that he had not. "I loved it, just as I love everything you do. You're a beautiful writer."

Jo pinked, her hands fluttering in agitation.

Of course Laurie had read her book. He was her dearest friend. It was the one proclamation that truly moved her. Yes, of course she knew he loved her, but until today she did not know he loved her book.

She didn't know why it made such a difference, but it did. Maybe because of the truth of it. The idea that, if he loved her book, he loved her, honestly and wholly. Regardless of all her crazed complexity.

The two of us. It's all in there.

Laurie wrung out his handkerchief. "I had to say something before I left. Before you meet someone else and marry him. I'd be hanged before I let that happen!"

Jo rolled her eyes. "Laurie, I'm not going to meet a man while you're away at school and elope with him. I'm going to be stuck here at home, with no hope of meeting anyone. The thing is, I'm never going to get married."

How could she make him understand that she would never marry, would never become someone's property, never give up her name and her writing, to play house with any man. Not even for him. No matter how she felt about him.

"You will not marry?" asked Laurie. "Honestly, Jo?"

She shook her head. "No, I'm not going to marry anyone, Teddy. Especially not you!"

He went pale, but whether from anger or disappointment, she couldn't tell. "Why *especially* not me?"

"We'd fight constantly. We couldn't possibly make each other happy. We are too alike, short-tempered and bossy. We would drive each other mad—like my mother and father. They have the same temperament, and so Father is either off to war or still in the South after the war is over. Yes, he is there to do good deeds, but he is also there to get away from Mother." At last, the truth of the Marches' marriage had to be said. Why was Father always away? Because it was more peaceful that way, for everyone.

Laurie refused to hear it. "We are *not* your father and mother."

Jo shook her head. "Your father married someone unsuitable and broke your grandfather's heart. This would be the same."

"No, not in the very least. This is our own story, Jo. Yours and mine, not my parents' or yours."

"We couldn't make each other happy," she said in despair.

"We could. We *already* make each other happy. Don't you see? We've been as good as married for years now." Laurie stalked to the window to look at the place where the little post-office he'd made for them to exchange notes sat in the hedge between their houses, a reminder of happier times. He took off his coat. Why was it always so hot in this room? If he didn't know better, he'd think Jo was trying to sweat him out of her life. "There's no one for me but you, Jo."

"Teddy," she cried. "I can't marry you. To be a wife and mother, to give up my writing? I can't! I won't!"

"We've been through this, Jo. I would never ask you to give up your writing. I know how important it is to you. And I would never want to take your talent away from the world."

I read your book, Jo. You're a beautiful writer.

Still, Jo forged on, desperate to make her case. "You wouldn't mean to, but it would happen anyway. Having a house to run, children—I'd never have time to write anymore. And you would hate having an author for a wife. It would embarrass you. I'm not smart enough or fashionable enough for you. For your society friends, like Lady Hat."

"You are! You're smarter than everyone put together! And I don't give a damn about fashion or fashionable society. You know that! You think too little of yourself, and you did well in New York."

"Well enough as Jo March, not as Mrs. Theodore Laurence. Lady Hat would be horrified by me, you know it. Everyone would think I'd married you for your money." She shuddered. "Literally everyone."

"So? Who cares? Harriet would accept you because you'd be my wife. My everything. You are everything to me, Jo," he said. "And everyone would be so pleased. Your people. Mine. Grandfather would be beyond thrilled." He pressed a fist against the windowpane in frustration.

"Oh, Teddy, I'm so sorry. But I can't even imagine it."

She stood next to him and put an arm around him to hold him up, the same way he had done in the pond just a few months before.

He turned to her, his voice quivering. "Really and truly, Jo?" he asked, with a look she would never forget.

"Really and truly, dear."

He went pale then. He couldn't look at her anymore. So that was it, then. She did not love him. Not the way he loved her. He had to live with that. He had to accept it.

"If you cannot even imagine a marriage between us, then you are not as much of a writer as I'd thought," he said, bitterly.

He didn't mean it. He was smarting, that's all. Jo shook her head, for once unable to form words to console her dearest friend even as her heart broke with his.

Laurie stood in the hall, holding his coat, his face a mask trying to conceal his pain, his complete and utter devastation at the hands of the one person he'd thought he could count on above all.

"Oh, Jo, can't you?" he asked, in a final effort.

"Teddy dear, I wish I could!"

There was a pause, and Laurie nodded briskly. "Good-bye, Miss March. Good luck with your sequel."

WHEN HE HAD left the house, Meg burst into the room. "Oh, Jo," she cried, "I just saw Laurie; he said you refused him! What have you done?"

Jo sank into her tuft and crossed her arms, determined she would not be moved. "I've done nothing that didn't need doing."

Meg seemed nearly on the verge of tears. "Oh, Jo, don't you see? You don't have to be alone to find your happiness in life. You love Laurie and Laurie loves you. It's a simple thing."

Jo shrugged. She couldn't explain.

But it's not simple at all.

"Not to mention that if you marry Laurie, you will never have to worry about money ever again," said Meg. "As if I have to remind you."

Jo forced herself to focus on her sister. To smile.

"Always with the mercenary proposition! I shall have my happiness without greed," scoffed Jo. "Besides, I shall write my way to success!"

"That may be," said Meg. "But what is success if you have no one to share it with? Just because Laurie is rich is no reason *not* to love him. You're a fool who doesn't know her own heart."

"I guess I'm a fool, then," Jo said as she flung her manuscript aside. "The biggest fool you've ever met!"

Then she banged her way down the old attic stairs, one at a time, leaving the pages where they landed on the floor.

I'm just an old Roman step, she thought. *As dented and abandoned as they come.*

There was no point in making up stories when her home and family, her dearest friend, were all so dramatic in real life.

When the shadows felt as if they could very nearly swallow her whole.

18

AUTUMN SPLENDOR

*J*o did not attend the farewell luncheon Laurie's grandfather threw for him. She did not help him pack his steamer trunk, did not so much as look his way through the glass windowpanes as everything was loaded up and packed off.

Once Laurie left for Cambridge, there was little rhythm to Jo's days. Because she couldn't sleep, she spent her nights up in the attic trying to work—though her meager scribblings were leaving her in anguish—and her mornings crossing out everything she'd written the night before.

She would kill off Roderigo one day only to bring him back the next. Then John Brooke would go off to war but meet someone else, a Southern belle, perhaps, and elope, though that didn't satisfy Jo's sense of proportion.

What Southern girl in her right mind would care at all about old Brooke?

He was hardly the kind of man who attracted high-society ladies, no matter which side of the Mason-Dixon Line they lived on.

Except for Lady Hat, apparently, who'd cooed and fussed over Brooke as much as anyone, according to Meg.

Jo had a hard time believing it.

She sat looking at her pages and considered the problem she'd written for herself. Maybe everything she'd read about society girls in novels was wrong. Maybe having a family name and money meant you were immune from looking for those qualities in a husband. Or perhaps it was just a perverse fantasy of Harriet's, to set her cap at a man whose own situation wasn't anywhere comparable to hers. Jo couldn't pretend to understand what it would be like to be entirely free of financial worries, given that money—or rather, the lack of it—consumed most of her available free time.

She would have liked to ask Laurie what he thought about Harriet and Brooke, but he wasn't here. And she wasn't going to write to him on that subject—on any subject—not if her life depended on it.

Not after how they had left each other, the last time.

Jo was resolute that she would not think of Laurie and his heartache, as it was too close to hers. No, she would not think of her heart at all.

So Jo was not at all certain that her work was going well. At this rate, her fictional sisters would end up as adrift as the real ones were, waiting for their lives to begin.

Even the fate of poor Beth was giving her fits. Every story line she tried didn't work. Beth overcoming her shyness. Beth learning to dance. Beth meeting Frank Vaughn, the sickly, made-up twin of Laurie's real-life friend Fred Vaughn, at a church picnic and striking up an unlikely romance. Beth the nurse, living at home, caring for her mother after a serious illness. (Even in fiction, Jo couldn't write Mama Abba's death. It was, she told Meg, *out of the question*.)

Or even once she had written Beth marrying Laurie, if only to give them both some happiness that eluded them in real life.

Wrong, wrong, wrong! Jo crumpled the page up into a ball. What a bunch of rot her sequel was turning out to be.

It was no one's fault but her own. All those hours spent on a story no one—not even the story's author—wanted to read.

Especially not the story's author.

If you cannot even imagine a marriage between us, then you are not as much of a writer as I'd thought, Laurie had said.

Theodore Laurence, she groaned to herself, heaving her quill across the room. *You've cursed me! Cursed me with your neediness, your loving me. Foolish, foolish boy!*

I'll never write another word.

Never!

WITHOUT HER BOOK to write, Jo turned instead to her daily chores, throwing herself into harvesting the bounty from Vegetable Valley, into learning more of the plain cooking that she'd begun before writing *Little Women*, if only to have something useful to do and to please her mother. Mama Abba was the one person who never grew cross at Jo, no matter how much difficulty she found herself in. Patient Mama would only smile and encourage her to try again, praising any effort Jo made to keep her temper in check. With such a person to emulate, Jo did want very much to please her. Mama's demands weren't nearly as impossible as Niles's.

It was on such a day, as Meg and Amy worked on harvesting Vegetable Valley and Jo struggled to learn to knead rising dough, that Meg received a letter from her dear friend Sallie Gardiner, whose wealth and connections had sometimes allowed Meg to travel in more fashionable circles, at least in Concord.

On opening the envelope, Meg saw that it wasn't a typical letter at all, but an invitation to an Autumn Splendor Ball. *The first of many*, Sallie wrote to Meg. *Or at least I hope it will be.*

The three March sisters, distracted from their squashes and pumpkins, their cabbages and turnips, went squealing through the house to learn if their mother would give them permission to go. "Of course, my darlings," she said, hugging Meg. "Of course you will want the society of other young people, especially"—and at this, she looked significantly at Jo—"when you are missing your usual company."

Jo frowned, feeling this was a criticism, though Mama took her by the chin and said, "It's all right, Jo. I would never make you accept any man who couldn't win your ardent affections. That is for you to decide."

Jo nodded, allowing Mama Abba to comfort her—even if she would not concede to needing comfort.

Now Mama Abba patted her daughter's cheek. "But I think

you would have to agree it has been a bit quiet around here since the younger Mr. Laurence went to Cambridge."

Amy snorted, "Since Jo *insulted him*, you mean. We should be lucky ever to be invited to anything again."

Mama gave her youngest a stern look, but she only said, "I think all my girls could do with a little bit of lively company. Music and dancing and other young people are a sure cure for loneliness."

Jo could hardly call herself lonely. She was surrounded by people constantly. Why, she'd hardly had a minute to herself since the day she climbed out of her attic garret, "Determined to live life," she'd announced to her sisters, "instead of only writing about it."

But a ball—especially a Concord ball, even one with Meg's dearest friend—didn't strike her as particularly exciting or noteworthy. Not after the delights of Manhattan and Dickens.

Still, as she walked to the Gardiners' a few days later with Meg and Amy, she had decided to find pleasure wherever she could. She may have been deprived of Theodore Laurence's company, but he was not the only boy in the world, nor the Marches' only friend.

If you cannot even imagine a marriage between us, then you are not as much of a writer as I'd thought.

Hmmpf.

After much discussion, the three March girls had all forgone the Worth gown this time. Jo had refused it utterly. It was too painful to be reminded of Laurie's kindness.

It's from a portrait of my mother when she was young . . . She

was laughing and so happy and so alive … Well, it's the one picture
of her that always reminds me of you, Jo.

After that, Meg and Amy had argued over who would wear
it until Mama Abba insisted neither would do so. "It wouldn't be
proper for one of my girls to be dressed so much more extrava-
gantly than the others. Especially for young ladies whose family
cannot afford to give them a proper debut. You are sisters and
equals and should look the part," Mama said, shaming them all
into silence. "Such a fine gown will save for another occasion. Like
a wedding," she added, looking at Meg.

That was that, then. There was no arguing with Mama Abba,
once she had made up her mind.

Instead, Amy had to settle for one of Jo's old evening dresses,
patched and improved. Jo wore the white tarlatan she'd worn to
the opera, while Meg wore Mama Abba's best dress, a dark green
jacquard with a froth of lace at the bosom. The color was a bit too
old for young Meg, but the dress itself was perfectly respectable
and lovely. Unremarkable and unlikely to draw too much attention
to the impoverished March sisters.

They walked over the few blocks to Sallie's in their finery,
planning to be of help to the Gardiners in the party preparations.
Coming early also had the added benefit of downplaying the fact
that they had no carriage to take them to and fro, like the other girls
of Sallie's acquaintance.

"We should have asked old Mr. Laurence," Amy whined.

"We aren't his responsibility," Jo said.

"He would have been happy to help, I imagine," Meg replied.

Jo gave her sister a look, and the subject was immediately dropped. Truthfully, Jo had been too abashed to face him after refusing his grandson's hand.

Meg fussed the rest of the way, saying her slippers would be dusty from the road before they arrived. But Jo said, "Who'll see your slippers under all those skirts! Honestly, Meg, you always think everyone is judging you."

"Because everyone is," said Meg, remembering Lady Hat's triumph at the Ducal Ball when she'd realized Meg's escort had left her. Her cheeks burned, thinking about it. *At least I shall not have to face Lady Harriet this evening,* she thought.

"A real ball," Amy sighed. Tonight would be her first. She was positively glowing with excitement, even in Jo's old dress.

The Marches could not afford to throw a proper debut for Meg, much less Jo or Amy, so the Autumn Splendor Ball would have to do for the youngest sister. Meg and Jo had agreed to chaperone *"as long as Amy doesn't make a fuss of it,"* Jo had said.

"I never make a fuss," Amy had fussed. Jo was about to argue, but Amy swore she would keep her swooning to a minimum. This time, at least.

When they arrived at the Gardiners'—a large fine house that Jo had used as the model for Aunt March's Plumfield in *Little Women*—Sallie was already at the gate to welcome them. "How well you all look!" exclaimed Sallie. "Your cheeks are so rosy, Meg! You'll be the envy of every girl at the ball."

Sallie was always unfailingly kind, forgoing any little digs at Meg's expense that another girl might make. She never mentioned the fact that they'd walked, or that their evening clothes were hopelessly out of fashion. Jo was quite glad to see her.

A little walk does us all some good, thought Jo. *Some exercise will also ensure I won't be cross with Meg or the other guests, if I expend my excess energy in more productive ways. And I will forget about Laurie, I will.*

Mama would be proud. Jo was finally learning to control her temper. You're growing up, Mama would say, and give one of her Mona Lisa smiles.

Jo secretly suspected even Mona Lisa must have been raging on the inside, as well—but she tried to learn her resolve, all the same.

Inside the house, there was still work to be done—and the March girls joined in, happy to do their part. Jo, Meg, and Amy helped Sallie set out vases of flowers and cut-glass bowls full of the last of the raspberries, heavily sugared. Of course, the sight of them reminded Jo of her own sad effort with sugared strawberries—the time she'd salted them by accident instead of sugaring, and served them with cream that had turned—but Laurie had been good-humored about it, and teased her only a little, enough to make her laugh at herself. Enough that she'd felt comfortable including it in *Little Women* for all the world to see.

She was thinking of the jokes he'd make at her expense now, seeing the raspberries. *Did Jo help you prepare them? No, thanks, I'll stay away, then.*

Laurie—always Laurie. At least he wouldn't be at the ball

tonight. He would be down at Cambridge, holed up his room, unable to enjoy even the meager delights of Concord society.

Jo felt a pang of sadness even picturing it.

How she missed him! Especially on a night like tonight.

There would be no one to laugh with, no one who would be interested in dancing with her, no one to confide her secrets to in front of the fireplace. She remembered the first time they'd met, how they'd both been hiding from the party. She smiled to herself at the thought.

How long ago that was! And what a strange little goose I could be!

"What's so funny?" Amy asked, passing by her with a bowl of apples.

"Nothing," said Jo. She wouldn't confess that she'd been thinking of Laurie even a little, especially not to Amy, who was still furious at her for refusing him. "Now, then, where do these peonies go? The rest of the guests will start arriving any minute."

"Over here," said Meg, patting the table next to where she sat.

"Oh?" asked Jo, giving her sister a teasing look, for in the language of flowers, peonies were supposed to foretell a happy marriage. She set the fat pink hothouse blossoms next to her sister. "All we need now is John Brooke." She turned the vase so the fattest blossom faced Meg.

"Did I hear my name?"

The girls turned to find John Brooke standing just behind them. The first to arrive, Jo noticed, besides themselves. *Eager to see someone here, perhaps?* Jo wondered.

"Mr. Brooke!" said Meg, exactly the someone Jo had just been thinking of. "How wonderful to see you." Brooke had continued to commute from Boston for Mr. Laurence, but had not been by for a visit in a while.

"Ladies," he said, and gave them a bow. "You all look lovely this evening. Miss Amy, how nice to see you out."

"Thank you, Mr. Brooke," said Amy. "It's nice to be out. I was starting to think it would never happen." She tossed her curls melodramatically.

Jo shot Amy a look of warning, then turned to Brooke with a critical eye. Dressed in a stylish (and new!) evening suit, he looked so well that even Jo had to admit he was handsome. His dark eyes were more lively than usual, and someone had cut his normally shaggy hair into a more elegant shape.

But Meg would not meet his eye. "How have you been?" she asked, politely. Jo noticed there was a kind of hitch in her voice.

"Very well, Miss March. Thank you."

Jo gave him a very saucy look and said, "We haven't seen as much of you since Laurie left for Cambridge, Mr. Brooke. Whatever have you been doing with yourself? Aren't you terribly bored?"

"Terribly," said Brooke, and Jo noticed just the barest hint of Laurentian sauciness in his own voice.

"What will you do now?" asked Meg.

"I've decided to stay in Boston with my young pupils," he said, "since I'm no longer needed here in Concord. I'm gathering my things from Mr. Laurence, so this visit may be my last for a while."

"Oh?" said Meg. Jo detected another quiver in her voice. "How sad. But surely you won't stay away long?"

Voices came from the hall before Brooke could answer. Once nearly empty, the room was now filling with guests. More friends of Sallie's were arriving every minute. Here came the Moffats, including Ned and his sisters Annie and Belle, who'd made a cameo in *Little Women*. Sallie Gardiner was already greeting Ned, and Jo had a sudden suspicion the entire Autumn Splendor Ball had been concocted so Sallie would have a reason to see him.

A marriage plot, indeed.

Jo was just about to protest that of course Brooke was needed here in Concord—"for poor Meg's sake," she was about to add, to torment her sister—when a flinty "Ah, there you are!" went up from across the room.

All four looked up to see—of all people—Lady Harriet Carmichael-Carlthorpe coming toward them from across the room.

"What is she doing in Concord?" Jo murmured, mostly to herself. Meg looked pale, but said nothing.

"Who is *that*?" asked Amy.

Jo whispered, "Lady Harriet. Laurie's friend."

Amy whispered back, "The English lady?"

"Yes. Don't stare."

"She is perfection." Amy could hardly stop herself. "Look at her dress! So many beads and crystals. It must have cost a fortune!"

"Shush," said Jo. "If you embarrass me, I will send you home to Mama immediately."

Lady Hat joined them, immediately hitching an arm through

Meg's on the one side and Brooke's on the other as if they were old friends. "My dears," she said, "how lovely to find us all together! What an absolute lark."

Jo's astonishment was so great, she could barely speak. What on earth could the titled and landed gentry be doing in provincial Concord, of all places? She nearly forgot her manners. "Lady Hat," she said. "I didn't expect we'd ever meet again."

"Nor I, dear Cousin Jo! But Mr. Laurence invited me and the Vaughns for a stay, you know, and we've just arrived for the ball. Surely Laurie told you?"

Jo stiffened at the mention of his name.

Laurie most certainly had not told Jo that Lady Hat might come to Concord, much less that she knew the Vaughns, whom Jo had only met once or twice herself, through Laurie. There was Kate Vaughn now, greeting Sallie and her mother, but no sign of Laurie's loud and ridiculous friend Fred. "I see. And where is Fred Vaughn, my lady?"

"Oh, down at Harvard with Laurie." She waved her hand. "That's why we were up north, to take him to university. Kate said your friend Sallie wouldn't mind if I came tonight. I couldn't resist the chance to say hello to *so many* new acquaintances."

Jo did not miss the look of significance Lady Hat gave Brooke, nor the sight of her hand on his arm. Nor did Meg, who'd turned pale.

"I'm sure we are all very glad to see you again, my lady," said Brooke. "All of Concord is honored."

Speak for yourself, Babbling Brooke. Some of us would have been quite pleased never to meet her again, thought Jo.

"My goodness! I never realized Concord was so charming. All these lovely woods and fields! It's no wonder the Laurences love it here. And you, too, Mr. Brooke." She gave his arm an affectionate and proprietary squeeze.

Thoroughly unconvinced by the lady's gushing over the provincial life in Concord, Jo was having a growing realization about Brooke and Harriet.

Are they a couple? Jo wondered. *They seem like one, surely they have seen each other in Boston, and it appears he is her escort this evening. But what about Meg?*

Before she could think, Sallie and Kate joined them, saying, "Hello! Hello, friends!" Sallie squeezed Meg's other arm. Kate introduced Harriet to Amy, who gushed, "A very great pleasure to meet you, my lady" and curtsied like she was meeting the queen herself.

In the middle of this stood John Brooke, a lone male presence in a ring of ladies. His eyes were only on Meg, even though Meg would look anywhere in the room but at him.

"And how have *you* been, Cousin Jo? Cousin Meg?" asked Harriet. "Terribly dull since Laurie went away?"

"Cousin Jo?" asked Amy, who had not been with them in New York when these nicknames were bestowed.

"Not at all," said Jo stiffly. "I've been quite busy."

"That's right! I remember Laurie telling me something about

your little novel. I knew things were different here, but I never dreamed I'd meet a real-live authoress!"

The "real-live authoress" would not be offended at such a label, though she was certain the lady meant it as an insult.

Society ladies don't write novels, Laurie had once told her. It would be positively scandalous, not to mention unprofitable—which was why so many Englishwomen, including the Brontës, had written under male pseudonyms.

Here in America, Jo thought, arguing with the Laurie who still lived in her head, *things are different.*

And indeed they were. While Harriet prattled on about Boston and Concord—*How dear! How charming everything is! How fresh and sweet and new!*—Jo watched her sister wilt. In her mother's borrowed dress—a gown meant for a much older woman, married and respectable—Meg looked wan next to Harriet's feathers, Jo decided. Perhaps she was wishing she'd worn the House of Worth gown after all.

Or perhaps it was the realization that Brooke and Kate Vaughn and Harriet were all staying together as guests in Mr. Laurence's house. They would be having meals together, and evenings in the parlor together. Now this outing, the Autumn Splendor Ball, where Lady Hat was positively *glued* to Brooke's side. Gloating just a bit, Jo thought.

Jo just didn't see how it was possible. Brooke and Harriet? Why on earth would Lady Hat want Brooke, of all people? She would be better off choosing someone like Fred Vaughn, perhaps, who was her own countryman and a gentleman, after all. Or even Laurie, although the Vaughns' fortune eclipsed the Laurences'. Still, Harriet could have anyone, so why would she want John Brooke, who was virtually penniless? A scholar without land or titles, dependent on the Laurences and families like them for work.

Still, it occurred to Jo that she herself disdained both lands and titles, and she didn't have a tenth of Lady Harriet's wealth. Perhaps they weren't so very different as she thought. Perhaps Harriet was following her heart, as Jo urged Meg to do. Except Harriet could afford to follow her heart and Meg could not.

Beside her, Jo could feel Meg trembling. It wasn't just Jo, then. She hadn't imagined it: Lady Hat had set her cap at Brooke, and this visit was meant to cement her place in his affections. *That* was a plot twist Jo hadn't seen coming.

But if John Brooke preferred Lady Harriet to dear, sweet, lovely Meg, then it was only for her wealth. Perhaps he had made the same calculations Meg had: that he could not afford their match, either. They had nothing to give each other, and Harriet—oh, Harriet—could give him so much.

Behind them, the musicians were tuning up. "Oh!" said Harriet. "If only there were enough young men to dance with! I'm afraid you will be busy this evening, Mr. Brooke."

"I am ready to do my duty for the young ladies of Concord," he said. The musicians were calling people to the dance floor for the waltz. "Would you do me the honor of dancing the first with me, Lady Harriet?"

Harriet gushed and took his arm. "Of course, Mr. Brooke."

Jo watched the two of them move into the first crowd of dancers while, beside her, Meg looked on the verge of tears.

It always comes down to money, Jo thought grimly. *Money, or the lack of it.*

John Brooke had a choice before him: love, or money.

Choose wisely, Brooke.

For your sake, and for Meg's.

19

⁓ↄ⊙ↄↄ⊙ↄ⁓

HARVARD YARD

*O*utside, the leaves collected on the ground, and the nights were growing cooler. Hour after hour Laurie went to his lessons—mathematics, history, Latin, and literature—with all the enthusiasm of a man walking the plank.

Or more precisely, that of a man who had already thrown himself headlong into the briny sea, and was now sinking as fast as he could.

He had wanted Jo to understand him before he left for school, to make certain she knew what he intended, so she would not run off with someone else while he was in Cambridge. But also so the two of them could finally acknowledge what was right in front of them.

That they were in love with each other, and had been since the very day they met. Tall, tomboyish Jo, with her mane of curls, her impudent tongue, and her generous heart. Jo, who had coaxed the shy Laurie out of his grandfather's study, who had made his lonely life so jolly by opening her home and her heart to him. Her sisters were his sisters.

Or so he had thought.

How could she not understand?

First, she had believed he was in love with Meg! Next thing he knew, she would be marrying him off to Amy or some other such rot.

He shuddered.

Laurie knew he'd had to say it before he lost her to some other chap—he'd seen the way that older gentleman looked at her at the Dickens reading. Fall would bring the harvest balls to Concord, and more church socials; it would bring a new crop of suitors, and one of them would certainly fall head over heels for Jo—just as he had.

Worse, Jo would marry. She would love someone passionately and with all her heart, as was her nature. And Laurie would have to stand aside and watch.

Oh, heartache! Oh, gloom! Was love ever so wretched?

Harvard was a glum distraction during the day, but nights when he should have been studying, he found himself invariably attempting to write to Jo, though it was no use.

Laurie would begin letter after letter with "Dear Jo," or "My dearest Jo," or even "Mr. Snodgrass," to try to keep his tone light-hearted. But there was no use in trying to be funny when Jo had sent him off to university without any hope of happiness.

Oh, Teddy, I'm so sorry. But I can't even imagine it.

He'd greatly misunderstood her feelings for him, that was clear.

The turn of her countenance he would never forget, nor the note of panic in her voice when she exclaimed, *I can't marry you. To be a wife and mother, to give up my writing? I can't! I won't!*

As if he'd ask her to give up her writing to be his wife—how could she think such a thing?

I'm not going to marry anyone, Teddy. Especially not you!

He would never forget the look on her face, never.

The pain, the actual disgust she'd felt.

He'd been so wrong about everything. He'd always thought their friendship would be the most important thing in the world to her, as it was to him. But she had turned him away without a second thought. She had never even said she felt the same about him, and it was obvious—glaringly obvious—that she did not.

Oh, she tried to cushion the blow.

I'm not smart enough or fashionable enough for you. For your society friends, like Lady Hat.

As if his acquaintance with Harriet could compare with his friendship with Jo! The Englishwoman was a fine person—attractive, cultured, moneyed. She had a fine title and a fine family. But none of that had ever mattered to Laurie.

He wanted adventure. Passion. He wanted Jo.

The way he saw it, neither one of them had ever wanted anyone else.

Was it too much to think that his dearest friend would also be his wife? That the girl he'd loved with all his heart would love him back? That he might have the kind of love in his life that his father and mother had known? His father had followed his mother all the way to her home country, such was the depth of his love.

Wasn't there more to marriage than the staid, careful accumulation of wealth?

Grandfather could send him to Harvard, and Laurie would dutifully become a businessman instead of a musician.

I would give up all my dreams for just this one.

Jo could refuse him all she wanted, but he would love her forever. His feelings would never change.

If only hers would.

Just then, the door burst open to reveal his friend Fred Vaughn, Harvard robes flying. "We're going down to the supper club, old sport. Join us?"

"I can't, Fred. I have this blasted Latin passage to translate before tomorrow."

"Hang Virgil!" exclaimed Fred. "There will be cricket. A little fresh air and exercise is all you need, man, and maybe some more interesting company."

"I'm not interested in company."

"Did I mention there's a halfway decent piano 'round the hall?"

Laurie looked at the sheaf of papers in front of him, the letters swimming. He'd never gotten the gist of Latin *or* Greek, despite Brooke's best efforts. *Babbling Brooke,* Jo had called him in New York. A joke on the fact that Brooke was the most reticent, close-mouthed person Laurie had ever met.

To his astonishment, he felt actual tears spring to his eyes at the thought of his old tutor. Not to mention the other people he was missing: Grandfather. Mrs. March. Dear Hannah.

Not to mention Meg and Amy and Jo—even if he'd sworn he'd make himself stop thinking about her.

How he longed for Orchard House, with its attic garret where the Pickwick Club met, and its little garden, and the hedge with their own personal post-office.

He'd give anything to be there now. Anything. Not here in his drafty room in Cambridge, watching the leaves turn brown outside while he was shut up with some moldy Latin.

"Are you all right, old chap?" asked Fred. "You look a little ill."

She will not have you, he thought. *She refused. Are you going to be miserable the rest of your life? Never to meet anyone else, or have any fun or happiness, because Josephine March has decided against marrying you?*

She doesn't love you.

You have to accept that.

Pick up the pieces and march forward.

It was the only thing to do.

There would be cricket, and new people to meet there. People who were not stubborn, obstinate Jo March.

"All right, Fred," he said, and abandoned his passage of Virgil. "Just give me a minute to get my coat."

20

LETTERS

For months the mail had been piling up on a table by the door, neglected by everyone, but most especially by Jo. "My Dearest Miss March," they all began, and then devolved from there. From Pennsylvania and Delaware, Ohio and the wilds of the Minnesota frontier—even as far away as London or Paris—girls were writing to Jo with one question: *What happens next?*

Every week, when Mama went into town to buy groceries and collect the post at the post-office in Concord village, she brought home at least three or four and sometimes as many as nine or ten letters about *Little Women*.

On the one hand, it was clear the book had touched its readers with the sweet and tender tale of four devoted sisters, their mother, and the boy next door.

On the other hand, all Jo's efforts to complete the sequel had been, so far, a total disaster. Her first effort had been too dull; the second too interesting, for all the wrong reasons. *Lacking in good taste*, as Niles had said, and *not serving your characters or your readers.*

So when those same readers were writing her letters with their demands on her time and imagination, along with their ideas for her sequel, Jo started to view the mail as an oppression, a constant reminder of her failure. She was disappointing her readers, all the young ladies waiting to find out the end of the story. Not to mention her editor, her family, and worst of all, herself.

"Christopher Columbus!" she exclaimed one day when Meg came in with the post, a full *fifteen* new letters all addressed to *Miss Josephine March, Authoress.* "Can't my gentle readers leave me in *peace?*"

"Apparently not." Meg opened one envelope. *"Dear Miss March,"* she read.

> *I am writing to tell you how much your* Little Women
> *has meant to myself and my little sister, and to implore
> you, please, to make sure that the Laurie in your book
> marries Jo. My sister Mary and I are quite determined
> that no other fate for Jo would be at all acceptable,
> and we have shed many tears over the prospect that
> this might not be the case. Please write us back and set
> our minds at ease over the fate of our favorite charac-
> ters. Yours truly, Anna Lake*

Meg looked satisfied and held out the letter to her sister. "There now, Jo. It's not just myself, then. Or Niles or Mama or even Laurie. The whole world knows the two of you belong together."

"What a bunch of rot," Jo exclaimed, snatching the letter out of Meg's hand. "I won't marry Jo to Laurie for anything! Especially not to please anyone!"

"Certainly not yourself," Meg muttered.

"What?"

"Nothing, dear."

The front door to the house opened, and Hannah and Amy came in, carrying empty baskets back from the Hummels, who had all come down with some kind of terrible cough once more. They'd gone to take the family some of the bounty from Vegetable Valley, since they had so much and the Hummels so little. The troubled family battled a variety of ills every winter, and it strained the Marches' pocketbook to keep their poor friends in tinder and coal to keep the winter wolves at bay. The Marches had known poverty, but they had never known abject poverty, and Jo was often stunned by the profound difference between having very little and having nothing at all.

"Now then," said Mama, taking off her gloves, "what's this row I'm hearing? My Meg and Jo arguing?"

"Not at all, Mama," said Jo. "We were discussing my reader mail, that's all."

"And how all her readers want Jo and Laurie to marry," Meg added, with a merry gleam in her eye.

"Don't tease her, Meg. It's her book and her characters, and she must be free to pursue their fates without anyone's input. Even ours."

"Even when she borrows us so mercilessly for her books, and writes us embarrassing fates, and makes us a national laughing-stock?" Amy demanded.

"You're hardly a laughing-stock." Mama smoothed Amy's glossy curls. "And yes, even then."

"Hmm," Amy said, and frowned. Her cheeks were pale, as if the thought of appearing in Jo's sequel were a humiliation. "I don't see why I shouldn't have a say in what Jo writes about me."

"Because it's not about *you*, goose," Jo said. "Not the real you. Just the version of you I've invented."

"If the character is an invention, why couldn't she be named something other than Amy March?"

"Christopher Columbus!" Jo exclaimed again. "Everyone's a critic."

While Jo scowled and stomped around, the youngest March picked up the bundle and read the return addresses. Two letters had traveled all the way from someplace called Rochester, Minnesota, and another all the way from San Francisco.

Amy thrilled to imagine the journey that letter had taken—perhaps on horseback across the Rocky Mountains and the plains, past Indians and cowboys and wagon trains headed for Oregon. Or else it had been sent on a steamship that traveled down the coast, then sent by wagon across the Isthmus of Panama, and up from Florida on yet another steamship. Perhaps it had been captured by pirates, ballooned on a desert island.

She said as much to Meg, who laughed and said, "*Marooned.* And what kind of pirate would want Jo's mail?"

"A bored one, I'd imagine," said Jo.

Amy pouted. "I don't see why you have to tease me," she said. "The two of you went to New York and had all kinds of adventures without me! I always get left behind! I only get to stay home and *imagine* an adventure. Jo's old mail is as close as I ever get."

Meg touched her chin and said, kindly, "You will have your own adventures one day, dearest. Jo and I never went anywhere, either, when we were your age."

"Jo won't even write me an adventure," said Amy.

"I told you, I don't want to describe so many foreign cities! Especially ones I've never even been to!" said Jo.

"But you will go one day—you've been invited to Paris and London. You'll be there before you know it! Unlike me, who shall never leave Concord," said Amy.

"Beth never left Concord and she was the happiest of us," said Jo.

"Beth was a saint!" said Amy. "And I shall never measure up to her. I'm sorry you're left with me, Jo! I know Beth was your favorite."

Jo reeled backward as Meg held up her arms, horrified. "Amy! Don't say such things!"

"All are loved equally," said Mama, trying to soothe her youngest, "in this peaceable cottage."

"That's not true," said Amy. "In Jo's book I am vain and ridiculous, and Beth is sweet and perfect and is gifted a piano."

They all turned to the piano in the middle of the room, which had stood silent for so long now; none could bear to play since Beth's death.

Next to the fire, Jo finally found her voice. "Do I not set aside money every month for your art lessons and charcoals and paints?"

"You do."

"And to keep you in ribbons and bows?"

"I have enough ribbons."

Jo shook her head. "Amy, you are as dear to me as Beth, and it grieves me to think you believe otherwise."

Amy set down her basket and sighed. "Of course I don't."

"There," said Meg, as she and Mama came between the sisters and enveloped both in a hug.

"We are all we have," said Mama, and they all heard the tears in her voice. "Love each other, my dears. Remember that. In the end, there is little else that matters."

The sisters resolved to remember. They broke off the embrace, and Jo ruffled Amy's hair. "You shall have an adventure someday, and in your own very real life—not just in my sequel."

Amy sighed. "It's just so tedious to wait for *someday*!"

"Darling," Mama said. "If you're so interested in Jo's letters, perhaps you would help her answer them?"

At this, Amy perked up considerably. The idea of sending letters to London and Paris and California was the most excitement she'd felt in weeks. "Oh! May I, Jo? Please?"

Jo heaved a great sigh. "I suppose *someone* should. I can't bear to write them all back myself."

"And it will be good for you, Amy dear," said Mama. "A less *teddy-us* way to practice your writing."

"But I insist on seeing every one before you send it," Jo cried. "I won't let you send anything that would embarrass me."

"Jo, honestly. Your sister would never embarrass you."

Amy flung herself down on the sofa. "I'm already *exhausted* thinking about answering Jo's mail, and I haven't even started."

"You do look tired," Mama said, smoothing back Amy's hair and letting her hand linger a moment on the white forehead, the pink-spotted cheek. "You may write three letters today, if that suits you. To get started."

So Amy went to work on Jo's letters, starting with the oldest. There were at least a hundred to get to, which would take Amy a month at this pace, and she grew tired just thinking about all the work she'd have to put in.

But she wrote carefully, in her best handwriting, as if she were Jo: *How pleased I am to hear you enjoyed my novel. I am hard at work on the sequel, and will take your ideas under advisement. Yours most sincerely, Josephine March.*

She worked for hours, until it got dark.

"There," said Amy, bringing them to Jo at dinnertime. She felt weary beyond measure, and fuzzy-headed, as if she'd been awake all night with insomnia. "Now tell me I didn't do a good job of it."

Jo took the letters and read them approvingly, though she

found several spelling errors and more than one comma splice. "If you're going to impersonate me, you have to use proper grammar! I thought this whole experiment was to give you more practice with your writing, not to showcase your deficiencies."

"Jo," said Mama, "don't chastise your sister. She is doing you a favor, after all." Then Mama's face changed. She looked alarmed. "Are you all right, my dear? You look pale."

Amy swayed a little and grabbed the table to steady herself. "I do feel a little strange. I thought I was just tired from all that writing."

"Were you playing with little Christina Hummel this morning? The sick baby?"

"Just keeping her from eating grass, Mama, while Hannah helped with the baking. She was stuffing leaves into her mouth by the handful."

"Hmm," Mama said, looking serious. "You're much too warm, Amy." She looked panicked, and Jo remembered that tone of voice, that fear. This was how Beth's sickness began. Always with the Hummels. Always with the fever.

Jo looked up at Amy's pale face and couldn't help but be reminded of Beth on her deathbed. "Hannah, get us warm blankets and a compress. Now!" she said, rattling their old, faithful servant.

Amy shook her head. "I'm fine, I'm telling you. There's nothing to worry about. If anything, I'm just a little cold."

Then she lay back on the sofa and closed her eyes.

Amy coughed into her hand, and they heard it: the beginnings of a rattle at the bottom of her lungs.

"Amy!" Jo cried. "You are terribly sick!"

"To bed with you," Mama said, and shooed Amy upstairs. "The mail can wait."

21

ANOTHER PROPOSAL

*A*my's illness, as it turned out, was not so serious as they had feared, thankfully enough. A cough and a low fever kept her in bed and from answering any more of Jo's mail, but it was hardly more than a little autumn cold, one that would surely go away after a few days of rest. The panic that had set in the house had been unwarranted in the end. Amy was not Beth, and she would not suffer her sister's fate.

Jo tried to turn toward answering the letters herself, but between the demands of her readers and the stubborn denials of her editor, she could hardly bear the thought of writing a word— not to the readers of *Little Women*, nor continuing with its sequel.

It was Laurie who'd upset her so, Laurie whom she argued with, constantly, in her own head. *Stubborn fool,* she'd call him. *Determined to ruin us both.*

To these scenes she always added some dash of melodrama. The wind rising outside. A blizzard. A cyclone.

Or else they were on a steamship in the middle of the Atlantic, waves dashing on the deck. Then they'd run into hidden rocks and the hull would split, sending them all to their watery graves.

I'm stubborn? When every word out of your mouth is an insult? You're killing me, Jo. I want you to be with me.

And to her invisible audience, Laurie or her readers or both, she'd always exclaim, *I won't marry Jo March to Theodore Laurence for anything! I belong to no one but myself, in fiction and in life.*

Jo was in the middle of writing such a scene in a chapter called "Heartache," which borrowed too heavily on Laurie's real proposal, when Brooke arrived to call on Meg one glorious October afternoon. From her attic Jo watched him walk up the lane, his lips moving as if he, too, were arguing with himself—or else someone else whose happiness and his seemed always at odds.

They had seen him only once in the few days since the Autumn Splendor Ball at the Gardiners'. It hadn't taken him long to gather his things from Mr. Laurence's house and have them sent to Boston. A trunk of books and clothes and who knew what else had gone out one morning. Meanwhile, Lady Harriet and Kate Vaughn were still visiting, and his hours had been taken up with picnicking with the two ladies and showing them around his favorite Concord places: the little pond where the geese gathered, the apple-trees laden with fruit. Jo and Meg had stood at the window and watched them walk down the lane together, arm in arm in arm.

When Brooke invited Jo and Meg to join them on one of these rambles, Meg had nearly begged off, saying she couldn't bear to watch Harriet gloat over Brooke. Only Jo's insistence that she'd feel worse staying home had convinced her to come along.

Still, she'd been unusually reserved and quiet, even for Meg. Brooke had noticed and said he hoped she was feeling all right.

"I'm quite all right, Mr. Brooke," Meg said. She'd returned to her governess position with the Kings on the first of September after having the summer off. "Just tired from overseeing my little charges."

"I certainly understand that feeling, Miss March," Brooke said kindly. "Do make sure you take care of yourself. I wouldn't want you to make yourself ill."

"Thank you."

Jo watched him watching Meg. Perhaps she'd been wrong about Brooke and Harriet; he did seem to still be interested in Meg. Perhaps he would choose love over money in the end, Jo could only hope.

"Oh, it must be so *difficult* to be a governess," Harriet said, clutching Brooke's arm. "You must have the patience of a saint to work with children."

"Only the ordinary kind, my lady," Brooke said. "But the work can be very rewarding, if you let it."

For the first time, Jo felt she understood Brooke, and pitied him. Not just the fictional version she'd made of him, but the real-live one. It couldn't be easy for him to find himself in Harriet's sights, after all. To be faced with such great temptation: love and happiness versus stability and security and position. That is, if the dowager lady allowed the match, of course. But if he won Meg's heart, then he was more than worthy, and Meg was worth a thousand Lady Hats.

Now, as Brooke came up the lane to the door of Orchard House, Jo looked at the messy scribblings of her manuscript and felt a rising despair that nothing she had written was approaching the version that would please Niles. *It's no use,* she thought. She'd written one book, and one would have to be enough. She had no sequels in her. She'd have to think of something else to write.

She tore up the sheaf of paper and took out a new one, her quill poised over the creamy, blank page. But nothing new was coming to her, either. There were no Roderigos to meet, no swooning ladies in towers, no Cherry King. There were only the leaves going yellow outside, and the rising wind, and the whole winter ahead of her with no Laurie, no Dickens. No money, either, for Christmas presents for her sisters or her mother or Hannah.

She thought of her father down South, going through another winter in his old boots and coat. How she had wanted the money from the sequel to send him some new ones!

But the blasted story wouldn't come. The future was just like the page in front of her—a blank. She was a failure. She couldn't conceive of a future for her sisters or herself, on the page or in real life; she'd stolen them for fiction and cursed them all as a result.

Brooke's knock on the door gave her a reason to get up. Jo ran downstairs to answer the door, for Meg was reading to Amy, who had turned the corner, and Mama was out on a call. Even Hannah was out back plucking a chicken for tomorrow's dinner; only Jo was idle and could greet their guest.

Of course, she thought, with not a little self-loathing.

"Hello, Mr. Brooke," said Jo, opening the door to see his serious face, his jaw working as if he were lost in thought. "Is everything all right?"

"Hello, Miss Jo," he said. "I hope so. Or that, if it isn't, it will be soon."

This was promising news. Jo felt her mood lighten just a bit. Perhaps this would be the longed-for moment she'd been expecting since their return from New York—that John Brooke would finally declare himself to Meg, and be done with it.

How much it would please Mama, and Meg, too, to have the question settled. If only Meg would accept him! And Brooke would keep Meg close to home. If she must lose her sister—and it was becoming increasingly clear that she would, if only Meg would allow herself her feelings—at least she would not go far.

So, Jo had been wrong about Brooke and Harriet, after all. She'd never in her life been so glad to be wrong.

She settled Brooke in the drawing-room, then clattered upstairs in a breathless rush and flung open the door so hard, it left a mark on the wall.

Amy let out an *eep* of terror, and Meg declared, "My goodness, Jo, is the house on fire? Why are you in such a hurry?"

"Brooke is here. For you, Meg."

Meg looked pale, then set down the book she'd been reading.

Jane Eyre, Jo noticed—how appropriate. One governess reading about another.

Meg was hesitating, pulling at the curl over her forehead. "I don't think I can talk to him now."

Jo yanked her sister to her feet. "Go, go," she said. "I'll read to Amy. Where did you leave off?"

"Jane has just left Lowood school. She is about to arrive at Thornfield Hall."

"Ah, this is the best part!" cried Jo. "Go on, I'll read it to her. See what Mr. Brooke wants! Don't you want to know?"

Meg froze as if in terror.

Jo held her cold hands. "My dearest, if you love him, you must accept him. You don't need to take care of anyone but your own heart."

"Oh, Jo! I can't."

"You must."

"Meg!" cried Amy, coughing a bit from exertion. "Tell us everything he says."

"Now, not everything needs to be shared," Meg replied, but she went down with a determined tilt to her chin.

Jo picked up the book Meg had discarded. "All right!" she said. "Now you shall hear all the most chilling parts of the story, for Thornfield Hall is haunted by a ghost."

Amy clutched the covers and coughed some more. "Don't tease me!" she cried. "You know I'm afraid of spirits, Jo March."

"I do not tease you, for Thornfield is haunted, I say. But I promise it will turn out all right in the end."

"For who?" Amy begged.

"For everyone. Or mostly everyone," Jo said, and began to read.

DOWNSTAIRS, MEG AND Brooke decided to go outside, the better to avoid being overheard by the rest of the family. They walked a bit down the lane, alone.

She heard the first of Mr. Brooke's questions, but she had to confess she missed the rest of it because of the roaring in her ears.

"Marry you?" she asked. "Is that really what you want?"

"It is. I have thought for a long time what I would do when I was finished as Laurie's tutor. Now I shall go back to Boston to my pupils, but before the winter I would like us to be married, Miss March. It's all I've thought about for some time. If you'll have me."

Meg was quiet for a while. They walked down the lane toward the stream, and Meg thought again about Jo's nickname for Brooke. *Babbling Brooke.* Her sister thought she was so clever, but Jo had woefully underestimated this quiet, honorable young man who reminded Meg so much of her father.

"Are you all right, Miss March?"

"Yes. I'm just thinking. It's a lot to take in."

They walked to the stream together in companionable silence, with only the sounds of their footsteps, and a few noisy birds, for company.

For some time Meg had been noticing her own feelings toward Brooke changing. In New York, for instance, she had been so pleased by his attentions at first, the quiet way he looked at her, as if trying to memorize her face against some future loss. The night of the Ducal Ball, he'd been everything she'd ever hoped for—attentive, careful, polite. Except when Lady Harriet appeared, and turned everything on its head. Only when they had returned to Concord had she started to believe she'd imagined the whole thing. Brooke had come by two or three times a week to visit with her. Surely he cared about her as much as she cared about him.

But since then, the story had grown more complicated. Lady Harriet had staked her claim to Brooke at the Gardiners', chatting with him and slipping her arm into his in a possessive way that Meg couldn't help but notice. It *was* possible that Lady Harriet was only trying to make Meg jealous, and that Mr. Brooke was too polite to remove himself from her grasp.

Or—and this was the possibility she couldn't ignore—he actually liked her attentions and was encouraging her. A wealthy, beautiful young woman wasn't something any man could afford to ignore, much less a poor man like John Brooke.

When they reached the fork in the road—when they had gone as far as they could without drawing too much attention to themselves—Brooke stopped, and said, "I know that my leaving for Boston makes my question more complicated."

"It's not that."

"What, then?"

"I was thinking Lady Harriet might be sorely disappointed by your asking me. And that you might be disappointed as well."

He took her hand in his, and she let him—but only because she couldn't think of a way of removing it without insulting him. "Lady Harriet doesn't factor into my thinking at all."

But Meg was determined. Brooke had said his piece; now she would say hers. "Why shouldn't she? She's clearly so fond of you. And—and I have no dowry. Whereas she is rich as Croesus."

Brooke clutched her hand more tightly. "You know that doesn't matter to me. I wouldn't ask you if it did."

"Perhaps it should matter to you."

Mr. Brooke became agitated. "What are you saying, Miss March? That you won't have me because you have no dowry and I only a modest income?"

"We'd be paupers. We'd have nothing to our names, nothing," cried Meg.

"We'd have each other. Isn't that enough? It is enough for me, my dearest. I wish I had more to give than my heart."

She looked down at their joined hands. She didn't pull hers away; she couldn't bear to let go, not yet. Not until she'd told him the truth. "It's not enough. Oh, Mr. Brooke, if you won't think of your future, you must let me do so for you. Don't marry a poor girl. I'm sure Lady Harriet would be glad to have you, if you asked her."

His shoulders sank, along with his dark brows. "But I did not ask her. I'm asking you."

She glanced down once more at their joined hands. *You must be firm. For his sake, don't be selfish now.*

"I cannot marry a poor man," she said. "I won't. Two wrongs

don't make a right, especially not in this case. I am very fond of you, Mr. Brooke, but there can be no question of us marrying. Not when neither of us has a penny to our name."

Now Brooke did indeed let go of her hand. He took off his hat and rubbed at a spot on the brim, saying, "I understand," so quietly that it was hard to hear him. "No, of course not, I cannot ask you to marry a man as poor as me. I have overstepped."

Meg felt her heart in her throat, but she choked it down. Poor heart, to be so denied. "I hope in time you will come to see the wisdom in this decision. And that we may still be friends."

For a moment it seemed even the birds had quieted down, as if the whole world were leaning in to listen. "A friendship so denied can never recover, I'm afraid, but I see you're resolved. I will not bother you any more, Miss March."

He bowed once, stiffly, and left her standing in the road, shaking and nearly ill, but determined. She had done the right thing for both of them. She had never been more certain she had done the right thing. They would be as poor as church mice! What was love but a burden? He would thank her one day, when he was the lord of Carmichael Hall, his magnificent bride on his arm, and they had everything they ever wanted and needed. She would give this to him; she would sacrifice her love for his happiness.

It was all she had to give him.

When Meg entered the house, her sisters pounced on her. "So! What happened?" "What did he say?" "What did you say?"

"Why do you look like that?" asked Jo and Amy in excitement as they fought to sit by Meg and hear all the delicious details.

Meg almost fell onto the sofa, her legs having given out underneath her. "He asked me to marry him."

Amy was petting the cat next to her. "And?" she asked her older sister, her eyes lit with the fire of romance.

"I said no."

"You refused him?" Jo demanded.

"I did."

Jo looked stricken. "Why?"

"Because he should be with Lady Hat. With someone who can provide him a better life than I can."

"But he didn't ask Lady Hat!" raged Amy.

"That's what he said," said Meg.

"You refused him," Jo repeated.

"Oh, Meg!" said Amy, who pushed the cat away from her lap in her agitation. "What is wrong with everyone in this family? I was so looking forward to the wedding!"

"But you love him," said Jo. "It's so clear. And so why can't you have your happiness? Who cares about money?"

"I do. I want him to be happy. He will be happier with her," Meg said, staunchly. "So will I."

"No, he won't! You won't! He loves you!" said Jo, raging and flinging her arms about in the unfairness of it all. "I've never met such a martyr in all my life! You refused him!" she exclaimed again. "Because you think he would be happier if he married someone with a large dowry? Meg, are you mad?"

"I must be," Meg said, tears pricking at her eyes, "but it was the right thing to say, and not you, or Mama, or anyone else can change my mind!"

"But you love him and he loves you!" Jo shouted. "It's enough! It has to be!"

"Is it?" Meg stood taller. "Look in the mirror, Josephine March!"

And she ran up to her room and slammed the door on her sister behind her.

22

SHADOWS UPON SHADOWS

*A*fter the first few weeks away—and once he was able to stop brooding over Jo long enough—Laurie was almost able to enjoy himself at Harvard.

Almost.

There was cricket and rugby after classes, plus the supper club, the debate club. And at all, there was the company of other young men from fine American families, some of whom were also at university against their will. Most of Laurie's classmates were New Englanders, but there were a few from as far away as Chicago and even Minneapolis who regaled their fellows with tales of living in the wilds of the Middle West. Evenings, they would read their lessons or play billiards with a glass of brandy or two. Weekends, they would go into Boston for their amusements: musical performances, lectures, sometimes even a dance where they would have a chance to meet the young ladies of Boston society—properly chaperoned, of course. When called upon—if not in one of his darker moods—Laurie would even favor them with a tune or two on the old supper club piano.

Fred Vaughn was Laurie's constant companion on these rambles, for Fred was a lively sort of fellow, given to Jo-like slang ("Hang it all!" was his perennial favorite), and always up for a laugh, if one could be had. In Fred's company, Laurie was able to forget about Jo for long stretches of time. In the middle of a rugby match or at a night of billiards with such lively company, it was impossible to brood on all he had lost.

Fred's company was good for almost everything that ailed Laurie except his studies. More than one professor had warned that Laurie would have to repeat his freshman courses if he didn't shape up soon. But because Laurie preferred to spend his evenings out of Harvard Yard, he was prone to miss turning in his assignments on time.

It was hard to feel like any of it mattered. His grandfather had insisted, so here Laurie was, but the old man couldn't make him study against his will.

He had missed the Virgil assignment, and another on Marcus Aurelius, but the Latin professor promised to give him a little more time to turn them in, as long as he did a spectacularly good job.

The history professor wanted a substantial essay about the Reformation in England, but as Laurie couldn't keep all the English kings straight, he didn't see how he'd manage to finish.

Instead he was up late with Fred, who'd found them a couple of girls from a good Beacon Hill family to squire around town to dances and dinners. Fred's girl was Amelia Perkins, a merry blonde with a wicked sense of humor that matched Fred's own. Her sister Caroline was Laurie's, less blond and more reserved than Amelia and (to Laurie's way of thinking) a bit dull, really, but pretty enough in her way. She didn't read much or like musical performances, declaring them too long and too crowded. But Amelia wouldn't go out with Fred unless someone escorted her sister as well, so Fred had begged Laurie to join him.

At the very least they made a cheerful foursome around town, riding in hired carriages, stopping for sweets at cafés after dark, and Laurie was glad at least to be out of his stuffy little dormitory, where he had too much time to think.

One night, Fred announced that Amelia and Caroline were hosting a society dinner at their house on Beacon Hill, and that all the Boston Brahmins would be in attendance—the Cabots and Elliotts, the Peabodys and Welds. Of course, half the Harvard student body would be in attendance, including honored guests Fred Vaughn and Theodore Laurence. "Do say you'll come, that's a good sport," said Fred when they received their invitations.

But Laurie had been souring on Caroline's company somewhat. She was a perpetual complainer, and though he was happy to help out Fred, he didn't want to be pulled further into the girl's orbit than he was already. Becoming a regular at her family gettogethers seemed especially beyond the pale, and so Laurie had been thinking about refusing the dinner invitation. Amelia didn't need her sister to have an escort in their own home, after all.

Instead, Laurie was thinking of going home to Concord for the weekend, on the pretext of seeing his grandfather. In reality, he was missing Jo and looking for an excuse to visit, if only to glimpse the old cottage, perhaps find out if she was as miserable as he was.

He hoped she was miserable! How terrible it would be if he saw her seeming happy and industrious without him.

I won't survive it. I won't.

But still.

"I think maybe I'll beg this one off, Fred," Laurie said. "My grandfather has called me home for the weekend."

"All the way to Concord for the weekend? You're joking."

"Not at all. He's leaving soon for London, and it wouldn't do to refuse him, you know."

Just then, a knock came at the door. It was the dormitory attendant announcing that Laurie had a telegram.

"From whom?"

"I believe it's from your grandfather," said the attendant, a young German with shaggy hair.

Laurie read the missive. It was clear from the note that Mr. Laurence had heard of Jo's refusal and knew his boy was nursing a broken heart, even as his was just as broken—he had been so looking forward to seeing the two of them together and Laurie settled. Perhaps they could cheer each other up.

"Grandfather is visiting this weekend," said Laurie.

Across the room, Fred Vaughn looked like the cat who'd eaten the canary. "How lucky! You won't have to go to Concord to see him after all. Which means you can come with me to Beacon Hill this weekend."

Laurie stifled a groan and only said, "I guess so. How fortunate."

MEANWHILE, BACK IN Orchard House, Amy's illness had, indeed, *not* turned the corner as her mother and sisters had believed.

Instead, it had gotten so much worse that she had been in bed for days.

Her mother and sisters had taken turns feeding her broth and tea, trying to starve the fever. They'd covered her with blankets and rubbed her feet, and yet over those days her skin had grown ashen, her sweet limbs wasting into emaciation. The cough grew so violent that Amy couldn't keep down any food, even broth, and the fever had grown, blossoming inside her small body like a lit fire, so that touching her skin felt like touching the stove.

For a week, Amy burned.

Sometimes she would rally, and sit up a little to eat. But other times she sank into a restless sleep, alternately kicking the blankets off and complaining of heat, then of freezing cold, though the autumn weather was still mild and the days were warm.

For her part, Mama hardly slept, so carefully did she dote on her youngest girl. The room had to be kept warm, but not too warm—the fire low, not allowed to die, but never blazing. A teapot on constant simmer had to be kept full of water and camphor, to loosen the phlegm in Amy's lungs, which she hacked up day and night.

After a few days, when she should have started getting better, she instead became worse, growing weaker, wracked with chills.

In a worry, Jo sat with her, spelling her mother off, to allow Mama Abba to get some sleep. Meg would tend to Amy, too, in the mornings before she went to the Kings' or in the early evenings when she returned. But as she needed all of her strength to tend to her little charges, the brunt of the sick-room fell on Mama and Jo and Hannah.

They sat with Amy and listened to the rattling in her lungs. A death-rattle, Jo feared, but then banished the thought. This was too much akin to what had happened to Beth, but Jo would not lose another sister.

"Don't leave me," she pleaded. "Don't leave us."

Amy opened her eyes to slits. "Oh, dear old Jo," she said warmly. "Go to bed, you're way too tired yourself."

Jo shook her head. "I'll watch over you."

"You can't change my fate," said Amy. "This isn't just a book."

"I can and I will," said Jo, a hand on Amy's damp hair. "Please get better. I can't bear it."

"I'm trying," said Amy. "But I am so tired of fighting."

"You have to."

In response, Amy closed her eyes.

"Don't die, Amy," Jo begged, openly sobbing now. "Please don't die. I'll be so much better to you. I'll even let you choose your own fate in my book, if you like. Whatever you want. You can have Laurie, even, if you really want him."

From the bed, Amy let out a faint chuckle.

Still, she burned.

But it wasn't up to Amy, or Jo, or Meg, or even Mama. It was only up to that Friend who listened.

Please, please, Jo continued to beg. *Don't let her die. I can't lose another sister. I barely survived Beth's death. Do not take Amy, too.*

But outside, the wind blew, and if that Friend were listening, no one answered.

23

DECISIONS

*T*he Kings? Why ever would I go live with the Kings?"

Meg was in shock, but Mama Abba was resolute. "I'll not let you become a danger to yourself and the Kings' children, Meg."

Because Amy is not improving.

That was the urgent point of the matter, however unspoken.

Jo wept at the thought of it, but it was no use. Meg was to be dispatched to the Kings, even though the doctor himself thought the precaution was unnecessary.

Mama was not convinced, having seen consumption spread not only within families but between them. She was sure Amy's visit with the Hummels had been how she'd come down with the disease. It wouldn't do to have Meg bring the sickness to her employers' house.

So Meg packed a small carpet-bag and went to stay in a spare servant's room at the Kings', who for their part were glad to have her staying longer hours.

From the Kings', Meg fretted and worried about Amy all day and cried herself to sleep at night. She would have been happiest living at home and tending to Amy herself in the evenings, which would have eased her worry. It seemed very hard to be banished from home during Amy's illness, and only wait for news.

They had already lost Beth.

They could not lose Amy, too.

If Jo suffered loudly and for everyone to hear and know, Meg kept her suffering inward. Losing Beth had made Meg all that more determined to make sure her family would want for nothing. No amount of money would ever bring Beth back, but somehow Meg had convinced herself that one was better off rich and miserable than poor and miserable.

And miserable she was, for she ached for John.

Her John, as Jo called him in the book. Her Mr. Brooke, who would never be her John except in fiction.

Meg had done the right thing, she knew, but it didn't hurt any less.

She tried to ease her suffering by spending more time with her young charges, though to be honest, she needed time away from them to rest. Her returns home to Orchard House in the evenings were the main reason she could be cheerful with the children on most days. But spending all day every day and night in their company was making her grouchy, so she took to having a ramble around the neighborhood after the children had finished their lessons for the day.

A little fresh air and exercise was all she needed. In the

November afternoons, it was dry and cool, and Meg wore Mama's plaid shawl on her walks down to the post-office to check for a letter from Father, or to look for a note from one of Amy's school chums to bring home, or to see if there were any decent fruit left on the Buttens' apple-tree.

It was on one of these rambles to the post-office that she ran into Mr. Brooke, who was still working for the elder Mr. Laurence.

She came inside to check the mail, as she had for the past three days, and at first didn't notice the man with his back to her.

As Meg walked in, she took off her plaid wrap, for it was a well-known fact that the inside of the post-office in Concord was close and stifling even in the howling winds of winter. She clutched the shawl in her hand and waited for her turn at the counter, distracted by thoughts of Amy, and of John Brooke, and of Jo and what an impossible, obstinate mule she had become—and so didn't hear the first part of the conversation between the post-master and the man in front of her. Only . . .

"So you'll be off, then?" asked the post-master.

"Yes. Tomorrow."

The man heaved a great sigh, and the post-master said, "When you return, be sure to come by, and we will toast your good health."

The man stood a little taller. "If I do come back, I will gladly take up that offer. Thank you, Mr. Taylor."

"Good luck to you, Mr. Brooke."

The mention of Brooke's name finally broke Meg out of her torpor. She looked up just in time to see John Brooke nearly bump into her, so distracted was he as well. "Oh!" she said, and he took her by the shoulder to keep from knocking her down.

"I'm so sorry," he said. "Are you all right, Miss March?"

Meg felt her face flame. "I—I'm all right. Yes. Thank you, Mr. Brooke. I didn't see you there."

"Nor I you."

They fell into an awkward silence. Neither mentioned *why* they hadn't seen each other much in the past few days, but it was there, between them: his request, her refusal. Like the sword of Damocles hanging over their heads.

Finally Meg said, "I thought you had already left for Boston."

"Not quite yet. But soon."

"Will you not come back to Concord?"

"Alas, no. Young Laurie has little need of a tutor now that he is in university," he explained. "And Mr. Laurence will soon be off to London."

She looked at his new coat—plain brown wool, with a coin pinned on his breast. He mustn't ever know the anguish she felt at seeing him like this. She would be cheerful, and wish him well, so that he would leave with her kind wishes, nothing more. She pasted a smile on her face and said merrily, "You will be sorely missed, Mr. Brooke."

"Will I?" He looked grim.

She startled. She'd meant the words as nothing more than a cheerful good-bye, but she realized he must have taken them otherwise. That she was making a jibe about his proposal once more. That she was laughing at him on the eve of his leaving.

"You will. You have been a kind friend to my family, and we will all miss you."

"All? Even you, Miss March?" His earnest brown eyes were full of pooling sadness.

Meg looked down at her hands. "Of course. Even though you would scorn my friendship."

"I didn't scorn it. I said your refusal would make it difficult for us to maintain our friendship. And so I was right, wasn't I? Because you can hardly bear to look at me."

It occurred to Meg that the post-master was still standing behind his counter, listening to every word. "I—I can look at you very easily, Mr. Brooke." And she raised her eyes to meet his, quickly, and then looked away once more.

"Very easily, yes."

Meg remained stoic. He mustn't see. He mustn't know she loved him, because that would be a disaster. She'd refused him once, for both their sakes. To save them both.

And ever since, Jo's words had haunted her: *I've never met such a martyr in all my life!*

Was she? A martyr?

Had she denied Brooke just to prove she could? She'd always thought she and Jo were so different—that she, Meg, had a much more dispassionate temperament, calm and thoughtful. *She* would never throw away a perfectly good marriage proposal on such quixotic principles as Jo's about maintaining her career, remaining free.

But she had refused John Brooke, just as Jo had refused Theodore Laurence.

And why?

What is wrong with this family? Perhaps Amy was right.

Meg had asked herself many times over the past week why she had refused Mr. Brooke, why she had *insisted on throwing him at Lady Hat*, to use Jo's words. Partly it was for the reasons she had told Brooke herself: She had no dowry. They would have no money.

Two wrongs don't make a right.

That's what she'd told him before sending him away.

But she'd had another reason, too, one that had slowly been making itself understood in her thoughts, when she was alone at night in her cramped room at the Kings', when she ate her solitary breakfast and directed her small charges in their lessons: She'd wanted to punish him.

Punish John Brooke.

And what was his crime? Not immediately snatching his arm away when Lady Harriet laid claim to it? Having the audacity to allow himself to be so petted and fondled by her that he made a fool of himself?

If he liked Harriet's attentions, let him have them for life, her soul had cried to itself, insensate. For Meg knew she was being ridiculous, but had been powerless to stop herself.

She was no better than Jo, who had denied herself everything in life on principle. Worse, even, because she'd done so out of jealousy.

And for all I know, I've ruined both our lives along the way.

Meg looked more closely at the coin pinned to his jacket and realized who had given it to him. Lady Hat, clearly. The coin was a love-token, engraved with her initials, HCC, and his, JAB. John Anthony Brooke.

Pinned over his heart.

Meg had thrown the two of them together, and they had stuck. Just as she had wanted, just as she thought was best for him.

Punishment, indeed!

She felt her lip tremble and looked away, quickly, toward the window, where some of Amy's school friends were on their way home for the day. Dear Amy, whose cough wracked her body. She would not be meeting her chums this afternoon, or anytime soon, and possibly never.

Just like poor Beth.

Where there had once been four March sisters, now there were three, and soon perhaps there would be only two.

It was all too terrible.

"Are you all right, Miss March?"

She was weeping. She'd tried so hard, but the tears started anyway. "Just thinking of my sister. How sorry I am not to be home with her now. How frightening it all is."

"Yes," said Brooke. "I was very sorry to hear of her illness. Mr. Laurence has sent for his physician to see if he can help."

Meg looked up, her eyes shining with gratitude. "Oh! That is very generous of him. Please tell him how much we appreciate it."

"I will. And Lady Harriet sent over some very good whisky to mix into a tea that she thought might help."

"That is . . . most kind of her. Please thank her as well when you see her next." Meg looked at the love-token. How gaudy it looked, engraved in gold. How much it must have cost. But then again, Lady Hat could afford to lavish him with gifts. "She is still in town?"

"Yes, for a few more days."

"And then back to New York?"

"I believe so. I don't really know where she's headed next."

"No?" Meg asked. "She wouldn't tell you where to send a letter?"

"No, I doubt she will want to hear from me anytime soon."

"What?" Meg asked. The politeness was all gone from her voice. She was in shock, plain and simple.

"I believe her last words were to tell me to go to the devil."

"How is that? Then you and she aren't—?"

"As I told you last week, Miss March, my heart is already accounted for. I have little notion of turning away from the object of my affection, even if she doesn't return it. Lady Harriet has been told so, quite clearly. In almost those exact words, in fact, earlier today."

"What about this love-token she's pinned to you?" Meg indicated the engraved coin. "I would have thought one would give such a gift only to a husband or, at the very least, a betrothed."

"Ah, I think her affections were leaning in that direction. I think she thought this token would be *the first of many*. Those were her words. But when I told her I couldn't marry her, she told me to keep it. To buy my passage across the Styx, I think she said."

Meg's face burned furiously. They were not engaged! She could hardly believe it. "But you kept it."

"Honestly, until you mentioned it, I'd forgotten it was there."

He smiled at her, and her heart eased. "Is that why you were crying just now, Miss March?"

Meg turned positively crimson; she could feel the spots burn on both cheeks. "Perhaps," she said.

"But I am still a poor man," said Brooke. "Poorer than ever, since I am no longer in Mr. Laurence's employ. I have nothing but the clothes on my back, in fact."

Meg touched the fabric on his arm. "But they are good clothes," she said in a small voice. "As is the man who wears them."

"Does that mean you have reconsidered?" Brooke asked, and this time it was he who could not meet her eyes.

Meg's heart leapt. "I suppose it does." She reached for his hands and held them. "If you'll have me . . . *my John.*"

24

⤜⤚◦⤙⤘

BEACON HILL

*A*n evening out was still an evening, and not to be turned down.

Grandfather had arrived in Cambridge. And, as it turned out, the Perkins family knew Laurie's grandfather as well and offered an invitation to the party that could not be refused.

So it happened on that autumn night that Fred and Laurie were fetched to the Perkinses' house in his grandfather's carriage.

It was a cool evening, foggy and raining, and the cobblestones of Beacon Hill were damp and slippery. The horses had trouble pulling the carriage, giving Grandfather ample time to question his grandson on his studies, for one thing, and how Laurie and Fred had been spending their too-abundant free time for another.

"I just hope you are not wasting these golden years of your youth," Grandfather lectured. "And your studies." Truthfully, he did seem to know a suspicious amount about Laurie's performance so far in his courses. Laurie was growing a bit wary; Grandfather mentioned both the Virgil assignment and the Reformation essay by name.

"I suggest you turn them in first thing Monday," the elder Laurence said. "And to make sure you do a good job of it, you will spend all day tomorrow with me."

Laurie groaned inwardly but said nothing. The visit was a warning: *Remember why you're here*, the old man was saying. *While I live, I have a say in how you live.*

As if Laurie could forget.

Beside him, he could feel Fred stiffen with repressed laughter. Fred's family didn't care if he received "gentleman's Cs," but apparently Laurie's grandfather did. It wasn't enough that his grandfather required him to *go* to Harvard, Laurie must actually *learn something* as well.

Despite himself, he remembered the look on Jo's face when she said she would cut off her hair and dress as a boy if it meant she could go to university. It shamed him to think of it—lively, curious, intellectual Jo would have loved the opportunity. And only because she was a girl, she was denied the chance.

In the next moment, though, he was angry with her all over again. She knew how much he despised going, and yet she couldn't give him *the one thing* that would have made his banishment to Cambridge more tolerable: her promise to marry him when he returned in four years, older and (he hoped) wiser.

If Jo wouldn't marry herself to him in fiction *or* in life, then he wouldn't bother to waste time on pitying her. She'd made her own bed and could lie in it, for all he cared.

He sighed.

Now they were pulling up to the Perkinses' house on Beacon Hill, the horses straining to keep their feet on the wet cobblestones. Grandfather and Fred managed to get down to the pavement in one piece, but Laurie was just halfway out when one of the horses slipped, jerking the carriage to the side, depositing Laurie in a puddle up to his knees and dirtying his good evening suit.

Fred hurried to help his friend up, but the damage was done: There was mud from his cuffs to his knees. "Look at you!" Fred declared. "You look as though you've just come in from a rugby match."

Laurie considered the mess his trousers had become and thought he spied a way to retreat without angering Grandfather. "I have to go home and change," he said. "This won't do at all."

"Nonsense," said Grandfather, as if he knew exactly what Laurie was up to. "Everyone's wet tonight. The Perkinses will have a fire going. A quick towel-off and you'll be good as new."

Still Laurie objected. "I can't go to dinner with mud on my trousers!" he said. "Grandfather, be reasonable! Let me go home and change into dry clothes."

But Grandfather was not having it; he sent the carriage away to wait for them. So Laurie stood on the sidewalk dripping, watching the guests go through the front door, all while deciding what to do. It was possible running away was his only answer.

But where?

More carriages were arriving, with more guests. Laurie watched them go inside in twos and threes: society matrons, young women in hoop skirts, gentlemen in top hats with long, wet mustaches. A couple of servants at the top of the stairs held out umbrellas to keep the guests dry at the threshold, and Laurie thought again how much he did not want to be here.

He should be at home in Concord with the Marches—with Amy, who was ill.

Of course, Jo had not written him to tell him so; he had to hear from Brooke, of all people. Still, his place was there in Concord, not in Beacon Hill, where he would be expected to play suitor to a girl whose company he could barely tolerate.

He should go and do as he pleased. If his grandfather cut him off because of it, then at least he would be free—free to pursue his music. Free to make a life wherever and however he wanted.

Like Jo.

No, he realized now, he could not go back to Concord, not until Jo apologized.

Until she *begged his forgiveness*. Until she *took everything she said back*.

Laurie would travel the world instead; he would show her! He would have his adventures without her, since that was what she wanted. He would go to Italy, to France. Anywhere unexpected; anywhere he could start anew, as he wanted. He could be poor and penniless and free—the way his parents had been.

He had just turned on his heel to leave when he bumped into a set of powdered bosoms beneath a wide black umbrella. A particularly jolly, familiar set, as it were.

"Laurie!" declared Lady Hat. "Is that you?"

"Hullo, old Hat," he said, his attitude brightening almost immediately. "I didn't know you were coming."

"Neither did I," said Harriet, "but your grandfather insisted we join him here. He thought you might need cheering up."

Laurie raised an eyebrow, as everything fell into place.

He suddenly understood.

If possible, Grandfather had been even more despondent than Laurie upon hearing the news of Jo's refusal. "There are more fish in the sea," the old man had said, in an effort to console—though it wasn't entirely clear which one of them he was consoling.

Other fish?

And so—if Laurie's suspicions were correct—this, it turned out, would be the fish Grandfather hoped Laurie would hook.

After all, like the Marches, the Lord and Lady Carmichael-Carlthorpe were the Laurences' old friends. And it would be just like the old man to bring Harriet to Boston as a surprise for Laurie, and then make sure she appeared at the Perkinses'.

"Where are you staying?" Laurie asked.

"Kate and I have gone to the Parker House. Mummy insisted. You know how it is."

"I do," said Laurie, sadly.

"It's comfortable there. Between you and me, we're all a bit tired from our Concord adventures."

"Oh? Did you see Brooke there?"

"Indeed. And those March girls," she said, sharply.

"Ah, yes," said Laurie.

"Well, I for one wish them all the happiness in the world," said Harriet with a toss of her head.

"Excuse me?"

"You haven't heard? About Brooke and Cousin Meg?"

"What about Brooke and Cousin Meg?"

"They are engaged to be married."

"Blazes!" said Laurie. "Old Brooke finally spoke his piece!"

"Rumor has it she refused him the first time. But apparently the man was not to be daunted."

Good for him, thought Laurie. "And she has accepted him?"

"She has," sighed Harriet.

He crossed his arms. "And you are all right?"

She shrugged. "As well as I can be."

His suspicions in New York had been correct, then: Harriet *had* set her sights on Brooke, just as she had the musician in London. The thrill of illicit romance, daring her mother's disapproval—Harriet thrived on all of it.

Now here she was, disappointed in love another time. The dowager had probably insisted on the rooms to keep an eye on her willful daughter, who gave her affections so recklessly to *undeserving men*.

"Honestly, I don't know how you stand living in the country," she was saying now. "So provincial. Small towns are so stifling, aren't they?"

Oh, Hat.

Laurie wasn't the least bit fooled by her dismissals: He knew heartbreak when he heard it, having so recently suffered it himself. "I suppose so, in some ways," he said. "Socially speaking."

He was surprised at how glad he was to see her. More than glad—he was relieved. There would be someone at the dinner whose company he would enjoy, besides Fred.

Harriet was spirited and cultured and witty, the life of any gathering. She would make the evening not just tolerable, but maybe even fun.

Besides, both their hearts had been broken by a March sister; perhaps this would remind them that one family could not possibly be the center of the universe.

There was more to life than Orchard House.

Wasn't there?

Harriet was lovely tonight in gold brocade, which brought out the unusual gold flecks in her eyes. He had never looked at her seriously before, having preferred Jo to any other girl, but he was surprised to find himself admiring her lively expression and fine figure. So different from Jo, who dressed in drab, even shabby clothes. Who refused to wear the beautiful polonaise he'd had made especially for her.

She'd given it to her *sister*, and still he'd refused to see the insult. Not until she denied him, firmly and irrevocably.

She would not marry him.

So why shouldn't Laurie learn to change his mind about women in general—and Harriet in particular?

Give me one good reason.

Lady Hat wasn't just the most vivacious girl in any room.

She was also wealthy and titled in her own right. A marriage to *her* would be Laurie's guarantee that he'd never again have to live by Grandfather's rules.

If he wanted to live abroad, he could live abroad.

If he wanted to be a musician, he could be a musician.

No one would ever again own him. He would be himself, free. Even Harriet, with her ancient name and title, would not be his master. He would chart his own destiny.

At last.

Lady Hat was watching him with a quizzical look on her face. "Is everything all right, dear boy?" she asked. "You look pensive."

But Laurie felt his troubles beginning to lift. There was light in the distance of his long, dark hour.

Perhaps his grandfather was right. Perhaps an old friend of the family could be the answer. A different family.

How had Laurie himself failed to see it for so long?

He held out his arm to her to lead her into the Perkinses' house on Beacon Hill. "Shall we go inside together?"

She took his arm and leaned into him a little. He felt the weight and accepted it gladly. "I thought you'd never ask."

25

~~~◠◠◠~~~

ALL ALONE

*M*ama! Come quick!" Jo cried from where she was reading to Amy in the sickbed. The entire household heard and came running: Mama and Hannah. Meg was still at the Kings'.

Amy had gone very still and very white. In the room the air was as still as she was. The curtains, open just a crack, didn't stir at all.

They held their breath and waited, fearing the end had come.

Until Amy took another small rattling breath, and coughed and coughed, the wetness in her lungs sounding like the wringing of a damp sponge.

Then the three of them crept out, slowly, and went to their separate private spaces to weep. The worst had not happened.

But it was clear that the worst was still coming, and they were afraid. Good Mr. Laurence's doctor had come and told them to "make her comfortable," which was all he would say about Amy's diagnosis.

Amy's illness had consumed them all for days and days. Mama, Hannah, and Jo took turns nursing the youngest girl during the day, feeding her broth and teas, putting mustard plasters on her chest to ease the cough, boiling camphor day and night to open up her lungs. Nothing had worked. Amy—who had always been small and delicate, though not frail—now positively seemed to shrink before their eyes day by day, hour by hour.

The worst was happening, and there was nothing they could do to stop it.

Poor Amy, who was always left behind, who had been too young to join them in New York, even as her artistic dreams spun fantasies of Paris and Rome.

She would never leave Concord.

She would never see the Colosseum, and the Prado, and the Uffizi.

Jo hadn't even been able to take her to the seashore, as she had Beth.

Every day was difficult in an unforeseen way.

There were times when Jo was convinced Amy was getting better, but then she'd come around a corner and find Mama weeping silent tears, her apron held to her face and her shoulders shaking. Jo would ease back around the corner, alarmed and unsettled to see her calm, collected mother so undone.

Jo herself was determined and grim sometimes, hopeful others, but always afraid.

She hadn't written a word in days. The sequel was utterly

beyond her now, and what was more, she found she didn't care a whit.

The fictional Amy was far less important than the real Amy, the one who needed her. Her characters would not have suffered anything worse than what her family was going through now.

It was hard, too, on Meg. There had been no celebrating, not even with what should have been her joyous news. John Brooke had gone back to Boston, and she wrote him every day to tell him what was happening at home in Concord.

What was happening was alternately dull and frightening.

Days, Meg worked at the Kings', trying to be patient with her little charges, who played and laughed and argued as all children do who are oblivious to the cares and worries of others. It was hard for her to be angry at them. Why shouldn't they be cheerful and argumentative, as usual?

It was only that she envied them, being so free of care. Neither illness nor poverty had touched them, while Meg had too much of both.

Nights, she tried to stay away from Orchard House, though sometimes she would walk home to find out if Amy or Mama or Jo needed anything. She wanted so desperately to help, but it was sapping her strength, and though Mama (and dear Mr. Brooke, who was becoming more and more a part of the family since he and Meg were betrothed) did their best to encourage her to rest and let the others take care of Amy, she couldn't bear to be away from her at such a time.

None of them could.

They haunted Amy's little bedroom, with its stuffy, camphor-scented air, with its constant noise of coughing, like they were the ghosts and she the living one on whom they fed.

She could not die. The horror of it would be too much for all of them. Not their dear little Amy, who was only fifteen. And worst of all, she wouldn't get to see Father one last time.

One evening, when Mama came down looking paler and sadder than ever, holding a tray of broth that had remained untouched, Jo said to her, "Is there nothing else to do?"

Mama shook her head. "I've asked everyone I can think of for their remedies. Nothing seems to make any difference."

They were quiet for a long time, listening to the weak sound of Amy's cough.

Finally Jo asked, "Do you think we should write for Father to come?"

"I think we must. Your father—he would never forgive himself if he didn't come. I think—I think she's waiting for him."

And Mama set down the tray, and the two of them fell into each other's arms.

MAMA SENT THREE copies of the letter, in case the other two were lost, but they all said essentially the same thing—

Amy is ill. Come home.

Come now.

There was no way to know if he would get the letters in time or, if he did, whether he would be able to come quickly enough. The last they'd heard, he was someplace in Mississippi, where there was a new school and a church being built. Even if the letters arrived, he might not make it home in time to attend the deathbed of his youngest daughter. He might not be able to risk the journey north with no money and little food.

But Mama said they had to risk it anyway, for all their sakes. It would take a miracle to get Father home, but if it would save Amy, if it would rally her spirits to see her father home again, Mama said she had to try.

They spent several terrible days waiting for word from Father, debating whether they should tell Amy or not. Would it help her more, or less? The snow had not started to fly yet, so the mail and the trains were still running, though both were somewhat unreliable, and the roads were passable.

Four days passed, then five. Mostly Amy slept and coughed. They fed her when she was strong enough, changed her soaked night-dress and sheets, kept her room warm, but little by little, they could feel her slipping away.

Jo watched the road with an intensity that even she hadn't known she could possess. Because Father had to come. He *had* to. Every other consideration was forgotten.

She was filled with fury.

How *wrong* it was that Amy had fallen ill because the family continued to show a little kindness to people less fortunate than they!

That Father had been gone for years upon years, first during the war, then during Reconstruction.

That there was no money for train tickets for Father, or doctors for Amy, or any other thing that would have made Amy's illness even the slightest bit more bearable.

That Mr. Laurence was away, and there was no one to help.

There was no justice when the Amys of the world sickened and died of poverty, and the Lady Harriets of the world flourished. When kindness and sympathy were punished and insolence was rewarded. No justice whatsoever.

Jo was starting to understand that there was a kind of anger that burns the humanity out of a person, a kind of anger that started in the brain and disoriented the body as it worked its way from muscle to bone.

How Jo felt was . . . furious.

Betrayed.

Utterly alone.

She felt like telling someone the intimate details of that betrayal and that aloneness, but there was no one left to tell. Mama was barely strong enough to survive this herself without Jo pouring out the weight of her own heavy heart. And Meg had John Brooke now.

Jo could feel a membrane slide between her older sister and herself, the thinnest windowpane, covered just so with frost. Enough to telegraph what there was beyond, but not enough to make out any of the detail. The effect was a ghostly reflection of the image that Jo had once been able to see so clearly.

She was losing Meg, too. Meg was John's now—and he was hers. If there was someone Meg would pour out her heart to, it would be him.

For a moment, just that moment, Jo hated everything about love. Because love was betrayal. Without it, there was no loss. Perhaps without it there was nothing, but even so—no loss.

At that moment, Jo believed that, between those two choices, it was the possibility of nothing—of not feeling, not aching, not even knowing—that might be worth it.

Love was madness, was foolish, senseless. Love was a problem, and yet somehow the loss of it was a worse one. Love made normal things, sensible things, make no sense at all.

It made Meg almost refuse a good man who loved her.

It made their mama give all their bread to the Hummels and wait forever for a chaplain husband who was practically a ghost.

It made Amy and Poppet speak in their own private language, the language of long-lost and now-reunited twins, shipwrecked together in the seas of some faraway world.

It made familiar things terrifying, and terrifying things familiar.

It burned the wings off moths, sending them headlong into the flame.

There was no escape, no recovery, no happy ending. You loved and you lost. Your heart beat and the beating left it bruised beyond recognition. You could feel it, or try not to feel it, or long for it, but you didn't get to keep it.

It didn't matter how, or even why. He loved you or he didn't. She died or she didn't. He left or he didn't.

In the end, you were always the loneliest person in the world, no matter who you were. Because that was what love was, the very raggedy edge of that feeling, the coming or the going of it. There was nothing else.

Only shadows.

Jo WAS NAPPING and didn't hear the knock when it came. "Hullo!" cried a voice. "Anyone home?"

Startled, she flew to the door and flung it open. Outside, it was dark and raining, so the dark figure in the doorway looked for a moment like Father in his blue Union uniform, come home as if Jo had conjured him.

Except the face had no beard. The figure's hair was brown, not white.

It wasn't Father. It was John Brooke, who had come back from Boston in his ordinary brown coat.

Beside him stood Laurie, looking sheepish in his own dripping hat and coat. "Oh, Jo," he said. "I came as soon as I heard."

Theodore Laurence had come home.

26

A RECKONING

*A*fter the two men were inside and their coats hung up to dry next to the fire—after the surprised hellos, the embraces, and (in the case of Meg and Brooke) a furtive kiss in the pantry—Jo took them upstairs to Amy, who cheered to see Laurie and rallied a bit, sitting up and whispering how glad she was that he'd come.

"You look—different," Amy wheezed. "Happier—than when—I saw you—last."

"I suppose I am," said Laurie.

"Don't speak, dearest," Jo whispered, smoothing Amy's pillow. "Save your strength."

"That's right." Laurie gave her small white hand a squeeze. "Let us do the talking for you."

Amy smiled weakly. He gave her a little doll he'd bought in Boston, a fancy one with a china face and a beautiful gown of gold brocade. Amy, who'd never received such a lavish gift, clutched it to her. "It—will—be my—most favorite—possession," she said.

Jo nearly wept. But then Amy's eyes rolled back in her head, and she went limp—fainted from exhaustion or happiness, or both.

Laurie made a startled noise. Alarmed, Jo rushed Laurie out of the sick-room and back downstairs while Mama and Hannah scurried around fetching smelling salts and more camphor. The beautiful doll was put aside on a nearby table in hopes that Amy would be cheered by it later, when—*if*—she felt better.

The four young people waited downstairs, the two girls trembling with fear that Mama would come downstairs to tell them that the worst had happened, the two men helpless to ease their suffering. For several minutes there was nothing but the sound of the wind rising outside. An autumn blow, with a hint of thunder. Everyone both tense and gloomy.

No one said as much, but it was there in the air, unspoken: Amy was unlikely to make it through the night.

"Your father?" Laurie asked, looking at Jo's dark eyes.

"I'm afraid he won't come in time," Jo said, quietly.

"Oh, Jo," Laurie said, for the third or fourth time.

Jo simply nodded. There was little else that anyone could say.

An awkward silence descended. Meg bustled into the kitchen for some tea and some bits of biscuit, leaving Jo alone with Laurie and Brooke.

Jo couldn't decide if she wanted to sob with relief to see Laurie there, or to slap him so hard his teeth rattled. For punishing her so. For ruining everything.

Except, wasn't this love, also? Showing up when you were needed, without being asked?

She softened. Everything was forgotten, everything forgiven, because he had come to her family in their most desperate hour. "I'm so glad you've come, Laurie." Her voice carefully neutral. She wouldn't cry, not now. Not if she could help it.

"I'm glad I could be here," said Laurie. "If . . . to see Amy. She's a dear girl, and I'm so very sorry she's ill."

"And thank you for bringing him to us, Mr. Brooke," said Jo warmly.

Brooke nodded. They were all emotional, and being as careful not to upset one another as they could.

For his part, Laurie was surprised that there was not a single teasing note in Jo's voice, nor the barest hint of sarcasm or mockery. She was genuinely glad to see him.

She doesn't know, he thought. *Brooke hasn't told her.*

But then, how could Jo know Laurie's news when Brooke himself had only just learned of it earlier in the day? No one knew. And Laurie was not relishing the telling of it—not under these circumstances.

Jo seemed not to notice his distress. "I hope your journey wasn't arduous."

"Not at all."

Brooke bent to build up the fire and gave Laurie a significant look as he passed. *Get on with it,* the look said, but Laurie would not. Let someone else ask if there was something they wanted to know; he would volunteer nothing if he could help it.

How different things were now than they'd been in New York, where Jo and Laurie had been each other's dearest confidants. Where the four of them had been so merry, going to the opera and eating in cafés and rambling up and down Broadway all day long! Laurie could hardly believe that had been just a few short months ago.

"How is university? Cambridge treating you well?" asked Jo.

"You'll be proud of me, Jo; my Latin has improved leaps and bounds," replied Laurie with a faint smile, even as Brooke snorted.

"And how is your sequel coming along?" asked Brooke. "Meg tells me you are working on the latest draft?"

Jo stiffened, as every writer does when asked about the progress of the current work. "Oh, it's coming" was all she said.

At last, Meg came in from the kitchen with the tea things and spent a few moments pouring and passing out cups, which gave them all something to look at and a way to pass the time.

"Thank you again for coming, Laurie," Meg said, sitting down with her own cup. "It's so good of you to be here now. I'm sorry if it will cause trouble with your studies?"

"Of course not," Laurie said. "Not even wild horses could keep me away."

A look passed between Meg and Jo, but Laurie couldn't guess what it was. Jo looked pale herself but not physically ill, as far as Laurie could tell. She was worried for her sister, nothing more than that.

"And so," Meg began, trying to sound cheerful, "will you tell us how you and Lady Harriet came to be engaged?"

Jo's teacup rattled.

Laurie looked uncomfortably at her.

Jo's face had gone positively ashen. "You are engaged?"

"John just told me congratulations are in order. How wonderful!" said Meg, her voice only the tiniest bit strained.

Jo said nothing more. She was speechless.

Laurie bit the inside of his cheek. Meg was merely making polite conversation, he knew, better to keep everyone's mind off what was happening upstairs. Was this subject any better, though?

Laurie sighed. Better to be out with it. Be direct with the truth, his grandfather always said, even if it's painful. As usual, the old man was right.

He leaned forward. "Thank you. It happened so quickly, it was too late for the post. It's not meant as a surprise by any means. But yes, I asked her in Boston. It's been agreed to all around. You can imagine how glad my grandfather was. I suspect that was his plan all along."

Jo now pretended to be very interested in her gloves. Meg looked at her, then back at Brooke. "But how did she happen to be in Boston? I thought she'd gone back to New York?"

"Her mother had some business in Boston, I gather. I'm not sure. But we met again at a dinner, hosted by some friends," Laurie began. "The horses slipped as I was getting out of the carriage, and I fell in the mud. You can guess what a sight I was."

Brooke chuckled, and Meg smiled, but Jo's mouth tightened around the corners. Laurie found himself enjoying her discomfort just a bit. *Let her see what her stubbornness has wrought.*

"Anyway, I was standing there dripping and contemplating going home for the evening, when who came along, carrying an umbrella and laughing at my misfortune?"

"There's nothing like a friend who can make you laugh at yourself," said Meg. She cut her eyes at Jo just for a second.

"Yes. It was nice to see a friendly face, and I told her so. She had come down on my grandfather's urging. He thought she might need a bit of company as well. He thought she was melancholy for some reason."

Jo looked at Brooke but said nothing. Had she guessed, or had Meg told her that Hat had set her heart on Brooke and been denied? Laurie couldn't tell. It wasn't like Brooke to tell tales of his rejected loves, even Lady Harriet. But Jo had a keen mind, and might have guessed.

It didn't matter. Harriet was his now, and he was hers. Everything past was prologue, including the fact that both of them had loved, and been rejected by, other people. Only the future mattered now.

"After we went inside, Harriet spoke to one of the family's servants and was able to procure me a new pair of trousers. She's quite resourceful that way."

Jo scoffed. Laurie went on with his tale. "At any rate, the evening was saved. We spent the whole dinner in conversation together, fairly ignoring the other guests. It was quite a scandal! But I'd nearly forgotten how much I enjoy her company."

"So what happened next?" asked Meg.

Jo stood up and paced the room in front of the fire.

"I saw her home that night. She was as lively as I've ever seen her. We joked that we were like the lovers in some novel, thrown together by fate. Roderigo and what's-her-name."

"Rodanthe," Meg and Jo said automatically.

He nodded, as if he hadn't known. "That's the one."

Laurie watched Jo pick up the poker and stab the fire furiously. Sparks flew off the logs and toward the hem of Jo's dress, where one left a little burn mark. How incautious she was. How maddeningly unreachable, in every way.

He went on. "I called on her the next day. All of this was at Grandfather's urging, you understand. He seemed quite determined to throw us together as much as possible. But it worked. A few days later, I asked and she agreed. It was settled quickly."

There was a moment of uncomfortable silence, then Meg cried, "Oh, Laurie, I'm so happy for you both!" She went to embrace him. "How happy you will be. And will you be married here in Concord?"

"London, most likely," Laurie said. "Though that's still a long ways off. Next summer, most like. I have promised Grandfather that I will finish my first year at Harvard before we wed. He'd rather I continued and got my degree, but he's thrilled, as you can imagine, since he and the dowager are old and dear friends. The joining of their houses and all that."

There was a long silence that stretched across the room like a cobweb. Had it only been two months ago he'd professed to love Jo forever? Only two? *Goodness*, Jo thought, *how fickle boys are!*

"So everyone is satisfied, then," Jo said. "That's wonderful,

Teddy. I'm—I'm so glad for you. And Harriet, of course. You're well suited for each other."

"Thank you," he said. There was a hint of steel in her voice. *You're well suited for each other* was an insult, but one only Laurie would have noticed.

She was still angry. *Good. Let her be angry*, he thought.

Meg watched Laurie and Jo looking at each other in puzzlement. Neither would give an inch. "So you'll make your home in Concord, then?" she asked.

"I suppose not. We haven't discussed it in detail yet. Harriet's estates are all overseas, and we will have quite a lot to do to manage them all." He looked at Jo. "It may be that we don't come back here very often."

"Well, if you are in London, Jo shall be there soon, to supervise the play based on her book," said Meg.

Brooke reached over for Meg's hand. "And we shall hope to be there for the premiere and visit you both."

Laurie arched his eyebrow. "The four of us in London! It will be just like old times."

"Jolly," agreed Meg, to fill the conversation, since the cat seemed to have gotten Jo's tongue once more.

"I need to check on Amy," Jo said, finally.

Meg watched her sister stand up straight to buck up her courage. Perhaps no one but a sister would have seen the little tremble in Jo's chin, the hurt in her eyes. Laurie certainly didn't seem to notice. Only Meg felt all the air go out of the room as she realized

Jo was very close to tears—that in another minute they would have a scene on their hands, and it would all come out at last.

Instead, Jo said, "Congratulations, Laurie. I hope you're very happy together." And she ran up the stairs and away before he could say another word.

27

DAYBREAK

After Jo's retreat, Mr. Brooke and Laurie retired to the Laurences' house across the lane and made plans to call on Amy the next day. Meg made excuses for Jo, but it felt like something had been broken, some connection irretrievably severed. Laurie would marry Harriet and leave Concord.

It was possible he might not come back, perhaps ever.

Beth was gone. Amy was lost in the land of shadow, and Laurie would leave them for London and the Continent. Meg would marry John, and Jo would be left alone with only her manuscript to keep her company. It was what she said she wanted, but why did freedom taste like ashes in her mouth?

Laurie was going to marry Lady Hat—who would have thought? For some reason, when Jo refused him, she did not imagine he would marry someone else. That had never factored into her imagination. What did she assume? That he would wander the earth alone, on his own, his unrequited passion for her burning within him?

Perhaps he was never as besotted as he had claimed. He'd left in early September; it was only the second week of November! Had he forgotten about her so quickly? Indeed he had. He wouldn't even look at her that evening.

The Marches spent a terrible night listening to the wind howl in the chimneys, and the house grew even stuffier and hotter than usual. Still Father did not come. They had to conclude he must not have received Mama's letters after all.

Meg didn't know if the next day would be any better. She could hear Jo rolling over in bed next door, stomping upstairs to the attic in a fit of pique. Jo's heart was broken, even if the stubborn thing didn't know it yet.

Oh! It was hard to watch her sisters suffer, especially when Meg herself was finally so content. It seemed too much to hope that Amy would get well, much less that Jo would find her happiness, now that Laurie was engaged to Harriet. Jo had no one but herself to blame on that score.

In the morning the air was clean, as if it had blown itself out. The sky through the curtains was an unbelievable blue, cloudless, with a hint of coolness. The trees were almost bare, the ground littered with crackling leaves.

As Meg had guessed, Jo had been up all night. She'd kept replaying the scene Laurie had described over and over in her head: Laurie falling into the puddle and the lady laughing. Harriet teasing Laurie as she, Jo, used to do.

There's nothing like a friend who can make you laugh at yourself, Meg had said.

Laurie had such a friend, but it wasn't her. Wasn't Jo, not anymore.

They would be married in London. They would not expect to come back to Concord often.

His friendship with Jo would die on the vine for lack of sunlight.

Jo could not believe that Laurie would marry the bosoms. The pretentious lady they'd met in New York, the one who'd gone on about the *uppertens*, was no kind of match for the funny, kind, energetic friend Jo had known for so long.

Perhaps he'd changed more in Cambridge than she'd realized.

During the night, when she'd realized sleep wouldn't come, Jo had actually gone into Amy's room and told Mama to go get some sleep. "I'll wake you if anything happens," Jo said. Mama, exhausted, kissed her hair and went to her room.

Amy had not spoken at all during the night, only coughed and coughed so hard, Jo thought the poor little thing's ribs would crack. *This is it,* Jo thought. *This is the dark hour. The shadowlands coming for Amy, just as they came for Beth. As they will one day come for Meg, and for me.*

Jo closed her eyes and prayed for Bethie and Amy.

She opened her heart to the pain and the grief and the darkness, letting herself feel the ache of loss and love. She wept for her little sisters—one gone, one going—the two little souls she cared most for, in the entire world.

And when she could weep no longer, she crawled into bed

next to her sister and slept as if she were halfway in the grave herself.

"Jo."

The voice was almost too quiet to hear.

"Jo."

She sat up with a start, disoriented. "Amy?!"

Morning had come; Jo could see the blue at the window. But even more surprising, Amy was awake and whispering that she would like to go sit outside. "To see—the flowers," she said.

It was autumn, and the flowers were brown and dead. Still, no one could bear to refuse her. Not now.

Especially not her big sisters.

Mama gathered her up and carried her downstairs and outside to her chair next to the remains of Vegetable Valley.

"How long—have I—been sick?" Amy wheezed.

"A fair while," said Jo. "Not forever."

"Don't fret about that," Mama said. "Enjoy the cool air. It's a beautiful day."

Amy smiled. It was.

They covered her with blankets to keep her warm. Meg brought her tea, and Jo rubbed her feet. Amy closed her eyes and let the sun warm her face.

They waited, watching her. The sun made her pale skin look the slightest bit pink.

For a while they sat outside and read to her. *Wuthering Heights* this time. Jo read:

1801.—I have just returned from a visit to my landlord—the solitary neighbour that I shall be troubled with. This is certainly a beautiful country! In all England, I do not believe that I could have fixed on a situation so completely removed from the stir of society. A perfect misanthropist's heaven: and Mr. Heathcliff and I are such a suitable pair to divide the desolation between us. A capital fellow! He little imagined how my heart warmed towards him when I beheld his black eyes withdraw so suspiciously under their brows, as I rode up, and when his fingers sheltered themselves, with a jealous resolution, still further in his waistcoat, as I announced my name.

"Mr. Heathcliff?" I said.

A nod was the answer.

As she read, Jo glanced up at Amy from time to time. Her sister didn't seem to move. She was as still and waxy as a statue.

A little while later, Amy took a deep breath and coughed. When she could speak again, she said, "I do—feel—better."

She took another breath, and another. Paused.

For the first time in weeks, the cough did not follow.

"Where is—my—doll—from Laurie?" she whispered. "Can I—have something—to eat?"

Meg and Jo, Mama and Hannah looked at one another, afraid and hopeful. "Of course," Mama said with tears in her eyes. "Anything you want, dearest."

The worst hadn't happened after all. The worst had passed them by. The shadows had been chased by the sun.

When they arrived to check on the patient, Brooke and Laurie were pleased to find Amy in much better spirits, and in returning health. She refused the broth Mama made and asked for bread and butter, which made everyone laugh with relief. As the day wore on and Amy sat outside, enjoying the outdoor air, her strength returned.

At first it seemed like she simply rallied, as many people do, for the change of scenery and the nice weather. Her color came back, and the cough receded little by little. The wheezing in her lungs reduced.

Mr. Laurence's doctor said it was the most remarkable turn-around he'd ever seen. "I didn't want to say so, ma'am," he said to Mama, "but I've never seen anyone recover from consumption for sitting outside. I shall have to try it on my other patients, and see if it works."

That night, when they brought her inside, she slept soundly, and she woke in the morning asking for johnny-cake and apples. Ravenous, she ate and ate until her mother said she must not overdo it and risk a stomachache.

Jo poked her in the belly and said, "Besides, you've emptied the larder. We'll have to go to town for supplies."

Everyone laughed. Their relief was palpable. Everything could be funny again, now that Amy was on the mend.

After two days of improvement, when it was clear Amy would live, Laurie and Brooke announced they were leaving once more. Laurie would return to his studies, and Brooke to his students in Boston. Once he and Meg were married, they would move there.

"We can leave now that we know we shall not have to part from you forever," Laurie said, and tweaked Amy's nose.

"Laurie! Don't!" Amy said, but she smiled. Jo thought how pleasant it was to see them tease each other again.

This was followed by a darker thought: the question of whether they would ever do so again. Now that Amy was better, Laurie had no reason to stay. There would be his studies and his wedding plans, and Harriet in Boston. He would not even return for Thanksgiving; he had plans with Harriet's family for the holiday.

Then in the spring, he would go away to England.

Maybe forever.

"So," said Jo to Laurie, "will you be home for Christmas, at least?"

Laurie picked absently at a fingernail. "I doubt it. Harriet will want me in New York, I think. And with Grandfather going to London for the winter, there won't be much call for me to come home."

"I see."

"I hope you return for our wedding, at least," chided Meg. "We've planned it for December, around Christmastime."

"Oh, is that so?" asked Laurie. "Brooke hadn't mentioned it."

It was the first Jo had heard of a Christmas wedding. Laurie squeezed Meg's hand warmly, and for a minute he was the old

Laurie again. "Of course I will be there. Wild horses couldn't keep me away."

One more visit, Jo thought. One more, and then he would be gone forever.

There are so many ways you can lose a person.

She wished she hadn't known.

MEG AND Jo went with the men to the train station to say their good-byes. After an awkward carriage ride, during which Meg and Brooke held hands and Jo and Laurie looked everywhere but at each other, the men bought their tickets for their departure. They were on the same eastbound express, headed to Boston.

Laurie cleared his throat and announced the train would be there in less than five minutes.

This sent Meg into paroxysms of despair. "Oh, darling!" she said. "I will miss you so!"

John held his bride tightly and urgently whispered declarations of love in her ear.

Jo and Laurie stood apart, embarrassed by Meg's tears. Jo was uncomfortably aware of a fifth presence at the train station, one who was visible to both even though she was absent: the figure of Harriet. Laurie's bride-to-be.

She could picture Lady Hat now, flouncing across Boston to pick out her wedding clothes. Probably the finest silks, the tiniest embroidery. Or perhaps she'd ordered her clothes from France, from the House of Worth. She could afford every luxury in the world. Between the Carmichael-Carlthorpes and the Laurences, there would be no expense spared. Unlike Meg, who would have to scrimp and save and make do with everything.

How could he think the bosoms would make him happy? Not *her* Theodore Laurence. Not ever.

But then again, he wasn't *her* Theodore Laurence. If he could profess his love for Jo and propose to Lady Hat all within the space of a season, then it was likely Jo really didn't know Theodore Laurence at all.

Meg was weeping openly now, but Jo had little patience for her sister's displays at the moment. "Ugh," she said. "I'll be glad when they finally get married so all this nonsense will stop."

"That's Jo, ever the romantic." Laurie chuckled.

"And once they're married, he will take her away," said Jo. "Everyone is leaving."

"It can't be helped," said Laurie. "You must think of their happiness and not yours. That's just how it is, I suppose."

Jo felt something within her wither. "And will you think of me, scribbling away in my attic, while you and Harriet spend your fortunes?"

Laurie smiled sadly. "I'll always think of you as a different sort of fortune, old friend. And I'll treasure our friendship, no matter how far away I go."

"But not enough to come back."

Laurie's mouth opened, then closed again. "I will be glad to meet you anywhere you go. You know that. We shall see each other in the West End, won't we? You with your play and me with . . ." His words dwindled into silence.

With a wife in tow. A wife of money and position who would keep him in England after Jo left. Their friendship would never be the same. They both knew the truth of that.

She'd refused Laurie on the grounds that she was not fashionable enough to be his wife, that his friends would laugh at her and feel embarrassed for him. But she had never considered the opposite—that if Laurie chose a more fashionable wife, the wife would always stand between them, casting a very long shadow on their friendship.

Or ending it.

Laurie! Engaged! It was ludicrous, and she was angry, except she didn't know what or why she was angry, only that she wished . . . oh, she did not know what she wished.

The conductor was calling for passengers. Laurie squeezed Jo's hand and climbed aboard. Brooke kissed Meg's hand once, quickly but with feeling, then climbed aboard after him.

The train began to pull away. Meg clutched her sister's arm and said, "Oh, Jo, what will I do these few weeks without him?"

Jo felt the weight of her sister's arm. "He isn't going for long, Meg. He'll be back by Christmas, and you'll be married."

"Soon," Meg said. The train was pulling out of the station, taking Laurie and Brooke with it. "But not soon enough."

Meg really was weeping now. Jo was horrified to feel a tear tremble in the corner of her own eye.

I will not weep, she thought. *I will not I will not I will NOT.*

I had my chance.

Laurie asked me first.

He loved me first.

But I let him go, and I don't deserve him.

I didn't want him then, and I don't want him now.

Not now. Not ever.

But Jo, of all people, knew a story when she heard one. Especially when the ending had been gotten so wrong.

28

MAKING PLANS

*A*s Amy's health continued to improve, the Marches were able to turn their attentions to something more pleasant: the preparations for Meg and Brooke's wedding.

Thanksgiving was a small affair, with the Laurences away, but there was much to be grateful for, not the least that Amy's smiling face with her oft-agonized "pug nose" was still among them.

"Still with the laundry-clip?" asked Jo as she passed around the platter of carved turkey and the boat of cranberry sauce.

"It will straighten, I swear, and since you already put it in your book anyway, I might as well continue to try," said Amy, sounding a little nasal, since her nose was pinched.

Jo threw a roll at her little sister and they all laughed.

"Not all of us are blessed with Roman features," sighed Amy, removing the clip. "Of course Laurie has a perfect nose, and a fortune. Life is never fair."

"No it is not, dearest, and the sooner we understand that, the better our lives will be," said Jo easily, without even wincing at the mention of her old friend.

Now CHRISTMAS WAS only a few weeks away. There was so much to be done, and there were so many reasons to celebrate. Amy's health. A new marriage. And a new engagement between Theodore Laurence and Lady Harriet Carmichael-Carlthorpe, to everyone's apparent satisfaction.

Meg was busy every hour now, working for the Kings during the day and sewing her trousseau by night. All of Meg's salary was going to purchase cloth and thread, new boots and bits of lace. Not to mention pots and pans, dishes and silverware, to set up housekeeping for herself and Brooke. Still, it was not enough. Mama gave Meg a few of her own things to help fill out Meg's trousseau. A few extra blankets, a spare set of kitchen curtains with a small rip in the corner.

Jo helped out, giving her little bit of writing income to buy food for the wedding feast and a gift for Meg of new gloves and a hired carriage to take Meg and Brooke to the church on the day of the wedding. If she'd finished her sequel and been paid, she would have been able to afford something more—a new dress, perhaps. But she had not finished, so she had not been paid. She would not be paid new royalties for her first book until the next year, and the money from the last check was running perilously low.

Their days were returning to normal, or the new rhythms that would approximate normal. Which meant that Jo could, and should, return to her sequel now.

But for no reason she could discern, Jo was more despondent than ever. She chalked it up to melancholy over their father's failure to appear. He had not even sent word that he was coming, that he'd received their letters. Mama had sent a new letter telling him that Amy was out of danger, but that one, too, had received no answer.

Niles had sent Jo several letters during Amy's illness, asking how the novel was coming, but Jo had not answered. There was nothing to say, not when every waking moment had been focused on Amy, on keeping her alive.

Now, though, Jo started to think again about her writing. It was absurd that she had written two versions of the story, neither of which had even come close to approximating what she wanted to say, what she meant to write.

The possibility of losing Amy had been too much to bear. They would have broken under the weight of it, Jo was sure. The loss of poor Beth had been so terrible, it was hard even to think about. To lose another sister, to watch dear Amy suffer and die, Amy who (unlike Beth) had always been strong . . .

To know that any of them, at any time, could be cut down by sickness and death . . .

The only relief was that it hadn't happened.

Jo still had Amy and Meg. She still had Mama and Hannah

and her home. And she must learn to be grateful for all she had. There were others with less, as Mama liked to remind them.

So it didn't matter that Meg would marry and leave home, that Jo could lose her best friend and ruin her career. They still had one another: Meg, Jo, and Amy. They were sisters, and they were still alive, together. It was enough.

THE PROSPECT OF Meg and Brooke's wedding was the one bright spot on an otherwise grim calendar, which seemed to stretch for weeks in either dour, dull direction. Not so for the one day circled in gold and pinned with lace on the calendar page: a Christmas wedding with friends and family, who would come to Orchard House to celebrate with them all.

There was much to do before the date arrived: invitations to write, sewing to finish. Jo worked on the invitations while Meg continued to work on her trousseau: sewing petticoats and day-dresses, linens and tablecloths, any one of a hundred little things a housewife would need for her future life.

The sisters often performed their tasks in Amy's room to keep themselves cheerful. The doctor had insisted she not set one toe out of bed until the cough was gone entirely, so every bit of wedding business became an opportunity for Amy to prove that she was well. She argued with Jo about writing the invitations, with Mama about helping to festoon the house, with Meg about the choices of flowers, as if the arguments themselves were proof of her improving health.

One afternoon, during another such argument, Meg told her there could be no question of roses for the wedding. "It will have to be the dried lavender and hydrangea blossoms, I'm afraid."

"No, no, no. Dried flowers are an abomination at a wedding. Can't you have fresh roses, Meg? A few at least?"

"I'm afraid not, dearest," Meg said with infinite patience. "All of the vines have gone dormant for the winter by now."

"*Christopher Columbus!* I keep forgetting it's already December," Amy declared, throwing a ball of ribbons across the room. "I feel like I've been in this bed for a *year.*"

Jo poked her head in. "Did I hear someone using my favorite expression?"

Meg frowned. "You've really rubbed off on her. In all the worst ways, apparently."

Jo sat down on the edge of the bed and tickled Amy's foot. "Don't listen to her," she said as Amy snatched her foot away. "I think it's perfectly adorable." Then she tweaked Amy's nose, leaving a black smudge of ink behind.

"Now look what you've done!" Meg said. She ran to get a wet cloth to clean Amy's face.

Amy grabbed the little hand-mirror from the bedside table and saw the marks from Jo's fingers all over her dreadful nose. "Look what you did!" she wailed. "You should be more careful."

Jo pinched her nose one more time for good measure. "Or you'll do what?"

"This!" And Amy stuck her finger in her own pot of ink and smudged it across Jo's cheek.

Jo only laughed. It was too much fun to tease her sister again, after so many alarming days. They were almost back to normal, if *normal* meant a constant low-level quarrel.

Meg came back with the cloth and clucked over the two of them as she cleaned them up like the mother hen she would some-day be. "You two are hopeless," she muttered, wiping ink from Jo's cheek. "What if Mama saw you behaving like this?"

"She wouldn't be at all surprised, at least by me," said Jo. "She *knows* I'm hopeless. Only Amy here would shock her."

Amy groaned under the pressure of Meg's cloth. "It's just that I'm so *booooored*. Can't I help with the invitations, at least, Jo? I promise not to get out of bed. I *promise*."

"I believe you," said Jo. "And I'd welcome the help, except your handwriting is atrocious."

"That just proves I need the practice. *Please, please* may I? I have to have something to do before I go mad."

"You're going to drive *me* mad," said Jo.

Jo met Meg's eyes. Her sister wore a *what-harm-could-it-do?* expression, and she shrugged. "If they're terrible, you could always redo them later without too much time lost," Meg said to Jo. "Let her try?"

Jo looked at Amy, who pressed her hands together in supplica-tion. "*Pleeeeease*, Jo?"

"Oh, all right. I suppose it can't hurt."

Jo went and fetched her lap-desk and writing implements, including blotting-paper, a few quills, and her best steel-nib pen, along with a sample invitation she'd finished a few minutes before for Amy to copy. "You practice with this. Take your time and don't be sloppy. I'll be back later to check on your work."

Amy gathered the writing-desk onto her lap and beamed at Jo. "Thank you! I'll do a good job, I promise."

"You'd better. Half your school assignments are illegible. We don't want wedding guests wandering into Walden Pond instead of Orchard House because they can't read your writing!" Jo reached out to tweak Amy's nose again, but the youngest March ducked her head out of the way. "Aha! You *are* feeling better!" Jo exclaimed, fairly skipping to the door.

In truth, she was glad to pawn the invitations off on Amy, even if it meant she had to redo them later. Something else was nagging at the back of her head all of a sudden, whispering ideas at her. *Try this,* it said.

"Where are you going?" Meg asked as Jo disappeared around the corner.

"To the attic," Jo called back over her shoulder. "I have a scene to write."

In fact, it was the cheerful teasing between the sisters that had inspired her, given a bit of juice to an enterprise that even yesterday she'd felt was still out of reach. With Amy taking over her one wedding task, Jo found she had the time and inclination to write a scene for her novel that had appeared, quite suddenly, in her head: the fictional family reunited and preparing a wedding.

What joy it was to write her way into happiness, even if it was fiction! In the first pages of her sequel, she could wave her wand and solve all their problems. The war was over, Father returned, the sisters were safely well and whole. The fictional John Brooke had gone to war, been wounded, and yet returned safely to Meg. *For life and love are very precious,* she wrote, *when both are in full bloom.*

It was like fortune-telling. If she could imagine it in fiction, it could still be real in life.

Selfishly she gave Meg three more years at home with her family before the wedding. She couldn't resist keeping her sister for herself just a little while longer. She had Father return to his ministry and Beth recovered from illness. And Jo—Jo was much the same as she'd ever been, alternately content and frustrated with her lot, because the author did not know what her character's story should be.

Should she go out into the world and come back wiser?

Should she stay, and learn to be content with her lot?

I'll figure it out later, Jo decided at last. Write happiness for the rest of the family. Her heroine she would leave alone for now.

As for Theodore Laurence, she did not write much about him, not at first. She left him away at school, as he was in life. She couldn't bear to think of him, or his very fancy, very suitable fiancée.

Was he making a good decision, one that would lead to everyone's future happiness? Or was it another mistake, one in a long line of rash, stubborn decisions that would lead to tears, cutting himself off from the friends who loved him most?

When it came to telling Laurie's fortune, Jo's crystal ball was blank.

The truth was that the fictional Theodore Laurence was as much a puzzle as the real one. She couldn't stop thinking of his words at their last parting: *I'll always think of you. I'll treasure our friendship, no matter how far away I go.* It left her breathless, on the verge of tears every day, as she composed and then burned letter after letter to him.

Don't go, she wanted to say. *Not so far away. Not where I can't reach you.*

Don't turn your back on life in Concord, not because of me.

You will always be my dearest friend. No wife can change that.

But she didn't know that a wife wouldn't change that. It was entirely possible that she would. Already Jo could glimpse the future Meg, the mother and wife, busy and bustling and content with her small lot. They would be sisters always, but things between them would change when Meg was not in the next room. She would have her own house, with her own husband and children, and keep her own counsel more and more. The secrets and stories the two of them shared now so easily would be different. Neither Meg nor Jo would mean to change, but the change was there, lurking just offstage, ready to make its presence felt.

If she could sense such a change coming between herself and Meg, how much more distance would there be between herself and Laurie? Not only the ocean between them but a wife. A fortune. An entire life lived apart.

Even if they didn't mean for their friendship to change, it would. It would without anyone trying to change it at all.

So she did not write much about Laurie, or about herself.

For Meg and Brooke, Mama and Father, Amy and Beth, she wrote every happiness.

She would give this to her sisters: the promise of a future as beautiful and bright as they were.

As they had every right to hope for, even if Jo did not.

29

AN ENGAGEMENT PARTY

*A*s it happened, Laurie wrote to Jo first, requesting her presence at a gathering of friends and family in Boston "to celebrate our engagement," he wrote. Himself and Harriet, he meant, and a small part of Jo mourned, remembering when the word "our" would have included her.

By then Amy was out of bed and puttering around the house more and more, helping Mama with her own small chores and beginning her lessons again. She'd done such a good job with the invitations that Jo gave her high marks for penmanship, something she'd never done before. So Jo's presence was not as needed at home as it had been of late, but still she hesitated, not certain if she *wanted* to go.

If she *should*. Could she bear it?

Mama, who seemed always to understand Jo better than Jo understood herself, took the letter from Jo's hands and looked at

Laurie's handwriting. *It would mean so much if you were there, Mr. Snodgrass,* she read.

She gave Jo back the letter and said, "You should go. You will never forgive yourself if you don't."

"But I don't much like Harriet. Mama, you should have heard her in New York. The snobbery was thick as molasses."

"You like Laurie," Mama said. "He's your friend. And you might not get many more opportunities to see him, if they do plan on living in England."

Jo made a noise of frustration and sank down on the sofa. *"Fine.* But I'm only doing this for his sake."

Mama turned to Meg, who was practically squirming while she braided Amy's hair. "What about you? I'm sure you'd see John while you were there, as he is sure to be invited as well. And your sister will need a traveling companion."

"Oh, Mama, may I?" Meg asked.

"Of course you may. Send word to Laurie as soon as you can, and Hannah and I will get your trunks."

A FEW DAYS later, the two sisters made the short trip by train to Boston, where Laurie and Brooke met them at the station in the Laurences' carriage. Jo had been nearly certain Harriet would be with them, though she was not. "You'll see her later," Laurie said. "Right now I'm glad it's the four of us together, just like we were in New York."

Jo was surprised but relieved. A few minutes without Lady Hat would be like old times—not just New York, but all the times they were together in Concord at picnics, in ponds. In the attic garret of Orchard House, playing out their small dramas on a home-made stage.

All at once the time stretched and telescoped. They weren't children anymore. They were adults, or nearly so. Everything would change. They would never again be as they were right now: four young people who knew each other's secrets. Who knew each other so well, they could finish each other's sentences.

But while Jo was afraid she might weep, Meg was so thrilled to be reunited with Brooke that she threw her arms around his neck in full view of everyone at the station, forgetting propriety completely.

"I'm glad to see you, too, my love." Brooke gently extricated himself from Meg's embrace while Laurie and Jo laughed.

Meg turned pink and straightened out her dress. All around them, people were staring.

"Get ahold of yourself, Meg," said Jo. "I thought *I* was the im-proper one in the family. We can't *all* be scandalous, now, can we?"

Laurie was nearly doubled over with laughter. "That's a sight I'll never forget," he said. "But love makes fools of all of us, I sup-pose. Should we head home before we're all arrested?"

"Good idea," said Jo, and they all piled into the carriage.

She was gratified to see her sister and Brooke reunited, but Jo had to admit to herself, as they drove through the pouring rain, that this visit was not something she was relishing. To meet Lady Hat again—to watch her preen and fuss over Laurie, to claim him, to fold him into her family like just another of her wealthy possessions—would be one of the hardest things she'd ever had to witness.

But she was here for Laurie, because he *was* her dearest friend, and would always be. For the sake of their friendship, which she had not given up on yet.

Meg kept her arm in Brooke's all through the ride and said very little. Brooke was quiet, as always, but Jo and Laurie chatted about any number of things: Amy's improving health. Laurie's classes, which he was still neglecting, to his peril. Harriet's mother inviting most of the Manhattan social register to the wedding.

"What about your sequel?" he asked Jo. "Have you given it up for good? When we were in Concord, you seemed to hint that you had."

Jo looked at Meg and Brooke, her sister's hand curled around Brooke's upper arm. "I might have started working on it again."

"Oh?" Laurie asked. "What scenes have you written?"

"Preparations for a wedding," she said, and gave Meg a wicked grin. "Oh, don't worry, it's all in excellent taste, I promise."

"And me?" Laurie asked. "Am I in this one?"

"I haven't decided yet. Perhaps I shall make you turn pirate."

Brooke smiled at them both. "What makes you think he isn't one already?"

They all had a good laugh, but for Jo it was still tinged with sadness. Everything was ending; she could feel it. Soon, Meg would move from Orchard House into a home of her own. But at least the newlyweds had decided to stay in Concord. Brooke would move to their little hamlet for good, giving up his pupils in Boston.

When they pulled up in front of the house, Mr. Laurence himself came to the door to greet them, holding out an umbrella so the girls could dash into the house. "My dear girls, welcome to Boston!"

"Hello!" cried Meg, while Jo said, "We thought you were leaving for London on the last boat. Have you decided to stay the winter?"

"I have, to help with the wedding planning," he said, ushering them inside. "We will all journey over together next year, when the weather breaks."

"Thank you so much for having us," said Meg, gently taking the old man's hand. "You're always too kind!"

"It wouldn't be a proper engagement party without some Marches," said Mr. Laurence. "The two of you are a welcome reminder of home."

For just a minute, under the umbrella, Jo met Laurie's eyes, and she felt the current between them that was always there, even if it was slightly removed for once.

It was clear Laurie was happy. He was content, and he was back to being her friend again instead of a jilted lover. After the terrible disagreement they'd had at the end of their New York trip, and later her painful refusal of his offer of marriage, she was relieved to find that he had regained his sense of humor. He was able to be kind, because he had found his bride, even if it wasn't her.

She was determined to be happy for him.

She *would*.

TWO NIGHTS LATER, the Laurence house was a splendor. Though never as grand as the Carmichaels' Manhattan manse, it was still a large, well-built brick house with fine drawing-rooms and dining-rooms filled with the creamy light of hundreds of candles, the smell of beef and lobster, the tang of good French wine.

Upstairs, the March girls were helping each other dress for the party—Meg in one of her pretty silks, Jo in one of Meg's old plaid dresses. "Like you're ready for the hunt," Laurie said when he saw her. "A Scottish lass in the heather." And he kissed her once on the cheek, warmly.

As he would a sister, Jo thought. She tried to think nothing else about it, but the warmth of his lips had left her fizzing, if only for a moment.

Downstairs, they were still setting candles and flowers around the room when there was a noise at the door, a clattering of umbrellas, shoes, and door hinges.

"Oh, you *wicked, wicked* girls!" Harriet exclaimed, practically flying at them. "Why did you not come to me immediately on arriving in Boston? I can't believe Laurie and Brooke have been hoarding you for two days already. I only *just* learned of your arrival."

Harriet and her mother were staying at a hotel, as was proper.

After the engagement party in Boston, they would journey with the Laurences to New York for another engagement party there.

Jo and Meg rose to their feet, alarmed at the cacophony of colors and noise that Harriet brought wherever she went. "Hello, Lady Harriet—" Jo began, but Harriet rushed on, "Mother and I were so *desolate* that you didn't come to see us right away. I *told* you, you must come to see me whenever you come to Boston."

She had never said any such thing, especially since she usually lived in New York, but Meg only said, "It's good to see you again, Lady Harriet."

"Please, call me Hat. We're practically family," she said.

"Yes, of course," said Meg. "It's good to see you . . . Hat."

Harriet was being entirely disingenuous. All this nonsense about practically being family, when a month ago Harriet had been envious of Meg to the point of turning green! *What rot.* Jo couldn't help needling her, and by extension Laurie, just a bit. "I'm afraid we're not in the *uppertens*," she said. "I hope that's all right."

"Oh, of course!" she gushed. "Mother might object, but I never would. A woman of the people, that's me."

Jo met Laurie's eyes. He looked amused, and at Harriet's expense, since a Carmichael-Carlthorpe never was and never would be *a woman of the people.* Jo was reminded yet again that it was unlikely they'd see much of each other after this, and so she only had to endure Harriet's snobbery for a few days. For Laurie, she would remember her manners.

"Very republican of you," said Laurie.

Jo grinned. "Yes, the manners of the country must be rubbing off on you. Next thing you know, you'll be swimming in mud-holes like we used to."

"Laurie!" said Lady Hat. "You swam in mud-holes? With Miss March?"

"In my defense, it was very hot that day."

"Scandal!" said Harriet, and took him by the arm. "I suppose I will have to civilize you, after all."

"If you can," Brooke said. "I found that prospect rather difficult myself. Some people resist all efforts at civilizing."

"Perhaps you should have tried harder." Harriet looked over Brooke coolly. Apparently there *were* still hard feelings, at least on Harriet's side. Meg either didn't notice or didn't care.

Then Harriet and her mother moved closer to the fire to get warm, and Jo leaned over to Laurie to whisper, "Who will be civilizing whom, I wonder?"

"Jo. Behave yourself."

"I always do, Teddy. I'm not sure your fiancée realizes that. We *lower classes* do have *some* manners, after all."

"Please, Jo. If you just tried to get to know her, I'm sure you'd find she's not . . . half-bad."

"Such high praise. No wonder you want to marry her. Or was it her . . . other attributes that attracted you?"

"Other attributes? Mainly that she wasn't you?"

"Of course she isn't me. Teddy, you're better off without me. Surely now even you realize it."

"I do, Jo. You were right. We've both found where we belong." He turned and looked at Harriet, who gave him a sly, private smile.

We have, thought Jo. *Finally, we both have.*

Even if it was not a place anyone would have expected.

The guests arrived, and Laurie and Harriet greeted them with grace and enthusiasm. As the party went on, the guests laughed and danced and drank toasts to Laurie and Harriet. In the midst of them all, Jo smiled and laughed and danced with her best friend as if it were for the last time. Perhaps it would be.

Tomorrow they would return home. Meg and Brooke would soon be married. And Jo would have her books, her writing, her family.

It was all she ever wanted. That would be enough.

It would have to be.

30

An Unexpected Guest

*B*ack at Orchard House a few days later, Meg had removed her silk gown and put on a different one. She turned around and around in the silver House of Worth dress, trying to see the back for herself. "Bother!" she exclaimed. "I can't get a good look at it."

Jo fetched a second hand-mirror from her own room and gave it to Meg. With one mirror in front and one behind, Meg was able, finally, to glimpse the back side of the most expensive, lavish garment that any March had ever owned and decide for herself if it was the one she'd wear to her wedding.

Several long seconds passed while Meg stared critically at her own reflection. "I don't know, Jo," she groaned. "I just don't feel comfortable being married in your dress."

Jo stamped her foot. "For the last time, it's not *my* dress!"

Once more, Jo thought how silly all this wedding business was. What difference did it make what dress she wore? Meg was beautiful in everything.

"But Laurie had it made especially for you. It's . . . personal."

"You didn't think so when you wore it to the opera in Manhattan."

"That was different. I wasn't getting married at the opera. It's bad luck to be married in another woman's dress!"

"Ugh." Jo flung herself down on the bed. "It's not another woman's. It's *yours*. I gave it to you."

"And Laurie gave it to *you*."

"I've never even worn it. I'm sure I never shall," she said. "My opera-going days are over, I'm afraid."

"Don't say that. You don't know what might happen yet."

"With you married and Laurie in England, how on earth would I manage to go to the opera? No," she said, "it's yours."

"Jo . . ."

"Be reasonable, Meg. You don't want to spend the little bit of money you've saved on a new dress when you already own the perfect dress. Even Sallie Gardiner did not have a wedding dress as fine as this one. You'll be the envy of every girl in Concord."

Meg gave a great sigh. She was still not convinced. It was true that when her friend Sallie had married Ned Moffat a week before, she had worn a very lovely but very local dress. Not this Parisian confection.

Jo said, "If you don't wear it, it will only sit around collecting dust until Amy is old enough to wear it. It will get old and brittle, and possibly fall out of fashion. Why shouldn't you wear it now? Be sensible."

In the little hand-mirror, Jo could see Meg's face break into a small smile. She *wanted* to wear the dress. But first Jo had to convince her.

Just then, through the crack of the door, Mama caught sight of them both. She put a hand to her mouth. "Oh, Meg," she said. "I only wish your father were here to see you."

Because of course they still had not heard from Father. No one wanted to say what they were all thinking: that if Father had not come to them during Amy's illness, and no one had heard from him since, it was likely that something dreadful had happened. He might have been seriously injured, delirious in some faraway hospital.

Or worse—he might already be dead.

So Mama's mention of him had them all in tears. Why was it, Jo wondered, that new beginnings were always so inextricably tied up with endings? Couldn't they have the joy and celebrating without the sense of impending loss?

Her sister.

Laurie.

It was all changing. From a vase by the window, she broke a small branch of primrose and tucked it into Meg's hair. The white buds were like pearls against Meg's dark hair, the only pearls they could afford.

Tomorrow she would be a bride, and not Jo's sister any longer. Or not *only* Jo's sister. A wife and someday, probably, a mother.

She looked at her sister in the Parisian finery. *Don't leave me,* she wanted to cry. *Don't leave me alone, Meg. I can't face the future without you.*

She had to, though. There was no other alternative.

After the wedding, Meg would leave Orchard House forever.

THE DINNER THE night before the wedding was a small affair, as the wedding itself would be the next day. As Brooke's former employer, Mr. Laurence had invited the Marches, Mr. Brooke, and a few of their friends to his house in Concord for a chance to toast the newlyweds in private.

Both the Laurences were there—*no, three Laurences*. Lady Hat, another bride-to-be, would be a Laurence by next summer. And Kate and Fred Vaughn, who had traveled from Boston with Laurie and Harriet. The four March women, plus Hannah, walked across the lane while Sallie Moffat, née Gardiner, brought her own new husband, Ned. And of course Mr. Brooke was there in a new suit of brown wool, looking a bit hot and uncomfortable at all the attention, in Jo's opinion.

Sallie gushed over Meg and whispered things that made Meg's face go scarlet. It seemed to Jo that everyone in the world had been given a partner except her.

You could have had one if you'd wanted one.

There was nothing to be done. The decision made, the choice irrevocable. Meg would wed Brooke in the morning. In the summer, Harriet and Laurie would leave America for England. If Jo had second thoughts about any of it, it was already much too late. Besides, she still hadn't finished her sequel, and had missed the Thanksgiving deadline.

As he had in Boston, Mr. Laurence met the Marches at the door to welcome them. Always a gracious host, he had included Hannah as a part of the family. ("Mercy, I would be afraid t' enter tha' house!" she declared when the invitation arrived.) Still, she had put on her Sunday best and gone timidly with the Marches across the lane, trying to hide behind Amy to escape notice.

It didn't work—Lady Hat looked shocked for a moment when she realized the Marches' servant was coming inside, too. But after a second she rearranged her face and was as gracious as anyone else.

They met in the drawing-room and chatted amiably until the servants called them in for dinner. Harriet sat on one side of Mr. Laurence and Laurie on the other, while Brooke sat at the other end of the table, Meg on his left side. Between the two poles of the dinner-table were gathered everyone in this world that Meg held dear, except Father. Except for Beth and Father, there was nothing more in the world she could ask for.

It was Laurie, at Jo's urging, who began the speeches. He stood and tapped his glass with his butter knife, drawing the room to attention. "Thank you all for coming," he said. "As you know, I am very fond of old Brooke here, though I have done as much as I can to avoid admitting so publicly. I am very fond of the Marches as well, and can find no better occasion to say so."

"Hear, hear!" said Mr. Laurence, and there were nods and murmurs of agreement all around.

Laurie went on. "I am pleased that my fondness has been so well placed, and that these two will finally stop torturing one another and all of us by declaring their love before the law."

A few laughs. Meg looked mortified; Jo guffawed.

"But as you also know, I am not a wordsmith. Because we do have a wordsmith among us this evening, I believe she should begin the toasts. Jo, will you say a few words on our behalf to the happy couple?"

Laurie's eyes were twinkling; he was teasing her. But putting her on the spot like this, in front of everyone—unforgivable! How *dare* he?

On the page, Jo could be witty, thoughtful, romantic. And if not, she could always revise and start over. In person, though, she was lucky to string two words together properly—and Laurie knew it.

The guests were tapping their goblets for Jo. She rose reluctantly to her feet, staring daggers at Laurie. *I'll get you for this, Theodore Laurence.*

She coughed. "Yes. All right. Let me think."

They were all watching. Finally she cleared her throat. "I won't say she 'walks in beauty, like the night,'" Jo said, "because I've seen Meg first thing in the morning, Brooke. It's not a pretty picture."

"Jo!" That was Mama, chiding.

Laughter all around the table. But they were among friends, and no one would hold Jo's impertinence against her here. Except perhaps Harriet, and Jo didn't care a whit what Harriet thought.

She went on. "I *will* say that you could not ask for a better bride."

Smiles now. She was winning them over.

"As Mr. Bennet said of Lizzy, I cannot believe that anyone

would be deserving of our Meg, but we could not part with her to anyone less worthy than you, Mr. Brooke."

She picked up her glass. The friends around the table did the same. "To the happy"—then a sudden noise, someone knocking at the front door—"couple."

The room fell silent.

Mr. Laurence and Laurie looked at each other, around the table. No one else was expected, surely? Jo couldn't imagine who could be coming over at such an hour, on such a night.

Voices in the hall. The servants, talking to the unexpected visitor. The visitor answering.

No one had the slightest clue who it could be.

In a moment the servant appeared, and behind him, a figure in a blue greatcoat, his head and beard gray. "I'm so sorry to interrupt—" he began, and was then himself interrupted.

"Father!"

"It's Father!"

The March women were up out of their chairs then, racing around the table to fling themselves at a shocked and laughing Mr. March.

Father had come home.

"You made it!" Jo exclaimed, her eyes wet with tears.

"In the nick of time, it seems," he said, and embraced them all.

31

⮜ഽ◯ ◯ഽ⮞

None but the Lonely Heart

Father hadn't known that the wedding was to take place the next day. In fact, he hadn't known about the wedding at all. It was only blind luck that he'd arrived at home after nearly a month of traveling, through all kinds of trials and dangers.

They settled him into a chair while the servants fetched him a good glass of brandy at Mr. Laurence's request. He sat down gratefully, exclaiming over all of them, wet with their tears. Jo sat on one side of him and Meg on the other, while Amy sat on the floor at his feet, each of his girls clamoring to be near him.

When he could speak, he told them all he'd experienced recently, how, after receiving Mama's letter, he had decided to come home during Amy's illness. He'd written a letter to tell the family he was coming, that Amy should think of her father in her difficulty, that he would be home as soon as possible.

"We never got the letter," Meg said.

"Hang the postal service!" said Jo.

"I can imagine you thought the worst had happened," he said.

"I was afraid of the same." And he cupped Amy's face in his big hands. "I can't tell you how glad I am to see that was not the case."

"So are we, Father," Amy said, and hugged his legs.

Little by little the story came out, how Father had left his position in Mississippi in mid-November, on foot, for what he'd heard was the nearest rail station that would take him to Washington, and from there he could go by rail up to Boston. But he'd been caught in some terrible weather, shrieking winds and rainstorms that went on for two days. The roads became impassable because of mud and fallen trees from the storm, so Father was forced to walk to Oxford, all the while afraid he would arrive home too late to see Amy one more time.

It was weeks before he arrived in Washington, dirty and hungry, but he kept going north as fast as he could, taking train to train to train, until he reached Boston and finally Concord, more than a month after receiving Mama's letter.

"Christopher Columbus!" Jo declared on hearing all he had endured. "It's a wonder you made it home at all."

"It is," said Father, pressing Mama's hand to his heart. "I'm like Ulysses, coming home to Ithaca. But with a much happier outcome. I'm so glad I'll be able to be here to see you wed, Meg." To Brooke he said, "I couldn't have chosen a finer young man for her myself."

"Hear, hear!" said Mr. Laurence. They all toasted the happy couple again, this time with the entire family present.

Jo met Laurie's eyes. How happy she was! It was possible she had never been happier and never would be again.

All evening, Jo watched her mother and father. Their heads

together, whispering hellos. The tears in not just her mother's eyes, but her father's as well. It was clear how happy they both were to be reunited.

She would never understand their marriage.

When Jo came around a corner unexpectedly into the cloakroom, she found them embracing, her mother's arms around her father's neck. Her mother weeping while her father whispered into his wife's ear in a soothing tone. Stroking her head. "It's all right now, my love," he whispered. "Everything will be all right."

Jo backed out of the room quickly, so as to not be noticed. She wasn't embarrassed, exactly—her parents had always been very affectionate with each other, at least when they were in the same town. But she was surprised. Mama was always so cool and collected, so unruffled by everything life threw at her.

With their father, Mama Abba was different.

To be fair, life had thrown quite a lot at her recently. Amy's illness. Meg's wedding. And the fear about what had kept Father from contacting them all those weeks. She had been shouldering quite a lot of worry. Now that Father was back, she was unburdening herself to him. Letting him comfort her as perhaps no one else could.

Because, as Jo was just realizing, that was what marriage was. The shouldering of each other's burdens. The knowledge that you weren't alone in the world with your cares, your fears. Your joys.

That was what Mama and Father shared, in whatever way they could, when they could. Whether or not anyone else could make sense of it.

Meg and Brooke, too—she could see it in their faces. Perhaps not everything, not yet. But that kind of understanding would come surely enough after the wedding. A home and children, a family, would bring them as close as Mother and Father were, in their own peculiar way.

Jo could see it in the way they tipped their heads together, the way they looked at each other with perfect understanding. Meg had chosen well for herself. The future Mrs. Brooke would be happy indeed—perhaps not the mother of twins, as Jo had written in her book, but a mother, surely.

Her children would love her every bit as much as Meg, Jo, and Amy loved Mama. Their "Marmee" in fiction and their beloved mother forever.

"Hullo, Cousin Jo." It was Laurie, coming up with a very full cup of punch to hand to her. "Shall we have some music, and dancing? I can't think of a better time for it."

She took the cup and instantly managed to spill some on her dress, as usual. "Are you going to be the one to play?"

"Of course. Do you have any requests for me?"

"Play Tchaikovsky's 'None but the Lonely Heart.' For old times' sake."

"For you, Jo? Anything."

Across the room, Harriet was watching them. Mr. and Mrs. March. John Brooke and Meg March. And Jo and Laurie, whispering with their heads together. She'd been watching them all

night, through the meal, the toasts, the excitement of the unexpected guest.

Laurie could feel her still watching as he sat down at the piano.
"Shall we have some dancing?" he asked, and began to play "None
but the Lonely Heart," as requested.

Meg laughed as Brooke twirled her around. Sallie and her
new husband joined them. Fred Vaughn bowed to Jo, and the two
of them joined the other couples. Laurie frowned to see it. Fred
leaned down and whispered something to Jo, who turned positively scarlet, and laughed at whatever it was Fred had said.

Fred Vaughn and Jo! Laurie nearly stood up and put a stop to the
whole thing right then and there. Not his dearest friend Jo March for
the fickle, bullheaded Fred, who courted girls by the dozens. Even
now, his previous conquest, Amelia Perkins, was crying into her pillow back on Beacon Hill. Lord only knew how many others there
were, scattered around Boston and Cambridge and even London.

But now here was Fred turning Jo around and around in a
dance. His hand on the small of her back, his other hand clasp-
ing Jo's own. For a moment Laurie could picture Fred bending his
head over Jo's white throat, kissing her neck . . .

Plunk went the song. Everyone turned and looked. Laurie
turned back to his music, keeping his eyes on his own hands.

There was no point in envy. Jo had refused him, hadn't she?
Once and for all.

Harriet, who had no partner since Laurie was playing, came
over to stand beside the piano, watching the dancers. "Penny for
your thoughts," she said.

"Oh, well," he said. "Just seeing how well everyone looks. How everything has worked out for the best."

"Truly, Laurie?"

She was by far the most elegant woman in the room, but Laurie couldn't help noting how unhappy she looked. "What's the matter, old Hat?" said Laurie. "You seem oddly glum. That's not like you."

She was watching Brooke and Meg as much as Laurie was watching Fred and Jo. "Funny, I thought it wouldn't bother me," she said. "I never expected to lose him to Meg. But they seem well suited to each other."

"Luckily you have gained such a splendid conquest in me."

Harriet sat next to him on the piano bench. Laurie made room for her. "Have I? I wonder."

Laurie still played, but he glanced over at her. "Is something the matter?"

Harriet joined in and turned the song into a pretty little duet, she playing the lower end and he the upper. "I don't know. Maybe it's seeing you here, at home in Concord. I feel like I don't belong."

She did not belong in the slightest, but Laurie would never have hurt her by saying so. She was entirely an outsider here, with the Marches and the Moffats and all the country folk. Only Laurie's and Grandfather's affection for her had brought her into this circle. But that's the way it always went—you met one acquaintance through another, and your circle widened.

"You belong because I belong. You belong to me, and I to you."

She made a little noise in the back of her throat. "That's just it, though. I don't think I do belong to you. Not really. Not like Jo does. All the Marches, really. But especially Jo."

Laurie's hands stilled, faltering a bit over the piano keys, while Harriet's kept going. The dancers were looking their way—Jo and Fred, Brooke and Meg—with curiosity. They'd noticed the change in the tune.

He was getting the distinct impression Harriet was trying to tell him something. But not here, where everyone could hear them. Alone.

When the song was over and the dancers clapped their appreciation, Harriet got up and quietly excused herself to go outside for a little fresh air. Laurie followed her.

When they were quite sure they were alone, she said, "Let's not make this a big scene, Laurie. Please."

He took her by the elbow. "What are you saying, Hat? That you don't want to marry me after all?"

"I think—no. No, I don't want to marry you after all." She threw up her hands. "Well, there it is, I suppose."

Laurie could hardly believe what he was hearing. "But you seemed so pleased when I asked you! I don't understand it. What has changed your mind?"

She smiled, but there was sadness in it. He could not ever remember a time when she had looked so serious, or spoken to him in such earnestness. She clearly meant every word. "I care for you a great deal. You know that. But it isn't love, not really. Not like Meg and Brooke."

"Meg and Brooke? That's why you're breaking our engagement?" he asked.

"I don't know. I thought maybe he would still change his mind about Meg. I thought—well, it doesn't matter. I was wrong, wasn't I? They're so *happy*."

It was beginning to dawn on Laurie what she was saying.

That she had loved Brooke, not Laurie. That she had accepted him only because her first choice had been denied. Because when you couldn't have what your heart most desired, what did it matter? After that, everyone else was just another *someone* to try to love.

Another wrong someone.

On that score, they were alike. *Exactly* alike, Laurie had to admit.

"Oh, Hat. I didn't realize."

"It's fine," she said. "I didn't realize it myself until tonight. Not the whole of it. I thought I was just jealous that he didn't love me in return, and that it would pass in time. But I think, perhaps, it was rather more than that."

"Oh."

"It's better we find out now, isn't it? Before we do anything irreversible. Besides," Harriet said, "I saw the way you looked at Jo just now. You still love her. You may not want to love her any more than I want to love Brooke, but you do. You can't help it."

Laurie's head was swirling. "But Jo refused me."

"It doesn't matter. I won't marry someone who's in love with another person. And neither should you. It's . . . small. And ugly.

And I think, despite all our faults, we are not yet that." She gazed at him wistfully. "One hopes."

Laurie sank down onto a bench. "We're finished, then." It was not a question.

"Positively wrecked." Harriet sat down beside him. "But we'll be all right. Our kind usually are."

"Where will you go?"

"Back to New York with Fred and Kate, I suppose," she said. "Fred Vaughn must have declared he was in love with me ten or fifteen times at the Perkinses' dinner."

"Did he?" This news should have bothered him, Laurie realized. But it didn't.

"I've never lacked for suitors. If it's not Fred Vaughn, it will be someone else." She shrugged. "Probably someone my mother picks. You know . . . steel, oil, coal, finance . . . the odd lesser lord." She laughed, sounding a bit more like herself again, if only for a moment. "What about you? You'll be all right?"

"I think so." Then, "Yes." Laurie took the hand of his former betrothed and kissed it.

She looked at him fondly, then nodded and drew a deep breath. "It's best if I leave first thing in the morning. You'll tell your grandfather for me?"

"Of course."

"I'm so sorry, Laurie. In a little while you'll see it's for the best." With that, Harriet got up and disappeared into the house.

Laurie cradled his head in his hands and sat watching the dark street, the windows still lit up behind him, their guests still murmuring, laughing. Grandfather would be disappointed, but Laurie was not. He felt instead strangely resigned, as he supposed a condemned man on a pirate ship must feel walking the plank.

You may not want to love her any more than I want to love Brooke, but you do.

You can't help it.

Was Harriet right?

He was still thinking about it when, not long after, the Marches emerged out the front door, leaving to return home. Mr. and Mrs. March. Meg and Jo. Amy and Hannah. Calling back their thanks to Grandfather for the hospitality.

As Laurie watched them cross the lane, the March women crowded around their husband and father, now restored. Content now that they were all together once more.

They would meet again at noon for the wedding, minus one.

By then, Harriet would be gone.

As Laurie watched them go, he felt the same wistful pull at his heart that he'd come to expect whenever he saw the March sisters together with their mother. A feeling of longing and belonging, all tied up together at once, in a way that somehow contradicted and completed itself. It didn't seem real or even possible, but there it was, every time he saw the Marches.

What is it, the word for that?

But as soon as he wondered, he knew.

Home.

32

THE HOUR OF GETHSEMANE

*P*erhaps it was the return of Father, or perhaps it was the sight of Laurie following Harriet out onto the porch in the darkness. Whatever it was, Jo was awake all night.

She lay down and tried to sleep, but sleep wouldn't come. Her mind would not stop moving—over the things she'd seen and felt. Over the thought of her sister's marriage, and her parents'. Laurie and Harriet. What it meant to be part of a family—not just a family that one was born into, but a family that one made for oneself. The people you loved and stood by, no matter what difficulties came your way.

Jo felt she understood it, even felt it now. She'd glimpsed the heart of things, the *why* behind every action, every decision.

The world opened itself up to her, and by extension, so did her book.

She went upstairs to the attic and lit the candles. She wrote all night, the words feverish in her mind.

There were the twins for Meg and Brooke, and Europe for a grown-up Amy, who went with fictional Aunt March to study painting. Father was home from war.

She sent herself away to New York to get away from Laurie's increasing attentions, where she was governess to two little girls who lived in a boarding house.

And Laurie—Laurie proposed to Jo, and Jo refused.

The scene wrenched at her as nothing else in her life had done. The Jo of her novel was not any different from the real Jo. Temperamental. Obstinate, even reckless. And afraid. Afraid to give herself over to a man, any man, body and soul.

Afraid of change. Afraid of making the wrong choice. Because in life, there were no revisions.

In a heartbroken fog, she sent Laurie to Europe, where he met Amy and Aunt March on their travels. She wrote that Amy became a fine lady, admired by society and with her choice of half a dozen suitors, including Fred Vaughn.

Jo laughed to herself when she wrote it. Amy would like this part of the sequel very much. All those art lessons had to be put to use somewhere.

But there had to be sadness, too. No life was ever untouched by tragedy. And so, like she had in real life, the Beth who had survived scarlet fever weakened, and eventually died.

Then Jo felt it utterly.

She wept when she wrote it. They had lost Beth. There would be no future for her in fiction, as there had been none in life. There was no pretending any more that a fictional future could make up for the real one. And the loss was as hard on the page as it had been in Jo's own life. A devastation. In its wake they had all been raw, and would be ever after.

When it came to Bethie, Jo could not write her way to someplace better, only more truthful. Not a castle in the air, but a castle on the earth, a gravestone to mark where she once had been.

It was the hardest thing she had ever done, and when she finished the scene, she was exhausted.

But she had to finish.

There must still be an end for Jo and Laurie.

She thought of all the readers who had written to ask her what happened to them. They must marry, these readers had said to her. And her own response—"I won't marry Jo to Laurie for anything!"

They must marry, but not to each other.

So Laurie married Amy, the fine lady. In grief over the news of Beth's death, they comforted each other. They came home to surprise Jo and Meg, Father and Marmee, already husband and wife. This contented everyone, for Amy was the kind of lady Jo could never be. Laurie belonged to the Marches, as he had wanted. And Jo—Jo belonged to no one but herself. On the page, as in life, she was alone, but free.

Jo wrote in a frenzy. It was a rough draft, and whole swaths were only just sketched out, but it was all there—the family in joy and sadness, broken but remade. Everyone's fate met her sense of satisfaction.

Outside, the sun was coming up, but Jo was still writing furiously. Her heroine ended the story as she began: temperamental and alone. Jo had promised her readers an end to the story, even if it was not the end they demanded. But no one could force her into a marriage. *No one.* Not even she herself.

The house was still asleep when Jo put on her coat to cross the lane to the Laurences' house. It was snowing softly, the air thick with flakes and silence. Her feet made soft swishing noises as she broke a path through the whiteness.

She would not wake the servants, or Mr. Laurence or Harriet. No one else needed to see her at that hour. She threw a pebble instead at Laurie's window, then another, to entice him to come.

A third pebble finally brought Laurie to the window. He threw up the sash and stuck his head out. His hair stuck up in every direction, his eyes still heavy with sleep. "Jo?"

"Come down, Laurie. I need to speak with you."

She could see the hesitation in his face. Was this some kind of trickery, he was wondering, some game she was playing?

"Teddy, *please.* I need you."

Then he knew she was in earnest. His face changed. "I'll be right down," he said.

In a minute he was coming out the door and meeting her on the porch. He, too, had thrown a coat over his night-clothes. In the morning light, with stubble on his chin, he looked like he had when he was young and would use ink to give himself a beard for the plays they put on in the attic. She wanted alternately to laugh and weep to see it.

"I hope I didn't wake the house," she said by way of apology.

"Not at all. I heard Grandfather snoring when I passed his door."

"And Harriet? Is she still asleep?"

Laurie looked at her with an expression of utter weariness. "What did you want to tell me, Jo? It's very early in the morning."

"I finished the sequel. I . . . wanted to give it to you to read. To see what you think."

He took the sheaf of paper from her. "Now?"

She was hopeful and stubborn and demanding, as always. "Of course now. It's not completely polished and, well, it's missing a lot of the middle . . . but it is done. Are you doing something else?"

He took the pages and began to read. She stood awkwardly nearby—too anxious to sit—watching him as he bent over the page, his brow furrowing. Now and again, he'd break into a smile or even a chuckle, as Jo had done herself.

He flipped page after page. Inside, she could hear the house begin to stir. The servants came down to light the fires. The cook made breakfast in the kitchen; Mr. Laurence thanked her for his tea.

Across the lane, Mama and Hannah would be doing the same. Readying the cake, and bringing out the best of the jam, the scones, the tea for the guests.

Jo should be there, helping, but she couldn't take her eyes

off Laurie, or wait for what he would say. He read fast, the pages smudging under his fingers.

No matter—she knew what they said. It was written on her heart.

His eyebrows rose and he coughed at a few pages—she peeked over his shoulder and saw it was the chapter called "Heartache," which she had written about his proposal.

He glanced up and she found she could not meet his eyes.

Still, like the pages, she didn't need to see them to know what they looked like.

There are no eyes like those in the whole world, she thought. Eyes like glaciers, like cold northern afternoons. Lapis eyes, blue-sky blue.

She hadn't known how much she loved them.

And that face.

She loved the frown. She loved the furrowed brow. She loved the one irritated eyebrow. She loved the total indifference, the moment one idea or another pushed her temporarily out of his thoughts. She loved it because she loved the sweetness, in the other moments, when he came back to her. The softening, when she came near.

Her heart was broken. She knew that, had known that.

Expected it, even.

What she hadn't and couldn't have imagined was the part that came after, the vast stretch of the thing, the way it settled in and took over every element of her life.

The way she lived with it. The familiarity of how she knew it.

The ease with which she could build a house in it, carve furniture from it, plant her own little dark garden with it.

She hadn't expected that.

Who knew a heart could break open so *expansively*?

Who knew whole kingdoms—with no master, no queen, no governance, obedient to no rule of law, accountable to no country custom, unruly to all logic whatsoever—could rise in a heartless wake?

Sometimes, now, she felt as if she might have imagined him. Her Teddy, the way he had been. The intimacy of their bond. The very watering-hole of it.

The way their relationship had defined and redefined every other in her life, including those with her sisters, her mother—even the way she had seen herself.

The way I see myself now, she thought.

He is my person. Everyone needs a person, and he is mine. Only he isn't mine.

He was, and now he's not.

That was a very grave problem indeed, and the more she felt it—how wrong she had been, how foolish, how ignorant, really, to not see it for what it was—well, that was of no consequence now.

She was exactly and directly as intimate with the absence of him now as she had been with the presence of him then.

She still stood at the sitting-room window of Orchard House every day, just as she always had. Only the view had changed. That face she had loved so well, the one she had been unable to see for all its brightness, that ball of light, the sun of her own small galaxy? Gone.

The shadow in its place was a void, a darkness beyond reckoning.

And so here she stood, dizzy from the weight of nothing at all.

This is how lovers die, she thought. *This is Romeo and Juliet. This is Roderigo and Rodanthe. It isn't because they choose to leave their life behind.*

It's because there is no life left in living.

At last, Theodore Laurence set down the final page. Around them, Jo could smell wood-smoke. In the distance, a loon laughed. "Well?" she asked.

"It's very good. Nearly perfect, in fact."

"*Nearly* perfect?"

"You haven't finished with your heroine yet. She needs . . . something more. Her own sense of contentment, whatever that may be."

"*She is content.*" Jo got up and stomped across the porch, her footsteps as loud as gunshots. "I've told you; I won't marry her off for anything."

"Yes, I am well aware." Laurie seemed to sag, as if someone had placed on his back a tremendous weight. Like Atlas, holding up the world. "But she must have something. Something more than her writing, as she faces her future."

"Why shouldn't her writing be enough?"

"She is accomplished and successful. But that isn't all she is. She is loving and bright and everything. But she is very much alone in the world."

Jo was furious, fuming. Why did a woman need a husband? Was she never enough on her own, without a man? *Who was Theodore Laurence, to order her about so?*

"If you will not marry in life, at least marry in fiction. Niles will demand it; you know he will."

Jo groaned. *That* was probably true. "But whom?"

"Not me, of course. But someone. Someone who will be a friend to her, and make her laugh at herself."

"Who?"

"She meets someone in New York. Another writer, perhaps. A Dickens type." A very faint smile flickered across his face as he remembered the older gentleman sitting next to Jo at the reading. "You and old Charley, together at last."

Jo smiled. He wasn't trying to change her life, she saw. Only her book. To draw the story to a close. "A scholar," she said. "A German professor. Mr. Bhaer."

Laurie laughed as she invoked the name from Vegetable Valley. "Very ursine. Yes, Mr. Bhaer, your old bore. But she returns home to see Beth before she dies, and leaves him in Manhattan. All seems ended, until Amy and Laurie return home . . . man and . . . wife."

Jo looked at him. "It was about art and music. And Paris. And Rome."

"I get it." He shook his head, aghast. "But, Jo."

"Keep going," she said.

"Fine, then." Laurie thought about it. "Let's say the professor arrives to bring Jo something she had written. A poem he found of hers, about her sisters. He says he would offer her his hand, except he has nothing to give her . . ."

"Poor as rats. Just like we used to be," Jo said. "Yes."

Laurie nodded. "So he says . . . his hands are empty."

Jo smiled. How funny Laurie was, concocting this end for her. "But she puts her hands in his and says, 'Not empty now.'"

Laurie smiled at her sadly. "A fitting end for your heroine. Engaged to a poor scholar, with none of those mercenary tendencies that would have made her accept her boy, when he asked. Happiness without greed."

"Yes," said Jo.

Laurie was giving her away. He was letting her go, as he must, and offering to marry her to another. It might be fiction, but it had the ring of truth.

She could already see it all—the professor with his German accent, his fond and foolish speech. Just what Laurie had declared for her all those months ago, when they had quarreled, and he went away. That she would meet someone else and love him, and that Laurie, heartbroken, would be hanged if he would stand by and let it happen.

Instead, he was the one who had met someone else, and she was the one who was heartbroken. For that's what it was, wasn't it? To watch someone you loved marry another.

She'd learned, all right. She'd learned it all too late.

There was a wedding to attend, but there was also a book to write, and so she went back to it. Because that was what writers with deadlines did, even on the days they were helping to throw weddings.

They wrote.

33

⁓⊱⊰⁓

WEDDING BELLS, SILVER BELLS

*T*he morning had dawned beautiful and clear. A brilliant winter day, the earth turned white. The grandest cathedral in Europe would not have been more perfect for the wedding of Margaret March and John Brooke.

Meg wore the silver Worth gown that Laurie had ordered for Jo. Her mother had done Meg's hair up in braids, tied around her ears and behind. Her friend Sallie Moffat had given a silver comb for Meg's dark hair, as her "something borrowed," and Jo had tucked behind it a bluebird feather she'd found, just so.

Meg had never looked so beautiful when she came downstairs to the drawing-room to find Brooke waiting for her. Dressed in his new brown wool suit, he seemed on the verge of disappearing into the wood.

Mama and Father sat together on a bench to watch, along with Amy and dear Hannah. Most of Concord had come to see the ceremony. The Moffats were there, and the Gardiners. The Emersons came, and the Kings, and the Nileses. Even the Hummels were there, and Jo was astonished to see Mrs. Hummel with tears in her eyes.

The minister spoke over the couple, who recited their simple vows. Meg looking shyly at her new husband. Brooke with a sheepish but unmistakably pleased grin.

Then it was done. "I now declare you man and wife," said the minister, and the assembled broke into applause.

Everyone except Jo. She could not applaud the loss of her sister, even to a man she admired as much as John Brooke.

When she had greeted all her guests, Meg turned to her sister and flung her arms around Jo's neck. "Oh, Jo!" she said, her eyes dropping happy tears. "I can't believe how happy I am! Truly, I could wish nothing better for myself."

"You will both be very happy, I daresay."

"How I would wish something similar for you. What will make you happy, Jo? Whatever it is, I hope you get it!"

"I have, dearest," she said. "Nothing makes me happier than seeing those I love content. As long as you are, I am."

A CAKE WITH a posy on it, baked with love by Mama Abba herself. That was how the March girls had celebrated every birthday for as long as Jo could remember, and Meg had especially requested the very same for her wedding.

So Jo had dutifully helped her mother and Hannah bake and frost and decorate the glorious layers of sponge for days—and was still helping her mother cut them—when Mr. Niles found her, trapping her at the table. "So, Miss March, am I ever going to see your sequel, or have you given up?"

She crossed her arms. "As a matter of fact, sir, I have most of it finished. I believe you will be well pleased."

He looked a tad skeptical as he asked, "And is there a happy ending?"

"Perhaps not the one you or my readers would have intended. But there is a certain truth to it. I am . . . moderately . . . er, largely . . . satisfied . . . on behalf of my characters."

Truthfully, the jury was still out, even to Jo's own mind.

"And what of their . . . let's see . . . *whalebone-corseted hearts*?"

Jo raised an eyebrow. "One only writes what one knows, sir."

"One writes what pays one's bills, Miss March. That's *what one knows*—but now, whether one admits it? Quite another tale entirely." Still, her editor looked merry. *Or perhaps just hungry,* Jo thought, watching Niles eye the cake in front of her. "And when can I expect it? This moderately or largely satisfying tale?"

She nodded up toward the general direction of her garret, her automatic response whenever anyone asked about The Book. "In a few weeks. I only need to add one last element, and it will be perfect." As she said the words, she desperately hoped they were true.

Niles quirked a smile. "*Perfect* is maybe less important than *done*, Miss March, but I will look forward to reading it, all the same. Tell me, is everyone married off this time?"

Jo smiled. "Very happily."

"Good," said Niles. "I think we'll sell loads of it, then."

"I hope so," said Jo. "I need the money."

Niles nodded. "Don't we all. Now. About that cake—may I?"

"Of course." Jo waved at the bountiful dessert table.

The editor regarded his author over the tops of his spectacles, then took the largest slice with a wink. "But why stop at one when you could have two? The second being for my wife, I mean." He helped himself to the second-largest piece as well.

She sighed. "The true question, Mr. Niles, is if you ever mean to stop at all?"

He laughed. "I suppose that depends entirely, Miss March, on the flavor of the cake. I'll let you know."

"I'm sure you will, Mr. Niles."

And with that, he disappeared into the throng of well-wishers crowding around Brooke and Meg.

Mama Abba followed him, hovering anxiously, for he had come the farthest, and thus somehow needed the most supervision, by Concord logic. As if he were a sheep that had strayed up the road from Boston, rather than a man with a coach.

Jo felt someone at her elbow and hurried to cut another piece. "Just a moment," she said, and reached for a plate.

"No need. I'll have one later, when everyone else has gone."

She looked up to find Laurie meeting her eyes, only somewhat awkwardly. Her heart turned over and over in its place, rolling about in circles beneath the carefully ironed tucks of her dress. *Like one of Bethie's kittens,* she thought, *when it couldn't quite get comfortable in the laundry-basket.*

How sad it was, though, to not be altogether comfortable around her own Teddy anymore.

But she smiled, because Teddy was still Teddy—no matter how much a mess she'd made of everything. "I didn't see you standing there."

"I know. I was watching you work. Most effectively, I might add. The way you handle a blade, Roderigo himself would be proud." He grinned, a sly twinkle alighting in his eye.

She wagged the aforementioned weapon in the air between them. "Well, I have been practicing. One must have prospects, and I fear cake-cutting shall be all that remains, if my next book is truly only moderately satisfying." She sighed—then smiled again. "But thank you for your help. With the ending, I mean. Truly."

"What I read was very nearly finished, and will no doubt be a smashing success. And if not? Ho, ho! Jo March, the great swash-buckler of cakes!" He laughed.

She heard the guests cheering huzzah to Brooke and Meg from the parlor, and realized they now had the room to themselves. *As we had a thousand times before,* Jo thought. *But a thousand years ago.*

It was a shame, and she knew it, so she steadied herself and determined to do better.

For he is my oldest friend, and it is not his fault that I have been a brainless goat.

"Of course," she said, as she licked one finger surreptitiously, "I will graciously make my considerable skills available to you at great discount, as our next Concord bridegroom," she teased. "I do hope I'll be invited, even if the wedding is in England."

"You won't be," Laurie said, quickly.

It felt like a slap.

Then he looked at her sadly, almost shamefacedly. It was a look she knew well. She'd seen it when he'd dropped the pie they'd spent an entire morning baking with Hannah. When he'd toppled her ink-pot and wrecked a week's worth of articles for the Pickwick Club. Whenever he couldn't say what she wanted to hear, or couldn't *not* say what she wanted to avoid—

"There will be no wedding, Jo."

"I see— I'm sorry, what?" She almost dropped the knife.

"You are?" Laurie looked disappointed. "Sorry, I mean?"

"What do you mean, there will be no wedding?" She was in a kind of shock, perhaps, because suddenly nothing was making sense.

"No wedding." He sounded miserable.

"Oh, Teddy." She impaled the knife into the cake and let go, straightening up. "Come here." She took him by the hand and pulled him out into the garden, where white wedding ribbons still adorned the veranda, blowing prettily amidst the creeping garden vines. The cat, who had been sniffing at the cake crumbs, followed them outside.

"Talk to me, Teddy." Jo took a seat on the top step, despite her own wedding finery. Laurie sank down on the step beneath her, right at her feet. "Tell me everything."

"There's nothing to tell. Nothing much." Laurie looked pale and sad, though she thought perhaps that could have been from a lack of sleep. He reached down to pet the cat absently.

"And Harriet?" As she said the name, Jo realized that in all the fuss and chaos of getting Meg dressed and ready, Harriet had been nowhere to be seen.

He shook his head. "Gone."

Jo looked confused. "But isn't she here? I could have sworn I saw her this morning."

"She left before dawn."

"She did? To go where?" The words almost seemed like nonsense, still. She struggled to catch up.

"Boston. Then perhaps back to New York. I may have misunderstood, but she seemed to suggest that Fred Vaughn might want to marry her." He jammed his hands into his pockets with a very Laurie-like shrug. "It all happened a bit quickly, to be honest."

"What? Whatever happened?" Jo hadn't seen or heard anything at all, so engrossed had she been in her writing. In truth, she'd been laboring all through the night, burning down lumps of candle-wax, one after the next, only registering the hours when she looked up to see that dawn had already broken.

Then she'd had Laurie read her pages, only to dive right back in.

It was like a kind of time travel, when the great rivers of words finally came, and whole days could pass with Jo hardly noticing anything at all.

"She's broken off our engagement."

Jo's mind was swirling. Had something gone awry at the dinner the night before? Harriet and Laurie had slipped away at the end of the night, which must have been when it happened, but it still made no sense. Why would Lady Hat break her engagement? They had seemed so happy. Happy, and perfect for each other. Content in who they were and the sort of life they were meant to have. Life in brilliant color and *uppertens* company.

"But—I don't understand!"

Laurie turned to her, a serious look on his face. "I've learned my lesson. Maybe I only learn things in the very hardest of ways, but I do learn."

"Learned what?" Jo reached for his hand and took it in her own. Her old friend looked so distraught.

He shook his head somberly. "There will be no more talk of weddings, Jo. I'll never marry. I can't make any woman happy."

"Don't be silly, Teddy. You could make any woman happy. You're kind and intelligent and artistic. Stubborn and argumentative, but never dull, either. What girl wouldn't accept you?"

Through the doorway behind them, she watched the wedding party continue on. Father was holding a glass to toast the new couple. There were cheers and huzzahs for John and Meg. Warm words and wise, for there was nothing better done than a good match well made.

"What girl wouldn't have me? You, Jo. You refused me, remember?"

She did. As she stood there watching Meg and John raise their glasses to each other, she felt her eyes prick with tears.

"And I might be a fool, but I know girls don't like to marry gentlemen who are in love with another girl. As I will be for the rest of my life, and so I am ruined for anyone else."

"Teddy," she said softly, as her heart beat against her chest. "What are you saying?"

"If you won't have me, then I won't bother. I will never marry. There's no point to it." He shrugged again. "It doesn't matter." He forced a smile.

Jo turned away. An instinct. There it was, the familiar panic. She couldn't look at him.

"Don't run, Jo." He sounded resigned. "You don't always have to flee. I don't know what I did—what anyone did—to make you so afraid."

"Afraid? Of what?" Still, she didn't look at him. She was like some kind of trapped creature, caught halfway off the step. She couldn't admit it was too hard to stay.

"Of love, Jo. Of feeling it. Of giving it. Of getting it."

Of losing it.

She closed her eyes and saw her Beth's eyes close, just like always. Saw her skin turning pale. Saw her fingers letting go of the sheet's edge. Saw her floating away as the wordless scream rose in Jo's throat.

The shadow. The silence. The soul-crushing, bone-crushing despair.

Promise me, Jo, Beth had whispered. For she knew how lost her sister would feel, how dark Jo could get without her.

Stay here. Stay in the world of the living. Keep the silence away. Promise me, Jo. You must live. You have so much to live for.

Keep writing your way back to the light.

Jo opened her eyes and sat back down on the step, hard. Her

breath was labored—truly, she was almost gasping, like she'd suddenly arrived at the end of some great, endless race she didn't understand and had no idea she'd been running in the first place.

Was that it? The great risk of belonging to someone else? Someone who could hurt you. Someone who could leave you. Someone you could lose. Someone you could love, and make all those other things a thousand times worse.

Was that why receiving a heart felt like having to give her own away?

Every cell in her body was screaming at her to flee, but every beat of her heart was telling her to stay. And now she knew. She did belong to him, because he belonged to her, and they belonged to each other. There was no wedding vow that needed to be spoken for her to understand that. Even unmarried, even under separate roofs, they belonged together. No suitable wife would ever care for him more.

He looked more miserable than she'd ever seen him. It wasn't Harriet who had done this to him—it was her. It was all so clear now. Even if nothing could be unsaid, nothing could be undone.

Jo felt the last of her resistance crumbling. "I—I know I hurt you, Teddy. I know I did. And I'm so sorry."

He waved off her apology. "Of course it would come to this. It's like the end of one of your stories. Who's the real Roderigo now?" He laughed—then sighed. "There could be no other fate for me. That I should love my whole life someone who does not love me in return—I suppose it's fitting. Poetic justice? Is that what you writers call it?"

Jo didn't answer him, because she was far too occupied with not answering him. *A lie. That's what the writers call it. Because it's too late for the truth.*

"I'm sorry," she finally said.

"Don't be." He stood up. "I mean, it's all right, Jo. You don't owe me your hand in marriage. You weren't put on this earth so I could feel love. I won't ask again."

He would not. She could see it in his face. The hurt that shadowed his eyes now when he looked at her. The resignation that set with his jaw. This wasn't her Teddy; this was her Teddy hardening into someone else, someone he was never meant to be. And what a terrible shame that would be, really almost a crime.

A world without a proper Teddy.

And in that moment—sitting on the splintering veranda steps of Orchard House, surrounded by Vegetable Valley, looking up at the first and last great love of her life—Josephine March knew precisely what to do. And even more, she knew she was going to do it.

Risk it. Embrace it. Maybe even, one day, lose it.

Love.

It would be her honor and her pleasure to go down with this particular ship. They could be dashed together upon the rocks, sink together to the ocean floor. Only blurry, ink-splotched pages to mark their watery grave.

Because it was always our story.

It just never had the right ending.

Jo finally knew, and a great calm settled itself upon her, the first peace she'd felt in a very, very long time.

"It's all right, Teddy." She reached for him, and he took her hand, helping her to her feet. "You don't have to ask again. Because I will."

"You will?" He furrowed his brow at her. "You will what?"

"Ask. I'm asking. This is me, asking."

They stared at each other. One of them glowing. One glowering.

He dropped her hand. "Don't jest. It isn't funny this time. It's cruel."

"My dearest boy," Jo inhaled sharply. "My only boy."

She felt lighter—free—and emboldened, glimpsing a happiness that was just within reach, after all. "I do not jest. I am, most entirely, in earnest. I—I have had a change of heart, Teddy." She stumbled over the words, searching. "Of my heart."

His face softened with hope, though she could yet see him holding back. She had wounded him so badly, so many times now. "And what does your heart tell you now, Jo?"

"That I—I want to marry you. After all. After everything." The words came tumbling out. "That is, if you'll still have me. Rotten as I've been. Rotten as I will most assuredly be again. But please, please don't let that stop you. Please, Teddy. Do say you will."

"Jo? Is this some sort of game?" He went very pale, grabbing for the fence-post at his side. "You can't be serious."

She took a tentative step toward him. "I am. Entirely serious. Harriet might be foolish enough to let you go, but I am not. Not twice, anyway."

"To be clear. Just so there is no confusion." His dark eyes sparkled. "You mean it? You *want* to marry me? You will marry me?"

"I do." She took another step. "And I will."

Now they were standing face-to-face.

"Jo," he breathed, leaning close. "Say it again. No, swear it. Swear it on the Bible. Swear it on this garden, on this family, on Orchard House itself. Swear it on Pickwick and on garrets and inkpots and scorch marks and—"

"Pickled limes?" Jo said, caressing his cheek.

"Watering-holes," came the husky reply as he grabbed her hand.

"My dear Teddy," she said, pulling him by his waistcoat. "Don't you see? We swore it the day we met."

He touched his forehead to hers. "And every day after."

Jo closed her eyes. "Every moment of every day."

Then he lowered his mouth to hers and kissed her, and she kissed him back, his soft lips warm against hers, as his arms encircled her waist and pulled her ever closer.

It was worth the wait.

34

WHALEBONES

*L*ove," Mr. Brooke announced, beaming proudly at the newly wedded and incandescently beautiful *Mrs.* Brooke, "is not just the stuff of poets." The doting husband paused to slip an affectionate arm around his young wife, who leaned on his shoulder. "In the immortal words of Catullus himself, '*Odi et amo. Quare id faciam fortasse . . .*'"

Jo stood in the doorway with Laurie, her breath catching in her throat as she took in the little wedding tableau.

Mr. Brooke and Meg.

What a lovely sight the two of them were! And what a happy family surrounded them! What a spectacular ending her eldest sister's marriage plot had turned out to be, cabbages and all.

After everything, they had found their way—from gossip and speculation and Jo's airy invention—to something far more important. Something more human, and more true.

From her place beside Meg, Mama Abba caught Jo's eye, looking from her to Laurie wonderingly.

Jo could feel her cheeks turning, and when Mama Abba inclined her head softly toward the stairwell, Jo nodded back, pausing only to whisper in Laurie's ear, "I believe Mama Abba knows."

"How could she? She couldn't possibly," he whispered back.

"You know Mama Abba, Laurie. Of course she could, just from one look across a crowded room."

"True," he said. "But the rest of them? Do you think they'll be surprised?"

"No more surprised than I am," said Jo.

"No more surprised than either of us," he agreed. Then he gave Jo's hand a squeeze, and sent her off to the stairwell, and to her mother's confidence.

MAMA ABBA WAS kneeling at the cedar chest that sat at the end of the little daybed when Jo found her. The chest was open, and even that much set Jo's heart hammering. Because the chest wasn't just a chest, she thought, but a kind of crypt.

For Beth's porcelain-faced dollies. For the March girls. For little sisters.

For childhood itself.

Mama Abba took up the most raggedy and beloved of Beth's toy children—but when she saw Jo's face, she looked startled. "You've gone and accepted him, haven't you?" She said the words even as Jo was still lowering herself to the clean-scrubbed wooden floor beneath them.

"I didn't *accept* him, Mama Abba. Not this time. I *asked* him."

Mama Abba dropped the old doll and reached for Jo's hand. "Oh, Jo."

"Tell me I'm doing the right thing, Mama."

"I can't tell you that, Jo. Not any more than you could decide Mr. Brooke was or wasn't right for Meg. Or that he was—what was it? A zucchini?"

"A cabbage," Jo said, ashamedly.

"You have to be brave. You have to make your own way. Your own choices. Just as you always have."

"Mama." Now Jo realized her mother was weeping.

Jo felt her own eyes begin to prickle.

She clasped her arms around her knees, staring across the room to the wall next to the bed, the wall where Amy had practiced drawing her sisters while they slept. There they still were, the smudged-charcoal faces of the four of them.

Now three.

Very nearly, two.

"It's all right, Jo. I've known it was coming; I've known it longer than either of you, I suppose. It's just—well, some small part of me must mourn it. Just for a moment. I've lost Beth. I nearly lost Amy. Today I'm losing Meg. Now I'll lose you, too."

"Except you haven't. And you won't. You'll never lose any of us." Jo was still studying the wall, the faces of the four sisters.

Because Amy's little mural had changed, and Jo herself had never noticed before.

Now the third figure in the little tableau—the one between the neat-looking Meg and the tousle-headed Jo and the *highly* angelic Amy—wore a pair of luminous white wings, an expanse of whitewash smudging that seemed to encompass all four faces in its folds. And a broad gold circle surrounded them, connecting all four of them.

The golden band.

That was how their father had described it.

Oh, Amy.

How frightened you must have been, even before you were sick.

How much you must have missed her, too.

Mama Abba took Jo's hand in her own. "It's all right, Jo. This is life. I will lose you, and you will lose me. Losing is part of having, my love."

Jo reached out to touch the wall. "I miss her so much, Mama. I think—I think I buried part of myself that day. With Beth."

The tears were coming so quickly, Jo could taste them.

Mama Abba touched her daughter's face. "You all did, Jo. All of you. I used to console myself that it was your *Pilgrim's Progress*, perhaps, just as it was mine. That we would all come out, I don't know, somehow—stronger."

"The *Slough of Despond*?" Jo wiped her face with her sleeve. "That's not how it felt. It felt like we just lost our way. I know I did."

"We all did. Meg, fleeing as soon as she could to make a home of her own with Mr. Brooke—"

"As if she could escape the shadow in ours," Jo mused.

Mama Abba nodded. "Amy, acting out for every scrap of attention she could beg from us—"

Jo smiled. "Good or bad."

"Your father, hiding his own grief in the pain of the wounded." Mama Abba looked away, and Jo wondered at the unacknowledged pain her mother must have endured, these long years on her own.

"Me, running like the devil from anything that could make me feel," Jo said, tiredly.

"Me, furious with your father for going, and with Beth for having to go. And beyond furious at God and every angel in heaven for taking her," Mama Abba said, finally looking Jo in the eye. "And for very nearly taking Amy." She shook her head. "I've been so angry for so long, Jo."

"Oh, Mama. You never said— I never knew. But you couldn't say, could you? Because you had to hold the rest of us, what was left of us, together."

"No, my dear girl. That was you. I've blamed myself for letting you, and I've blamed myself—and your father—for needing you to. And then, one day, I just stopped."

Jo touched her mother's cheek. "I wanted to help, Mama. Any way I could."

"I know that, Jo. At least, now I do. And it's how I made my peace with it. Do you know why?"

Jo shook her head.

"Because of the letters that come addressed to you, by the hundreds. Because of the way your little sister speaks of you when you aren't there to see it. Because of all the other little sisters—the ones you'll never know or meet—who you've made believe they could tell a story of their own."

Jo could feel her heart hammering inside her chest.

Tell her.

You can tell Mama.

Jo began slowly, because they were not words she had ever spoken. "There were times, Mama Abba—there was a time—when the shadow of death seemed too great to outrun. When I thought I would not come back from it. I could not. When I stood at the edge of the Mill Dam and wondered if I should just—"

Mama Abba pulled Jo into her arms. There it was, that wordless, reassuring warmth. That was her mother. Jo could remember it—the brush of her sleeve, the smell of her cloak—from her earliest days.

Now Jo was sobbing so hard, she could barely get the words out. "And I thought—I thought that no one with that sort of darkness in them could, by any right—"

"Love and be loved?" Mama Abba stroked her shaking curls.

Jo nodded, burying her face in her mother's shoulder.

"Yet here you are. Because you're Josephine March, the bravest soul I've ever known. And that girl never leaves a fight, not before it's over." Mama Abba pulled back, raising Jo's chin with a steady hand. "There is nothing little about you, Jo. And I'm so, so proud to call you my daughter."

Jo smiled as Mama Abba pulled the familiar handkerchief from her sleeve—the one with the cross-stitched AM—and dabbed at Jo's tears. "Do I have your blessing, Mama Abba?"

"To be married? To a boy I raised almost as my own? What do you think?"

Jo smiled, taking the handkerchief from her mother. "I think I must look even more of a wretch than usual."

Mama Abba placed Beth's porcelain dolls carefully back in the cedar chest, closing the lid with a thump.

"It's your life, Jo. Write it however you like. Just write it true."

NOBODY—WELL, ALMOST NOBODY—NOTICED when Jo and her mother slipped back into the party. Meg and Brooke were leading the dancing; Grandfather Laurence was complimenting Hannah on the luncheon; Mr. March was sharing a plate of cake with Amy, who had frosting on the tip of her nose. The scene was a sublimely happy one.

Only Laurie was pacing at the edge of the festivities.

"And?" He looked nervously from Mama Abba to Jo when Jo reappeared by his side. "Are you all right? Did something happen?"

"Yes. And—yes." It was all Jo could manage, but her eyes were shining with love, and before she could even attempt to say more than that, he stopped her.

"Wait!" He stuck his hand in his jacket pocket and came back again with something in his hand. Something small and light. He opened the box and put it into her palm—a ring of sapphires encircled with diamonds.

"What is this?" she asked, her eyes wide.

"It belonged to my mother." Laurie coughed. "And don't worry. I never gave it to Harriet. She insisted on using one of those fancy New York jewelers. She picked out her own ring and is returning it to Tiffany."

Harriet. It already seemed like a lifetime ago.

"My mother would have loved you, Jo. Knowing that, it makes me feel . . ."

"What?" she asked, leaning closer to him, suddenly giddy.

"I don't know. Just . . . feel, I suppose. You make me feel so much, Jo. You always have. When you ask me what I'm thinking about, or how I'm feeling—"

"How do you feel, Laurie?" she asked, teasing.

"How I feel is you." The words came husky from his throat, and from his heart. "My home."

She squeezed his hand. "Theodore Laurence. We may make a writer of you yet."

He raised an eyebrow. "No, thank you. There's already one writer in this family." He grinned.

This family.

Jo leaned closer—but he stopped her.

"Please, Jo. Let me do this properly. I've been waiting for such a long time," he said, as he slowly got down on his knee. Savoring every moment.

"Oh!" She had no words for once. She felt so happy, she wanted to laugh. And he looked so happy, she did.

The room went hushed as Meg and Brooke, Mama Abba and Father, Grandfather and Amy all looked on at the sight of Laurie proposing to Jo one more time. Amy's mouth dropped open as if she couldn't quite believe what she was seeing.

Neither can I, thought Jo.

Meg leaned her head on Brooke's shoulder. Her eyes held Jo's, blazing with sisterly love. Jo felt her own eyes begin to prickle before Laurie even said a word. As if there hadn't been enough said already.

"Will you have me, Jo?" he asked. Something in his tone was so raw—as if he still didn't quite believe he could ever have the answer he sought. "Will you? I know I'm not worthy. I know I'm not perfect. And I've done this all wrong, I know—"

Jo moved a finger to his lips. "You know me, Teddy. Just as I know you. And that's enough, so much more than enough. Why—it's perfect."

His eyes were twinkling now, but it wasn't the usual Teddy twinkle. They were sparkling with tears. Unembarrassed, unabashed, almost proud. Running down a face full of joy. Then he wiped his eyes with his sleeve and laughed. "You still haven't answered the question, Mr. Snodgrass."

Jo reached down and held his hand tightly in hers.

Then she took hold of his other one, pulling herself down until they were both on their knees, face-to-face. True equals.

"Yes, Mr. Weller. I'll have you and I'll love you, just as I always have. For now, and for always, old boy."

"Old Snod." He cupped her face with both hands and drew her toward him, kissing her with such passion that it felt to Jo like the sun itself was embracing her.

A kiss like that can explode a person into nothing.

Into everything.

Finally.

I love you. I love you. I love you.

Jo pulled away, gasping. "Teddy!"

Laurie grinned back at her, lacing his fingers through hers. "The point at which whalebone corsets melt? I think we've found it." Then he dropped his mouth near her ear and whispered, "And I'm quite certain we'll find it again . . . and again . . . and again."

All she could do was nod as he slipped the ring on her finger, and marvel at the feeling of it.

The family broke out in applause, and then Jo and Laurie realized, dazedly, that they were not alone.

They never had been.

They were surrounded by love. Love for each other, love for their family, a love that would sustain and carry them all their lives.

Beginning now.

"To Jo and Laurie," said Meg, lifting her glass.

"To the Cherry King and his Queen," agreed Amy.

"To my dear children," said Mama Abba.

"May they find happiness in each other for the rest of their lives," said Father, looking at his wife. "And may we."

"It's about time!" shouted John Brooke, to the delight of everyone present.

And so it was.

A Brief Historical Note

~

Jo & Laurie is a work of fiction inspired by *Little Women*, by Louisa May Alcott, and also by the life of Alcott herself. Because Alcott chose to use her own life—growing up as a fledgling writer in a cottage full of sisters in Concord, Massachusetts—as the inspiration for her first domestic fiction, using what we now know about "Lu" Alcott has allowed us to reexamine and rethink her beloved literary stand-in, Jo March.

In general, we tried to follow the basic touchpoints of Alcott's original story line—certainly the spirit of it—as well as her original cast of characters. From smaller details (like Amy's infamous punishment for smuggling pickled limes into her school, her burning of Jo's first manuscript, the scorched dress Jo was forced to wear to Sally Gardiner's ball, and *The Pickwick Papers*) to the larger beats (like Beth's death, Laurie's rebuffed proposal, Jo's trip to New York, and their father's absence), we took great efforts to continually reconnect our story to Alcott's. When we chose to depart from the world of the established fiction, or from explorations based on questions raised by the established fiction (see: Jo and Laurie's romance), those decisions were usually inspired by

Alcott's personal history or the letters of Louisa, Bronson, and May Alcott.

The Alcott family did live in Concord, Massachusetts, at Orchard House, named for the forty apple trees Bronson Alcott planted. Lu Alcott described the home, in a letter to her editor, as "damp and earwiggy"—she wondered at how disappointed her readers would be to see it. When they were young, the Alcott children were allowed to draw on the walls, and Bronson Alcott referred to his girls as a "golden circle," which inspired the image our Amy draws on the March girls' bedroom wall.

Like the March family, intellectually minded Bronson and social-work-minded Abigail "Abba" Alcott had four daughters—Anna ("Meg"), Louisa ("Jo"), Elizabeth ("Beth"), and Abigail May, called May ("Amy"). Anna married John Bridge Pratt, who like John Brooke, was not a man of means. Elizabeth died of scarlet fever at the age of twenty-two. May trained and ultimately became a successful painter who married a Swiss businessman and lived in Paris until her untimely death at age thirty-nine, eight weeks after childbirth; our Amy's brush with death was inspired by May's own sad, sudden fate.

Both Jo's and Louisa's father was a chaplain in the Civil War, where Louisa herself served as a nurse, though Jo nurses only Beth. The fictional Mr. March and the real Mr. Alcott both struggled to earn a living for most of their lives, pressuring both Jo and Louisa into early careers writing for the penny press under a variety of names. (Louisa wrote as Flora Fairfield and A. M. Barnard.) Even at the height of her success, Louisa's letters unfailingly mention the price of every expenditure she makes—including booking second-class passage to cross the Atlantic—something every writer alive can understand, including the authors of this book. (Ha!)

The romantic musician "Laurie" is, according to Alcott herself, a hybrid character. He's based on a Polish musician, Ladislas "Laddie" Wisniewski, with whom Louisa spent time in Paris, and Alf Whitman, an actor Louisa performed a Dickens play—*The Haunted Man*—with at the Concord Dramatic Union.

Thomas Niles really was Alcott's editor at Roberts Brothers Publishers in Boston. He also posthumously published Emily Dickinson, as well as most of the major American Renaissance writers. The first publication of *Little Women* was, indeed, a sudden and phenomenal success—a print run of two thousand sold out and went into reprints almost immediately. Alcott's royalty, in lieu of the one-hundred-dollar advance she was otherwise expecting, became the sustaining income of her extended family for years to come.

The pressure to resolve the marriage plots of *Little Women* is how *Good Wives* came to be published immediately after (in the United States, the two books are now published as one, under the title *Little Women*). At the time, Louisa steadfastly and openly refused to allow the fact that her readers were overwhelmingly *shipping* Jo and Laurie to influence the marriage plots in the second book; she famously said, "I won't marry Jo to Laurie for anything." Of course, Louisa herself never married.

When our own story's departures were not inspired by Alcott's history or letters, they were framed by the historical context of literary or popular culture in mid-nineteenth-century America, especially in the greater Boston area, about which much has been written. Charles Dickens really did tour the United States for speaking engagements in both 1842 and 1867, traveling with his wife to speak at Steinway Hall, as in our story; Alcott did refer to "old Charley" with affection in her letters, upon hearing that he had died. Also in our story, Jo refers to feminist essayist Margaret Fuller's "Manifesto of Femality"; there is no question Alcott would have known of that text as well. The couturier Charles Worth was a famed dressmaker of the period—especially to the *uppertens*—though he had no salon in New York City. Just as Meg is married in the "Worth dress," it was the custom of the time for most brides to be married in the finest dresses they owned, as opposed to purchasing new ones. Finally, the language of flowers was a Victorian code that assigned meanings to different flowers, which were sometimes used to send messages. Though, in our case, vegetables have been quite useful as well. ☺

Finally, it is through Alcott's own letters that we know there was a day in 1857 when the author stood at the edge of the Mill Dam, in Boston's Back Bay, and contemplated jumping. The high highs and the low lows of one of the most successful writers the world has ever known is strangely relatable to our modern reader and writer friends, so we thought it was important to share that moment with Lu's doppelgänger Jo in our retelling, too.

—MS & MdlC

ACKNOWLEDGMENTS

WE WOULD LIKE to thank the little women and one little man (ha!) who helped bring this book to your hands: our awesome editor Stephanie Pitts, "fourth sister" Jennifer Klonsky, and brother-from-another-mother agent Richard Abate. Pickled limes and peppermints for you all!

Thank you to everyone at Penguin, especially Jen Loja, Shanta Newlin, Elyse Marshall, Felicia Frazier, Emily Romero, Christina Colangelo, Alex Garber, Carmela Iaria, Kristie Radwilowicz, Eileen Savage, and Cindy Howle. You've hidden our scorch marks so beautifully, we might actually enjoy this ball.

Thank you, as always, to the third musketeer, Rafi Simon, and fourth musketeer, Susanna Hoffs, as well as the YALLkids, Tori Hill and Shane Pangburn. (Pickwick Club, please come to order!) And to our own beloved Lady Hat, undying thanks for lending us your fabulous name!

Thank you to our families, especially our own *Marmees*, Marilyn Ross Stohl and Ching de la Cruz, who gave us our copies of *Little Women* and encouraged us to chase Jo March up into her writing garret. Thanks and love to our dearest Emma, May, Javi, Mike, and Mattie. Everything we write is for you.

And lastly but mostly, a huge and enduring thank-you to you, Dear Reader, because *Christopher Columbus!* The thanks we feel for you is not little at all.

—Margie and Mel

READ ON FOR MORE
FROM MARGARET STOHL
& MELISSA DE LA CRUZ

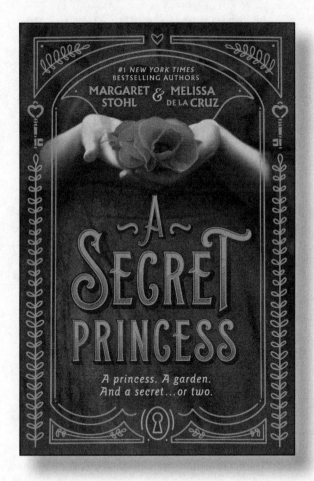

1

*M*emory is a liar. It can hide truths in fantasies, make the misery of one time appear to be the happiness of another. It mutes faces, words, sounds, and sights. It covers everything in a delicate lace that softens the harshest of realities. Take, for example, the morning of January 7, 1865, when Sara Crewe first arrived at the Select Seminary for Young Ladies and Gentlemen.

Memory will tell Sara that, on that morning, the rising sun was filtering through lilac fog, and the seminary's pale stone rose up in the distance like something out of Tennyson. In truth, there was no sunshine through the icy rain. The fog was not a pastoral lilac, but an industrial yellow, and the seminary was no castle, but a fortress. Sara looked out of the window of the smart carriage her father had rented for the journey and found herself shocked by the sight of row homes and factories and turning gyres. This was nothing like the England she'd imagined.

"Is it always this wet?" she asked. "And cold?"

Captain Richard Crewe sat close beside her; even after such a long journey, the smells of dancing lady orchids and sea spray clung to his shirt. It was a trick of the brain, to be surrounded by gray and cold while the senses danced with sunlight and color.

"England has seasons, the same as almost anywhere else," he said. "In the winter, it is cold. In the summer, it is warm. But, yes, it is almost always this wet."

Sara cut her sharp green eyes up at her father, who hid a grin behind his beard—thick, black, and struck with shocks of gray like lightning in a storm cloud. Captain Crewe's ability to maintain frivolity in the midst of anxiety was one of the traits Sara loved most about him.

Sara was not laughing, however. She was sure her father had tried every trick, joke, and story he could think of, but since she stepped onto the dock in London, nothing had stirred the stone from her face. She supposed being angry was easier than being sad.

"I'm stronger than you think, you know," Sara said quite suddenly, no longer hiding behind the conversational pretense of the weather. She stayed facing the grim outside world, but she could feel her father's eyes on her face.

"Oh, Sara." His voice was the heartbroken sound of wind through bare trees. "Dear heart, that's not why—"

"Isn't it?" Sara asked, turning sharply on Captain Crewe. "You think that I am too soft, too . . . spoiled. But I can help run the hacienda—"

"I know you can," Captain Crewe said, harsh and cold. "And one day, we shall need that from you. But not today."

Sara knew from that tone, as final as the closing of a curtain, that the conversation was over.

CAPTAIN CREWE TOLD the carriage driver to let them off at the end of the long drive leading to the school. With the fog gathering around them and pulling at the hems of their clothes, they began to walk. It was an unsettling landscape to Sara. No sun, no color, no birds or animals at play. Not even the sound of children laughing at this so-called school. Somewhere, a church bell chimed the hour, and the deepening sound reminded Sara of the crashing of the tide in a gale. Thinking of the tides and sea storms crushed something in Sara's heart anew. What was a place without an ocean? What chance was there for happiness without the sea?

The old gray estate that housed the seminary rose before them like the base of a great mountain. Lights blinked on and off behind tiny windows that looked down at them with a cold and assessing nature. It was a grand, judgmental building. A craggy old man sitting alone on his hill and looking with suspicious eyes upon the world as it rapidly changed about him.

"'Time's glory is to calm contending kings,'" Captain Crewe said, staring up at the seminary. "'To unmask falsehood and bring truth to light, / To stamp the seal of time in aged things, / To wake the morn and sentinel the night, / To wrong the wronger till he render right—'"

"'To ruinate proud buildings with thy hours,'" Sara interrupted. "'And smear with dust their glittering golden towers.'"

"You've been studying," Captain Crewe said.

Sara refused to accept the joy that her father's pride often gave her.

"Well, I had to do something on the way here."

"Aye. By the time I return to fetch you, you'll know more Shakespeare than I."

"Who is to say I don't already?"

Sara and her father traded glares until the corners of the captain's lips quivered. His sober countenance only held up for another moment before he threw back his head and laughed. It was a loud, prideful, and utterly joyous laugh, and above all else, it was the thing Sara loved most about her papa. Richard Crewe was the German-Irish son of servants, a war veteran who made his fortune in the Far East, and a person who chose independence over food, education over shelter. He was a man who had no right to laugh after all he'd endured. And yet, he laughed like a man born with all of the eases of the world at his disposal. Quite forgetting the decorum her Filipino-Spanish mother had drilled into Sara to ensure she could never be denied due to bad manners, Sara hurled herself against her father and wrapped her arms securely around his chest.

Sara pressed her temple against the beat of her father's heart until she felt his hand grasp the back of her neck.

"Come now, little Sara. Truly, you must be the most solemn child . . . Please, my love, if you keep this up, I'll be forced to take you directly back to Manila, and your mother will have both our heads."

Captain Crewe attempted a laugh, but it was hollow. It made Sara cling to her father all the tighter.

"Sara. Sara, that's enough of that, you hear?"

With a gentle yet jarring force, Captain Crewe grasped Sara's shoulders and pulled her back to where she could stare directly up into his face.

"What has happened to my brave little girl, hm?" he asked. "The one who chased a hawk from the baby goats at the age of three, who scolded her cousins for sitting idle at six. Why, when you were no taller than my kneecap, you crossed through the jungle with no more than your wits. The one thing Sara Marie Crewe has never been afraid of is an adventure, and I won't have her starting now. Straighten your back, dry your eyes. Show them where you come from. Who are you?"

Sara did as she was told—straightened her back and dabbed her eyes—and said, "I am Sara Crewe, daughter of Richard Crewe of Munster, Ireland, and Munich, Bavaria, and Matea Reyes of Manila and Pampanga, the Philippines."

Captain Crewe smiled, and Sara thought there might have been tears in his eyes.

"Yes, you are," he said.

The sound of quick steps on the gravel turned both their heads. Materializing out of the sickly yellow fog was a black pillar of a woman. The minimal light was caught by and reflected off the heavy set of keys that hung at her hip. She was dressed all in black, as if in mourning, and her dark hair was pulled back in the monarch's tight bun. She began to speak immediately, even before she was fully upon them.

"I thought I heard footsteps on the lawn," she said in a surprisingly deep voice. "This ridiculous Manchester fog. I hope you did not become lost on the way to our quaint school, Captain Crewe. I promise, in the height of spring, this estate is as beautiful as—"

The woman ceased speaking almost immediately upon seeing them fully. Her mouth hung agape; breath caught between two words. Sara could practically feel the heat of the shock and confusion playing behind her eyes. It was an expression Sara had become used to since setting foot on English soil. This woman was expecting a flaxen-haired, rosy-cheeked girl of proper British stock. She glared at Sara and her father as if they'd eaten these imaginary people and now dared to stand in their place.

Finally, the woman managed to speak.

"Captain?" she asked warily, as if afraid of the answer. "Captain Crewe, I presume?"

Sara's father removed his bowler hat and bowed his head gallantly.

"Pleased to make your acquaintance, Headmistress Minchin. And this is your newest pupil, Miss Sara."

Sara dipped into a curtsy, fluid and elegant, as her mother had taught her.

"Charmed, Mistress Minchin," she said.

The mistress in question attempted what Sara thought was a smile. Instead, it more mimicked a chittering mouse drawing its lips back over wide teeth.

"Yes," Minchin said. "Charmed. Absolutely charmed."

From her mouth, the word *charmed* was biting as a curse.

SARA AND HER father followed Minchin through the tall main doors of the seminary. Sara expected a flood of warmth to chase off the cold of the outside, but she was shocked to find that the interior of the citadel was the same temperature as the exterior. She burrowed even deeper into the mink scarf tucked around her neck.

"The child does not much care for the cold?" Minchin asked this of Captain Crewe, even though she was looking directly at Sara.

To Captain Crewe's credit, he did not address that statement as the slight Minchin was probably hoping it would be.

"The Philippines is a land of sunshine," he said. "Sara has never known cold."

Minchin's smile was of genuine malice this time.

"What blessings," she said. "Some children are born, live, and die only knowing cold. Well, I'm sure Sara will have ample time to adjust to the seasons here at the seminary. Our winter is quite robust."

Minchin strode on, and Sara's eyes began to adjust to the changing light. The ceiling of the entryway was vaulted as high as a cathedral they'd visited in London. The sounds of laughter, talking, and many footsteps seemed to gather from throughout the building and collect there, for even though there were no pupils in immediate sight, Sara could hear them. It brought the image of ghost children chasing each other about the rafters to Sara's mind.

The floors, ceilings, and walls were all of the same monastic gray stone; the only light shone from flickering sconces. Very little had been changed from one century to another. In one way, Sara loved that aspect of her new home. When her parents told her she was to be shipped off to an English boarding school, her first thought was of castles and battlements and abbeys. As Sara walked the halls with her father and the brittle Minchin, Sara removed her hands from her muff long enough to brush her fingers against the walls as some fleeing princess, delicate lady, or resolute nun might have long ago.

"I shared in my correspondence that Sara is quite intelligent," Captain Crewe said. "I expect for her to have a thorough education."

"Oh yes," piped Minchin. "We do pride ourselves in providing the necessary foundation for any young lady of means and grace. Our girls must master several languages, at least one of the fine arts, the intricacies of home life—"

"When I said education," Captain Crewe said, "I did mean a *true* education. Sara's mother and I have already taken steps to secure her with the trappings of good breeding. I rely on this school to make her familiar with more collegiate matters. Languages, yes—she is already quite conversational in French—but also the sciences, geography, history, literature. Things she will truly need in life."

The note of sarcasm in Captain Crewe's voice was sharp to Sara's ears.

The headmistress endeavored to straighten her back even further and lifted her chin defiantly. As a trader in these trappings of good breeding, Sara was sure she took the speech with some offense.

"I cannot speak for the Philippines, I'm sure," she said. "But here in the queen's own country, we understand that if a young woman is to aspire toward anything, it must be house and home, where she is needed. Beyond this, yes, I am sure there are collegiate matters, as you say, that she may undertake. But she will find that all that truly matters lies within the confines of the four walls of her own dwelling. But, yes. I suppose since Sara is such a special child"—Minchin looked down at Sara from what she believed was a physical and moral height—"we may make allowances."

As THE TOUR concluded in the heavy, wet air that hung all about the seminary, Sara stood silently and watched her father speak of dollars and cents with the peckish-looking woman. They discussed a timetable for payments, addresses where invoices were to be sent, and a lawyer in town that he'd employed as a go-between for matters that required immediate attention. She turned back to look up at the looming manor. It seemed to reach out to her with long, sharp fingers, snagging on her gown and binding her to it. She had a sudden and desperate urge to cry out, to flee, to run all the way back to the Philippines if that's what it took. But her feet kept their place even as her spirit rattled against her ribs like a prisoner rattled against their chains.

"My solicitor at Barrow and Skipworth will be along presently with the full amount," said Captain Crewe as he creased his billfold and returned it to his chest pocket. "But if there is ever any need, do not hesitate to contact me. In any case, we shall be back in the summer, to see Sara's progress."

"Oh, I'm afraid that's quite impossible." The headmistress said this in an unnervingly casual tone, all while counting crisp banknotes with the efficiency of a merchant.

"What?"

It was the first time Sara had spoken since arriving at the seminary, and it was a disruptive sound even to her own ears.

Minchin managed to give Sara her full attention when she said, "Parents are permitted on campus just for a Parents Day ceremony in the autumn, and the school operates year-round. Students only leave under very special circumstances. We believe that this arrangement allows for as few distractions as possible, thus expediting a pupil's education through routine and focus. It is an unorthodox approach, but we have found it to be quite effective."

"I assume you include holidays in this . . . approach?" Captain Crewe asked.

"Yes, of course," Minchin said. "Many parents send gifts and greetings for the season, but rarely do I allow a student to leave for something as fleeting as a local holiday. We still employ all the usual festivities, I assure you. Easter service, philanthropy during Christmas, and all the rest."

Sara understood this perfectly, but she could see her father grasping for an explanation that seemed less absolute, less final.

"Allow me to be sure I am understanding things clearly," Captain Crewe said. "Apart from these Parents Day ceremonies, when are her mother and I meant to see Sara?"

"During Convocation," Minchin said. "At the age of seventeen. Only then is a seminary student deemed fully prepared to rejoin society."

Sara turned devastated eyes up to her father. She withdrew her hand from her muff and clung to his coattails like she did when she was a child.

"Papa, please," she whispered, ignoring all of the lessons on decorum that he and her mother had painstakingly imbued in her over the years.

Captain Crewe inclined his head to the mistress, excusing them, and gently drew Sara aside. She felt a choking swell in her chest, but she held down that urge to cry. Her voice—usually even and strangely calm—shook with the effort.

"Papa," she said with urgency. "Das ist keine Schule, es ist ein Gefängis."

Captain Crewe raised a dark, bushy eyebrow at his daughter and once again looked on the edge of a smirk.

"German now? Has it really come to that?"

German was a language solely for Sara and her father. They spoke it while only in the gravest of confidence, a fact that often angered Mrs. Crewe, who could only pick up bits and pieces. But Sara felt the danger pressing in around her, and her most powerful instinct was to escape, by any means necessary.

"Do you not find this place inexplicably odd?" Sara asked. "A school with no holidays, no education, and no students from what I can see."

"Yes, it is rather unorthodox," Captain Crewe said, glancing back at Minchin, who'd begun to tap her foot impatiently. "But it is the only boarding school of note in this damned country that will accept you. Or rather, accept your papa's money."

Sara refused to accept that as an excuse.

"Then why not Spain? France? Switzerland? America?"

"Do you assume that your mother and I have not explored all options?" Captain Crewe answered, affronted. "You are a brilliant girl, as durable and beautiful as a narra tree. Wherever you are planted, you will thrive. But this is not just concerning an education, my princess. The day when you should marry is fast approaching, and all the cosmopolitan education in the world won't rival a British title."

Sara followed her father's logic in only a cursory way. He was a sensible man—his words and reasoning often made sense—but he might as well have been speaking in Farsi for all Sara understood.

"Papa," she said slowly, as if speaking to a child. "If their schools refuse your money, how do you imagine their families will accept your daughter?"

That seemed to freeze the captain's blood. He stood still and rigidly tall. The child in Sara saw the stony look in her father's eyes as disappointment. However, the more astute side of her—the side that said little but saw much—recognized only hurt.

"You do drive to the heart of things," he said. "Times are changing again in the Philippines, Sara. All that your mother and I have done could be taken away in an instant. Here, in this cold, dreary place, you will find protection. Little can touch an English duchess in this world of ours. You will grow lovely enough to catch the eye of any stuffed lord or earl. And you are wealthy enough to secure the best of them. I shall ensure that."

Minchin coughed in what she probably hoped was a demure way, but the crudeness of the gesture shattered the private moment.

"Captain, I must insist," she said. "Young Sara needs time to become familiar with her new home."

At that, Sara felt her heart beat once, hard, in her chest. Again, every atom in Sara's body screamed at her to protest. To fall onto the ground and rave like a tempestuous child. To resist this new home as a body resists a virus. But she withheld. She smoothed her gown and lifted her chin. She stilled her trembling lip and poured cold iron down her back. When she and her father returned to Minchin, Sara thought it would be very difficult for anyone to sense the terror in her heart.

"I expect all our requests in regards to her care and upbringing to be addressed," Captain Crewe said. "If there is ever a concern, my representative speaks for me."

Minchin dipped her head in answer. The captain then turned his full attention to Sara.

"I shall send you books. Great, big, fat ones like you like:

English, French, German. Perhaps even one or two by those cynical Russians that you favor."

"Truth is not always cynical, Papa," Sara said in solemn answer. This inspired a laugh in the captain, a gasp from the headmistress.

"Oh, do not be shocked, Mistress Minchin," Captain Crewe said, still laughing. "Sara's mind is sharp and known to cut deep on occasion."

The mistress appeared sincerely terrified by the prospect.

"Well, then, I suppose I am off," the captain said. "I'll be back in—what is it, October?"

"November," Minchin said with a quickness. "November, Captain. Details will be shared promptly."

November. It was only just now the start of January. Sara calculated the days in her head, lining them up in a row as a captive might on a cell wall.

"November, then. There, that is not quite so long, is it, princess? The time will fly by. With all your studying and entertainments, why, you won't even have time to dwell on Manila and your old papa. Come now, let us not dawdle. Give me a hug for luck on my journey home."

Sara did not hesitate and threw herself quite inelegantly against her father. She heard the breath forced from his lungs, followed by a chuckle. In childhood, Captain Crewe had always encouraged Sara to hug him with all her might, to knock him over if she could. Of course, as a small child, she never managed to unseat Captain Crewe. But she wasn't a child anymore. With shaking fingers, the captain gently drew Sara away. He cradled her cheek in his large, callused hand, a hand that Sara had clung to every day for the entirety of her life. She refused to cry, not in front of the dreary headmistress, who continued to look at them as if they might transform at any moment into the congenial white family she'd expected. And Sara refused to cry in front of her father. To him, she was a mooring in a turbulent sea, and she refused to display any behavior that contradicted that sentiment.

Sara stood with Minchin as they watched Captain Crewe make his way down the drive. His shoulders hunched against the wet, and the black tails of his overcoat flapped about him like the wings of a raven. Memory would tell Sara that the sun victoriously broke through the blockade of clouds, and bathed in a ray of gilded light, Captain Crewe turned and blessed her with a smile. Yet, as has already been established, memory is an unscrupulous liar. Captain Richard Crewe did not turn to look at her one last time. He drew farther and farther from her, fading into the writhing screen of fog. Sara opened her mouth to call his name, but only a gasp left her throat before her father became lost to the gloom.

Sara exhaled the breath she didn't realize she had been holding and watched it crystallize in the air before her.

Sara turned her head to see Minchin's eyes—now malicious and judgmental, where only a minute ago, they were the very sparkling image of compliance—glaring down at her.

"Do you not speak, girl?" she asked, not bothering with forced charm, which Sara appreciated. If this was to be her home for the next two years, then it was best that she knew where she stood.

"I am quite fluent in several languages, Mistress Minchin."

The woman's lip turned up in a sneer.

"The Queen's English will serve," she said.

Without waiting for Sara to follow, Minchin turned and vanished through the open doors of the seminary, which gaped before her like the mouth of a ravenous, cruel, and cunning monster.

This we do not for ourselves, she reminded herself. *But for those who came and those yet to come.*

Don't miss Melissa de la Cruz's *New York Times* bestselling fantasy-romance duet!

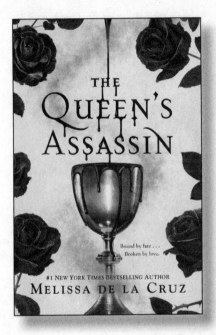

READ MELISSA DE LA CRUZ'S
BESTSELLING TRILOGY ABOUT
AMERICA'S GREATEST LOVE STORY!

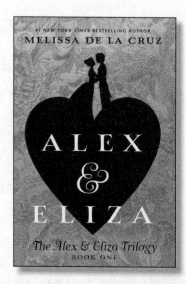

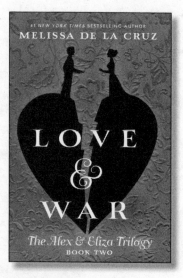

CALLING ALL FANS

OF RETOLD FAIRY TALES . . .